MADAME I EMPERORIUM

BOOK ONE

THE PORCELAIN NECKLACE

Best Wishes

Alan Dunn

Alan Dunn

Also by Alan Dunn

Historical Fiction:

The Collier and his Mistress
The English Dancing Master

Crime Fiction:

Die Cast
Ice Cold
Payback
Stage Fright

Madame Klein's Emperorium
Book One
The Porcelain Necklace

Copyright Alan Dunn 2024

ONE

The sound of a key in a lock travels far. Creatures from different worlds, from different planes, from different times or existences, their hearing attuned to just such a soft discord, may sense such small tremors . . . and act on them.

In a distant Elsewhere and Elsewhen a beast reared its head from feeding on something that might once have been human. Its name was Atraxa. It had heard the key's summons and began to move. It recalled its instructions.

'If the door opens, the Klein may pass through. She will not stay long. One hundred and twenty-seven years ago she remained for seventy-five minutes. Two hundred and two years ago? One hundred and thirteen minutes. Last year she visited four times, her longest stay fifty-six minutes, the shortest twelve. She is becoming more wary as she grows older.

'I will not be able to send you further messages, her proximity is a barrier. So you will remain in the vicinity of the Gateway and, if the key turns, if the door opens, if the Klein passes through, you will know. You will find her. You will bring her to me. She is mine and she must be kept alive.'

Atraxa was not alone. Seflapod would be somewhere close. Seflapod was one of the Old Ones, the Souleaters, the Maker's first creations. Seflapod would have heard the key turning as well.

'There may be other lives with the Klein; if so, they're yours. But the Klein must be kept alive and brought back to me. We have much to discuss.'

TWO

It was Saturday morning and Maia was ready for work.

The apartment was tidy (she always left it that way in case her father should return while she was out) and her schoolbooks were stacked neatly on the kitchen table as a reminder of impending homework. She paused at the front door before going back to check her father's bedroom, hoping that he might have slipped in during the night when she was asleep. There was no-one there; the bed hadn't been slept in.

The study hadn't been used since she'd looked in the previous evening. Nor, more importantly, had the workroom. The kilns remained cold. Shards of dry clay still littered the floor, sketches were scattered over tables and pinned to walls. She'd examined all of them many times for hidden messages, but her father had left without writing her a note. She didn't need a diary or a calendar to tell her that he'd been away for nine weeks and three days. Or that her fifteenth birthday had fallen, uncelebrated, in the middle of that period. Or that she missed him more and more with each passing day.

His absence hung in the air like warm dust. The shelves were filled with his creations: pots and vases of all shapes and colours; tiles and plates decorated with strange landscapes; porcelain heads - life-size - rendered and painted in such detail that they seemed ready to speak to her; and sculpted animals, some of which she recognised, others that were the product of his fertile imagination. She picked up one of the animals, coloured with her father's favourite lustrous blue glaze. At first sight it appeared almost human, but it had a bear-like head and a scorpion tail, a long, twisted

5

horn that curved halfway down its back, and an open mouth full of far too many teeth. 'It's surprising I don't have nightmares,' she said to the monster, replaced it carefully on the shelf. Her hand crept to the necklace she always wore, made by her father and given to her on her ninth birthday. Each of the beads of glass-hard blood-red porcelain was embedded with minuscule gold runes. 'For good fortune,' he'd told her.

'Please be here when I get back,' she said to the necklace, as she had done every day for almost ten weeks.

Maia fastened her black cloak around her shoulders, closed the door behind her and hurried down the rattling stairs into the street. She strode along cobbled lanes strewn with untidy autumn leaves. It had rained heavily during the night, but the sky was now blue and the town glowed with a polished sheen. She turned a corner into a narrow lane where the buildings bent towards each other as they climbed. A canary in a cage sang from a balcony high above her head.

'Good morning, canary,' she whistled.

The bird chorused its reply and the two harmonised for as long as it took Maia to reach the end of the lane. They finished with a flourish of syncopated arpeggios as Maia stepped into the town square. She inhaled deeply, closed her eyes, and smiled. She was standing outside Mrs Vogt's bakery and could smell fresh bread. 'A good idea,' she said to herself, pushed open the shop door and, at the same time, lowered the hood of her cloak. Her hair was bright, sleek electric red, so red that it dazzled and shone. It was cut in a short bob that framed a heart-shaped face and green eyes above a nose that was just a little too large, with a prominent bump at its bridge, and a wide mouth that promised laughter. Maia felt that her eyes were too close together and her brows, naturally arched, made her look as if

6

she was always on the point of asking a question. She thought herself plain.

'Hello Maia.' The young man behind the counter wiped his hands on his apron as he spoke. He was thin and spindly, as if he'd grown too fast in a kind summer. His long hair was imprisoned beneath a blue cap.

'Hello Tom. I'd like two - no, make that four - croissants please. Madame Klein has a special this morning and they may want to share . . . Oh, but her client might have a companion. Better make that six, just in case.'

'Six it is, baked with my own fair hand.' The young man busied himself, selecting the largest croissants for his customer. 'I've been experimenting,' he said as he transferred each croissant into a crisp white bag, 'I've a new recipe if you'd like to try it: banana, oatmeal and blueberry bread. It tastes rather good, though I say so myself.'

'That sounds delicious.' Maia smiled as she spoke and the young baker blushed slightly. He was painfully aware that he was blushing and ducked below the counter to find a bread knife, took a deep breath before reappearing.

'It's really warm this morning,' he said, hoping that might be a good enough explanation for his reddening cheeks. He cut a slice from a blue-tinged loaf on the counter, offered it to Maia. She took it graciously and devoured a large, unladylike mouthful.

'Mm,' she said through the crumbs, 'that's absolutely delicious! Even better than last week's, what was it? Cranberry and beetroot?'

'And a touch of carrot,' the young man said proudly.

'Will you go into production, then?' Maia nodded as Tom offered another slice. 'You're very good at this, Tom, developing new recipes.' She closed her eyes as she chewed. 'This is so good! I must . . .' She reached into a pocket and brought out her mobile, urged Tom into position behind the loaf and leaned towards both of them. 'Smile,' she said, pressed the button and examined the result. 'That's what you get when you use your loaf!'

Tom tried to calm himself. 'Would you send me a copy? For publicity? And please, take the bread. I doubt that anyone else will want to try it and my mother . . . well, she wouldn't even consider . . .' His words ran out.

'Then she's missing something. And her customers are missing something as well. I'll speak to her when I next see her and tell her . . .'

'No! Please, Maia, don't tell her, don't say a word. She already thinks I've too much imagination, thinking up new recipes. Daydreaming. She says I'm often in another world altogther.'

Maia shrugged. 'Perhaps other worlds are good places, Tom.' She nodded to herself, confirming the answer, then gathered her thoughts. 'You *do* have a good imagination; you've been making up stories for as long as I've known you. Do you write them down? If you do I'd like to read one of them some time.'

Tom's thoughts jostled and pushed each other. Yes, he wrote his stories down; yes, he'd love it if someone read them, especially if that someone was Maia. But if she said they were good, could he believe her? If they were awful then she'd probably still say they were good, just to avoid hurting his feelings. So what was the point of showing them to her, to anyone? 'No, I don't put them on paper,he said.' He was relieved at the lie. 'They just stay in my head.'

'In that case,' Maia said, 'you can *tell* me one of them sometime, when we're both less busy. If you'd like to, that is.'

'That sounds good,' Tom replied, and he meant it. Just him and Maia, somewhere private, the two of them. How could that be anything other than delightful? And he'd have time to picture the occasion, to imagine what would happen, to savour the anticipation.

Maia paid for the croissants. 'What time do you finish?' she asked, eyebrows raised.

Tom thought he'd never seen anyone so beautiful. 'About noon,' he said, 'Mum started everything off this morning but I took over at five. She'll be back in a few minutes.'

'Let's make it noon, then? That's when I have a break. I'll meet you under the statue, you can tell me a story. Okay?'

Tom panicked. Was Maia aware of the exquisite torture she was performing on him? He could have made an excuse, he was good at excuses. His mother might have needed him to do some deliveries. He had homework, a friend was coming round, he was going shopping, there were chores to do, logs to cut for the oven, an elderly aunt was visiting. He was about to choose the most plausible of these when he heard a voice, identical to his own, say 'I'll see you at George. I'll bring some bread. And cheese?'

'Things get better! I'll bring some coffee.' She glanced at the clock over his head. 'Better rush. See you later.' She turned and left, waved without looking back, fingers fluttering, and the bell above the door rang in jubilation. Tom watched her hurry across the square. His mother bustled in from the back room where the ovens were still working, her face round and ruddy and dusty with flour. 'Was that Maia I saw? She's a lovely young lass, that one, a real credit to her father. So sad about her mother, though.' She would have gone on with the familiar story but her gangly son bent and kissed her on the forehead. 'Goodness me, what was that for? What have you done? Burned a batch?' She sniffed the air.

'I haven't done anything, Mum!'

Tom's mother stared at him. 'No, I don't think you have. You don't look guilty enough.' She peered more closely. 'Then why are you grinning?'

'I didn't realise I was. Perhaps . . . Perhaps it's because I feel good.'

She stood on her toes and pulled his face towards hers, returned his kiss on *his* forehead. 'That's fine, Tom, nothing wrong with feeling good. I wonder,' she teased, 'if it's to do with a certain customer - no, don't say a word! I'm pleased you're happy.' She sniffed again. 'Goodness me, I'll be the one burning batches of loaves, not you.' She hurried away.

'You're so embarrassing,' he said silently to her retreating back, unaware that there would come a time when he would long for her gentle, teasing, loving smile.

In the centre of the square was a tall plinth on top of which was a sandstone statue of a soldier riding a horse. He was holding one hand high in the air, and there were some who said that the hand once held a sword; but the rain and the frost and the hard sunshine had worn away the sword almost as quickly as they'd reduced his face to a featureless mask, and dissolved the words carved at the statue's base, and softened his uniform to a most unmilitary t-shirt and shorts. Everyone called him George, as if he was a familiar friend rather than a lump of stone.

Maia liked George's horse better than George himself. The horse had lost its equine characteristics and looked, Maia felt, like an okapi, thin-necked and stocky-legged, out of proportion. And so the horse became Oscar the okapi, George's faithful companion.

'Good morning George,' she said as she passed, 'good morning Oscar. I like your wig, Oscar. Very fetching.' During the night several pigeons had roosted on Oscar's head, and they'd left their mark in the form of long white strands of what looked like hair.

On the steps at the foot of the plinth sat two figures. They were engrossed in flicking small pieces of gravel from one of the steps into a plastic cup lying on its side. If one of them was successful there were cheers and fist bumps; failure was met with groans. They were dressed similarly in faded jeans, their hooded sweatshirts hiding their faces. Maia knew them anyway. 'Morning Friz,' she said, 'morning Slip. You're up early.'

Two heads turned in one motion, recognised Maia, then returned to their game. The larger, wider of the two pulled down her hood to reveal a pale, square face surrounded by curls of cropped ginger hair and littered with freckles. 'We're not up early.' There was pride in her voice. '*We* are up late.' She took a piece of chewing gum from her mouth and spat on the ground, then replaced the gluey material beneath her tongue.

The other figure rose to his feet. 'Friz,' he said, 'don't spit, it's disgusting.' He was taller than his friend and long black twists of hair tumbled around his dark, handsome face. 'It's just not stylish.' He shimmied a dance step, slid left and right, pulled an imaginary hat over his eyes. 'Unlike me, who's style personified.'

Maia smiled and went on her way, then turned, as if she'd forgotten something. 'Won't they be worried at St Anthony's if you've been out all night?'

'Not if they don't know,' Friz said menacingly.

Slip sighed. 'We haven't really been out all night,' he explained. 'We did think about it, but it was too cold. So we stayed in, talked, then came out before breakfast.'

'No breakfast?' Maia said. 'You should go to see Tom, he's been making some new bread and he's giving away free samples. It's very good; worth a visit.' As she moved off in

11

the direction of the Emperorium she saw Friz and Slip, sullen teenagers, transform into eager youngsters, and smiled again - with them, not at them - as they made their way to the bakery.

The buildings that faced the statue on three sides of the Square seemed at first glance to be similar simply because they were dressed in the same uniform of white render and black painted wood. They leaned into the square like old friends sharing gossip, each with its own personality. Here and there the render was rubbed away to reveal rich red-brown brick. Some of the windows and doors were embellished with deep blue or red or green paint. Shops had been made of the ground floors: an ironmonger's, a butcher's, a hardware store, one shop whose windows were filled with musical instruments, another sparsely - though elegantly - decorated with three mannequins wearing white silk dresses. Fruit and vegetables from the greengrocer's spilled out onto the narrow pavement and rubbed shoulders with tables and chairs from the cafe.

The muddle of styles and smells and sounds came together in a harmonious whole, save for the fourth side of the square containing the shop where Maia worked. What appeared at first to be a bright new building facade was actually a printed plastic sheet stretched over scaffolding on both sides of the Emperorium. All the buildings except Madame Klein's had been demolished. A few years before there'd been a mixture of proud homes and small businesses, a clock repairer, an electrician, a taxidermist and a perfumier. One by one the shops had been sold into disuse and allowed to become so dangerous that they'd been knocked down; only Madame Klein's Emperorium remained, a polished brass plate beside a glossy black door announcing its presence. The name gave no indication that this was a shop, nor what was sold inside, but behind that door the establishment spread wide and deep and high. Everyone in the town knew that, whenever they wanted something unusual or difficult to obtain elsewhere, they'd find it in the Emperorium.

Maia peered through a gap in the screen at one side of the door, though she already knew what she'd see. Beyond the scaffolding was a wasteland of rubble and burned timber, broken glass and cast-iron drainpipes, roof-tiles and cables and old doors, sheets of rusty corrugated metal, sinks and toilets and plumbing leftovers. Only the Emperorium stood proud, and that never ceased to captivate Maia. It was as if an adventurous primary school teacher had told her class to make any shape of building they wanted from any scrap box or bottle or tube (yes, Alfie, you can glue a perfume bottle to a plastic chocolate box if you want, as long as you paint it in bright colours and - yes, you can put a door in the roof if you want, Chloe) and had assembled them at random into one large display of architectural insanity made real.

Maia knew the Emperorium well, it had been her second home for as long as she could remember. When she was young she'd stayed there with Madame Klein whenever her father had to travel, and that had been often. Madame Klein had become a friend, a surrogate grandmother, a teacher, a comforter and - in the end - her employer. Maia loved her and the Emperorium itself.

Maia let her eyes wander over the miscellany of impossibility that was the Emperorium's outer shell. In most of the walls, some of the ceilings and even in one or two of the overhanging floors, windows had been placed. The curves and slides and dimples and projections of the irregular polyhedrons (such a delicious word, Maia felt, tasting of tea and digestive biscuits, smelling of chalk and dry sand, feeling like lemon sherbets) were made of different materials: timber and brick, concrete, clay, steel and glass; the roofs were dark grey slates and terracotta pantiles, thatch and shingles and asphalt; and chimneys grew like mushrooms, strange colours and shapes, all at different angles, some shimmering with smoke, both dark and steam-pale, while others were soot-clad and silent.

The Emperorium had, according to Madame Klein, been built into and around and over and under and through the gaps between other buildings. It had been knotted and tied into backyards and unused basements, tunnels and lofts, hidden rooms and bricked up bedrooms. It had stretched and grown through alleyways and passages, footpaths and ladders and stairways, cellars and sewers and garderobes, chambers, sculleries, cupboards, storerooms, privies and coalholes. There was, according to Madame Klein, a map of the building kept safe in the library, although you might need a map of the building to find the library.

Maia always felt that the Emperorium looked a little untidy. Top-heavy. Ungainly. She felt that the whole building, if it could be thought of as a single building, was in danger of being blown over by even the weakest passing breeze. It had certainly been shored up in places. There were buttresses (flying and flightless), wall-ties of numerous sizes, clamps holding walls together, beams supporting roofs, even beams supporting beams. Planks of wood were balanced on bricks and pushed up into floors that sloped at precipitous angles. Doors and frames had been braced, walls riveted, staircases propped up, pipes welded. And so far it had worked. Nothing serious or essential had yet fallen down.

The signs fixed to the scaffolding had, Maia noticed with displeasure, been over-painted again. Some of it was too familiar. 'Pawquine and Grovelle Properties,' she read aloud, spitting out the words. 'A prestigious development of luxury apartments and retail opportunities.' There was nothing different in any of that. But beneath had been added 'Work begins this month; special discounts for off-plan purchases.'

'That's new,' Maia said to herself. '"Work begins this month". Surely Madame Klein can't have . . .' Maia didn't usually run, not unless she was engaged in some sporting activity or was sure no-one was watching. But an onlooker might certainly have said that she scurried along the pavement and pushed open the door to the Emperorium with a little more haste than she normally displayed. 'Madame Klein?' She peered into the gloom, saw a stocky figure approaching. 'Madame Klein,' she exclaimed, 'have you seen . . ?'

A voice interrupted her, caressed and stroked its purring words. 'Of course I've seen ze silly sign, nonsense of ze highest ordure. But you're late, child.'

Maia said nothing but tilted her head to one side as if listening; on cue the grandfather clock in the hall began to chime, closely followed by the mantel-clock behind the counter and, far off in a distant bedroom, Madame Klein's alarm.

'I set zem slow,' the voice said, honey and sandpaper, 'so zey don't get ahead of zemselves.'

Outside, the church clock began its sonorous early morning peal. Maia smiled. Madame Klein was her normal cantankerous self. She said the sign was nonsense and so it must be nonsense. 'I'm sorry I'm late, Madame Klein. It won't happen again.' Maia held out the croissants. 'I thought you and your guest might like these with morning coffee.'

Madame Klein stepped forward. She was small and old, her grey hair tied in a bun, her black cardigan and white blouse hanging from sloping care-worn shoulders. Her face was lined, narrow red lips and pinched nose a perfect right angle. The thick lenses of her wire-framed glasses magnified deep blue eyes which glinted as they returned the smile. 'You are a very kind young lady, just like your farzer. How is he today?'

15

'I haven't seen him this morning, but I'm sure he's well.' Nothing Maia said was untrue, she reasoned, but Madame Klein was looking at her as though she knew there were other words hiding behind those she'd just spoken.

'Zat is good.' She held up the bag of pastries. 'We we will have ze crescents as soon as we return.' Her shoes tapped as she pattered into the room. 'But Mr Li is already here and you must look after ze shop and his son Ten until we return. Now where are zhey?' She looked puzzled.

Maia told herself not to be judgemental: 'Ten' wasn't necessarily an unusual name; and it was unlikely that Mr Li had had so many children that he'd run out of inspiration after the ninth. 'They're probably looking round, I'll see if I can find them.'

'Zank you, my dear. I'll get my bag.'

Madame Klein retraced her steps and Maia went in search of the Li family. The first room of the shop, that immediately to the left as the front door was opened, the room with the counter and till where Madame Klein had been waiting, contained dry goods, groceries and foodstuffs piled high on uneven shelves stretching to the ceiling. The room to the right of the entrance was equally well stocked with hardware and grey-brown boxes whose labels explained that the contents were 'screws, brass, cross-head, 25mm, 8 gauge', or 'clippers, toenail, large' (Maia wondered if the adjective referred to the clippers or the toenails), or 'forks, table, medium, chrome-plated', or anything else anyone could ever imagine. Madame Klein had never turned a customer away because the item required wasn't in stock.

Children who entered the Emperorium usually went straight ahead, through the door marked 'Toys - adults prohibited'. Was Ten Li young enough to qualify as a child, Maia wondered, would he be captivated by the toys on display? Or would he be more interested in the books on the first floor, up the stairs on the right? She could hear voices in that direction and she climbed towards them.

'I still don't see why we're here, Dad.'

Maia frowned. The voice was American with a mosquito whine that both threatened and irritated.

'We could have been in Paris or London or Berlin,' it continued.

Maia wished she had some insect repellent.

'But you insisted on stopping in this, this . . . tumbleweed town, in this falling down shop selling . . . well, I can't tell what it's selling. It looks as if it tries to sell everything and ends up selling nothing. I mean, some of these books are years old. And I can't see any graphic novels. Where's the Marvel? Where's the DC?'

'Just humour me, Ten, please.'

That, thought Maia, was where the son inherited his whinging selfishness. The father's voice pleaded and cajoled where it should have required or insisted. She climbed softly up the stairs, slowly, keen to hear how the conversation would unfold.

'You haven't even told me why we came here.'

'I told you I came to see Madame Klein. She's a very special person.'

'Meeting this Madame Klein is an appointment, Dad, not a reason. And she's weird. She looked at me as if I was an idiot. She looked down on me.'

'You're taller than her, son. She couldn't look down on you unless she was standing on a chair.'

Oh yes she could, Maia's inner voice protested, she could look down on anyone. Madame Klein may have been short in height but she was tall in self-confidence and attitude. She'd almost reached the top of the stairs and began to drag her feet so that father and son Li would know she was approaching. 'Hello?' she called, 'are you up here?'

17

The head that poked out from the book room door was owl-faced with a squat nose and blinking eyes, hair buzz-cut short. He was wearing long shorts and a black T-shirt that was just a little too tight around his middle.

'Are you Ten?' Maia asked. 'Is your father here? Madame Klein says . . .'

'I'm here.' Another face appeared, clearly the son's father, equally round-eyed and round-nosed and round-bodied but also with round-framed spectacles. He bustled towards Maia, ignored her outstretched hand. 'Where is she?' he asked as he pushed past her.

'In the main room,' Maia frowned her disapproval, 'bottom of the stairs and turn right.' Her words followed him but he made no gesture or expression of thanks.

'You're welcome,' Maia said under her breath, though not as silently as she'd hoped.

'He has a lot on his mind,' the son explained, 'he's normally very polite. But thank you for coming to get him.' He made as if to follow his father but Maia stood in his way.

'Madame Klein asked me to show you round. I think she and your father need to meet in private.'

The younger Li blinked. He was bigger than Maia in all dimensions but probably only a year or two older. He looked as if he might argue with her so she adopted Madame Klein's manner and used her tall voice. 'My name's Maia, I'm Madame Klein's assistant. I'm sure we could find some books here that might interest you.' She leaned closer to her charge. 'I think you're probably into something alternative, something different, something cutting edge. Perhaps . . .' she slid past him and into the book room, 'something a little challenging.' She paused beside the door when he didn't move. 'Follow me, then!'

Madame Klein was waiting for Mr Li at the bottom of the stairs. She was wearing her businesswoman's face, all friendliness and efficiency. 'Should we begin?' she asked and, before he could reply, led him back up the stairs to a door with two painted wooden signs on it. The first, in rather florid script, read 'Private, No Admission'; the second was more plain and angular, it said 'Hic Movet Aliud Tempus'. Madame Klein saw Mr Li's gaze fall upon the Latin words.

'Zis is my motto,' she said, 'a rough translation is "Time passes differently in zis place". My customers lose track of zhe time, you zee, zhey become zo involved in what zhey do.'

The door was framed, not with wood, but with glazed tiles, each decorated with a pattern that seemed to move whenever the eyes tried to focus on it. Madame Klein took a lanyard from around her neck, it had three keys on it; she used the smallest to open the door and ushered Mr Li to the corridor beyond. She locked the door carefully behind her.

The corridor seemed, illogically, to grow taller and wider as it faded into the distance; the floor was uneven, the ceiling sagged; if right angles had ever existed here, they were now long extinct. There were doors at irregular intervals on both sides, all without names or numbers.

'Zhank you for zhe information you zent me,' Madame Klein whispered, 'it was mozt helpful.'

'I don't know why I'm doing this,' Mr Li said. 'I must be mad. My son thinks . . .'

'Your zon is grieving, as are you. He underztands your needs, even if he doesn't approve of your methods. He loves you, zhough he doesn't often zay zo.' She paused. 'And please zpeak zoftly.'

Mr Li did as he was told. 'He *never* says he loves me. Not since . . . I think he blames me.'

'Zhat is what people do: zhey find zomeone to blame. And zhey always zeem to blame zomeone close to zhem.'

Madame Klein seemed to recognise his need for reassurance. 'I'm not a medium, Mr Li. I don't contact zhe spirits of zhe dead. Zhere is nozhing after life. All I do is help people explore zheir pasts. Focus on zhings zhat happened. React wiz zhem.'

Madame Klein counted the doors on the left and opened the third. She fumbled in the darkness and switched on a bright light to reveal a long narrow room. The walls were painted with an urban scene. To the right a railway ran through a small town centre into its suburbs. Behind were green fields with farm animals, some hillocks, snow-peaked mountains in the distance.

The far wall, shorter than the others, framed an industrial backdrop with factories and refineries, warehouses and old canals, gasometers and chimneys and piles of coal.

The railway tracks curved round to the left. There, running back towards the door, was a different town, more fields, this time filled with crops, and eventually, close at hand, a port with docks and cranes and boats of all sizes. Mr Li looked closer. 'It's very clever,' he said, 'I swear I can smell saltwater, and I can hear seagulls. But when I was focused on the industrial scene up there,' he gestured at the far end of the room, 'there was a clang of metal on metal, foundries, smoke and sulphur fumes.' He nodded. 'Like I said, very clever, there's been a lot of work put into all this. And it does look a little like my hometown.' His hand flew round the room. 'But I told you, my wife killed herself by stepping in front of a train. I'm not sure why showing me a painting with a railway will help.'

'No, I can see why you might zhink zhat, Mr Li.' She tapped her way forward and waved him after her, knowing without looking back that he would do so. 'Zhe detail is zo clear. And when *we* ztart moving . . .' she whispered, 'everyzhing moves! Look closer! Look closer!'

Miniature cars and buses and trucks began to drive along flat paper-tarmac roads and, in doing so, became more like their real selves. Children played in schoolyards; shoppers hurried along busy streets; there was life.

Mr Li did as Madame Klein had told him to do, he looked more closely, tilted his head as if he was hearing individual conversations. And then his brow furrowed. He moved in front of Madame Klein, stared at a leafy suburb. 'How did you know? It's my house. My home.' He wiped his forehead. 'But you had my address. You looked it up on the internet, street map, you made this especially for me. That's why you charge so much, it's because of the effort you put into making these images.'

Madame Klein raised a finger to her lips. Then she pointed at the door of Mr Li's house. It opened, and a figure appeared on the porch. It was a woman, blonde, wearing a bright yellow sweater and black slacks. There was no detail in the face save a line of red for lips and two black dots for eyes.

'My wife! That's what she was wearing when . . .' Mr Li stopped. 'It's not my wife. It could be anyone.'

The figure began to move and, as it did so, its features resolved, became more precise. And Mr Li spiralled down into the world of his own life, his own past, and he heard his wife scream back into the house, he heard familiar words, the last words his wife had spoken to him: 'You care more about your work than you do about me and your son! Find someone else to be your housekeeper, your childminder, your gardener, your . . . your slave! I hate you!' From an upstairs window wide eyes in a young, round face watched the woman slam the door and run down the drive, wrench the car door open, climb inside and screech down the road.

Mr Li was standing on the lawn, Madame Klein beside him. She took his arm. 'You aren't here. You can zee but you can't ztop anyzhing happening zhat has already happened.'

Mr Li pushed the arm away. 'I already know what happened.' There was anger in his words, though it appeared to be mostly directed against himself. 'She drove to the playing field close to the railway. She parked up. I was ringing her but she didn't pick up, I texted her but she didn't reply. She climbed over the fence and waited until there was a fast train then walked in front of it. That's what happened.' He shrugged back tears. 'It was a mistake to contact you, to come here to see you. I want to leave now.'

Madame Klein shook her head. 'Come wizh me.' She took Mr Li's hand and they were immediately elsewhere, looking at a familiar car parked beneath some whispering aspens. She led him easily towards it though he fought her all the way; he had no strength; she was omnipotent. She pushed him into the front seat of the car, beside his wife. Her head was slumped on the steering wheel. She was crying.

'I tried to tell her,' he explained through his own tears. 'I tried to tell her I did it for her and for Ten. The long hours. Staying away. Pushing myself.'

Madame Klein nodded.

A phone rang.

'That's me,' Mr Li said, 'I rang her. I tried to talk to her but she didn't answer.'

His wife ignored the phone. Her tears became a racking, wheezing wail of despair.

'Honey, pick up the phone. Talk to me.' The words did nothing. He reached out to touch her, to put his arm round her, but he wasn't there. He had no presence. He turned to Madame Klein. 'What can I do?' he whispered.

'Nozhing,' she replied. 'Zhis is what happened.'

Mrs Li controlled her tears, wiped her nose on her sleeve. 'The trouble is, Tony, you don't need me. You don't need *me*. Anyone would do. And I want you to need *me*.'

Mr Li tried to explain. 'She used to get low, get down. She told me she'd self-harmed before we met. And I suggested counselling, but she said she was happy, she didn't need it. I thought . . .'

'You didn't zhink, Tony. Zhat was zhe problem.'

'I left her a message. I told her I loved her. I told her I wanted her to come back safe and sound. I told her I needed her. But she didn't listen. She normally got over the lows quickly, easily. If only she'd listened. If only she'd listened . . .'

The phone buzzed. Mrs Li looked at it as if it was something strange. She opened it, read who the missed call had come from, smiled, then touched the screen and lifted the phone to her ear to hear the message.

'She *did* listen! But if . . . Why . . ?'

Mrs Li's smile broadened. She sniffed, wiped away the remains of her tears. 'I love you too, Tony,' she whispered. Rain began to smear the car windscreen. 'I didn't mean to hurt you either. It's just that, sometimes, it gets too much. Yes. Yes, I'm coming back. Right now, I'm on my way.'

'Carrie,' Mr Li whispered, 'just come back.'

They heard the yelling at the same time. Their heads turned to the fence where a distant figure rushed towards them screaming for help. Mrs Li threw the car door open and climbed out, reached the fence at the same time as the boy she'd heard. He was breathless, his face dirty with tears. 'What is it?' she asked, sinking to her knees so her face was level with his, her fingers hooking the wire mesh of the fence. What's the matter?'

'My sister,' the boy gasped, 'we were playing and she, she got caught . . . An' she can't get out.' He coughed and wheezed, eyes wide. 'She can't move an' the express, it'll be

23

here soon, an' she can't move, an' . . . Help, you've gotta help!'

'Ring for help, Carrie, use the phone!'

As if hearing her husband's voice Mrs Li looked back at the car. In the distance a train signalled its approach with a banshee scream.

Mrs Li scrabbled and scrambled up and over the fence, landed unevenly beside the boy. 'Show me where,' she said, and the two ran towards the tracks. The wasteland they crossed had once, in more prosperous times, been a marshalling yard; now it was flat and scrubby, overgrown with thornbush and sharp-edged, scolding plants. Only two tracks remained, running along the valley bottom.

'She's over here,' the boy said. A small figure was crouched on the tracks, crying, dragging at her foot. Mrs Li saw immediately what had happened. There was a switchgear allowing trains to swap from one track to the other and the girl had caught her foot between the iron rail and the angled switch. The mechanism was automatic. The girl's foot was trapped. Beneath her own feet Mrs Li could feel the vibrations of the approaching express.

'A branch . . . or a piece of metal,' she yelled at the boy, 'find one! Quickly!' She turned to the girl. 'I'll get you out,' she said calmly. The girl, no older than four or five, face streaked with tears and pain, whimpered. She was in shock. Mrs Li bent down beside her. 'I know it hurts, but I'll get you out.'

The boy returned dragging a piece of wood almost as tall as he was and a length of painted copper pipe. Mrs Li discarded the wood immediately, hefted the pipe.

'The train,' the boy warned, 'it's coming!'

Mrs Li didn't need to look up, she could hear and feel the train's remorseless charge. She jammed the metal pipe between the two pieces of rail and pulled heavily on it. There was no movement.

'It's coming!' the boy screamed.

Mrs Li pulled again, sure she could feel some movement. 'One more,' she hissed, 'when her foot comes free pull her away.'

Mr Li and Madame Klein were ghosted beside them. 'She can't do it,' he shouted, unheard by all except Madame Klein.

'Was zhere any report of a child killed?' Madame Klein asked.

'No. No, no-one except . . .'

'Zhen she can do it. Perhaps if you helped?'

'But you said we couldn't affect things that happened!'

'Is zhere any harm in trying?'

Mr Li moved opposite his wife, looked into her eyes as she strained at the metal pipe. He placed his own hands over hers, ignoring the train's dragon breath, pushed as she pulled though he could feel nothing, pushed with his mind and he could feel everything.

And there was a small metallic click.

Mrs Li's face froze into a mask of physical and mental effort and the two rails moved apart a further fraction. 'Harder!' her voice cracked, and it was unclear whether the exhortation was aimed at her invisible husband or the boy, but both did as they were told and with a scream the girl was free and falling backwards away from the tracks into her brother's arms. In the same moment the metal pipe cracked and snapped, the points clicked back into place, and Mrs Li fell back too, onto the tracks.

The train passed through, and on, and beyond, its brakes screeching it to a distant halt two more miles down the track, and Mr Li and Madame Klein were left alone. The two children were already limping into the distance, fabricating tales of falling from a tree, their memories of what really happened already locked away in future nightmares.

'I think, for a moment, I felt her hands in mine.' Mr Li raised his hands, as if expecting some mark to be there. 'I think, as she fell, I saw her look at me, not through me. I think . . .'

Madame Klein's voice was suddenly tired. 'Don't zhink, my friend. Come, we must go. Now you know zhe truth. You have what you wanted. I hope it makes it easier for you.' She linked her arm in his, both guiding him and using him to support her, and led him slowly away to the long corridor they'd left only - she checked the time on her pocket watch - an hour before. She reached for the chain round her neck. 'I need to lock zhe door and zhen we can talk, if you vant.' She lifted her head, inhaled deeply. 'But we must hurry. Zhere is zomezhing in zhe air. We have taken too long.'

THREE

Young Li followed Maia into the book room.

'And you're Ten, I believe.'

'Sort of. Ten Moku Li is my full name. But Ten will do.' He looked around the room. Books were stacked on shelves that were too high, that threatened to fall over, with no signs or labels to show their subject matter. 'And you're . . . Maia? Is that right?'

'That's right. Full name Maiolica but that's a mouthful, so Maia will do. Do you like reading? I love reading, I read anything and everything, rather undiscerning in my tastes I'm afraid. How about you, Ten?'

'I don't read a lot. Not books, that is. I check things out on the internet.'

'Ah, the internet. Doesn't work here. Blind spot. No mobile signal either. But you don't need either to read a good book.' She looked at him closely again. 'Do you like graphic novels?'

Ten looked puzzled. 'Yeah, I do. How did you know . . ?'

'The thing is, we don't stock ordinary books here, we try to keep something special for everyone who comes in.' She ran her fingers along the spines of the nearest books. 'Have you heard of Enki Bilal?'

Ten shook his head. 'I mostly like Spiderman. And Batman. That sort of thing.'

'Perhaps I can suggest something new, then? How about Jean Giraud? Druillet? Corben? Jodorowsky? Alan Moore?'

Each name brought a puzzled shake of the head.

'Then we'll start with Bilal. The Nikopol trilogy.' She pulled a book from the shelves. *'La Foire aux Immortels* in its original French, but this is a translation, of course.' She handed it to him and he held it gingerly as if it might sting or

27

bite. 'You can sit down,' she said, turning the spine of *One Hundred Graphic Novels You MUST Read* to the wall. 'I normally choose the floor. There's a bell attached to the shop door, it'll ring if anyone comes in, so if you hear it and I disappear, don't worry. I'm reading *Cold Mountain*, Charles Frazier, almost perfect writing.' She took a battered text from the shelves and slid to the floor. 'Of course, it has *some* flaws, just like any writing. I mean, there's never any novel published that couldn't do without a little further editing. Don't you think?' She glanced at Ten. His face was buried in his book, eyes wide. He turned a page then turned back again, puzzled, as if a new revelation had forced him to rethink something he'd just absorbed. Maia was content.

When the doorbell chimed a few minutes later Ten didn't seem to hear it. Maia climbed to her feet and clattered downstairs but slowed when she saw the two pairs of feet, then trousered legs, that were waiting for her. She forced her face into a smile as she completed her journey.

'Ah, good morning young lady,' said the smaller man, a broad grin on his dough-pale face. His grey hair was slicked to his scalp and he wore large, black-framed spectacles on a fat nose. 'Is the delightful Madame Klein at home?' He seemed to be quivering with pleasure, his small body dancing while his feet remained fixed to the ground. When he wasn't talking his tongue moved round the inside of his mouth, as if savouring the taste of the words he'd just used.

'I'm sorry, Mr Grovelle, she's with a customer at the moment.'

'You recognise us? I'm so very, very pleased. That is . . .' He turned to his companion. 'She recognises us, Mr Pawquine! The day has suddenly become better, sunnier, kinder.'

'Well,' Maia said, 'you do come into the shop at least once a week. And have done for the past year. So I should . . .'

Mr Grovelle ignored her interjection. 'And would you know - yes, of course you'd know, a beautiful and intelligent young woman like yourself - would you know how long she might be? You see, Mr Pawquine and I would be very pleased to see her, if that were possible.' The ends of his mouth moved higher up his face, his chin lower, to form a semicircle of insincere contentment. 'Isn't that right, Mr Pawquine?'

Pawquine was as wide as Grovelle was short. He bulged. He had an explosion of white hair and a cylindrical pig-like nose. His eyes were too close to each other and wandered the room in search of something to focus on. 'Ah . . . yes . . . indubitably, Mr Grovelle, quite right, correct in . . . um . . . everything you say, of course. As my old schoolmaster used to say, quoting Horace, I believe . . . Or was it Boris? Norris perhaps. No matter, I can recall the words as if he'd spoken them yesterday: "quid pro quo per ardua ad astra," and who are we to disagree with such words of wisdom spoken so . . . um . . . where was I?'

'Madame Klein is busy,' Maia said, 'and she'll probably be busy for the rest of the day.' She squeezed past the men, held the door open for them. 'I'll tell her you called.'

Grovelle's mouth opened a little, though his smile remained fixed, a ventriloquist in the making; his lips were wet and shiny. 'But my dear, you don't know *why* we called. I'm sure we could wait here for the venerable Madame Klein, I'm sure she'd want you to extend your hospitality to us until she's able to speak to us in person, as it were.' He took a step away from Maia, a step back into the shop. 'I think she'd like us to wait. Do you agree, Mr Pawquine?'

'I couldn't agree more, Mr Grovelle, unless I was actually saying your um, your words at the same time as you. Two minds thinking . . . thinking . . . thinking, um, deeply, that's it, deeply, and truly, madly deeply, as one, "mens insana in corpore sanctus," as we used to say in the old Bulldog Club.'

Mr Pawquine also stepped away from Maia. 'We'll wait,' he growled.

Another voice entered, a deep, gravelly voice aged in oak vats and toasted over hot coals. 'I think Madame Klein would rather you waited outside the shop.'

'Mr Chavanel,' Maia whispered as an elderly man approached from the grocery room. His hair was grey and tightly curled, and he wore a dark plum velvet jacket with a yellow paisley cravat at his neck. The walking cane he carried in his left hand was long and thin with a silver handle.

'I think you should go,' the man said politely, ushering Grovelle and Pawquine away with a flick of his hand.

'I think, um, we'd rather, um . . . "carpe diem," comes to mind, a fish on a bicycle is like a man without a . . .'

Chavanel's fingers touched the handle of his cane lightly. 'You're beginning to annoy me.'

Grovelle and Pawquine looked at each other and their unspoken words hurried them to the door. 'One day, Yves,' Grovelle warned, 'you'll go too far.'

'And we'll be waiting, on that day. At least, um, he'll be waiting,' Pawquine said, pointing to Grovelle, 'and I'll be right beside him. Right behind him. "Non sinister sed dexter".'

Maia held the door wide and the two men were hastened on their way by Chavanel's softly spoken 'Boo!'

'Thank you, Mr Chavanel,' Maia said. 'I didn't hear you come in.'

The old man lead the way back into the grocery room where there was a stiff-backed chair in front of the counter. He lowered himself into it. 'I was already in when you arrived, having coffee with Madame Klein.' He pointed at the mug on the floor as if he was keen to demonstrate his truthfulness. 'I don't sleep well, I was out for an early morning walk and I noticed a light on as I passed, so I knocked and she invited me to join her.' His eyes flicked towards the door. 'I hope you didn't mind my interruption.'

Maia twisted her face. 'I don't think they would have left otherwise.'

'Still wanting Elise to sell?'

Maia nodded.

The old man shook his head. 'She won't do it.'

'They say they're offering a very good price.'

'She won't sell at any price. She has her reasons. She's *very* attached to the place.'

Maia heard the stressed word and looked at Mr Chavanel; his face remained impassive. He was the only person she'd ever heard call Madame Klein by her first name. He was the only person she'd seen who was permitted to touch Madame Klein - albeit with a gentle hand on her shoulder or in the small of her back - without a deadly frown. And when they greeted each other it was with three kisses to each other's cheeks. They clearly knew each other well, but neither had ever told Maia anything about their own or the other's past.

'Madame Klein's consultation seems to be lasting a long time.' Mr Chavanel had taken a watch from his waistcoat pocket. 'I hope she doesn't overtire herself.' He settled himself in his seat again. 'We aren't getting any younger.' His eyes closed then snapped open immediately. 'Don't worry about me, I'm quite happy sitting here. If anyone comes in I'll call you. You have someone to look after, I believe?'

'Oh yes. I'd almost forgotten about Ten.' She took the first few steps back towards the book room when the door at the top of the stairs was unlocked and flung open; Mr Li, followed closely by Madame Klein, hurried through. The old woman peered back through the open door. 'Maia!' she hissed. Maia was by her side in an instant, brushing past Mr Li who was dabbing at his eyes with his sleeve.

'Can your young eyes zee anyzhing?'

Maia stared down the corridor. 'Nothing, Madame Klein.'

'Be sure! Be very sure!'

Maia had never seen the old woman so agitated. 'Perhaps a haze? Smoke? Or a mist?'

'What colour, child?'

'Blue?' Maia squinted. 'A little blue?' She hesitated, and Madame Klein noticed.

'And?'

'There's a strange smell. Oily?' She turned her head a little to one side. 'And I can hear something. Breathing? Deep breathing.'

'Bazhka!' Madame Klein tugged Maia away from the door. 'Chavanel,' she yelled, 'zhe girl, she can zmell Bazhka!'

Maia had never seen Chavanel move so quickly, so gracefully, to join Madame Klein. His walking stick had been replaced by a long, thin metal blade, so polished it drew light into it. 'Come away from the door, quickly,' he muttered, and Maia did as she was told, but not before she saw something appear at the far end of the corridor and move rapidly towards them. It wasn't running, it moved with a skittering, scuttling, insect-like urgency in jumps and bounds, and it made an inhuman chittering sound as it approached. Its skin was leathery, its eyes - too many eyes and legs and limbs - were fixed on her, its mouths were open . . .

Madame Klein slammed the door and turned the key in the lock. From the other side there came, moments later, a faint scratching sound, as if a mouse was asking politely to come in. 'Just in time,' she gasped. 'I must be more careful.'

'What was that?' Maia whispered.

'You zaw it too? You zmelled it and heard it and zaw it? Zhat is not good.'

Chavanel shrugged. 'I've been telling you she was ready.'

'No! She's too young.'

Chavanel slid his blade back into its sheath. 'You were younger, belle dame.'

'I'd been prepared.' She looked at Maia but replied to Chavanel. 'She's too young.'

'If it's me you're talking about,' said Maia, summoning her confidence, 'then please talk to me directly.'

'Too young. And too proud.' Madame Klein squinted at Maia. 'And probably too vain.' She took the stairs slowly, one at a time. 'Come. Wizh me, now.'

'But . . .'

'But me no buts, young lady. Mr Li needs zome refreshment. And I zhink I need a glass of tea also.'

In the building site at the side of the Emperorium Pawquine was kicking stones and pebbles with his worn and dirty shoes. Grovelle was picking his way fastidiously between pools of dirty water and slick mud.

'She won't sell, Grovelle.' A small rock spun from Pawquine's inaccurate toe and splashed Grovelle's well-pressed trousers.

'Then she needs persuading, Pawquine.' He brushed the dark material with well-clipped fingers and shook his head. 'And do be a little more careful, if you please, these trousers will need cleaning now.'

Pawquine looked at his own crumpled trousers and food-stained tie, his frayed jacket cuffs. He felt the dead lettuce curves of his shirt collar. The he peered at Grovelle's trousers. 'Looks perfectly clean to me, old boy.' He bent down and picked up a stone, threw it angrily at a length of old drainpipe and was rewarded with a metallic clang. He smiled triumphantly. His teeth were uneven and yellow, decorated with small pieces of food. 'We've tried persuading her,' he said, 'it hasn't worked.'

'Then perhaps we need to persuade her more. Or differently.'

'Differently?'

'Differently.'

Pawquine pretended to think, his brow furrowing. 'Oh, I see. "Differently." I know exactly what you mean, my dear fruitcake. Differently.' He turned the word over in his mouth several times, tasted it, then spat it out. 'No. No, I'm afraid I have no idea what you're talking about, old bean.'

Grovelle looked around him then took a step towards his partner and whispered. 'We have to threaten violence, Pawquine.'

'Violence, Grovelle? Violence? Threaten *violence* to Madame Klein?' He shook his head. 'I very much doubt that the *threat* of violence would do anything to nudge the old bat towards a sale. I honestly believe that *actual* violence may be called for and I know that I for one would love to be involved in the aforementioned, ah, use of physical force.' He licked his lips. 'Are we talking about bruising here? A little blood? Or do we go straight for the removal of a limb or two?'

'We do none of this, Pawquine, we are not to be seen considering such actions.'

'But you said . . .'

'What I say and what I mean may be two different and opposing things, Pawquine, but they have the same outcome. We need to employ the assistance of others.'

'Employ?' Pawquine thrust his hands into his pockets, as if protecting his loose change. 'Employ someone as in pay someone?'

Grovelle nodded his oily head. Behind thick-lenses his eyes glinted. 'Employ as in get someone else to do the dirty work, Pawquine. Then it's nothing to do with us if Madame Klein is injured. Or maimed. Or worse.'

'That would be so sad, Grovelle.'

'That Madame Klein should be hurt?'

'No! Oh no, no no no, you misunderstand me! It would be sad that she would be hurt and that I would have played no part in the hurting.' He chortled, a liquid bubbling sound, as if he was trying to cough up a large ball of congealed phlegm. 'Do you know anyone who might do the deed? *Habeas corpus*, as it were, *pro patria mori*?'

Grovelle took a deep breath, puffed out his pigeon chest. 'As it happens, Pawquine, in my youth my actions and my companions were not always beyond reproach and I'm sure I can recall some names, some numbers, some individuals who might help us.'

'Or I could do the job myself!' Pawquine struck a pose as if he was about to lay an egg. 'I dabbled in the martial arts, y'know. Haa-YAA!' He kicked out with one leg, almost overbalanced, kicked again in a vain attempt to right himself. He spun round and fell against a stub of brick wall so old that the mortar holding the bricks together had melted away. The wall collapsed and the timber frame it had been supporting sank by a few centimetres. A buttress attached to the frame moved slightly. Doors creaked. A window broke, nails popped and sheared, slates cracked, gutters and down-comers shivered and shook, chimney pots and the stacks below them swayed dizzily, shrugged, seemed to right themselves.

But something had changed.

Pawquine, dirty and dusty, lay on the ground and looked up at Grovelle.

Grovelle, twitching with anxiety, looked down at Pawquine.

They both turned their heads slowly. 'What happened?' they said together.

Everything around them looked almost the same, but different enough to be worrying. Different enough to make them feel they were being watched by something more unpleasant than them. Different enough for Pawquine to crawl backwards towards the gate, for Grovelle to walk though puddles muddying his mirrored shoes, for them both to find and hold onto each other and whimper.

The sound was nothing at first, little more than a rumour that a sound might shortly arrive. It became louder, a whisper, it increased in volume, it grew and flexed its muscles, found freedom, stretched itself into a murmur and a mutter and a mumble, developed a real voice that shouted and yelled and roared and snarled, that bellowed its anger to become a whirlwind of hatred and desire and malevolence.

The scream dragged with it a physical presence, and that was the creature that appeared before them. It seemed both to flow and burst through a wall, shattering stones and blocks but at the same time leaving them intact. It had its back to Pawquine and Grovelle. It was tall and wide and clad in a coat of midnight blue leather. Its breath rasped, it smelled of engines and sulphur.

Pawquine looked at Grovelle. Grovelle looked at Pawquine. Pawquine took a breath but Grovelle shook his head, raised a finger to his trembling lips; but it was too late. 'Do you think it's seen us?' Pawquine whispered.

The creature turned slowly. A hood cloaked its face, and from deep within came a hard, metallic, gasping voice. 'I hadn't seen ya. But now I has. My name is Atraxa. What's yours?'

'He's Grovelle,' sobbed Pawquine, 'he's in charge.'

'I am not! He's the leader, his name's Pawquine.' Grovelle was in tears.

'Grovelle? Pawquine?' The creature tasted the words carefully. It took a step toward them. 'I don't like them names. I think I'll call ya . . . Food!

Madame Klein and Mr Li were drinking tea in Madame Klein's private rooms. Maia and Chavanel were outside in the shop.

'I think you owe me an explanation,' Maia said. Her hands rested on the counter, fingers stretched and playing an irregular, urgent tattoo.

Chavanel pretended to examine the jars of jams and preserves, the tins of fruit. He took one down, turned it gently, replaced it. 'I owe you nothing, young lady.'

'"Young lady"? My name is Maia, you've used it often enough to be able to remember it.'

'I haven't forgotten it. But I choose, for the moment, to be more formal than usual.'

'And why is that?'

'For the same reason you're asking questions as if I were a criminal? As if you were a judge?'

Maia considered his words. 'I'm sorry,' she whispered.

'So am I, my little Maiolica.'

'Not so little, Monsieur Chavanel.'

Chavanel turned to face Maia. 'Perhaps I was right to call you a young lady, then.' He sat, reluctantly, in the stiff-backed chair reserved for the Emperorium's older customers. 'You need to talk to Madame Klein. I need to be there with you, as a referee and friend and advisor. As her *Craquelleur* - and I know the word will not be familiar - as her warrior. There are things I feel you ought to know, but only Madame Klein can tell you. I shall urge her to be open and honest with you, however . . .' He shrugged. 'The *Belle Dame* has a mind of her own and purposes I'm unaware of. She is so much more than she seems.'

Maia waited. The silence lengthened. 'And?'

'And nothing. Anything else is up to the good lady.'

A door slammed above them, footsteps sounded on the stairs. Chavanel was on his feet, ready to draw his rapier from its walking stick sheath, when Maia's hand on his arm halted the action. 'It's Ten, Mr Li's son. He was upstairs, looking at books.'

Chavanel sat down again, his fingers still holding the handle of his walking stick. Ten walked into the room, he was clutching seven or eight books. 'These are fantastic,' he said, 'I started reading this one . . .' he held up one of the books '. . . then I looked into this one, then I realised I had to have them, so I've looked at a few and these are the best. At least I think they are.'

Maia stepped in. 'Monsieur Chavanel, this is Ten. His father is in with Madame Klein.'

Chavanel inclined his head to thank Maia for her courteous introduction, then turned his attention to Ten. 'So many books; that's a lot of money.'

'My Dad'll pay. He owes me.'

Chavanel looked as if he was going to say something but caught the insignificant shake of Maia's head.

Ten placed his books on the counter. 'Do you know how long my Dad's going to be?' he asked Maia.

'Are you in a hurry? Madame Klein usually isn't, you see. In a hurry, that is. You're welcome to sit and read,' she pointed him to a second seat in the window. 'I can make you a cup of tea if you want?'

Ten looked at Maia as if the tea she offered might be poisoned, the seat made of knives. 'All I want is . . .' he began, but he was interrupted by his father's voice, the sound of footsteps approaching. Maia noticed a smile of relief and pleasure and anticipation cross his lips for the briefest of moments, but it was quickly defeated by the return of his surly teenage expression. 'He's here,' he said through pinched lips, 'about time too.'

The weary, jaded Mr Li who had accompanied Madame Klein into the depths of the Emperorium only an hour or so beforehand had been replaced by a new man, a calm, happy man, a man who hurried straight to his son and embraced him. 'Ten,' he said, holding his son's shoulders and staring into his eyes, 'I have so much to tell you. Your Mom . . .'

'I zhink, Mr Li, zhis conversation would be better in private?' Madame Klein, close behind her client, nodded wisely.

At that moment, outside in the building site, Pawquine knocked against the brick wall that collapsed, allowing the timber frame it had been supporting to sink, creating the small movement that had allowed things to move, to change. And it didn't go unnoticed. Maia felt the change, a slight adjustment of perspective that made her blink and hold out her hand to make sure the counter was as solid as it ought to have been. Madame Klein frowned. Chavanel reached again for his swordstick. And there was, suddenly, a smell of oil and the sound of cracked, guttural breathing.

'Yves, zhe door has opened!' Madame Klein closed her eyes.

'But you locked it. I saw you.' Chavanel was on his feet, looking around him.

Madame Klein was concentrating. 'Zhe door has moved!' Her eyes opened wide, full of fear. They flicked to the top of the stairs. 'Get everyone out!'

Chavanel was already pushing Mr Li and his son in the direction of the front door. 'You too,' he nodded at Maia.

'I'm staying with Madame Klein,' Maia said.

'You're coming with me!' Chavanel grabbed her by the arm

'What's going on?' Mr Li protested, while his son twisted away to get the books he'd left on the counter.

The staircase didn't explode. It didn't collapse. It was as if the space it occupied folded in on itself and was reduced to rubble; in its place was a long, dark corridor. Maia blinked. Madame Klein was no longer there, Chavanel had disappeared, Ten and his father might never have existed. Instead there was a wall of a creature that stepped closer to Maia, a creature whose head was hidden beneath a hood attached to a long midnight-blue coat which swept almost to the floor. Maia stepped back and tripped over something, found that she'd stumbled over Ten's silent, motionless body. The creature's face swung towards her.

It had only one eye, flecked with yellow, with a vertical slash of a pupil like that of a reptile. In its other socket was a lens of some type, set in telescopic metal. It whirred, turned quickly, and it bent forward as if it wanted to see more closely. Its face was painted with blue and white swirls, but the paint was old, and beneath it the skin looked like rust. It turned its head slightly to one side and the other, as if it was trying to scent the air. Its nose was a series of vertical slits above a circular mouth lined with cruel, rasping teeth.

It stared at Maia and Ten unmoving beneath her. 'Two humans. One male, post-puberty,' it said, and its voice was cracked and buzzing; its lensed eye looked past her at Ten's body. 'Unconscious. Otherwise undamaged. Limited intelligence. Probably of no value. Query: ignore, destroy or reclaim?' It licked its lips lasciviously and Maia could see its tongue, a livid bright blue, wash over serrated teeth. 'Second human is female, post-puberty.' Its voice grew louder. 'Atraxa, I have a female.'

It bent closer, too close. Maia could hear the rasp of air being forced into and out of its mouth, she could smell rot and decay. 'Are you frightened, human female?' The sleeves of its coat rose up either side of her head. The tips of its fingers appeared; at least eight of them crept from each sleeve, some thin and rope-like, others thicker, like a baby's arms; several were tipped with twisted corroded metal, glistening with viscous liquid.

'Why should I be frightened of you?' Maia whispered, aware that she was indeed desperately frightened.

Its head came closer still, but its feet were still planted on the floor halfway across the room. The analytical, dispassionate part of Maia found time to wonder how it kept its balance.

'Pain, human female, that's why you should be frightened of me. Pain.' It turned its head again. 'Atraxa? I repeat, I have a human female in my care. What would you like me to do with it?' It licked its lips again, opened its mouth in a grin. 'It has been a *very* long time since I fed.'

Maia tried to duck her head below its fingers, slide away to one side, towards where she thought the door ought to be. The creature moved its arm to prevent her, shook its head. 'Beware, human female. I might just decide to tap my fingers together.' It wriggled two of the thinner fingers then held them in front of her eyes. As she watched they seemed to change shape, become sharper, straighter, longer. They reared back, then hurtled forward. She felt them slide over the top of her head, parting her hair, and bury themselves in the wall behind her. 'You may turn your head to look, human female,' the creature said. She did so, watched it withdraw its fingertips from the wall. Three inches of metallic flesh appeared; the tips must have penetrated plaster and brick. 'Imagine what would happen if I tapped my fingers together,' it explained, 'with your head between them. Do not move. I am a little nervous, Atraxa should have responded by now.'

'Atraxa 'as responded, Seflapod,' came a weary voice, slow and thick and hard as iron, from somewhere both beyond and within the room. 'I 'ave two adult yuman males.'

'But we were told to find a female. I have found a female. My single female is therefore worth more than any number of males.'

'Is your female *the* female? Is she the right age?'

It was clear that the creature standing over Maia, threatening her, was subservient to the other.

'I have already said. It is female.' The head moved closer. Its tongue snaked out of its mouth, scented the air. 'It is post-puberty. It is . . . tender. It is . . . fresh.'

'Then it's worthless, Seflapod. We seek an old woman. Y' should dispose of yer tender female.'

'And your two males?'

'They ain't tender. They 'ave age, they 'ave experience. They might be useful in 'elpin' us find the old woman we're lookin' for. I'll question 'em. Then I'll dispose of 'em.'

'Then I will do the same with this one.' The creature turned its attention back to Maia. 'We seek a human female,' it rasped. 'She resides here. She is not tender. Where is she?'

Maia realised they were looking for Madame Klein. 'There are quite a few women - females - who live here,' she whispered, 'I don't know which one you mean.'

The single organic eye stared at her. Its artificial companion moved closer. She could hear its whirring and, beneath that, a deeper rhythm, a regular triple-time beat of an inhuman heart. She felt one of the hands creep around her head and two fingers hovered over her. One of them was metallic, sharp and nervous; the other glowed with a narrow beam of light.

'Do you tell the truth, female?' The creature's voice was suddenly soft.

'Yes,' Maia lied.

'I think not. I will be specific.' It turned its head to one side as if straining to hear a distant whisper. 'The human female is old. She is called the Klein. Where is she?'

42

Maia took a deep breath. 'I don't know,' she said, aware that she wasn't actually sure where Madame Klein was.

The creature inhaled. 'I can smell your innocence, female. I can see your truthfulness. You do not know where she is. Therefore you are of no value to me.'

Maia felt the creature's grip on her head tighten. She saw the sharp finger pull back, twitch with anticipation.

'But you are so very . . . very . . . tender.'

Maia closed her eyes. There was a scream, but it wasn't - to Maia's surprise - her own. She opened her eyes to find the creature still standing above her, but instead of its deadly sharp finger poised to pierce her skull there was a stump dripping violet blood onto her blouse and skirt. Part of her wanted to complain that the outfit was almost new and would, had she not bought it from a charity shop, have been very expensive. But the more sensible part of her forced her to squirm through the creature's legs where she saw Chavanel, sword in hand, its blade stained with the creature's blood. He motioned her to move behind him as the creature spun around. It held up its hand, the remaining fingers writhing. 'You hurt me,' it hissed.

'Good,' grinned Chavanel. 'That was only a beginning. *En garde*!' He took up a fencing stance, one hand on hip, sword arm extended, his weight on the balls of his feet. He danced forward but the creature swivelled easily, quickly, brought from beneath its coat a curved scimitar. It sliced at Chavanel's head and the old man avoided the blade only by staggering backwards, pushing Maia with him as he went.

'Stay there!' Chavanel ordered Maia as he regained his balance, jumped to one side and aimed the point of his blade at the creature's chest. It retreated a step, blocked Chavanel's thrust with its arm and pushed the blade away. It swung the scimitar again, faster. Maia could see only one outcome. The creature was far bigger than Chavanel, stronger, quicker, and Chavanel could do only limited damage with his sword. It was pushing Chavanel back with a flurry of strokes, knocked the sword from his hand and giggled. It held up the stump of its finger; it was growing back. 'I don't think your head will do the same when I cut it from your body,' it cackled. 'But perhaps I'll cut off a hand or foot to begin with. So you can feel pain and fear together.'

Maia reached down and found a half brick amongst the rubble at her feet, threw it with unerring accuracy, and it struck the creature's head. It spun towards her. 'You should not have done that, tender girl!' it spat. Its arm seemed to extend, it snaked towards her even as she was reaching down for another brick to throw, long fingers curled around her neck and began to squeeze. At the same time it stamped hard on Chavanel's sword, broke it in two. Chavanel himself had his back against a wall, there was nowhere to escape, and the creature's sword moved slowly towards his chest. 'Two together,' the creature said, 'tender and aged.' The creature's tongue slithered into its mouth, appeared again shaking with anticipation.

Maia's sight was fading, she couldn't breathe, and though she punched and kicked against her assailant its grip didn't lessen. The creature's sword was resting on Chavanel's neck. 'Yes,' it said softly, urgently, 'oh yes.'

A book spun across the room and hit the creature on the forehead. Its eyes swivelled, and a second book hit the telescopic lens hard.

'You hurt my son!' a banshee voice screamed as Mr Li hurled a third book which struck the creature on the neck. It took a step towards Mr Li, dropped Maia who breathed in a gulp of gloriously dusty, dank air. She had to do her part. With a chorus of coughing she heaved a fusillade of bricks at the creature, not caring which part of its body she hit. The creature was holding its sword aloft in a vain attempt to block similar missiles now coming from Chavanel as well. He reached for his broken sword and crawled forward, raised it high and stabbed what was left of the shattered blade into the creature's foot.

'Atraxa!' the creature shrieked. 'I am under attack! Assistance is required!' The onslaught of Maia, Chavanel and Mr Li (who had run out of books and turned to throwing tins of fruit and vegetables) drove it back. It limped, blood flowing from its wounded foot, and stumbled over Ten's body. It bent swiftly and scooped it up, used it as a shield. The flood of projectiles ceased. Maia was gasping for breath, covered in dust and blood, though none was her own. She looked at Chavanel, he had several cuts on his forehead, his clothes were torn in places. Mr Li was wild-eyed, wide-eyed, he stared at her, pleading.

'Who's attackin' ya, Seflapod?' the weary voice demanded.

'Tender girl! Old man! Book man! I am injured. I have exerted, I have had to regenerate. I require assistance.'

'Ya deserve no assistance. Take a life, recover. Have ya found the Klein?'

'No.'

'I'm interrogatin' the two males. *You* can help *me*. Take a life.'

The creature looked at its assailants in turn, then at Ten's body. 'This one stirs. That is good. There is life in it. It will suffice.' It raised one hand which seemed to change shape, it spread out over Ten's scalp and down, over his eyes and mouth and nose, it glowed slightly as the creature inhaled.

'No.' Mr Li whimpered.

'Yes!' the creature hissed.

'No!' Mr Li hurled himself at the creature. 'You will not take my son!'

Mr Li was a big man, he caught the creature in its stomach and kept going, pushed it to the ground. Chavanel was quick to react; as the creature attempted to find its scimitar with its free hand he leaped forward, stamped on its arm. The creature tried to roll, to scramble to its feet, but Maia was there too, adding her weight to the struggle, trying to pull the creature's hand away from Ten's head. She felt a surge of triumph as Ten, eyes flickering open, fell to the floor, but that victory was short-lived; the creature used its free arm to throw Chavanel away, ignored Maia, and forced itself to its feet. 'I will feed!' it yelled, extended its arm again, one finger sharpened into a glowing point, and thrust it at Ten.

Mr Li was quicker.

He threw himself in front of his son.

He seemed almost surprised when the finger pierced his chest, when a faint glow covered his body. Then he collapsed to the ground.

The creature was immediately rejuvenated, It stood taller, stronger, suddenly more confident as it looked around the room. 'Atraxa,' it announced, 'I have fed. Such memories! Such delicious guilt! Do you wish me to feed more?'

'Seflapod,' the disembodied voice whispered, 'we 'aven't found our prize. My males 'ave been unhelpful, they seem incapable of thinkin' at all. We 'ave t' search for Klein ourselves. You must join me.'

The creature looked longingly at Maia, at Chavanel, at Ten. 'I will return,' it said to them. It looked up, tasted the air, then turned and charged through a wall.

'What happened?' Maia coughed, 'why has it gone? It could have killed us, but it didn't.'

Chavanel rose to his knees. 'I don't know,' he said. 'I know what it is, but . . .' He looked at Mr Li's body, at his son sobbing over it, stroking his father's bloodied head. His eyes searched the room further. 'Elise!' he called.

'She's not here,' Maia said, reaching out a hand to him.

'You heard them! They said they were looking for her!' There was desperation in his voice.

'If she knew they were after her she might have tried to escape,' Maia said. 'Or she could have tried to lead them away, to stop them . . .' She looked at Ten sobbing over his father. 'To stop them hurting anyone else.'

'Then we must find her before they do.' Chavanel climbed wearily to his feet. 'Come, Maia.'

FOUR

Atraxa had cornered Pawquine and Grovelle, they were crouched in a circle of dampness between two piles of rubble, hugging each other and mumbling incoherently. Atraxa scuttled to and fro as if it had many legs. Its movement was similar to its speech, swift and purposeful. Its skin was, like Seflapod's, roughened by dirt and paint; unlike its taller colleague, its face was wide. Its hood was lowered to reveal black, oily, braided hair falling onto broad shoulders. Its mouth seemed to stretch the whole width of its face; even when it stopped talking its lips seemed to pulsate with a life of their own, as if something was trying to escape from behind them.

'Your humans are less resilient than mine,' Seflapod said, 'and there are fewer of them. Yet you have let the Klein escape.'

Atraxa spun round angrily. '*I've* let 'er escape? Weren't she inside the building? Weren't yer inside the building? Then *you've* let 'er escape.'

Seflapod's voice was steel. '*You* are my senior, Atraxa, as *you* often remind me. Therefore *you* are responsible for *my* actions. Regardless of how the Klein has evaded us, *you* are accountable for the loss.' Seflapod licked its lips and whispered. 'Until you are, as seems inevitable, removed from your position of leadership.'

Atraxa pointed a sharp angry finger at Seflapod. 'If that 'appens then I'll make sure y're right by my side on the trip to the vats.'

Seflapod pondered the threat, reconsidered its animosity. 'Then perhaps we should seek the Klein together?'

'That was my order to y'! So why isn't y' doin' it? She can't 'ave gone far.'

Seflapod sniffed the air. 'I could smell something in the building, it must have been her, but the stench was old. Yet now?' Seflapod raised its head again. 'I have it! Faint. Distant. But definitely the Klein!'

The creatures raised their heads and howled their triumph.

And they were gone.

Madame Klein had been injured. Her right arm was clearly broken, it was too painful to move and was hanging limp by her side. She was talking to herself. 'What happened? Two Bazhka already zhrough, more on zheir way unless I can do zomezhing.' She staggered across the square, dazed, not entirely certain where she was going or what she was doing. And she was tired, so tired. She reached the statue in the middle of the square and sank to her knees. They were after her, the Bazhka were after *her*, she'd heard them say that. But why?

Her eyesight was poor at the best of times and she'd lost her glasses somewhere in the fight, somewhere in the explosion of sound and the destruction of the doorway. So she sensed rather than saw two shadows on the ground in front of her, heard breathing. She waited for the blow to fall.

'You alright, Madame Klein?' The voice seemed worried, concerned.

'We heard a noise from the Emperorium, sounded like an explosion.'

Madame Klein turned. The blurred figures were too small to be Bazhka. 'My arm's broken,' she said, 'zhere was an accident, I can't zee straight. You are . . ?'

'Friz.'

'And Slip. We're sort of friends of Maia, she . . .'

'We've been in your shop before,' Friz interrupted.

Madame Klein nodded. 'Yez. I remember. But you must help! Zhere is zomezhing bad and I must go back to close zhe door.' She chewed at her bloody lip. 'But did zhey come zhrough zhe door? No!' She shook her head. 'I must get away, zhe Bazhka are after me. But why? Why me?'

'I think she's gone loopy,' Friz whispered.

'Deffo. One sandwich short of a picnic.'

'Yep. Only one oar in the water.'

'You must help! Zhey will be here soon, zhey will know where I am.'

There was another noise from the direction of the Emperorium, the howl of a hunter baying after finding the scent of its prey. Slip and Friz looked at each other then, together, bent down to haul Madame Klein to her feet. They tried to be gentle but she whimpered as they raised her from the steps.

'Which way?' Friz asked urgently.

Slip looked around. 'The bakery, it's nearest. We can hide there.'

They half-carried, half-dragged Madame Klein across the square, glancing behind them as they made their slow way to the bakery. It was Slip who saw the creatures first, one leaping over the fence beside the Emperorium, the other bursting through it. The larger of the two lowered its head and began running toward the statue, the second danced and bounced around the first, its maniacal laughter echoing around the square. In the distance a police siren promised help, but Slip knew it would be too late.

Friz was taking most of Madame Klein's weight. 'What's . . . happening?' she asked.

'You don't want . . . to know. Just keep going.'

The door was close, but the creatures had already reached the statue and had seen their prey; they sped across the remaining few metres, eyes wide, mouths open and slavering. Slip flung the bakery door open. Mrs Vogt was behind the counter. She looked up, saw Madame Klein, Slip and Friz; her eyes widened as she took in the creatures beyond. 'Through the back!' she yelled, opening the counter hatch.

Somehow, with Mrs Vogt's help, Slip and Friz pushed and pulled Madame Klein through the counter opening and into the room beyond. Mrs Vogt slammed the door behind her just as the shop-front disintegrated. The creatures hurtled through the debris, fragments of glass and splinters of wood filled the air, rained onto the loaves and cakes scattered across the floor.

Mrs Vogt slid two bolts across the door, leaned her back against it. She slid slowly to the floor. 'What are they?' Her voice trembled. 'They . . . I've never . . . Monsters!'

All heads turned as the other door, the one that lead to the bakery itself, was thrown open. Tom appeared, hands and arms coated with flour, tousled hair escaping from beneath a crumpled white hat. He took in Madame Klein, Slip and Friz, but his attention was only on his mother. He ran to the door. 'What's happened?' he demanded, 'I heard . . . well, it sounded like an explosion. 'Are you okay?' He examined his mother closely, looking for signs of injury.

'I'm not hurt, I'm just . . . There are creatures. Monsters. Outside.'

As if waiting for the cue, the door shook as it was struck from the other side. Mrs Vogt pushed herself away from its vibrations.

'Monsters? What type of monsters?'

'Zhey are called Bazhka, boy.' Madame Klein's face was as white as the flour dusting the floor. 'Zhey are evil.'

Tom pulled his mother towards him. 'Will they be able to get through that door?'

Even as he spoke a long sliver of metal thrust its way through one of the door panels.

'Zhey will get in,' Madame Klein nodded. She glanced over her shoulder. 'You must all go. Zhrough zhe bakery, lock zhe door. It is me zhey're after.'

'There's no way out,' Mrs Vogt said. 'It's just the ovens and a storeroom. We keep flour there. Sugar. Butter. And yeast.' She shook her head. 'Though we don't have much, I ordered some yesterday but it hasn't arrived yet.'

'It's alright, Mum, don't worry,' Tom said.

Slip and Friz looked at each other. 'Shock,' Slip diagnosed.

'I hope they don't make too much of a mess,' Mrs Vogt continued as one of the door panels disintegrated.

Tom swung round to stare at Madame Klein. 'What do we do?'

Madame Klein struggled painfully to her feet. 'I'll go out zhere, zhey might go once zhey have me.'

A large tooth-filled head framed with oily braided hair peered into the room. 'Well well, Seflapod, I think we've found the old woman. An' I count four others. Two each. Tasty!' The head retreated and two hands with too many fingers continued to pull the door apart.

Tom pushed Madame Klein down into his mother's arms. 'They aren't going to let any of us go!' He looked around him. 'Mum, show Slip and Friz where the flour is. Bring some bags out of the storeroom, as many as you can carry. And the fans, the floor-standing fans, get them out and plugged in.'

Mrs Vogt seemed very calm. 'But you know what'll happen, Tom,' she said over her shoulder, 'we can only use the fans when the floors been wetted, there's too much flour around. It'll blow everywhere. There'll be such a mess.'

Tom pulled the wincing Madame Klein into the bakery. There was very little door left, but the creatures didn't seem willing to rush in.

'After you, Atraxa,' the first said.

'Yer may 'ave the privilege of enterin' first, Seflapod,' the second growled.

'But you are the senior. The honour should be yours.'

'And y're the junior! So y're expendable.'

There was a moment's silence. 'What did you see, Atraxa? Are they armed? I have already suffered damage today.'

'They're unarmed. The Klein's injured. The others are nothin'. Tender.'

'We should go in together.'

'There's no room! Get y'rself in!'

Seflapod was pushed into the room; it was empty. The open door beyond led into a further room from which a cloud of heat was emanating. Seflapod took a slow step forward. Atraxa appeared behind him. 'I smell food,' Atraxa said,' I smell tender!' He barged past Seflapod and into the bakery.

'Now!' Tom yelled. He held a floor fan in his hand, on the other side of the bakery Friz held the second. They switched them on, directed them at the open sacks of flour on the floor in front of them. The flour blossomed upwards to form a cloud of white, a flour storm that engulfed Atraxa and billowed into the room beyond to coat Seflapod with faint white dust. Both creatures darted back in alarm. 'It's . . .' Atraxa's long tongue snaked out of his mouth, licked the flour dust away from his eyes. 'It's . . . 'armless! Seflapod, they're tryin' t' escape through the cloud! Back!'

Both creatures threw themselves towards the door again, found themselves jammed together in their blind haste and anger.

Madame Klein and Mrs Vogt were lying on the floor covered in wet sackcloth. Tom and Friz, wielding their fans, wore their dampened robes like cloaks. 'Now,' Tom said to Slip, 'Light it.'

Slip was holding a rag of sackcloth soaked in cooking oil, heated in the bakery oven. He flicked the long-handled oven lighter and the flame danced. He touched it to the rag and the flame flared. And he threw it into the whirling storm of flour. It dropped to the floor.

'It didn't work!' Slip yelled.

'It should have blown up,' Tom cried, 'it's one of the things we learned, no naked flames near flour. Mum always said to watch out!'

Mrs Vogt appeared at her son's side. 'You have to do it properly,' she said. 'I don't know, if you want a job done . . .' She picked up the lighter and the rag and strode forward as two monstrous shapes appeared.

'No Mum!' Tom yelled, but Slip and Friz held him back. A long arm wrapped itself around Mrs Vogt's waist, another circled her neck. 'The food comes to us unbidden,' a voice giggled.

'This one is not so tender,' a second voice rumbled.

'You threatened my son,' Mrs Vogt whispered. She lit the rag and waved it in the air around her.

Slip and Friz pulled Tom to the ground as the world exploded.

Maia and Chavanel saw the front of the bakery consumed by a gout of flame. They saw its walls sag and break and collapse to the ground. They staggered across the square, coughing and spluttering as they met the cloud of dust billowing towards them.

'Careful,' husked Chavanel, 'we don't know what happened. The Bazhka could be waiting for us.'

'Bazhka?' Maia said, 'you haven't even told me what they are!' Her eyes were streaming, she could barely breathe, and her nostrils were filled with the smell of burning oil and scorched flesh.

'Listen to me!' Chavanel said, his hand clutching hers. 'We have to find Madame Klein, the Bazhka came for her but she's the only one who can help us get them back where they came from.'

'And where's that?'

'Inside the inside of the Emperorium. Locked away.' He pulled her after him.

'But they *were* inside and they got out. How can we lock them back in? There's no door, let alone a lock.'

'That's why we need to find Madame Klein. Come *on*.'

They crept forward, found themselves stepping through rubble, broken bricks and fragments of jagged glass, splintered window frames. Chavanel suddenly froze, raised a finger swiftly to his lips and pointed ahead. Looming out of the swirls of smoke was a figure lying on the ground, too long and bulky to be human. 'Bazhka?' Maia whispered.

'What else could it be?'

'Perhaps it's dead.'

Chavanel shook his head. 'It takes a lot to kill a Bazhka. But injured? Perhaps. Wait here.'

He took a step forward. Maia followed him. Chavanel turned his head to growl at her but saw the determination in her face. He shrugged. They took another step forward, then another. The creature seemed to have two heads and thick sturdy limbs, at least four of them. Chavanel took a deep breath of smoky air and heard Maia hold back a snorting laugh. 'Oh no,' she said, 'it's George! And Oscar!' She anticipated Chavanel's bewilderment. 'The statue in the square,' she explained, 'and his horse.' Her laughter subsided quickly. 'But they're blown up. Lying on their sides.' She moved closer. 'Chavanel! Look!' She pointed beyond the sandstone statue to another figure.

Chavanel followed her outstretched arm and nodded. 'Bazhka. We go round.' He motioned her to one side, and that was when Maia's face was struck by a drop of water, then another, then many more. 'Rain,' she said, as if hoping that the summer downpour would wash away the horrors she'd experienced. Instead the deluge captured the dust and smoke in the air, dragged it downwards. It revealed, just ahead of them, the body of a Bazhka, another a little further away. The clothes of both creatures had been ripped and torn, the skin beneath was blistered and blackened. Maia took a wary step forward, picked up a broken piece of wood and prodded the nearest body.

'I think it's dead,' she said.

Chavanel pulled her arm back. 'I doubt it. Damaged, injured, unable to function, yes. But not dead. Bazhka don't die easily.' Something caught his attention, he raised his eyes from the Bazhka to the ruins of the bakery where figures were emerging from the rubble. 'Madame Klein!' he yelled, vaulted the bodies of the Bazhka and sprinted forward. Maia took a less direct route, she couldn't take her eyes from the still, dark blue bodies of the Bazhka. Their limbs were bent and twisted at unnatural angles. Parts of them seemed missing altogether. There were no signs of life, no rise and fall of breathing in crushed chests, no groaning. Her attention was drawn by Chavanel calling her name, and she ran to join him.

He was kneeling on the ground, Madame Klein's head resting on his lap, the rest of her hidden by a piece of sackcloth. Her eyes were open. Maia's instinct was to sink down before her and weep joyfully because she was alive, but there was fire in those old eyes, and they darted to one side: 'Zhere are ozhers,' she whispered, 'who need help more zhan I do.'

That was when Maia found Tom. It was as if he was mimicking Chavanel, kneeling on the ground, a figure resting a weary head on his lap. But that was where the similarities ended. Behind him stood Slip and Friz, heads bowed, arms round each other. And the figure in Tom's arms, eyes closed, not moving, was Tom's mother.

'Is she . . ?' Maia knelt down beside Tom, put her arm around him, knowing the answer.

'She's not breathing.' Tom shook his head wearily, his voice low and surprisingly calm, as if the body he was cradling was asleep and he was trying not to wake her. 'No pulse. I had to learn first aid, when I started working in the shop. I tried mouth-to-mouth, I tried CPR, but . . .' He wiped the hair from his mother's eyes. 'She rescued us. She set the flour alight. If she hadn't then those *animals*, those *creatures*, those . . . They would have killed us all.' He stretched his head to look around, saw the Bazhka's bodies.

'They're dead,' Maia confirmed.

Tom nodded. He raised his head to look at Maia, his eyes filled with an ocean of tears. 'That's good. Because if they weren't, I'd have to kill them myself.'

'The police will come. What do we tell them?' Slip was taking in the scene around him.

'Yeah,' said Friz, 'how do we explain those?' She shrugged a shoulder in the direction of the Bazhka.

Madame Klein's voice carried to all of them. 'We need to get back to zhe Emperorium. Zhis is too dangerous.' With Chavanel's help she struggled to her feet. 'Come, all of you. Now!'

Maia found herself moving towards the old woman without actually giving any instructions to her feet. Slip and Friz seemed equally compelled. Only Tom remained where he was.

'You can do nozhing for her, boy,' Madame Klein's voice and words were harsh. 'She is dead. We must save zhe living.'

Tom's face twisted into a grimace of disgust. 'If you think I'm leaving my mother, then . . .' He was unable to finish.

'Zhen stay, stupid boy.' Madame Klein turned her attention to Maia. 'You must help me back, zhe door will ztill be open and I must close it.' Maia could see that Madame Klein's face was grey, and not with dust. Her forehead was striped with blood congealing from a deep cut. Without Chavanel's help she would have fallen back to the ground.

'Don't we need to wait here, to tell the authorities what happened?' Maia asked

Madame Klein was already starting her slow, painful way back towards her shop. 'Zhat,' she said over her shoulder, 'is zhe last zhing we must do. And zhe stupid boy will only make zhings worse! Now help me!'

Maia took up position opposite Chavanel, supporting Madame Klein's arm, carrying and dragging her round the Bazhka' bodies. Slip and Friz trailed close behind them. Chavanel said little, but when he spoke his words chilled Maia. 'I don't think the Bazhka are dead, Elise.'

'I *know* zhey aren't dead.'

Maia looked back over her shoulder. 'But if they aren't dead . . . And Tom's still there . . . He's nearer than us and they'll . . .'

'Zhey aren't interested in zhe stupid boy! It was me zhey came for; and I am zhe only one who can zhend zhem back!'

Maia had seen Madame Klein using words as weapons: she had watched her being rude to customers, attacking them with honeyed insults; she had herself experienced (and had been close to tears because of) the old woman's temper, her bitter tongue, her sarcasm; but she had never heard her sound like this: weak, hurt, afraid, and lashing out at those who needed sympathy. She increased her pace, felt Chavanel on the other side of Madame Klein do the same.

Chavanel wasn't looking back at the creatures. His gaze was fixed on the door of the Emperorium on the far side of the square. It was creeping closer.

Slip danced in front of them. 'She's mad, talking about Tom like that, it's not right.'

'Don't matter,' Friz announced. 'So she's a bit loopy? Them things back there are loopy. Or we're loopy, 'cos we've actually seen them. My Gran went a bit like that. Least *she*,' Friz gestured towards Madame Klein, 'is *our* loopy.' Her brow furrowed with concentration. 'Does that sound as daft as I think it does?'

'No,' Maia grunted, 'it sounds . . . really sensible. Could you just give a hand?'

Friz ducked under Madame Klein's arm, took Maia's place. Maia hurried ahead. The front door was wide open, leaning slightly in its frame. All was quiet except for someone sobbing.

'Do you want me to go in first?' asked Slip nervously, his trembling voice indicating clearly that he'd prefer her to decline the offer. Maia shook her head and stepped into the shop.

The air was heavy with dust, but Maia could see clearly enough the two figures on the floor ahead of her. Ten Li was resting his father's head on his lap, gently stroking his face. There were streaks of tears in the grime coating the man's forehead. Ten looked up as Maia entered. 'He's dead,' he whispered, 'my Dad's dead.'

It was too much for Maia. In the space of a few minutes she'd seen Tom's mother and Ten's father killed. Somewhere inside her a voice urged her to kneel beside the grieving boy, to put her arm around him, to share her own tears. But she was unable to move. Instead she began to shake, her breath shuddered in her lungs and began to escape in a deep wail of anguish.

'Shut up, girl!' Madame Klein was suddenly behind her, still supported by Chavanel and Friz. The sharp words had the desired effect: Maia was silenced. 'And you, American boy, listen! Your fazher is not dead, he has been taken. But he soon will be dead if you don't do as I say.' She turned her attention to Chavanel. 'Help me sit down, over zhere, on zhat chair. Maia, come here, zhere is not much time. Wide girl, dancing boy,' she addressed Friz and Slip, 'zhrough zhe door in my private rooms, bring zhe mattress and bedcovers, be quick!'

Ten was bending his head to his father's lips, his fingers were seeking a pulse from wrist and neck. 'I can't find any sign of life,' he said.

'Zhat's because zhere *are* no signs of life. But zhat doesn't mean he's dead.'

Maia had found her voice. 'But that doesn't make sense . . .'

'Zhat's because you are a stupid girl who knows nozhing! He is *not* dead. He has been *taken*, his mind has been . . . I have no *time* for zhis!' Madame Klein sank into her seat, frail and injured but belligerent as a cornered fox. 'Here,' she motioned to Slip and Friz who had appeared with the mattress, 'on zhe ground, in front of me. Zhen put Mr Li on zhe mattress - gently, very gently - and yes, cover him wizh zhe quilt. You, American boy, stop zhis snivelling, I need to zhink!' Madame Klein closed her eyes. Her voice grew softer. 'I feel almost ready. I know what I must do.' Her eyes snapped open. 'Maia, in my room you will find a zkirt and a shawl, and a hat. Get zhem. Put zhem on. Quickly.'

Maia hurried away. As soon as she'd gone Chavanel shook his head. 'I'll do it, Elise.'

'Do what, Yves?' Madame Klein's voice was thin and weak.

'The Bazhka are still alive and will soon be awake again. You need them inside. They came for you, but you can't draw them back in because you need to put up a shield, yes? So Maia is your decoy.'

'If she does as I say zhere will be no danger.'

'There was meant to be no danger from Bazhka, Elise. But they got through.'

'And we must get zhem back again! I need you wizh me, beside me, Chavanel, in case . . .'

'In case of what?'

'Zhey cannot take me. You know zhat.'

'But you said it would be safe. A contradiction, ma cherie?'

Maia came back into the room. Madame Klein's skirt was too short, too wide at the waist, but Maia had found a belt to tie it round her. With the shawl draped over her shoulders and the hat hiding her hair she might, at a distance, pass for Madame Klein.

'You must go outside, my child. Zhe Bazhka will be recovering. When zhey see you, zhey will zhink zhey see me. Zhey will come after you. Now listen, listen carefully. When zhey chase you, you must be like me: not too fast. But zhey must not catch you. When you come in you must go ztraight zhrough zhe house and up zhe stairs but do not go zhrough zhe door. Instead go into zhe book room, wait for zhe Bazhka to go past, zhen lock zhe door behind zhem. Zhat will hold zhem for a while, I will do zhe rest.' She bent her head and took off the cord containing her keys. 'Zhis key,' she said, '*ce clef, le plus petit*, zhe smallest. It will lock zhe door. It will lock all zhe doors.' She coughed loudly. 'Can you do zhis for me?'

'Of course, Madame Klein.'

The old lady nodded. 'Zhen do it!'

Maia stepped outside.

Tom didn't hear the noises at first. They were too slight: the hesitant tap of a fingernail, the slide and scrape of cloth on rough flesh.

He was cradling his mother in his arms, his tears running down the dust on her face. He was waiting, hoping that, if he held her for long enough, her eyes would flicker open and she'd smile at him. She'd tell him everything would be alright. But he knew deep inside that his hope was a wish, and that this wish wouldn't come true. That was when the sound tugged at the fringes of his consciousness, nagged at him, insisted that he pay attention; and so he looked up. A limb (it was encased in the sleeve of a coat so it was probably an arm, though Tom wasn't willing to assume anything about these creatures) twitched and lay still, then twitched again, and again, until its movement became purposeful.

It wasn't revenge that gripped Tom, it was injustice. His mother was dead, she'd died trying to protect him and others from these creatures, yet they were coming back to life; his mother wouldn't live again. They moved, yet his mother was still. He laid her down, gently, slowly, and kissed her on the forehead, on the cheeks, on her lips. He could taste dust and the salt of his own tears. 'Not in vain,' he whispered, pushed himself to his feet.

There was no groaning, no sign that the creatures were injured or in pain. It was as if their bodies were absorbing life, growing themselves again. The mound of flesh and fabric, a stain of midnight blue, gathered itself together and coalesced into two recognisable figures. As they rose to their feet (the fleshy shapes were at the end of tattered trouser legs so must have been feet) the creatures looked around them, scented the air. They glanced at Tom once and dismissed him by ignoring him, began dragging themselves in the direction of the Emperorium.

Tom searched the debris around him, found a piece of long, thick timber. It had nails projecting near one end and he found himself smiling grimly at them. 'Not in vain,' he said to himself as he picked up the beam and set off after the creatures.

A few moments before they'd been dead. Now they were slithering and lurching almost as fast as Tom could run. 'Stop!' he yelled, but if they heard him they ignored him again. And then they paused, their bodies rigid.

'Atraxa do you see her?' The voice was harsh and grating, as if the words were passing through a throat made of sandpaper.

'I sees 'er, Seflapod. Oh, 'ow I sees 'er.'

'We shall capture her!'

Just as Tom thought he'd catch them, fight them, kill them or die trying, the creatures moved again, even faster. Tom could see why. In the distance, outside the Emperorium, a dazed Madame Klein was wandering to and fro, searching the ground.

'Look out!' Tom screamed, and Madame Klein glanced upwards. She might not have seen Tom but she certainly noticed the Bazhka. The creatures were panting, baying their desire to get to her, and Madame Klein ducked inside the shop doorway. The Bazhka were close behind her, Tom at their heels. He hurtled after them, followed them into the battered remains of the shop. He leaped over a pile of rubble, heard voices screaming at him, but they were nothing more than insect sounds and he swatted them aside. The blue coated figures were at the top of the stairs, through the door, and he was close behind them, yelling after them. And then the door slammed behind him. The creatures slid to a halt. They turned slowly and sniffed the air.

'She is not ahead of us, Atraxa. She did not come through the door.'

'But this,' the creature licked its lips, 'this man-boy, 'e did come through. What should we do with 'im, Seflapod?'

'I sense no barrier beyond the door, Atraxa. We must break the door and obtain our objective.'

'But the man-boy's in the way.'

'Then we must break it as well.'

Atraxa sniggered. 'Shall we eat it after we break it? Or while we're breakin' it.'

The creatures slid towards Tom.

Maia pulled off Madame Klein's clothes as she thundered down the stairs. 'I did it,' she cried, I locked them in! What do we do now?'

Madame Klein took a deep breath. Her voice was weak, a monotone. 'Zhe door will hold zhem for only a few minutes. I must build a barrier.' She closed her eyes. 'Zhey are back inside, I must do zis now.' There was a faint crackling sound in the air, and a pale green aura appeared around her.

Maia was looking for someone. 'I thought I heard Tom,' she said, 'and I saw him chasing the Bazhka this way. Where is he? What happened to him?'

Ten shook his head. 'You mean you didn't see him?' He was kneeling, stroking his father's head. 'Well I think you'll find you've just locked him in a room with those monsters.'

Maia's eyes widened. 'No! No, I can't have done!' She took a step towards Chavanel. 'Why didn't you stop him?'

'We tried.' Chavanel sounded old and weary. 'He didn't hear. Even if he had heard us, I don't think he would have come back.'

'He definitely won't be coming back now,' Ten said.

Maia turned on him. 'At least he was trying to do something brave, not like you, sitting there crying like a baby.'

'My father is dead!'

'So is Tom's mother! That's why he decided to do something about it!' Maia looked around her. 'I'm going back to unlock the door and help him, is there anything I can take as a weapon?'

'Nothing can harm the old ones, not permanently,' Chavanel said. 'But I have my sword stick. I'll come with you.' He held up the broken blade, winced with the effort of doing so. 'We must be quick.' He pointed at Madame Klein. 'She's building a barrier and we don't want to be on the wrong side of it.'

Friz rose to her feet. 'I'll come too,' she said, 'I'm strong, I might be able to help.' She reached for a piece of metal that had been supporting the shop's counter. 'And Slip here is quick and sly, he's always handy in a fight.'

Slip didn't seem as keen as his friend. 'Hold on,' he said, 'don't you think that's a little stupid? Or even a lot stupid? Or even completely mad! I mean, we've seen what those things can do.'

'You don't have to come,' Friz said. 'Stay here and look after him.' She pointed at the American. 'You've something in common.'

Maia was already running up the stairs, Chavanel beside her, Friz close behind.

'What did she mean by that?' Ten asked.

'Probably that I'm a coward.' He sniffed, wiped his nose on his sleeve and clenched his fists. 'She knows just how to get to me, that one! Damn!' He stamped up the stairs after them.

'Assholes.' Ten kneeled down again beside his father. 'I'm sorry, Pa. I'm sorry for the things I said about you, and to you. You . . . You tried to protect me, I know that. You were brave. You didn't think of yourself. And now . . .'

He looked up. Madame Klein was muttering something, words in a language he didn't recognise. He climbed to his feet, took a cautious step closer, then closer still. He kneeled down to hear more clearly what she was saying, then started when Madame Klein's eyes flicked open. 'He is not dead,' she hissed, 'your fazher is not dead. Look at him.'

The glow that bathed her body in electric green was expanding, he could feel its charge as it crept over him, raised the hairs on his arms. It slid towards, then over and around his father, cocooned him in the same light. And he saw his chest move. He was alive.

'Go after zhem. Tell her, tell zhe girl, tell Maia.'

'Tell her what?'

'Tell her . . .' Madame Klein's voice was weakening as the aura grew stronger, as the hum of electricity grew louder.

'Tell her . . . Dis-lui . . . C'est trés importante . . . very important . . . Clef! Le clef!'

'If you think I'm going . . .'

'Tell her! "Tu es le clef!" Or . . . He dies!'

Ten jumped to his feet and looked at his father before reluctantly climbing the stairs. 'I can't believe I'm doing this,' he said, 'I can't believe it. It can't be real. It cannot be real.'

Maia unlocked the door and threw it open. She rushed into the corridor beyond, Chavanel and Friz close behind her. Tom was backing slowly towards them, the two Bazhka hugging the walls of the corridor in an attempt to split his attention and better their chances of overcoming him. When Maia and the others appeared the Bazhka stopped abruptly.

'I'm so sorry,' Maia cried, 'I didn't see you follow them through. And I thought they'd . . .'

Tom interrupted her. 'They said they could get break the door down even if it was locked,' he growled.

Maia looked at Chavanel. He shrugged. 'So what do we do now?' she asked.

'Four,' one of the creatures said. 'Can you take two, Atraxa?'

'Two? I could eat all of 'em, Seflapod.'

'And then we progress to our goal.'

'Can I 'ave the girl? She smells fresh and sweet.'

'There are two of the female gender, Atraxa.'

'I'll 'ave 'em both, then!'

Chavanel stepped forward to stand beside Tom. 'Maia, Friz, back through the door,' he said.

Friz pushed Chavanel aside. 'You go back if you want, old man.'

The larger of the creatures drew itself up to its full height, its shoulders against the ceiling, head pushed forward, jaws dripping. 'Enough!' it said in a voice so soft it wept with malevolence. 'You are in our way. Remove yourself and we will not harm you.'

'Seflapod might not 'arm you, little 'umans, but I might. I most *definitely* might.'

The doorway became suddenly more crowded as Slip eased into the corridor to shelter behind Friz. 'I knew you wouldn't manage without me,' he said, 'you need someone to watch your back.'

'Five? Are there more?'

Ten was the sixth to join them, his mouth open, ready to scream. He couldn't take his eyes away from the creatures. 'I only came because . . .'

He was unable to explain why he was there. Behind and below them there was a rush of hot air and a thunderous explosion. Maia, and those around her, fell to the ground then scrambled quickly up again, expecting the creatures to use the confusion to attack them; but they were met with the spectacle of the monsters retreating, backing away from them, scurrying down the corridor until they rounded a bend and were out of sight.

67

'What happened?' Maia asked. 'Why did they go? What was that noise?'

'That was the sound of a door slamming,' Chavanel said. 'That was Madame Klein putting up a barrier. That's why they,' he gestured down the corridor, 'went away. Even if they attacked us, even if they killed us, they wouldn't be able to get through to her. The world is safe again. For a while.'

'They killed my mother,' Tom said, dropping his wooden club. 'I'm going back to get some type of weapon, then I'm hunting them. I'll find them.'

'They won't be hiding, Tom.' Chavanel put his arm round Tom's shoulder, for support as well as comfort. 'But you do need to find a better way of defending yourselves.'

'Hold on.' Maia's voice was sharp, it halted all speech and movement. 'We need to go back. We need to help Madame Klein, she was hurt.'

'I agree,' Ten said, 'I'm only here to pass on . . .'

Chavanel turned to face them, his face clothed in age and fatigue. 'I'm sorry Maia, all of you. You weren't listening to me. When I said there was a barrier, when I said the door had closed, slammed, I meant that the Bazhka couldn't get through. But nor can we. We can't go back.'

'Oh yes we can,' Ten said, 'through this door and down the stairs, that's where we go. At least, that's where I go.' He turned on his heels and pushed past Slip and Friz.

'Go on then,' Chavanel said, 'go back. We'll come with you, just so we all know what choices we have.' He ushered the others through the door after Ten, linked his heavy arm with Maia's. They trudged wearily down the staircase to find themselves in front of a translucent pale green wall. It sang with blades of crackling green and razor white electricity.

Chavanel was weary, his hair seemed whiter, his face greyer. He spoke to all of them. 'Nothing can get through. Nothing at all. Including us.'

'How do you know?' Ten asked. 'What makes you the expert in . . .'

Maia interrupted. 'I can see her. I can see Madame Klein. And Ten, she's right beside your father.'

'Don't touch the barrier!' Chavanel warned.

'Can't she see us?' Slip asked, raising a hand to wave.

'She's got her eyes closed.' Friz pointed out.

Maia squinted. 'Can you see beyond her? Where the shop door used to be? There are two people standing, not moving either. I think . . .'

'It's Pawquine and Grovelle,' Tom said.

'Please everyone, you must listen to me.' Chavanel straightened his back, made himself taller. 'Time works in a different way in the Emperorium. The outside world is often, as now, out of synchronisation. We've speeded up, or the world has slowed down. And as you move deeper into the Emperorium then you might find other things that are different. I'm not sure, Madame Klein didn't often talk about being inside.'

There was a chorus of voices: 'How can time move differently . . ?' 'What do you mean, move deeper inside . . ?' 'What about my father?' 'What about those monsters?' 'It's a shop, we can't exactly go far!'

'Be quiet!' Maia's voice was strong and loud, and everyone turned to look at her.

'I'm sure Mr Chavanel will explain everything if we give him the chance. We know nothing of what's happened, what those creatures are, where they came from . . .' She sniffed, wiped her nose with her sleeve, and realised that her blouse and skirt were torn and blood-stained, and her face was dirty. The others were as dishevelled as she was. 'I'm tired and frightened. I'm sure you feel the same. But Mr Chavanel seems to know something about what's going on. He can lead us out of this, I'm sure. But we have to listen to him.'

'He's not going to lead us anywhere,' Tom said. 'He didn't say "we" he said "you". I don't think he's planning . . .'

'The Bazhka,' Chavanel interrupted, his voice weak and slow, 'are difficult to kill, you've seen that. But they can kill others in many ways. Some of them have poison in their teeth or their claws or their talons. One of those two,' he nodded back into the building, 'certainly did.' He turned his back. His shirt was torn, he lifted it to reveal three parallel lines of blood welling from purple black wounds.

'Tis but a scratch,' he smiled, 'Ask for me tomorrow and you will find me a grave man.' His smile became a grimace.

'What's he on about?' asked Ten. 'Has he gone mad?'

'Shut up, you idiot!' Maia knelt down in front of Chavanel. 'Does it hurt? Is there anything we can do?'

'You can do nothing, Maia. And yes, it hurts.' He hung his head on his chest and closed his eyes. His mouth opened as if he was trying to force words to come, but there was no sound. He waved Maia closer, breathed in deeply. 'I told Elise you were ready.' He smiled again. 'I'm sure I was right. You should . . . look for a guide. A map. Find . . . the Library?' His head fell forwards one last time. Maia felt his neck but found no pulse; there was no rise and fall of his chest, no trace of breath on his lips. She kissed him gently on the cheek. And she made up her mind that she would cry later, when she had a chance to be alone.

FIVE

Maia washed Chavanel's face and folded his arms over his chest. Tom and Friz helped her pile bricks and rocks over his body. Ten looked on but offered no assistance. They stood in awkward silence until Slip interrupted their sorrow.

'We can't just stand here doing nothing,' Slip said. 'Those things might come back and I don't know . . .' He looked around nervously. 'I mean . . . Well, it's weird,' he stared into the electric green barrier, 'seeing Madame Klein in there and knowing we can't get to her. As far as I can see the wall-thingy curves round the whole of the building. Or rather, where the building was.' He took a few anxious steps up the stairs. 'I can see through a window,' he said, 'the barrier goes right over the top of us. It's a dome.' He slid back down to join them. 'I can't figure out,' he said, stepping daintily through the rubble, 'where those creatures could have gone. I mean, it's not that big a building.' He glanced uneasily up the stairs. 'They could still be pretty close.'

'It's obvious, isn't it.' Ten stalked over to join them. 'The door was a portal to another world. The monsters . . .'

'Bazhka,' Maia interrupted sullenly, 'they're called Bazhka.'

'Yeah, well, the Bazhka managed to get through somehow. The old woman was meant to be some type of gatekeeper - not that she was any good at her job - and she let them through. She's had to put up this barrier now, so we're stuck on the inside. And although she said my dad wasn't dead, I reckon the old witch was wrong about that. 'Cos he looked dead to me. So life is basically . . .'

'Don't talk that way about Madame Klein!' Maia turned to stand in front of Ten. 'She did everything possible to save us!'

'Well perhaps she didn't try hard enough!' Ten's face was contorted with anger. 'I could ask my dad what he thinks, except I can't! Why? Because he's not breathing and he's not moving and he's locked inside some barrier with the mad crone whose fault this whole farce is anyway!'

'If she said your dad isn't dead, then he isn't! So now it's our turn to try to help him.'

'And exactly how are we gonna do that, little miss know-all?'

Maia backed down, her voice small. 'I don't know.'

Tom spoke up from her side. 'None of us knows what to do next. Your dad might still be alive, Ten. I mean, if you look at Madame Klein she doesn't seem to be on the other side of the barrier; she's actually in the barrier. And Chavanel said time was distorted, so . . .'

'Clutching at straws, aren't you?'

'At least *you* have a straw to clutch. My Mum *is* dead, that's certain.' Tom's voice was calm and even and angry. 'I held her. No heartbeat, no breathing, no life. So I don't care what anyone else is doing, I'm going to find those monsters and kill them.'

'So what do we do?' Slip joined them.

'Let's think what we know already,' Maia suggested.

'If you look beyond the barrier,' Tom began, 'you can see those two men . . .'

'Grovelle and Pawquine,' Maia said.

'Yes, they've hardly moved in the last fifteen minutes. So time does seem to be passing at a different rate.'

'And space,' Slip added, 'that must be distorted as well. When the Bazhka disappeared down that long corridor it looked as if they were miles away, way beyond where the far end of the shop would have been.'

Friz joined in. 'The Bazhka are dangerous. They're strong, they come back to life when you think they're dead, they're poisonous.'

'And they came here for a purpose.' Maia's eyebrows were leaning towards each other, she chewed her lip as she concentrated. 'Did anyone else hear anything they said? They were definitely looking for Madame Klein.'

'They feed on a person's life force, or something like that,' Ten said, 'not just their bodies. With my Dad it was as if he was being drained of all his energy.' He gulped his tears away. 'That monster took his soul.'

Maia reached out, put a hand on the young American's shoulder. He brushed it away, 'I don't like being touched,' he said.

'Chavanel said we'd have to go deeper into the Emperorium,' Slip said. 'And that we'd need a guide. Did he mean a guidebook? He said it would be good to begin in the library, so we could get a map.'

'Even though we don't know where the library is? And even if we find it, and there's a map, we don't know where to head for? Sounds stupid to me.' Ten shook his head, stalked away from the rest of them.

'Any better ideas, Yank?' Tom didn't try to hide his annoyance.

'Yeah, as a matter of fact. Even if there is some sort of time shift, if we wait here then the authorities will arrive and find a way to take the barrier down. And if we're still here, they'll get us out. But once we move away . . .' He drew a finger across his neck, 'then we're done for.'

'Stay if you want,' Tom said. 'I'm going. Anyone else coming along?'

There was silence.

'Those monsters might be waiting for us,' Slip said.

'At least here we know what to expect,' Friz added. 'And there's plenty of food to keep us going, the whole of the contents of the grocery!'

Maia pondered. 'We'd probably be safer here than going on, but . . .' She took a step closer to Tom. 'But if we did, then the basic problem still continues. If the barrier does disappear then we might get rescued, but the Bazhka, perhaps loads more, can come through. We need to stop them. We're probably the only ones who can stop them. So I'm with you, Tom.'

Slip and Friz looked at each other, as if each was daring the other to go first.

'And then,' Maia continued, 'there's the fact that going into the Emperorium gives us choices. If we stay here then all we're doing is waiting for someone to rescue us. But if we go on, we might do some good. And if we don't, if we can't find the library or there's no map of the Emperorium inside it, then we can always come back.'

'I don't really like standing around doing nothing,' Friz said 'and you're right about options. Plus, it'll be a bit of an adventure.'

'An adventure that gets you killed!' Ten was angry again. 'It's not one of your stupid video games, you know, you don't disappear for a few seconds then start the level again. You don't have a few lives. You can't look for cheats to get you through a difficult stage.' He pointed at the rocks covering Chavanel's body. 'You die here and you're permanently dead.' He glared at Friz. 'I think I'd rather be permanently alive.

'No-one's making you come with us,' Tom said. 'I'm going to see if I can find some different clothes, some knives, food, a rucksack. I want to be away inside an hour, two hours max.' He didn't look back as he headed for the door.

Maia went to follow him. 'I'm heading up to Madame Klein's rooms first, see if there's any running water so I can have a wash. Then it's what Tom said. Clothes and so on.'

'I'm not hanging around here,' Friz announced. 'You coming, Slip?'

'We're a team,' Slip said. 'Will we need sleeping bags? Tents? Torches, definitely torches.'

'Let's see what we can find. Come on, we're wasting time.'

Slip and Friz left Ten alone. He sat down on a dirty, dusty, ripped armchair, his eyes focused on the still figure of his father lying in front of Madame Klein, cloaked in a dirty blanket and a shimmering green haze. He wasn't dead, according to Madame Klein, but he wasn't alive either. And he was neither in the outside world nor in the world of the Emperorium. He was incapable of moving from his existence in that strange limbo, just as his son was incapable of any action that would take him further away from his father.

There was hot water in the taps in Madame Klein's apartment. Maia showered the grime and sweat from her body and, wrapped in a clean dressing gown, searched the 'Teen's and Women's Wear' room for anything suitable. It was difficult, not knowing what lay ahead, to choose exactly what to wear and what to pack. After laying underwear, overwear and outerwear on Madame Klein's single bed (metal-framed, thick-mattressed, floral-quilted with three well-stuffed pillows) she dressed herself in multi-pocketed trousers, a T-shirt and fleece. She discarded anything that required other than simple care, divided everything remaining by two, and managed to fit it all into the bottom of a large backpack. She added soap and a lightweight towel, a pair of trainers (for when her feet grew tired of the walking boots she'd chosen to wear), matches and plastic bags.

She looked in the mirror and decided that she was presentable, then reached for the necklace her father had given her and took it off. It was, she decided, too precious to wear; if she was in danger it might get broken. She placed it gently, reverently, in her zipped pocket.

Atraxa and Seflapod were stopped in their tracks. The voice which had commanded them to halt was familiar, though distant and fragmented. It held memories of honey and treacle laced with broken glass. Its owner didn't speak to them often, not directly, and its presence unsettled them, pained them. They listened with eyes closed, strained to hear the faint whisper.

'I have read you and understood you,' the voice said. 'Your lack of success was unfortunate.'

They bowed their heads, waiting for their punishment, anticipating the pain which would grow inexorably to become and agony that was unbearable for some. They waited for it to begin.

'And yet . . .'

They said nothing.

'I sensed, Atraxa, just a moment ago, something near the entrance. It was weak, Seflapod, and has no self-awareness. It was almost like the Klein herself, but different, new. Its appearance was sudden. It interests me.'

They waited.

'You must return to the entrance.'

Atraxa was obliged to speak first, though he had no wish to encourage the Maker's anger. 'The Klein 'as built a barrier, Master. She's hidin' inside it. Perhaps . . .'

'You must listen more carefully, Atraxa. I know the Klein too well. I told you, this is different. This is new.'

'There were six humans, Master,' Seflapod said, 'five of them fresh. Two females and three males. Could it be one of these . . .'

'You are so far from me I can barely feel your presence. But when you get there, when you sense them, I may know. In my prison, in my darkness, the feeling is like a feather caressing the air in a distant room. You are my eyes and ears, you touch and taste and scent the world for me. So you must return to the entrance. Now!'

And the voice was no longer there.

Maia hefted the pack onto her back and turned at the door to look round the dusty room. That was when she noticed, lying on the floor beneath the dressing table from which it must have fallen, a sheet of writing paper. She might have ignored it, but it was half-filled with Madame Klein's tiny writing. Maia picked it up; it had her name at the top. She read it eagerly.

Dear Maia,

I can't sleep and am awake long before Mr Li is due to arrive for this morning's consultation, so I thought I'd set down some important matters before you arrive. This is, of course, so that I can think things through myself. I have no intention of giving this letter to you because I don't feel you're ready to receive it.

You are a talented young lady, worthy of the destiny I have planned for you. And yet you are, in many ways, so young. You have years, but you lack maturity, And that worries me.

What worries me more is that we do not have much time. I have noticed increased movement within the Emperorium. Nothing as serious as an incursion, or even an attempted incursion, more a sense of disquiet, fleeting glimpses of strange creatures, unusual sounds and smells.

Perhaps the greater problem lies with me. I no longer have the vitality of my youth, and this has become apparent, particularly to Chavanel. He is urging me to hasten your induction, but I'm yet to be convinced that you're ready. Is it that I'm unwilling to retreat into the background, to allow you to take over?

The problem of your father is more certain. His disappearance is a threat to our existence, I can put it in no other way. He is clearly in danger, lost somewhere in the Emperorium. Should I share this burden with you? What would you be able to do, how would you be able to help?

And now, as I come to the crux of the matter, the doorbell sounds. It's Chavanel, his ring is his signature, and carries with it a sense of urgency. I will continue later.

I return to this letter after Chavanel's arrival, he's resting downstairs. My disquiet may have encouraged him to speak out. He spoke to me with a candour, a forthrightness that is alien to him. It required courage; I am not usually open to the persuasion of others, particularly when it indicates that I have not been thinking clearly. He has convinced me (though I haven't given him the satisfaction of knowing that he has been successful in his endeavours) that you should be told something; the question remains, what and when?

I will begin at my beginning.

A long time ago, when this world was a very different place, a few people believed that the world was being ruled by superstition and fear. They decided to take action. They decided to prove that being Human was more important than worshipping false gods. They called themselves 'Truthsingers', and I am only the latest to bear that name with pride. We devote our lives to keeping Humanity safe. I am a Gatekeeper. Your father is

And the letter finished. No more writing, no more pages. Maia turned it over in her hands, held it up to the window, tried to make more words appear. It made no sense. Truthsingers? Gatekeepers? And Madame Klein had mentioned her father, she knew that he'd disappeared, and was in danger. And he was somewhere in the Emperorium. Why hadn't she said anything? Why had she kept up the pretence, asking how he was every day? Why had she hidden the truth?

Tears coursed from Maia's eyes, sobs burst from her mouth. She fell to her knees, certain that she would never rise again.

'Maia? Are you okay? I heard something.' Tom was knocking politely on the door.

Maia took a deep breath, almost choked. 'I'm okay,' she managed to croak.

The door opened gingerly. Maia quickly folded the letter and pushed it into her pocket.

'You don't sound okay,' Tom said. 'And you don't look okay. You've been crying. You look a mess.'

'It just hit me. Chavanel, and your Mum - oh, Tom, your Mum! And everything else that happened, and . . . I feel so helpless!'

Tom wanted to hold his arms out to her and hug her, comfort her, but he was frightened that she would misinterpret his kindness and think him too forward. So he coughed and spluttered and blushed instead. 'Everyone else is almost ready. We're just deciding what food to take and then we're going to share it out so . . . If you want to come down and help . . .'

Maia sniffed, wiped her nose on her sleeve. 'Yes, I'll be down soon, just let me tidy myself up. Please don't tell the others I was crying.'

'No. No, I won't.' He moved towards the door, speaking as he did so. 'I was crying too, when I was looking for clothes, when I was by myself. Don't feel you have to hold things in.

And if you need someone to talk to . . .' He turned but Maia had already gone into the bathroom. His words were unheard.

'Where do we start?' Maia asked.

They were standing in front of the shimmering green wall, reluctant to leave and fearful of what might be waiting for them, but aware that staying where they were wasn't wise.

Tom was the first to reply. 'The long corridor where we last saw the Bazhka? It sounds as good a place as any.'

'I'm not sure I want to be that near to them,' Slip said nervously. 'I mean, we've got knives but I don't want to be so close to a Bazhka that I have to use a knife.'

Maia had a small axe in a leather sheath hanging from her belt. 'None of us have any experience in using a weapon, I'd rather not get too close to a Bazhka either.'

'Are you sure Madame Klein didn't stock guns?' Friz asked Maia. 'Or flamethrowers? She always said she could get anything.'

'I can't recall a customer ever asking for a gun,' Maia said.

Tom had found a longbow in the sports section and it was slung over his shoulder. 'I need somewhere to practise with this,' he said. 'And we need to decide which way to go. It's not as if we have many choices, that long corridor is the only direction we can go.'

Ten was pretending to read. 'You've got it all wrong,' he said over the spine of his book. 'Try squinting.'

'Squinting?' Tom was already on his way up the stairs. 'What do you mean by that?'

'Reduces the amount you can see, the amount of information you have to digest. What did Chavanel say about where to go?'

'Get a map from the library,' Maia said, 'but we don't know where the library is.'

'Well I know where I'd start looking. If I was coming with you, that is.'

'And where's that, smart guy?' Tom seemed about to punch Ten.

'Where are there books in this ruin?'

'In the book room, of course.' Maia looked down her nose at Ten. 'But the book room isn't a library, it isn't beyond the door, it isn't inside the inside of the Emperorium. And I know every book in there, I helped order them, I put them on the shelves, I know what the stock is. And there's nothing like a map of the Emperorium in there.'

'Just offering a suggestion,' Ten said. 'You don't have to follow it. Go on, go hunting for monsters instead.'

Maia looked at Tom. 'What do you think?' she asked.

'I don't know,' he snapped. 'I think we ought to go down the corridor.'

'Friz?' Maia asked. 'Slip? Any thoughts?'

The pair looked at each other. Friz said 'Corridor' at the same time as Slip said 'Book room'.

'And I was going to go to the book room first,' Maia said. 'That's two votes each.'

Ten shook his head. 'I get the casting vote, then. I say book room.'

'You don't get a vote,' Tom said, 'you're not coming with us.'

'Perhaps I've changed my mind. Perhaps I want to come as far as the book room to see if I was right. And if I'm wrong, perhaps I want to stand beside the door and count the seconds as you disappear down that long corridor.' He clicked his tongue, mimicking the 'tick-tock, tick-tock' of an old clock.

Maia shouldered her way past Tom. 'For goodness sake, let's go to the book room first. It shouldn't take long to see if there's a map there. Come on.'

She pushed her way up the stairs and into the book room. It didn't seem to have suffered from the Bazhka trail of destruction, none of the books had fallen onto the floor and there were no cracks in the ceiling. Maia ran her finger along one of the shelves and checked it with approval, there was no trace of dust; that was good, she'd tidied the room only the weekend before. 'Come on, then, books about maps or maps themselves? There are some local ones over there,' she waved vaguely towards a bank of shelves.

'There's nothing here,' Tom announced without much of a search, 'it was a stupid suggestion.' He glanced pointedly at Ten. 'We need to go.'

Maia looked around helplessly. 'Like I said before, I can't recall anything that might fit the bill. Perhaps we'd better do as Tom suggested.'

'Squint,' Ten said. 'Think laterally. I can remember, quite a few years ago, I used to play computer games a lot and whenever I got stuck I'd ask my Dad for help.' He looked down. There was a long silence until he swallowed his grief, bit his bottom lip until a spot of blood showed. 'Anyway,' he went on, 'in one of the games you could only get through if you'd collected enough jewels or weapons or icons or something, and my Dad always told me that the people who designed the games wanted the players to think carefully. No solution would be too obscure. So think. What are you looking for?'

'A map,' Maia and Slip said together.

'Is this a library? It doesn't look like a library to me,' Ten said. 'You look for a map in the library.'

'Find the library, then?' Maia offered, noticing Tom edging towards the door.

'Look for books on libraries,' Slip said, already heading back to the shelves.

Ten was scathing. 'Too obvious. You need to find a path to the library.'

'A map, then. But we've already been there!' Friz's frustration was showing.

'An entrance?' Maia suggested. 'A gateway? A door?'

'There's only one door I'm going through,' Tom announced, 'we're wasting our time here.'

'A door?' Ten smiled. 'I wonder . . .' He took a purposeful step towards one of the shelves.

Maia was puzzled. 'That's books of biography, what can possibly be of use down there?'

Ten waved her closer. 'Try that one.'

She looked down to the bottom shelf, turned her head sideways to read the spine of the book Ten was pointing to. 'A Biography of Jim Morrison,' she said. 'What's that got to do with . . ?'

'My Dad again. When I was young he tried to get me interested in the music he liked. Jim Morrison was the lead singer of one of the bands. The band was called the Doors.' His smile became a grin as he pulled the book from the shelf.

It took them all a while to realise that nothing had happened.

Tom broke the silence. 'I told you!'

Maia was curious. She could remember most of the books in the room but just behind the biography Ten had pulled out was another, the letters on its spine faded by time and almost illegible. She pulled it out. 'The Open Door,' she read, 'by Helen Keller.' She flipped it over. 'And there's a quotation on the back. "Life is either a daring adventure or nothing at all."' She giggled. 'That's weirdly coincidental given what you said before, Friz.'

Friz didn't say anything. None of them said anything. They were all listening to a distant grinding of rusty locks being turned for the first time in ages; they heard the slamming back of bolts; they winced as hinges creaked and complained loudly. And they all turned in the direction of the sound. Tom was the first to see it, and he began to laugh. To the right of the entrance door another door had appeared, but it was no larger than a hand.

'Oh, that's great,' Tom roared, 'all that time, all that thought, all that effort and we find a door that only a mouse could get through. Someone's joking, someone thinks we're fools, someone,' he looked around wildly and his voice became louder, 'is making me angry!' He tugged at the handle of the full-size door and slammed it against the wall. 'This is stupid,' he said, turned to Ten, 'you're stupid, and the rest of you are stupid for even listening to him. I'm off.'

Maia made to follow him, to put her hand on his shoulder, to bring him back, but Slip's wild cry refocused her attention.

'There's someone there! A real person, a tiny person. Look!'

The small door had opened and a figure was standing in front of it, waving wildly. A distant voice seemed to be calling, but the words were carried away. And then the figure began to move, and to grow.

'Like I said, squint!' Ten leaned forwards towards the figure. 'It's not a small door, it's a big door. It's actually a very big door! It's just a long way away. And that figure is running towards us, that's why it's getting bigger.'

'You're right,' Maia said, 'it's all to do with perspective.' She turned to Slip and Friz. 'Can you see it yet? You have to believe what Ten said, that it's a large door quite a distance away. And that figure is definitely a girl!'

The girl stopped abruptly, spun around to look at the door, then turned back to them and raised her hands to her face. 'You have to hurry!' she yelled, her voice so distant th4y could barely hear it. 'I have to close the door soon!'

Slip and Friz took tentative steps towards the girl. 'Do we go or not?' Friz asked, her words directed at Maia.

'I don't know what to do! Tom's already gone, I . . .'

The girl took a few more steps. 'You . . . are . . . in . . . danger!'

'She says we're in danger,' Slip pointed out the obvious.

'I'd go if I were you,' Ten advised. 'When Tom the superhero comes back in a sulk because you haven't followed him, well, I'll show him where to go.'

The girl moved forward again. 'Bazhka . . . are . . . coming!'

'You go,' Maia said to Slip and Friz, 'just go! I'll get Tom.' The two took another step in the direction of the door but went no further.

'I think we should come with you,' Slip said.

'Best not split up,' Friz added.

Maia's eyes widened. 'Do as you're told! Go! Now!'

The two friends began a shambling, staggering run down the long path towards the door, their heavy packs threatening to tumble them to the ground if they moved too quickly.

'Stay here,' Maia said to Ten, 'I'm going to find Tom.'

'I wasn't planning on going anywhere.'

It didn't take Maia long to find Tom. As she rounded the corner she saw him lurching back towards her. 'Run!' he shouted, 'Bazhka!' He tried to grab her and pull her down the stairs to the remains of the shop but she managed to pull him to a halt. 'No, this way,' she hissed, tugging him back into the book room.'

Tom was angry. 'They'll easily find us here, they'll know where . . .' He looked around him. 'Where are they?'

Ten jerked his thumb at the distant figures of Slip and Friz, almost at the door. The girl was still waiting halfway down the path, gesturing urgently. Maia grabbed Tom's hand and dragged him after her. She stopped abruptly, looked back at Ten. 'You aren't staying, are you?'

Ten nodded. 'I'm going to try speaking to them. I need to know how I can help my Dad, assuming he's still alive.' His fingers were dancing nervously in front of him. 'They can talk, they can think, it must be possible to reason with them.'

From outside the book room door there came the sound of heavy claws sliding to a halt. There was a baying scream of delight. 'I smell food!'

'Or on the other hand,' Ten said, already running, 'I could just come with you.'

As soon as the girl saw they were all heading towards her she turned back to the door. Ten was a few steps ahead of the other two, Maia a little behind Tom, unsure of who was dragging and who was being dragged. She could hear the snuffle and scrape of the Bazhka, their breath and their claws, she could almost feel the sharp poisoned talons reaching out to grasp her. But she didn't dodge to one side, she didn't look back. The door was getting closer, not big, not large, but massive. The left half of it was already shut, the right was closing slowly but determinedly. Its timber was rough, tarred, heavy, it seemed obvious that it would shut before they got there. Maia's lungs were on fire, her pack was bouncing and scraping along her back, hitting her head, slowing her down, but she didn't dare stop to throw it off. The she noticed Friz, feet braced against the closed door, back thrust against the open one, trying to slow its progress. The girl noticed and joined her, Slip too.

'We can do it,' Tom grunted, and Maia found an extra sliver of strength in his words.

Ten got there first, ducked behind the door. Tom and Maia arrived together, knocked Friz and Slip and the girl into the entrance, and the door slammed shut behind them. On the other side there was a double crash of bodies, two screams of frustration, a muted scratching on impenetrably thick timber. The girl was the first to rise to her feet. She turned a huge wheel and metal bands slid into place to hold the doors secure. She turned to face them.

'Welcome to the Library. Would you like to come and meet the books?'

'You have lost her,' the voice said, even fainter than before.

'Na, not lost, Master. Not even misplaced. We know exactly where she is.' Despite the desperate chase neither Bazhka was out of breath.

'She is behind a door, Master. It is a solid door. But Atraxa and I might break it down.'

'Thank you, Seflapod. That will not be necessary.'

Atraxa waited for another instruction, or an expression of displeasure, but there was nothing. 'Is 'e talkin' t' you?' he whispered to Seflapod.

Seflapod shook his hooded head.

'What d'y' want us t' do, Master?' Atraxa asked.

The silence seemed to be framed with a distant happiness, not a laugh, nothing audible, just a sense of wellbeing. And then the words came. Their transmission must have required huge effort, they were forced and urgent but distant, more feelings than words. 'She is remarkable. So much like the Klein, but so different as well. No bitterness, no anger, no longing, no hatred even. But innocence. And fear, yes, fear, but that should be expected in one so young. Yet this is tempered by optimism and love, plentiful, abounding love. All these emotions and I can feel them, even when she's so far away. I sense her presence directly now as well as through you, Atraxa and Seflapod. Oh, it's just a trace, but there is so much potential there. And I know where she is. Thank you, Atraxa and Seflapod, for finding her and shepherding her.'

Atraxa looked at Seflapod. 'Did y' 'ear that? Did I 'ear "thank you"?'

Seflapod looked equally puzzled. 'I heard those words, Atraxa.'

'She is in the Library. She thinks she is safe. She does not know that I know where she is.' Now the voice laughed, a manic giggle that grew into a raucous, coughing, churning whirlwind of hilarity. 'And I know exactly what to do next. Oh, it is many, many years since I could anticipate such pleasure. Such playthings!'

'Master, we've no idea what y're talkin' about. Just tell us, what d'y' want us t' do?'

'Atraxa, and you, Seflapod, both of you, should return the way you came. You should find your way to the main entrance of the Library where other Bazhka will shortly be gathering. You will report to Excubitor. And you will prepare yourself for a war. Yes, a war.'

'Excubitor?' Atraxa said to Seflapod. 'If ever there was a Bazhka with 'er 'ead up 'er own . . .'

'Atraxa,' the voice said, 'do not test my patience. And do not annoy me while I'm bathing in the fragrance of this new creature, this fresh and vibrant human. Do not interrupt me with your petty squabbles.'

'Yes, Master,' Atraxa said. The Bazhka made their way back towards the book room and the long, endless corridors beyond.

The girl was in her late teens or early twenties, Maia guessed. She was no taller than Maia though a little thinner, dressed in a worn striped blouse, a plain blue cardigan that had seen better days, and black trousers that were slightly too short, frayed at the ankles, and couldn't hide her bare feet. Her blonde hair was tied back with an untidy elastic band and she wore horn-rimmed glasses on the end of her nose. She had a pencil behind each ear and many more in the pockets of her blouse and cardigan.

'Is this really the Library?' Maia asked. They were in an entrance or lobby, but the only light was from the glass-panelled doors ahead of them.

'I certainly hope so,' the girl replied, her voice clipped and precise as if she was playing a role in a play. 'Because if it isn't, then I've come to work in completely the wrong place.' She held a hand up to her mouth to silence her giggling.

'Look at the floor,' Tom whispered, 'covered in dust. No-one's been here . . .'

'No-one's been this way for many years,' the girl said, 'unless you count my own footprints when I came to open the door for you.' She drew circles in the dust with her big toe.

'Thank you,' Maia said.

'You're welcome.' The girl fished in her pocket. 'Now then, we won't get very far unless you have some form of identification. I've made up some temporary tickets for you, let me see.' She gave a small card folder to each of them, spoke their names as she handed them across. 'Maia, Tom, Slip, Friz and Ten. I do hope I've copied the names correctly.'

Maia's name was written on her card in a spindly, uneven hand, and she could tell from the expressions on the others' faces that they were equally surprised to have been correctly identified. 'But how did you know . . ?'

'Your names? The books told me, of course.' She motioned to them to follow her towards the doors.

'The books told you?' Tom clearly didn't believe her.

'Books know everything,' the girl replied. 'Finding the right one is sometimes difficult, but when they come to you with a message . . . Well, if that happens, they're always right.'

'Are you a librarian?' Slip asked.

The girl seemed affronted that he'd need to ask. 'Do I look like a librarian?'

'I don't know. I mean, is it possible to look like a librarian? Is there a librarian's uniform?'

'Of course. This,' she pirouetted once, 'is exactly how a librarian should dress.'

'Including no shoes?' Ten asked.

The girl looked at her dirty feet. 'I took my shoes off at my desk. And then, when the books told me you were about to arrive,' she glared at them in turn, 'pursued by Bazhka, well, I hurried to the back door as quickly as possible. And let you in.' She lifted her feet in turn. 'Hence the slight grubbiness.'

'Shouldn't we get a move on,' Slip said, glancing at the door behind them, 'just in case . . .'

'Oh, they can't get in now,' the girl said. She reached into another pocket and brought out several small squares of brown card, threw them in the air and giggled as they floated to the ground. 'I tore up their tickets.'

'That's stupid,' Tom said, 'not having a ticket isn't going to prevent a Bazhka getting in.'

'You clearly haven't met the Head Librarian.' The girl paused in front of the glass doors. 'I think we should go in now. I'm sure I don't have to tell you, but,' her voice became a whisper, 'please be silent.'

She pushed open the doors and they were overwhelmed by noise. There was a constant fluttering and buzzing, a counterpoint of high-pitched whistling, the mutter and grumble of heavy wheels turning slowly, and loud yelling, the words blending and twisting round each other in a clamorous cacophony of sound. They were standing at the top of a staircase and below them a vast prairie floor was littered with desks of all shapes and sizes, and at each desk a librarian (the women wearing blouses, cardigans and trousers or skirts, the men with shirts and ties, all with thick-rimmed spectacles) sat scribbling, reading aloud from books open in front of them.

There were books everywhere, on every desktop, scattered on the floor and on vacant seats, on trolleys standing still, on trolleys being pushed by brown-coated porters, on trolleys linked together being pulled by electric trains. There were books on bookcases, on staircases, on and in suitcases and briefcases and packing cases, they were packed into nooks and crannies, they tumbled out of sacks and bags and boxes. They sat, preening, on the cliffs of shelves reaching high to an invisible glass ceiling, so tall that they were shrouded in pale clouds.

And they flew.

Flocks of books twisted and turned in formation, while others beat steadily between the shelves in neat V shapes. Here and there gigantic volumes performed slow, lazy circles on unseen updrafts, while lower down small booklets darted here and there as if they were looking for food. Murmurations and sussurations of books danced in delight. The fluttering noise they heard was the rustle of paper, not wings.

'Impressive, eh?' the girl yelled.

'Are they all books?' Maia asked.

'Books? Books? They aren't *just* books. They're . . .'

'That one must be huge,' Slip said, pointing at a distant rectangle of darkness silhouetted against the pale blue sky.

The girl squinted. 'That's an opus. No, sorry, a grand opus. Or is it a magnum opus? Difficult to tell from this distance. And on the shelves below it there are flocks of volumes and tomes. We have every type of book here, I had to learn all their names. There's Rolls, different breeds of Codex, Manuscripts and Typescripts, even Filmscripts and Playscripts. There's Palimpsests, Potboilers, lots of different Remainders,' she said proudly, counting each word on her fingers. 'Overhead, now, they fly across every day at this time, those are Periodicals. Usually very colourful. And Magazines, Journals, Brochures, Pamphlets, Anthologies.'

'But books aren't alive,' Ten said, eyes darting from shelf to shelf, from stack to stack, finding clear evidence that he was wrong.

'This is the Library,' the girl said pride in her voice. 'And of course books are alive, look at them! The Head Librarian says they have,' she adopted a voice that was definitely not her own, '"an existence entirely separate from their writer".' She quickly reverted to her own, piping trill. 'Can't see what she meant by that, but she kept asking me to repeat it, so it must have been important. She told me that some people say the reader is more important than the writer in making books live.' She spun around, dancing from one dirty foot to the other. 'I've seen every type of book in the Library. Proofs, Revisions, Prose Anthologies, Poetry Anthologies, Essays and Tracts, Juvenilia, Primers and Texts.' She leaned close to Ten. 'I've even climbed the stacks late at night and seen some of the rarest books there are. Chrestomathies,' she said slowly, struggling with the pronunciation, 'Delecti. A single, solitary Enchiridion.' She nodded her wild enthusiasm, turned - to Ten's obvious relief - to Maia. 'And as for Genres and Sub-genres. You have NO idea! The books I've seen!'

'You were very clever to get us in here,' Maia said, hoping that flattery might distract the girl, 'and you kindly prepared our library cards. You know our names. What's your name?'

'My name?' The girl seemed confused. 'My name is . . . is . . . '

A thunderous voice cut through all thoughts and sounds. 'PENCIL!'

'Whoops,' the girl said, 'that's me. Head Librarian wants me.' She ran off, swerved between desks and bookcases, vaulted a trolley that had fallen on its side, blocking her way.

'She's loopy,' Tom said, appearing at Maia's side.

'In a nice way,' Maia answered. 'And she did rescue us.'

'How on earth are we going to find a map in here?' Slip asked. 'It's not like any library I've been in.'

'That's because you haven't *been* in any library, except the one at school,' Friz punched Slip on the shoulder, 'once, and that was only because you were hiding from Big Carrie.'

'Well I knew she wouldn't go in there. She didn't even know how to spell "book".

'She can move fast,' Ten said admiringly.

'Who, Big Carrie? She certainly caught me when . . .'

'No, the girl. Dirty feet. What's her name? Pencil?'

The girl was heading for a high dais made up of concentric steps which led up to a circular desk. At its centre a woman spun in a high-backed chair, a megaphone at her lips. 'Pencil!' she screamed again, 'Paper!' She looked down at the desk. 'Shakespeare!' There was a ripple of raised heads in a large group of desks nearby.' History Plays!' Some of the heads looked down again. 'Queen Elizabeth!' Two figures climbed to their feet and trudged towards the dais.

'Hang on,' Maia said, 'she just said "Queen Elizabeth". I'm sure Shakespeare didn't write a play about Elizabeth, he stopped at . . . Henry VIII?'

'Don't look at me,' Tom shrugged.

'You're right,' Ten said to Maia, 'and even that was a joint effort.' He looked around him. 'Slip was right too, this isn't a normal library. It's more like an aviary.' A book, no more than a few inches across, appeared in front of him and hovered uncertainly. He flapped at it with one hand and it zoomed away, only to return as quickly as it had departed.

'It likes you,' Maia said.

'Must be a pretty stupid book,' Tom muttered under his breath.

The girl reached the foot of the dais and bounded up the tall steps. She handed the woman something and pointed back in the direction she'd just come. The woman looked directly at them.

'Customers!' She yelled through the megaphone. For a moment all talk stopped as every librarian looked up at them, classified them, then the hubbub resumed again, curiosity satisfied.

'Customers! Report! To! Me!'

'I think that's the Head Librarian, and she wants us to go to see her,' Maia said. ' Come on. She doesn't look as if she likes to be kept waiting.' She began a slow passage down the stairs and across the floor of the library, the others following close behind in single file. At each desk they passed a head was raised in slow curiosity, then lowered again quickly as if the glance hadn't been worth the effort. There were no greetings, no smiles. 'This is what it's like when you've done something wrong at school and you're told to come out to the front of the class,' Maia whispered.

'And have you noticed the people?' Friz was looking around her. 'Those glasses they wear, every one of them. They aren't glasses! They're sort of . . . part of them. Part of their heads.'

Slip peered closer. 'They look like antlers, or horn, or bone. But the lenses are real. Just not glass. They look liquid.'

'They're writing with both hands at the same time,' Tom said, 'and they only have two fingers and a thumb on each hand. And I'm sure their ears are a slightly different shape. Larger than ours. More curved.'

'Natural selection?' Ten said. 'If you work in a Library, looking at books all the time, you need good eyesight. Magnified eyesight. And if you write a lot then being ambidextrous would help, plus you don't really need lots of fingers.'

'Large ears to hear what others are saying above the noise of reading aloud?' Maia suggested. 'Don't keep looking at them, you might offend them.'

They reached the foot of the circular dais and climbed the steep stairs to the top where the two workers were in earnest conversation with the Head Librarian and where, a few steps further down, their guide was hopping excitedly from foot to foot.

'Is your name really Pencil?' Ten asked. 'You said you were a librarian, but you don't look like the other librarians, do you. You've got four fingers on each hand and normal sized ears. And your glasses come off.' He bent closer. 'And there're no lenses in them! You're a human,' he accused her, 'just like us. Actually, I think you're just a pencil sharpener. A fetcher.' He looked at the workers below. 'I bet you don't even have your own desk.'

'I didn't say I was a librarian,' the girl said, affronted, 'you just assumed that. And yes, my name's Pencil.' Her animation abated; she stood still, her voice defensive. 'What's wrong with that? It's a good enough name. And everyone has to start somewhere.' In a gesture of defiance she looked directly at Ten, raised her finger to her lips and hissed 'Shh!' When Ten opened his mouth to speak she repeated her 'Shh!' then added, 'I'll be a librarian one day. Which is more than you'll ever be!'

Maia had been trying to hear what the Head Librarian and the workers were talking about, but Ten and Pencil's argument had drowned out every word. She glared at both of them and that was enough to bring silence. As the workers left, heads lowered, Pencil stepped forward. 'These are the new customers, Ms Inkwadi.' She stepped to one side. 'This is Ms Inkwadi, she's the Head Librarian. And a very important person. Ms Inkwadi, these are Maia, . . .'

The Head Librarian drew herself to her full height, towering over all of them. 'Thank you, Pencil, I know their names. You can go now.'

'But Ms Inkwadi, *I* rescued them, I think . . .'

'Pencil, go.'

Suddenly crestfallen, Pencil stepped slowly away from them. She descended one step, then another, almost managed a third before deciding that the Head Librarian's attention had been refocused. She crouched down, made herself as small as possible.

Maia stared up at the Head Librarian. Her white blouse was pressed and the buttons winked like all-seeing eyes, the pleats in her plaid skirt were like razors, her brown brogue shoes were polished to perfection. Her skin was dark as fresh chestnuts and - to add to her height - she wore a tall, rich blue cylindrical headdress which widened at the top like a flower seeking the sun. It was decorated with swirls of white beads forming words and pictures and abstract shapes. The light glistened in her circular silver earrings that promised, like wind chimes, sweet music. Her face was set, neither smiling nor frowning.

'Welcome to the Library.' Her voice was low and lilting. 'As Pencil told you, My name is Ms Inkwadi and I am the Head Librarian. You may each borrow up to five books, the checkout desk is situated beside the exit doors. Although this is both a lending and a reference library we have other, more important functions as well, so you may not browse the shelves. Any book you require will be brought to you. Do you have any questions?'

'We need,' Tom said quickly, 'a map of . . .'

'I just need to satisfy my curiosity,' Maia interrupted, mouthing 'Sorry' in Tom's direction before hurrying on. 'I'm sure I heard you mention a play by Shakespeare called "Queen Elizabeth", but he didn't write a play of that name.'

'Are you a Shakespearean scholar?' Ms Inkwadi's eyebrows climbed a fraction to demonstrate that she wasn't used to being contradicted.

'No, but . . .'

'Then listen carefully.' She raised her megaphone again. 'Stools! Six of them!' There was a bustle below and six stools, carried by younger versions of Pencil, were carried to the top of the dais. 'You may as well join us again, Pencil, since you'll only strain your ears trying to listen to what we're saying.' Pencil climbed the stairs again gleefully.

Ms Inkwadi waited until the stools were set in front of her and occupied then began to speak again, like a teacher, with the weary familiarity of someone who has spoken the same words many times before. 'I do not wish to repeat myself. Engage your brains with your ears and digest every word I say.' She waited until she was sure that she had her listeners' undivided attention. 'This Library's primary purpose is to look after books. Every book ever written finds its way here. Many are healthy, sustained by being read often. But others are less fortunate. They've been forgotten, they're neglected, uncared for. Unread. It's my job - the job of everyone here - to nurse them back to health, if we can.'

Out of the corner of her eye Maia saw Ten raise his head and sigh. She hoped that Ms Inkwadi hadn't seen him.

'Some of you may not understand this. After all, you come from a different world with different values. But I assure you, I speak truly.' She reached into a desk drawer and pulled out a small thin book with a pale green cover. The faded letters on the spine (the title of the book and the author's name) retained a glimmer of their original gold colour, but they were illegible. In comparison to the other volumes flying around them, flittering and rustling and buzzing at them, this one appeared lifeless.

'This is the last remaining copy of a book of poetry by Mary-Anne Pottinger. I know little about her. She wasn't famous, there are no other books by her. Look inside.' The Head Librarian opened the book gently, reverently, and turned it towards them, showed it to each of them.

'Blank pages,' Friz announced.

'Is it like that all the way through? Slip asked.

Tom bent closer. 'I think there *are* some words, but they're very faded. I can't tell what they say.'

Ms Inkwadi took the book back. She ran her fingers over the page. 'I can feel the indentations of some of the letters,' she said. She held the book at an angle in front of her. 'I can see some of the letters, or the shadows they once cast.' She held the book up to her face and inhaled deeply. 'I can smell the sense of the words. Allow me, this is from the preface.

These poems were written by my mother to her only true love, my father. I only found them when I cleared out her papers after she died. I never knew she wrote poems. I don't know if they're any good, but when I read them I'm comforted by them, so I've had them set and printed so my family can see how devoted she was to my father. So, dearest aunts and uncles, brothers and sisters, children and grandchildren and all those of my family yet to be born, these are the words of my mother, Mary-Anne Pottinger, who lived and died a prairie-woman. I miss her.
Ivy Tweddell, October 1886.

She turned the book round again. There were now letters on the page and, when she turned that page, a list of contents. 'Mary-Anne's poetry book was given to a large family, I believe, probably well over a hundred copies. And her books will still exist, locked away in boxes and cupboards and attics. But they aren't read. That's what these people do.' She waved her arm at the workers beneath her. 'They read dying books. They bring them back to life.'

The perpetual low mumble was there for a reason, Maia realised. And the lack of curiosity from the Librarians was understandable, they didn't want to waste any time. They wanted to read. 'Can everyone read like you?' Maia asked. 'With your fingers and nose as well as your eyes?'

Ms Inkwadi's eyes drooped and she seemed suddenly very tired and very old. 'Alas, no. Few have the talent. But we do what we can.'

'But what about Shakespeare's "Queen Elizabeth"? Surely that would be read by many people. But I've never heard of it.'

'That, my dear is a very different matter.' Ms Inkwadi rose to her feet again. 'Shakespeare returned to Stratford from London about 1611. He wrote a couple of plays, some collaborations, but he ought to have been more productive, more creative. Scholars have suggested a missing play, a lost play. That play is "Queen Elizabeth". It's been seen, up there, in the heights.' She gestured towards the high shelves. 'We have several of our best hunter-librarians on the job, but it's strong, elusive. That means it's being read. But since there is no record of its existence, we can only surmise it was a single handwritten copy, and that it's in the possession of a collector.' She grinned. 'Imagine that, an unknown Shakespeare play but so loved by its owner that he - or she - reads it regularly. A rare thing indeed.' Her saintly smile disappeared. 'But let us turn to more mundane matters. Do you wish to borrow some books?'

For some reason Maia's stool seemed to be closer to Ms Inkwadi than those of her companions. She looked around. Tom urged her to speak with an urgent nod.

'We'd like to borrow a map of the Emperorium,' Maia said.

The head Librarian nodded. 'Not unheard of, but an unusual request. May I ask why?'

'We need to find our way to . . .'

'Yes?'

'Well, it's not so much finding a place as knowing where we are at any given moment.' Maia turned to her friends. 'That's it, isn't it?'

There was a mumble of agreement.

'There is only one copy of the Map of the Emperorium,' the Head Librarian said, 'for reasons which will become obvious. And it's in the reference section of the Library. You may look at it, but you may not take it away.'

Tom erupted. 'What sort of a library is this? Your books fly about all over the place, you read them aloud to keep them alive, you don't let people see what books there are on the shelves, and you don't lend out the very book we need!'

'Tom,' Maia said, rested a hand on his arm, 'I'm sure that if we explain we might be able to copy the map out, it shouldn't take long. And if we explain why we need it, what happened to bring us here, then . . .'

'There's no need for that,' the Head Librarian said, 'I know your story. Remember how you got here? The books told Pencil you were coming. How did they know? Because someone, somewhere, is writing your story. I know all about the Bazhka. I know about your mother, Tom, and your father, Ten. I know that you seek revenge, Tom; that you, Ten, are here by accident; that you, Slip and Friz are here for adventure. As for you Maia, I know things about you that I shouldn't know and that I can't tell you.'

'Who's writing a book about us?' Maia asked, stung by the Head Librarian's words. 'Who would know what we've been doing? It's not one of us.' She looked around to seek confirmation from her companions. 'And what do you know about me? Why won't you tell me what you know?'

Miss Inkwadi rose abruptly to her feet. 'The poems of Mary-Anne Pottinger need me more than you do, I'm afraid. Pencil, take our young guests to the hostel, make sure they have what they need. I shall see you in the morning. That will give me time to seek out the Map. When you see it you'll understand why making a copy would be useless.' She looked directly at Maia. 'I will tell you tomorrow whatever I think may help you. Until then, sleep well.'

'But we need the map now!' Tom looked as if he was about to vault the desk and attack the Head Librarian, but when she smiled at him and whispered, 'I understand,' those simple words calmed him; his clenched fists fell to his side. Ms Inkwadi spun her seat around so her back was to them all, they could hear her soft deep voice teasing words from the book she held.

'That's it,' said Pencil, 'come on. I'm to look after you, that's what HL said and that's what I'll do.' She leaped down two steps. 'We shouldn't waste time, it'll soon be nightlights and a long day tomorrow. Let's be going.'

SIX

The Library was beginning to dim, and at every desk glow-worms of warmth and brightness burst into life to keep the darkness at bay. 'Shift change due,' Pencil announced, 'if we hurry we'll miss the worst of it.' She scurried down the steps and led them away in the direction of the high metal arch of a bridge which grew impressively large as they neared it. Their route wasn't direct: Pencil avoided large groups of librarians, many of whom were packing bags and clearing desks; others seemed to be heading out to the workstations.

Maia tried to stay close to her guide. 'Pencil . . . is that really your name? Do you mind if I call you Pencil?'

'It's the name I'm used to. If you can think of a nicer one then please use it.'

'Okay. I was just wondering how I might find out where the book is that Ms Inkwadi was talking about. You know, the one that tells my story.' She glanced around her. 'Our story.'

'Ask a librarian,' Pencil replied. 'If you're allowed to borrow it, any librarian could find it for you. Just let them know the name and the author.'

'But I don't know who's writing it! Or what it's called!'

'They couldn't find it then.'

'Agh!' Maia growled. 'But how did you know about us being at the back door, about us being in danger, if someone wasn't reading the story?'

'I told you, one of the books told me. *They* knew! They often read one another. When it's something interesting then they read aloud and you get whole flocks of books together, all listening in. And they're such gossips. That's how I knew about you, and the HL too. Except she's so good at asking books questions, she reads them in such detail.' She paused. 'Perhaps she'll find the story about you all and bring it tomorrow. It'll be unfinished of course, a work in progress. And you know what? I'll be in the story now. Well I never. I'm almost famous.'

Maia tried to make sense of what Pencil was saying but had to give up. They were characters in a story that was being written in real time? Was the writer reporting what happened or determining what happened? She hated not understanding something and sulked her way into silence.

Slip was curious. 'Where do all these people live. The librarians, that is, and the porters and everyone else. There are thousands of them.'

Pencil was pleased to talk. 'They live here, in the Library. When the books designed the Library they knew the librarians would need somewhere to live. There are towns and villages all the way round the outside, and farms and factories. We have everything we need.' Pencil's pride was evident in her voice and her expansive gestures. 'And the Library's at the centre.'

Maia found her voice again. 'But what's the Library at the centre of?'

Pencil seemed confused by the question. 'The world, of course. The Library is the world. The world is the Library.'

Ten was close behind Maia. 'I don't think you'll get much sense out of that one,' he whispered. 'Not the brightest of buttons.'

'How far is the hostel, Pencil,' Slip asked. He seemed impressed by all that was going on around them, pausing every few seconds to examine a new wonder.

'Not too far, near the main entrance. It's the place where visitors stay. Not that we have many. In fact, I can't remember when I last took anyone there.'

103

'How long have you been here?' Friz asked. 'Were you born here? What's it like outside? Do you go home at night, or do you stay in the hostel?'

Pencil's face contorted. 'The HL says I'm a bear of little brain, I think that means I'm not very clever. I'm no good at remembering things. Some things, that is. I can remember the books I've met, but not always the people. Strange, isn't it. I don't stay in the hostel because I'm not a visitor, so I keep my stuff under a desk, and that's where I sleep. Under a desk. It's because I always need to be ready, if anyone wants anything.'

'Like a pencil,' Ten said softly.

'Not just pencils,' Pencil added without malice, 'but other things too. Paper mostly. Membership cards. The HL taught me how important they were.' She raised a finger, remembering something else. 'Sometimes I fetch water for the Librarians. And I run messages. Sometimes I read books, if the words are easy. It's a busy life. What else did you ask?'

'What about your parents?' Friz added. 'Don't you go to visit them?'

'No parents. No family at all. I mean, I know I must have had a mother and a father, but . . .' Pencil's gaze grew vague and misty. 'I dream sometimes about a man, I think he must have been my father. He's handsome and he smiles at me and tells me he loves me. A bit like a fairy tale.' She looked around her. The bridge was almost above them, its steel arch painted a muted green, its roadway filled with the passage of librarians. It was supported by four towers built of massive stone blocks, and books had taken up residence in its arches. They fluttered softly.

'Bedding down for the night,' Pencil explained. 'And I think this is the hostel.'

They were standing in front of a squat two storey brick building. The front door was quartered and reached the whole height of the building. The windows were shuttered, the shutters dusty, their dark blue paint flaking and peeling. Pencil pushed the door and it creaked open reluctantly. 'Hello,' she called to an echoing vestibule, 'is anyone in?'

'Of course someone's in,' a deep gravelly voice replied, rough and grinding, 'why else would the door be open? Who are you and what do you want?'

Pencil seemed unwilling to say anything. Maia stepped forward, the rest of the group pushed in after her. 'We've just seen the Head Librarian, Ms . . .'

'I know who the Head Librarian is. I suppose she said you should stay here for the night. Would've been nice to get some notice. How many are you?'

Maia was about to say 'five' when Pencil darted forward. 'Six,' she said.

The voice considered the request. There was no sign of its owner. 'Rooms or dormitory?'

'Rooms, please.' Pencil had found her confidence again.

'I suppose you want en-suite. That means with bathrooms, in case you didn't know.'

'That would be good.'

'I'll have to give you the courtyard, then.'

'Would it be possible to get something to eat?' Maia asked. 'We've had a difficult day, you see.'

'Food? You want food as well? That's a little presumptive, if you ask me. Not that anyone ever does ask me anything. Step forward, then, let me see you all.' A dim lantern appeared. It revealed only a wall with plain brown wallpaper. 'I said, let me see you! Names as well.'

'You could say please,' Tom muttered.

'I could indeed, but I'm the one with the rooms, you're the ones who need them, so the pleases and the pleading should really be coming from you. Yes?'

'You're right,' Maia said, silencing Tom with a raised finger. 'I'm Maia.'

'Tom,' said Tom sullenly. The rest recited their names as they stepped into the light. Pencil whispered her name, head down.

The lantern was raised abruptly and grew brighter. The brown wall resolved into a woven smock or shift. At its base two red boots appeared, large as suitcases; a belt was wound round its waist and from it hung an assortment of knives, cleavers, axes and other sharp implements, each in its own scabbard; at the end of its sleeves hands grew, each cucumber-sized finger wearing rings richly adorned with jewels; and higher still was a round head framed in plaited brown hair. The figure was hunched; if it had stood upright its head would have burst through the ceiling.

'My name,' the figure announced, 'is Mistress Unthank.' It was not the abrasive, harsh voice that had been speaking to them a moment before. This voice was melodious, mellow, gentle, it sounded as if it was about to burst into song. 'I'm the cook and housekeeper at the hostel. I hope your stay refreshes you; if you need anything just call my name.' The words hugged the listeners, pulled them close as if they were saying 'There, there, everything will be alright'.

'Your voice is different, was that you speaking before?' Maia asked.

'It certainly wasn't. As if I'd talk like that!' High up on the mountainous slopes of Mistress Unthank's left shoulder something moved. Or slid. Or crept. It was difficult to define the type of movement, the light was too dim for that, but it wasn't the motion of any creature with four legs or fewer.

Mistress Unthank bent down and lifted her lantern higher at the same time. 'This is Mr Forritt,' she announced, 'not to be confused with the small semi-domesticated weasel-like animal bearing a similar name. He's the warden of the hostel.'

'I am indeed.' The owner of the voice rippled across Mistress Unthank's shoulder and descended her arm. 'Thank you for the lift and the introduction, dearest,' he said as he reached the ground.

'You're welcome, my lovely.'

'The pleasure is all mine.' The creature standing in front of Maia and the others was half their height, but that was only because his body was long and many legged, like a caterpillar or centipede. His front, the part that reared up vertically, was almost human in that it had two eyes (though very large) in a hairless head. His nose was a small circle in the centre of his face, his mouth a single horizontal opening from which a thin, feathery tongue flickered. He wore a bright red coat with four sleeves from which his hands, each with four fingers and two thumbs, protruded. When he spoke his hands moved as if he was conducting a hidden orchestra.

'I wish to dispel any possible confusion,' he said. 'My name is not a direct homophone of the aforementioned mustelid.'

'That's the family ferrets belong to,' Mistress Unthank explained.

'Thank you, my dear, I believe our guests know or would have inferred that. May I continue uninterrupted?'

Mistress Unthank grinned and nodded.

'Very well. My name is Forritt, spelled f-o-r-r-i-t-t. That is my last name, my first name is Reddy, spelled r-e-d-d-y. You may call me Reddy or Mr Forritt, it matters not at all.'

Ten raised his eyebrows and leaned towards Slip and Friz. 'Really? "Ready For It?"'

'You are probably unfamiliar with life-forms in and around the Library and are therefore curious about the way Mistress Unthank and I look. We're Changers. Our bodies regularly metamorphose into something different. We're unaware of

107

what the change will be.' He looked down at his many arms and legs, sighed deeply. 'I trust you have no personal or intrusive questions about my own appearance?'

Maia and friends shook their heads quickly. Pencil looked as if she was about to say something but decided it would be better not to do so.

'In that case I shall continue. The rules of your stay are as follows. Meals are served, in the courtyard, when they're ready. Bedding is provided, towels and washing materials are provided. Please do not wear outdoor footwear on the beds.' He looked directly at Pencil for a few seconds; she stared at her feet. 'If you have any queries or requests please ask Mistress Unthank or myself. You'll probably get a more pleasant response from Mistress Unthank.' He looked up at the cook. 'Have I missed anything, my dear?'

Mistress Unthank shook her head and smiled. She opened her mouth and began to mime eating, then tapped her wrist and described two circles with one fat finger.

'You can talk now if you wish,' Reddy Forritt said with no attempt to hide his exasperation. He scuttled away through an unseen door.

Mistress Unthank pointed them in the direction of an archway through which they could see trees and sunlight, hear birdsong and fountains. 'Dinner will be ready in two hours, little ones. No doubt you'll want to freshen up, I'll take you to your rooms. Follow me.'

The courtyard was square with two rooms on each side. At its centre was a stone table with a woven canopy overhead, and on the table were bowls of fruit and vases of flowers. There were fountains and neatly clipped hedges, several small trees. Insects droned their delight at the intoxicating mix of sunlight and pollen.

'I need a shower and a change of clothes,' Friz announced.

'Yeah,' Slip added, 'I wondered what the smell was.' He escaped Friz's grasping hands for only a few seconds, found his head immersed in the pool surrounding the fountain. The two, splashing and laughing, headed for their rooms.

'Me too,' Tom said quietly. 'I need to talk to you later,' he said to Maia, 'we need to figure out where we're going, what we're doing.'

'We all need to be involved in that, not just you and me.'

'Really? Do you think the others care?' He shouldered his bag and stalked into his room.

'I'm pleased you told him that,' Ten said. He looked around him. Only Pencil was still with them, though she was focused on persuading butterflies to land on her fingers. 'As you know, I didn't intend coming with you.'

'I do recall that.'

'But things have gone beyond what I wanted. And, given the choice, I'd rather go back than move on, and I'd rather move on than stick around here.'

Maia nodded. 'I can understand why you'd want to go back, but I don't think that's an option. The Bazhka will be hanging around the back door in case we decide to go that way. Why wouldn't you want to stay here? It's safe. You like books.'

'It's weird, that's why! Talking caterpillars and flying books, lady mountains and outdoor indoors. I mean, this place, outdoors in the sunlight, is inside the Library which is inside the Emperorium. It doesn't make sense. And I have a feeling that anyone who stays here for long doesn't get to leave.'

'So you come with us, wherever we go.'

'That doesn't fill me with much hope. I mean, you're almost normal, but laughing boy Tom? The comedy duo? I wouldn't want to place my life in their hands.'

'Perhaps they feel the same way about you.'

Ten shrugged. 'I'm sure they do. But since neither they nor I have any choice, there's something I need to tell you.' He looked around suspiciously, checking that no-one could hear. 'The only reason I came to find you was because Madame Klein told me to give you a message.' He shrugged again. 'When she spoke it was as if I didn't really have any choice. I just . . . came to find you.'

'Yes, she's persuasive like that.'

'And then, what with the Bazhka and the Library and so on, the message got pushed to one side and . . . Well, this is the first chance I've had to tell you.'

'And what did she say?' Maia asked patiently.

'She said, and these are her exact words, "Tell her, dis-lui, c'est trés importante, very important, clef! Le clef!" And then she said, 'Tu es le clef!'

'Your French is good! But it doesn't actually mean much, does it? The same thing in English and French: "tell her, it's very important," and then "the key" repeated.' She mulled over the words again. '"Tu es le clef."'

'The key? That key?' Ten pointed to Madame Klein's key, still hanging round Maia's neck.

'I can't imagine it would be anything else. And I already know it's important because it opens any door in the Emperorium, according to Madame Klein. But that's useless if we don't know where we're going. And for that we need the map which the Head Librarian says we can look at but not borrow.' Maia rose to her feet. 'Thank you for the message, but it doesn't really help. I'm going to shower now.'

'Okay. I need to ask Mistress Unthank if there's anywhere I can get a change of clothes. I didn't quite have time to pack for a journey where I'm bound to get killed. What's appropriate clothing for wearing at your own funeral?'

'Mistress Unthank would be, in this instance, the wrong person,' Mr Forritt's grey-slate voice said. He flowed towards them tugging a four-wheeled cart behind him. 'She's food and housekeeping, I'm everything else. I noticed you had no luggage.' He jerked his head behind him. 'This should fit you. All clean, all pressed, all free of charge.'

On the back of the cart was a leather sack. Ten opened it carefully, unsure whether this might be a trick. He pulled out several vests, three shirts, four pairs of shorts that were probably undergarments, five knitted socks and two pairs of thick overtrousers. He held each item against him in turn; they all seemed close to his size.

'That's very kind,' he remembered his manners, 'where did you get them?'

'My wardrobe,' Mr Forritt said. 'They fitted me many changes ago. Doubt I'll need them again.' He slid around, tugged the cart after him. 'Mistress Unthank's idea, not mine. Give them back when you return.' He shrugged several pairs of shoulders. 'If you return.'

Maia grinned. 'I'm looking forward to seeing everyone's faces when they see your new outfit.'

Ten took the bag and headed for his room. 'I stopped caring years ago what other people thought of me.'

Pencil had crept closer to sit beside Maia. 'I don't have a change of clothes either,' she said, looking around as if expecting Mr Forritt to appear with a bag for her.

Maia wanted only to rest, to wash away some of the terrors of the day, to lie down and think. But instead she forced herself to smile. 'Do you want me to come with you to collect your clothes? You said you slept under a desk. I'm not sure if that's right, but I don't mind going with you. If you're going to be in trouble with Ms Inkwada then I'll tell her I asked you to stay here with us. And there are things I'd like to ask you about the Library and the books, and how you came to work there.'

Pencil shook her head. 'No, you don't understand. I don't have a change of clothes.' She stood up. 'These are my clothes. I have a paper bag with my nightie in it. And my brushes I found, tooth and hair. At night I go to the washroom and wash everything I have, hang them out, they're normally dry by the time I wake up.' She looked at her feet. 'I don't have any shoes either.'

Maia was horrified. 'Does no-one help you out? The Head Librarian, does she know? I'm sure she'd find something for you if she knew.'

'No! You can't tell her! All I want is to be a librarian, and if she thinks I can't look after myself, how will she be able to trust me to look after books? Please don't tell her.'

Maia pulled Pencil to her feet. 'I won't tell her. But . . .' She made her mind up. 'You're about the same size as me. I've brought too many clothes anyway, I was going to leave some behind. You can have them if you want.'

Pencil's eyes widened. 'Your clothes? You'd give them to me?'

'Not all of them, just some.' Maia looked down at Pencil's feet. 'And some shoes. You can have my spare shoes.'

Pencil was dancing in Maia's outstretched arms. 'Clothes? And shoes?' She stopped and her brow furrowed. 'Are they Librarian clothes?'

Maia thought quickly. 'They're not like the Librarian's clothes here, Pencil, but they're exactly the same as Librarians would have where I come from. I'll show you.' She led Pencil to her room and emptied her sack out onto the bed. 'We can split them equally, one for you, one for me. I packed in a hurry so I brought too much.' It took only a few seconds until Pencil was skipping back to her own room clutching half Maia's clothes and her trainers. Maia watched her go.

'That was kind of you.' Mr Forritt was perched on the roof immediately above her door. 'Kind, but silly.' He crawled down the vertical wall. 'That girl will never come to anything. She's been here before, with other guests, not very often, but often enough to know the rules. She never remembers what we've told her, though. That's why I came back, to tell her to leave. Can't have Library understaff staying here.'

'Are you expecting other guests tonight?'

'No, we never get many anyway. Now in the old days we'd be turning people away by midday. But not now.'

'Then there's not a problem with her staying, is there.'

'It's against the rules. She can't have a room.'

'Then she can share with me. One of us can sleep on the floor.'

'That's what she's used to, I suspect.' Mr Forritt sighed. 'I dunno. I give my clothes away to one of them, let another stay when I oughtn't. Next thing you know I'll be offering to tell you captivating stories by candlelight after you've had your meal.'

Maia suddenly appreciated the rules Mr Forritt imposed upon himself, the way he disguised his kindness with a hard, brusque exterior. 'Stories?' she said. 'That sounds wonderful! Would you?'

'You silver-tongued little so-and-so! But my word is my bond, you've got me now. I'll have to consult Mistress Unthank, make sure I can find something suitable for your delicate young ears.' He headed back up the wall and over the roof. 'Your new friend might as well have the room she's in, no point in her sleeping on the floor,' he growled grudgingly as he disappeared from view. 'Five sets of sheets, six sets of sheets, what's the difference?'

Maia and Pencil were the first to reappear at the table in the centre of the courtyard. The air was still sweet and warm though the day had dimmed and lanterns had been lit. Maia's clothes fitted Pencil well; they might have been taken for sisters, though Maia looked younger yet behaved like the elder. The others commented on the similarities when they arrived. Even Tom seemed to have regained his calm. 'I'm sorry about what I said before, the way I behaved. When I think about what's happened I think it's all my imagination, that I'll wake up from a nightmare. But I won't, will I?'

'I don't know, Tom, I honestly don't know. But I suspect this is our new reality.'

Slip and Friz introduced Pencil to the pitch-and-toss game they'd been playing in the town square, but lost interest when she beat them every time.

When Ten appeared dressed in Mr Forritt's old clothes he was surprised to find that they met with unanimous approval. Even Tom remarked that Ten looked good in brown. Maia was pleased that her gentle warning to the others had been listened to and acted upon.

Mistress Unthank had prepared a meal (served by Mr Forritt) which was unlike anything they'd tasted before. There was undoubtedly meat of some type in a sauce which contained some sweet fruit. There were many-hued vegetables, roasted and mashed. Nothing was familiar, but every plate was emptied. They were given a sweet fruit pie and something that might have been chocolatey, and a succession of drinks that cleansed the palate and refreshed the body. When they were full they attacked the kitchen to thank Mistress Unthank, forced her into a corner while they washed and dried and - under her careful direction - put away every plate and mug and pan, every piece of cutlery, every glass.

'I must thank you all profusely,' Mistress Unthank declared, 'I have never known guests behave so kindly or work so effectively. I have two reasons to be sad, however,' she dabbed the corner of one eye with a tea-towel. 'First, I know that you must be on your way tomorrow, and that will be a cheerless goodbye. And second, I'm aware that Mr Forritt has managed to trick you into asking him to tell a story, and that will make ALL of you very sad indeed. That's if you don't fall asleep within two minutes of him starting!'

Mr Forritt appeared in the doorway and cleared his throat until he was sure he had everyone's attention. 'I should point out,' he said proudly, 'that Mistress Unthank is my dearest, my lovely, and my darling wife. She is, as you may have guessed, a Changer like me, hence the disparity in our sizes. But we are simply opposite sides of the same coin, complementary in all we do, and entirely knowing each other's character.' He coughed gently. 'And she loves my stories!'

They strolled into the garden and gathered round the table. Mr Forritt stood at its centre while his wife leaned out of the kitchen window and encouraged him with gentle insults.

'This,' Mr Forritt declaimed, 'is the story of my first change. In those days I was a handsome young man . . .'

'Couldn't afford a mirror though,' his wife called across to them.

Mr Forritt ignored her. 'And I could have had my choice of any one of many, many young ladies . . .'

'Blind or needing glasses, I believe.'

'I asked the most beautiful of them to be mine . . .'

'And she was daft enough to say yes!' Mistress Unthank guffawed.

'And every day with her has been happier than the previous one!'

Mistress Unthank's loud laughter was interrupted. From somewhere in the hostel a bell tolled, deep and resonant.

'You expecting anyone, Reddy?' Mistress Unthank asked.

Her husband was already heading for the entrance. 'I'll see who it is,' he said, 'send them away. Now, no telling them what happens.'

Mistress Unthank waited until her husband had left the courtyard. 'He's such a sweetie,' she said, 'that rough voice and grumpy manner, it's all a front. He worries so where the next Change will take him. His Changes seem far more cruel than mine, at least I'm only getting bigger. I have the same number of arms and legs I've always had. But he . . .'

Mr Forritt hurried back into the courtyard accompanied by a tall figure wrapped and hooded in a dark blue cloak. He made no introductions, just stood back to let the stranger throw off her hood and reveal herself.

'Ms Inkwadi!' Pencil exclaimed. 'What are you . . .'

'Silence, Pencil. I need you all to listen,' the Head Librarian said abruptly. She was struggling with three leather satchels slung over her shoulders, she wriggled her way out of them and dropped them on the table. The headdress she'd been wearing earlier was gone, her black hair was pulled back by a headband but strands of it had escaped and she was forced to sweep them back from her eyes. 'I'll explain what I know,' she said, her eyes fixing each of the group in turn, 'please don't interrupt. If you have any questions I'll try to answer them when I've finished.'

She undid the buckles on the first satchel and brought out a sheaf of papers. 'These are application forms for membership tickets, over two hundred of them. They were received a few hours ago. Each of them is from a Bazhka. And they're waiting for the Library to open tomorrow so they can all come in.'

'Why is that so important,' Ten said, 'just don't let . . .'

'I asked you NOT to interrupt!' Ms Inkwadi's eyes widened with anger. 'There are some rules which cannot be broken. Anyone who applies for a ticket to borrow books from the

Library must be given one. Possession of a ticket guarantees entry to the Library. I cannot prevent this army of Bazhka coming into the Library as soon as the doors open in the morning. And it would be naive to assume they wanted anything other than finding all of you. And before you say anything, there is more.'

She pushed the application forms away, stared at them again. 'I used to think that books only talked to librarians. Not talked with voices, of course, but with the words on their pages. Tell me, Pencil, when the books told you that our guests were about to arrive by the back door, that they were being pursued by Bazhka, did they speak words?'

Pencil shook her head. 'They opened in front of me and I read the words. They were easy words, though, I didn't have any problems with them. I knew what they meant.'

'Can you remember the words?'

Pencil's face contorted. 'I'm not much good at remembering. But . . . one of them said "DANGER!" Capital letters, I remember that. "DANGER! OPEN BACK DOOR! HELP NEEDED!" That was one of them. And another said something about taking tickets. And the names to put on them. That was it.'

'Two books? Only two books? Try hard to remember, Pencil, it's important.'

Pencil nodded. 'There was a third book, it looked like a story book, pictures on the front. But it didn't open for me, it just fluttered.'

'Did it do anything else?'

'Well, it sort of bumped into the two books that were telling me to do things. That's all. It was a bit clumsy.'

'Thank you, Pencil.' The Head Librarian closed her eyes. 'I just hope there's time for this,' she said to herself, then flicked her eyes open again. 'I'm not used to books that give commands, that order people to do things. Instruction books, yes, but the books that spoke to you, Pencil, seem to have been taking self-awareness to a ridiculous degree. I've known for some time that our books were sentient, but this takes things to extremes.'

Ms Inkwadi stood up. 'Earlier today I told all of you,' she pointed at Maia, at Tom and Ten, at Slip and Friz, 'that I knew certain things about you. I told you that someone must have been writing about you. I knew that much because your book, your story, had come to me and I read about you. I believe that this book, this story, was the one that ordered Pencil to rescue you. I kept it close by me. But when I opened it not long ago, this is what I found.'

She opened the second satchel and took out two books. The first was the size of a paperback but its cover was plain white. She flicked its pages and they were empty. She dropped it on the table. 'This book is dead. But earlier today it was alive, vibrant even, so full of life it was giving orders to Pencil!' She lowered herself into her seat, put her head in her hands. 'I don't like books dying.'

Maia leaned forward. 'Can I speak, Ms Inkwadi?'

'Go ahead. I have more to say, but I need to gather my thoughts.'

'What can have happened to make the pages go blank?'

'The writer stopped writing. But even with that, the words would still exist. It can only be that the writer destroyed the book. There is no other explanation.'

'But why?'

'I don't know, I can only guess. I think that the writer knew about the Bazhka wanting to come in. When those doors open they can ask for any book on any subject and my librarians are duty bound to find it for them. If that book existed, even if it was still being written, it would lead them directly to you. Its death gives you a chance to escape.'

118

'No!' Tom slammed the table with his open hand. 'That is . . . it's just unbelievable! I'm sorry, but I can't get my head round all this. Books that think and talk. Someone writing about us even as we're doing things. It's impossible! It's not real!'

Maia placed her hand on top of Tom's. 'We have to believe it, Tom, it's happening. We just have to accept it and find out how to deal with it. We have to trust what people like Ms Inkwadi tell us.' She turned her attention to the Head Librarian. 'Thank you for coming to see us, to warn us. But you've a second book on the table. And something else in the third satchel. What else did you want to say?'

Ms Inkwadi nodded. 'You need to escape. I believe that you'll be captured or killed or . . . I don't know what might happen to you if the Bazhka find you.' She reached for the second book on the table. Its leather cover was inscribed with the remnants of interlocking curves, but many years and many hands had worn them away so only a faint pattern remained. When the Head Librarian opened the book - slowly, reverently, afraid she might damage it - the pages were yellowed and frayed. The binding was coming adrift from the spine. The book lay like an old cat, waiting for the end of its days.

'This is a history of the Emperorium.' The Head Librarian was whispering. 'It is a dangerous book because it contains facts, and ideas, and thoughts. No-one except each Head Librarian knows of its existence. It isn't listed in any index. It is kept locked away. I am the only one to have a key. No-one reads it except me, and that is only when I am alone, in my private rooms. There is a precedent, however, that the Head Librarian may pass on some details if she or he feels that it would be dangerous not to do so.' She swallowed. 'It's written in a language few would understand. I can make out many of the words, but not all. I'd like to read you a brief summary written long ago by one of my predecessors.' She took out a scrap of paper from the front of the book and began to read.

'"Many centuries ago, some people with more wisdom than others began to believe that Gods did not exist. They called themselves Truthsingers."' Ms Inkwadi stopped, looked at Maia, because she'd heard the stifled intake of breath that came with the word 'Truthsingers'. 'Are you familiar with the term, Maia?'

Maia nodded but offered no explanation.

'Perhaps we can return to that later. I'll go on. "Truthsingers were, for the sake of their own lives, a secret society. They believed in the supremacy of mankind and in the development of the natural scientific method. There was no room in their lives for myth or religion. If anything couldn't be explained by rational thought and empirical observation, then that was because the right questions weren't being asked, or the right tools weren't available to investigate the matter." Are you all with me so far?'

'It's like being back at school,' Slip said.

'At least there you knew there'd be a bell sounding for a break,' Friz said longingly.

Maia looked at Ten and Tom, her eyes asking questions. They both nodded silently. 'I think we're okay with that,' she said.

'I've no idea what you're talking about,' Pencil objected.

'It doesn't matter, dear. I'll go on anyway. "Truthsingers lived across the known world and travelled widely. On hearing rumours of whole towns disappearing, buildings and inhabitants, a group of Truthsingers travelled to a distant land and found people being enslaved by a powerful being. The Truthsingers refused to believe that this creature, despite its powers, was a god, and the creature in turn was captivated by their attitude. Using their knowledge and curiosity they engaged with the creature and found its powers were not unlimited; it could not cross a boundary of fired clay. They imprisoned it by making manacles and chains of metal inside a shell of porcelain." There is much more than this, I'm aware that we're running out of time.'

'I don't like the sound of this,' Ten said. 'I've read too much fantasy, I can guess what's coming next.'

'Shh,' Maia hissed, 'you have to let her finish.'

'I know this sounds like fiction,' Ms Inkwadi said, 'but I can assure you it's entirely true.' She lowered her eyes to the paper in her hand. '"The creature, which called itself the Maker, was itself enslaved. It could not move. It could not escape. But it used its mind to build worlds in different planes. It populated some of these with its own creations, such as the Bazhka; it enticed humans to others; and, at the very periphery of its influence, people moved into these worlds by accident. Most of them stayed.

'The Truthsingers were aware of the Maker's influence and sought to understand it and reduce it, or at the very least contain it. The porcelain that was so useful in chaining the Maker was used to build doorframes and archways providing the only entrances and exits to the Maker's lands. The Maker could build worlds, but his creatures could not enter them unless the doorway had been destroyed or the door was opened for them, and only Truthsingers possessed keys." This is a very brief summary, there is much detail that I've left out. But what I've said is true.

'I can tell you a little more that might help you. When I return this book to its safe home I shall write in it that I have shared knowledge about it with you. I shall write your names in the book, just as I and my predecessors have done for hundreds of years. But I'll go further. I will break my vow of confidentiality and tell you that the last person to see this book, with me present, was Madame Klein.'

'She travelled here! She knew! She knew all this!' Maia was astounded. 'And she said nothing!'

'She probably knew more than this, Maia. She could read the book herself, more fluently than I could.'

'Why didn't she say anything?'

'I don't know. To protect you? Knowledge can be a dangerous thing.'

There was a cough from the kitchen window. Everyone turned to face Mistress Unthank. 'The most important knowledge I've learned in the last half hour is that these young people are in great danger. If the Bazhka intend entering the Library then it's most likely every door is guarded. Tomorrow they'll come in. We have to find somewhere for our guests to hide.'

'I don't think hiding will be good enough,' Tom said. 'The Bazhka who were chasing us knew we were there, in the book room. And they know we're still in here, why else would they want to come in? If we hide, they'll turn the place upside down until they find us. And who knows what damage they'll cause, how many books they'll destroy, how many people they'll kill while they're looking for us. There must be a way out.'

Ms Inkwadi shook her head. 'All the doors, including the back door, are indeed being watched. There's no other way to get in or out without . . .'

'Except for the roof.' Mr Forritt climbed nimbly onto the table. 'There are windows on the roof, most of them only open an inch or two for ventilation, but some of them are more like doors. I've been out of them before. In the line of duty, I should say, not out of idle curiosity.'

'Reddy, you little devil!' Mistress Unthank's words were coloured with pride. 'You never said you'd been up there! I knew you'd been a hunter, but on the high stacks? It's dangerous up there.'

'I didn't want to worry you, my love. It was a long time ago,' he said wistfully. 'When I was a man.'

The Head Librarian cut into the conversation. 'Can you find your way back?'

'I think so,' Mr Forritt nodded.

'Hold on,' Ten said, 'are you telling me that we can only escape from the Bazhka by going up on the roof of the Library?'

Mr Forritt and Ms Inkwadi looked at each other; they nodded in unison.

'That's the roof that's so high we couldn't even see it? The roof above the clouds? The roof where that, what was it, the Giant Opus was flying. And when we get up there we climb out of a window? How do we get down?'

'Carefully?' suggested Mr Forritt. 'Seriously, when I was up there I saw a stairway leading down, inside one of the buttresses. It probably goes down to ground level. I can show you the way.'

Ten ignored the offer. 'You just said there's a stair "probably" goes down to ground level. That means you don't know for certain. That means it might not be a way down. And even if it is, where are we going to go when we get to the bottom?'

Tom climbed to his feet. 'Do you have any better idea? 'Cos if you do, you should tell us. Now.'

Ten too was on his feet, staring at Tom. 'As a matter of fact I do. We know the danger we're facing now, we know about Bazhka. The ones who chased us to the back door may not even be there. And if they are, we can sneak past them, or attack them, or bribe them, get past them and go back to the entrance to the Emperorium.' He jabbed his finger in Tom's direction; his voice grew angrier. 'Then we wait to be rescued. That's my idea. Okay, it's risky, but not as risky as jumping out of a window at the top of a building so huge it's got its own weather system inside it!'

'Boys,' Maia said softly, 'I think you should listen to this.' She brought a piece of paper out of her pocket and unfolded it. 'This letter is from Madame Klein, it's to me, I found it in her bedroom. It's . . .' She looked at Ms Inkwadi. 'I'll let you read the whole thing, it's not long, but you'll understand why I gasped when you mentioned Truthsingers. For the rest of you, this is the important part.' She cleared her throat. Her voice was small but everyone heard every word. '"The problem of your father is more certain. His disappearance is a threat to our existence, I can put it in no other way. He is clearly in danger, lost somewhere in the Emperorium. Should I share this burden with you? What would you be able to do, how would you be able to help?"' She raised her head and there were tears in her eyes. 'I intend finding my father who's lost and in danger somewhere in the Emperorium. So I'll accept Mr Forritt's kind offer of help and try to find a way out over the roof. I don't really care whether any of you come with me or not.'

'I'm coming,' Tom said softly. He put his hand on Maia's shoulder and she covered it with her own.

'Us too,' Friz added.

'Hold on,' Slip said, 'you didn't even ask me!'

'What would you have said?'

'I'd have said I was coming, of course.'

'Well shut up then.'

They all looked at Ten. 'You helped us find our way here,' Tom said, 'you suggested the book room, you found the right book and the door. I don't know about the rest of them, but I . . . I'd be pleased to have you along.'

Ten looked puzzled. 'Why are you being so pleasant all of a sudden?'

Tom grinned. 'If a Bazhka sees you, it'll probably think you'd make a better meal than any of the rest of us. So it's self preservation, really. The more of us there are, the better the chance of me surviving.'

'You can't run as fast as us either,' Slip added. 'A Bazhka would go after you first.'

'And we can put some of the provisions in your rucksack,' Friz joined in. 'Less for us to carry.'

'And you're so miserable and grumpy,' Tom added, 'that having you along makes the rest of us seem happy and cheerful.'

'It's because they like you, luvvie!' Mistress Unthank yelled across the courtyard. 'It's because they think you're part of their team!'

'Is that really it?' Ten asked. 'You're not all just making fun of me?'

'Nah,' Slip said, 'if we wanted to make fun of you we'd throw rotten fruit at you. Fill your bag with stones. Tell you you're really handsome.'

Ten relaxed, though he was obviously unfamiliar with the others' humour. 'I can't pretend I understand you and the way you all think, and your jokes just aren't funny. But . . . But I didn't really want to see those two Bazhka at the backdoor anyway. And while there's a chance I might get my Dad back, well . . . I'll come with you.'

Pencil opened and closed her mouth, scratched her ears, then dredged up courage from somewhere deep inside her. 'I'd like to go too,' she said.

Maia looked as if she was going to reply, but the Head Librarian was quicker. 'Don't be silly, Pencil, why on earth would they want you to go with them? You'd be more of a liability than a help.'

'I think what Ms Inkwadi means is that you're probably needed in the Library,' Maia added, attempting to be conciliatory. 'After all, who would supply her with pencils and paper and everything else you do?' Her words did nothing to take the hurt and disappointment from Pencil's face.

The Head Librarian ignored Pencil's wounded pride. 'I brought something else as well, hoping that it might help you, but I'm not sure it will be of any use.' She reached for the last satchel and gingerly opened it. 'Two of my librarians were injured just capturing this brute.' She undid the catch and lifted the satchel by its base. A locked steel cage slid onto the table. Inside it, trembling with fear or rage or a mixture of both, was a book. 'This,' said Miss Inkwadi, 'is the Map.'

The cage was only a little larger than the book. The Head Librarian took a key from her pocket and reached for the lock. The book opened slightly, as if it wanted to trap her fingers inside its pages. 'Stop it now!' Miss Inkwadi ordered, but the book ignored her, shook itself angrily.

'I can't see any point in even trying to open the cage, let alone the Map,' the Head Librarian said. 'It won't let anyone go near it. It'll just fly away if we let it out.'

'Do books often do this?' Maia asked, bending to look more closely at the caged creature.

'Books can be dangerous because of the ideas inside them, but usually they just want to be read. They're only violent if they think they're going to be damaged. I've no idea why this one is behaving so badly.'

Pencil joined Maia. 'Are you frightened?' she asked the book. 'I wonder why you're frightened. 'Cos these nice people here aren't going to hurt you. They need you. They want to look at you.'

The Map shivered, but it seemed less angry.

'Nobody here wants to harm you,' Pencil said soothingly, stretched out a hand and placed it on the cage. Her finger slipped through the bars and gently stroked the Map's cover. 'There, there.' She whispered soft words to it.

'I'm sorry to interrupt,' Mr Forritt said, 'but we need to get ready to go. It's a long journey to the rooftops and those Bazhka will be desperate to find us.'

At the word 'Bazhka' the Map reacted violently, hurling itself against the bars.

'It knows!' Maia said. 'If the . . . monsters,' she chose her words carefully, 'can't find us then what will they do? They'll look for the Map so they can follow us.'

'It's alright,' Pencil whispered, 'we won't let anyone harm you. You can go with these nice people. They'll look after you.' She looked pleadingly at the Head Librarian. 'I know it's not meant to go but if it stays . . . And it's so frightened.'

Tom butted in. 'We need it. Ms Inkwadi. I'd guess that if it's left behind it'll be found and misused, damaged, hurt. It'll help the monsters track us and find us. In this instance, couldn't you break the rules? Just this once?'

The Head Librarian pursed her lips, her face coloured with indecision.

Mistress Unthank had somehow made her way from the kitchen and squeezed herself through the narrow (for her) doorway into the courtyard. She stood behind the Head Librarian and rested her giant hands on Ms Inkwadi's shoulders. 'If you ask me, which you aren't doing, but I'm going to tell you what I think anyway, there's no decision to be made. They take the Map with them. Their need is greater than your pride in the Library and its rules.'

Ms Inkwadi looked at Mistress Unthank's hands, felt their strength and weight, and made up her mind. 'Very well, you can take the Map,' she said resignedly. 'But once I've opened the cage to let it out I must leave. I have the whole Library to think of, and all those who work there and depend on it for their livelihood. If I'm asked then I don't want to know your whereabouts. I don't want to know which way you went.' This time the Map was still when she opened the lock and lifted the door to the cage. She took it out and placed it in front of Maia. But when Maia tried to open it, the Map remained stubbornly closed. Maia held out her arms. Ms Inkwadi tried to pull the book open, but even her strength and familiarity could do nothing to persuade the Map to open. 'Map,' she said, 'you're being silly. You're embarrassing me.'

'Can I try?' Pencil asked.

'Why would it open for you when it won't do so for me?'

Pencil smiled. 'Come on, Map, we really can't do without you.' She stroked the cover gently, her gestures matching the tenderness in her voice. There was no resistance at all when she reached one hand round and softly pulled the book open.

'Well I never,' said Ms Inkwadi. 'Who would have thought that . . .'

Maia touched Pencil lightly on her shoulder. 'Can I try?' Pencil nodded and closed the Map. Maia tried again to open the book and had as little success as the Head Librarian, though the Map did at least condescend to lie still when she tugged at its cover. Maia looked at Ms Inkwadi, head on one side. 'I think the Map is saying that it would like Pencil to come with us. And Pencil herself would certainly like to do that. Does she need your permission?'

'Strictly speaking, no. But she's, how shall I put it . . .'

'Slow?' Ten interjected. 'Well, it's true, isn't it?' he added when Maia scowled at him.

'I'm not slow,' Pencil pointed out. 'I just think differently. And I can't remember things. But I can be useful.' She smiled her thanks at Maia. 'And I wouldn't be a burden.' She turned her attention to Ten. 'At least I *want* to come with you.'

'That's it then,' Maia stood up, 'Pencil and the Map are coming along. Mr Forritt, when do you want to leave?'

'As soon as we can. Meet back here in half an hour? We can look at the Map together. With Pencil's help, of course.'

Pencil's grin split her face. Ms Inkwadi rose to her feet. 'I've a feeling I'll miss you more than I know,' she said to Pencil. 'Be good. Look after the Map. And don't annoy your travelling companions too much.' She gathered her belongings together, cleared her throat to draw everyone's attention. 'I do hope I see you all again. I will instruct all the staff to tell the Bazhka nothing about your visit, to refer all enquiries directly to me. If I have any advice, it's this. I've only once left the Library, many years ago when I was a newly appointed Senior Librarian. I was sent to recover a valuable book that had been lent out. The Head Librarian of the time told me to recruit a guide at a rather disreputable inn called O'Carolan's Terpsichory, it's at a crossroads in the corridors. I'm sure the Map will show you the way. My advice is that you should seek a guide and a guardian there.' She bowed her head, raised her hands to her heart. 'Goodbye and good luck.' She left without looking back.

It was Mr Forritt who took charge, filled the silence with a hearty 'Let's go, then. Time to be busy busy busy.'

'I think they all understand the need for haste, my dear,' Mistress Unthank said. She sighed heavily. 'I'll prepare some food for you all to take with you.' She ducked hurriedly through the doorway and headed back to the kitchen, Mr Forritt close behind.

As each of the others headed for their rooms to pack everything they'd so recently unpacked, Maia led Pencil (the Map, in its satchel but without the cage, clutched under one arm) to one side. 'I was just wondering,' she said, 'did you say anything to the Map when you whispered to it, the first time? When you calmed it down?'

The answer came too quickly. 'Me? Nothing, I didn't say nothing; I mean anything. Like you said, I just tried to calm it.'

'I see. You didn't ask it to open just for you? Like, when it felt your fingers and no-one else's?'

Pencil stopped at the door of her room, indignant. 'I wouldn't do that! And anyway, it wouldn't have followed *my* orders. After all, I'm slow. And I'm not even a librarian.'

'But you don't have to be a librarian to talk to books. To know books.' Maia smiled disarmingly. 'Do you?'

'No. Suppose not.' Pencil stroked the Map. 'I may not be a librarian, but I do know books. I *love* books. Sometimes you just have to find the right words. Ms Inkwadi wasn't really saying the right words. She was angry, and the Map doesn't like angry people.' She giggled. 'So I might have said *something* to it. Because I do so want to come with you.'

'And I'll be pleased to have you along. But it'll be dangerous. Why do you want to come?'

Pencil sighed. 'There's nothing really for me here. They'd never let me be a librarian, I'd be fetching and carrying for them forever. But there's something else as well.' Pencil held out one free hand, pointed to her clothes and her shoes. 'You're the only person who ever gave me anything. You're the only person I can remember who was ever kind to me as if they meant it.' She paused, looked down, ground her foot into the floor with embarrassment. 'And because I like you.'

'Thank you, Pencil, it's a long time since anyone said they liked me. I really like you too.'

'By the way,' Pencil added, 'when you brought that letter out of your pocket this came with it, you dropped it on the ground.' She held out her spare hand. In it was the necklace Maia's father had given her.

'Thank you,' Maia said, 'thank you so much. That was a gift, it means a lot to me.'

'It's beautiful. Why don't you wear it?'

Maia felt the necklace's reassuring weight in her hand. 'I took it off because I wanted to keep it safe, but I suppose there's always the chance it might fall out of my pocket. I'll pack it away in my bag, I think.'

'If someone had given me something special like that I'd wear it all the time. What's it made of?'

'Porcelain. And it's got special writing on each bead, but I don't know what it means.'

'Porcelain.' Pencil rolled the unfamiliar word round her mouth. 'Like the chains the Truth people made to lock up the evil creature, in Ms Inkwadi's story?'

Maia looked at the necklace. She felt a sudden need to run after Ms Inkwadi, to see if the runes on the necklace were similar to the writing in the History of the Emperorium, to ask if she could tell what they meant. But it was too late, they would be leaving shortly. Instead she refastened the band of red porcelain around her neck. As soon as she did she felt a sense of relief, of calm, as if the necklace or its runes were protecting her, hiding her from some distant, watchful, unwelcome eye. 'Thank you,' she said, fingers counting the beads. 'Thank you. I'm coming to find you.' Perhaps her luck was changing. After all, her father had said the necklace would bring her good fortune.

SEVEN

Excubitor was organising her troops. She took pride in her ability to think, to consider options, to plan and strategise. That was why she was pleased that the Maker had given her the task of destroying the Library. That hadn't been his primary order, of course; that was more straightforward: 'find a human girl travelling with four other humans; bring her to me.' But that would be easy, the Library and the land around it were not so large that humans would be difficult to uncover, no matter where they were concealed. Part of her hoped that the humans would be hiding; it would be entertaining to torture the Librarians into revealing their refuge.

Even if the humans were found easily, in the open, there would be an excuse for a formal execution and, once blood flowed . . . Controlling more than two hundred Bazhka wasn't easy at the best of times. That was why the Maker used her so frequently. Everyone, including Bazhka, feared her.

It wasn't that she appeared terrifying, at least, not in the way that many of her army did. She didn't slither, she didn't drool, her jaws weren't too large and her teeth didn't project. She didn't enjoy causing pain for its own sake but considered it a very effective tool - probably the most effective tool there was - in persuading others to do as she wished. Her willingness to hurt was well known and that was why she was feared. But that in itself would have been useless had she not been so physically superior. She was taller than most of the Bazhka in her command and cleverer and more devious than all of them. Beneath her dark blue skin thin plates of flexible armour protected her joints and muscles. Her speed was matched only by her endurance: her reactions were so quick they appeared to those watching as anticipations, yet she had the stamina of a pack of wolves. She was strong enough to wield her battle sword (as big as an adult human) as if it were a rapier, yet could use a sharp knife to cut and slice and pierce with precision and accuracy. She didn't enjoy killing; she preferred to make her opponents suffer in long, screaming agony.

She was positioning her army at each of the Library building's doors. She'd wanted them at each of the gateways as well, but there were too many of those and all of them were open. Passage to the Library and its outlying towns and villages from the corridors had always been easy.

The building itself was large and high. If she'd had another day, Excubitor would have had her fliers survey the whole Library from above to determine if there was access to the roof or high up in the walls. But the Maker's orders had allowed no time for that; even now her troops were straggling reluctantly into position, complaining as they always did that they hadn't had time to feed. She'd already had several disposed of for minor offences, despite them being told that looting would be allowed after the incursion. Those that remained were well-behaved, noisy enough to let those inside the building know they were there, quiet enough to make them think they were in no immediate danger.

It would soon be dark. Excubitor climbed to the top of a small mound in front of the main doors, allowed the setting sun to frame her, to silhouette her, so that her army would see her. She shook her braided hair, her red eyes blazed behind the visor of her helmet skull. She raised one arm and was rewarded by each of her Bazhka doing the same in obedient silence.

'One day, Excubitor, your pride will be your downfall.' The faint voice was in Excubitor's mind alone, as was her reply.

'If you say so, Master.'

'Ever obedient?'

'As always, Master.'

'And why is that?'

It wasn't the first time the Maker had asked her that question, and she was sure it wouldn't be the last. 'Because you made me, Master. I am yours to command, to praise, to scorn, to abandon even. And to unmake if you wish.'

The voice sighed. 'Excubitor, do you realise how tiresome you can be with your unswerving loyalty? You always do as I ask without comment or complaint, no matter how difficult the task.'

'That is my purpose, my Lord.'

'Then I have some news for you. I was able, until a few moments ago, to sense the girl you seek. I was becoming familiar with her presence, I could smell her, taste her. But something has blocked that sensation. It is . . . disturbing. And so your task has become more difficult than it was.'

Excubitor blinked but showed no emotion. 'Why does that make the task more difficult, my Lord? We seek a human girl. There can't be many in the Library. Therefore we will find her.'

'You are so confident! I like that. But I'd hoped to give you some indication of her movements within the Library. She will try to escape. I don't want you to lose her. She's important to me, though I don't yet know why. It's a long time since I felt so uncertain. So curious.'

'Do you wish me to storm the building now?'

The voice didn't reply. After a while Excubitor broke the silence. 'Master? Do you wish . . .'

'I did hear, Excubitor. I had considered doing that, despite the fact that it would go against the rules and principles that I set up in the first place. The Library is a neutral place. Access is free to those who apply to enter. Having this convention means that I, technically, have access to every

134

piece of knowledge there is about the human world and the Emperorium. I have no need to monitor what is going on personally, the Library does it for me. And it has been useful in the past. But has the time come to break that tenet, to enter outside the permitted hours? I am tempted to do so, I am impatient, but . . . Promise me the girl will not escape, Excubitor, if you enter as planned in the morning.'

'Master, every door is guarded and will remain so, even when we enter the building. I have fliers on the roof. I will have reinforcements at hand late tomorrow to help with the search if, as I expect, the girl and her comrades decide to hide. However, there may be some destruction if that happens.'

'That doesn't matter, Excubitor, the Librarian and her staff will have broken the rules by secreting her in some obscure room and I will then be justified in ordering the Library's destruction. Illogical in view of my earlier commitment to the Library's neutrality, I know; but in seeing the lack of logic and acting despite that, I'm demonstrating my own wilful godliness.'

'Yes, Master. But I will find her. And I will bring her to you personally.'

'Then why do I feel worried, Excubitor? That is, of course, a rhetorical question. I am worried because I sense that this girl is important, though I don't yet know why. Is she the one who will release me? Perhaps she will destroy me. Her aura was enigmatic.'

'I will find her, Master.'

'I'm sure you will, sooner or later. Or she'll find me. Either will be interesting.'

They gathered round the table as Pencil opened the Map. It was similar to other atlases they'd seen, pages filled with charts and plans and drawings. Pencil flicked through until

Maia stopped her. 'This isn't getting us anywhere,' she said, 'we need a page that shows the whole of the Emperorium, like a projection of the globe? You know, every country? Somewhere near the front, perhaps?'

Without Pencil doing or saying anything the Map's pages turned to reveal, close to the front, as Maia had predicted, a double sheet where left and right edges appeared to match.

'That was impressive,' Tom said. He examined the page closely. 'I don't recognise anything at all.'

'Did you expect to?' Maia said sharply, 'this is a new world, a different world. And we don't know how the Map works.'

'Just ask it,' Pencil suggested. 'Books like helping people.'

Maia ignored Ten's exasperated sigh. 'Map, where are we please?' she asked.

A pinhead of blue appeared near the bottom corner of the left page.

'It does as you ask!' Friz said. 'But why does it respond to you, Maia? I thought it would only do what Pencil said.'

'She had a few words with it,' Maia explained, 'when you all went to your rooms. She told it that it should be ready to help us all. Tom, can you try next?'

Tom spoke up eagerly. 'Map, do you have a page which shows the Library, and where we are in the Library? Oh, and the place the Librarian suggested we look for a guide, what was it called?'

'O'Carolan's Terpsichory,' Ten said. 'It's an inn.'

The pages flicked again. This time they remained open to show a grey-shaded circle surrounded by what looked like a town with buildings and roads and, near a clearly drawn outer perimeter, fields. There were lines projecting from the grey circle.

'The grey bit,' Mr Forritt said, 'that must be the Library.'

'And where's the inn?' Slip asked. As he spoke a red dot appeared well beyond the perimeter of the Library's land.

'How do we get out?' Maia asked. 'How do we get to the inn?'

The map's pages flicked again. The blue pinhead and its red counterpart were shown reasonably close to each other, and the curve of Library town's border showed a break in it where a road passed through it. But beyond that break the road leading to O'Carolan's Terpsichory twisted and turned, it was at least ten times as long as a more direct route would have been. Other roads wandered in a similar serpentine way.

'Perhaps it's hilly terrain?' Ten suggested. 'You know, the direct route actually takes you over the tops of mountains? There are no relief lines shown, though. No different colours either, high land is normally coloured brown.'

'Map, what's this place?' Pencil placed her finger on the page between the red and blue dots. Pages flicked, details appeared, all the colours and shapes normally associated with maps were filled in. But the entrance points, the places (only two or three, it appeared) where roads crossed the new territory's borders, weren't fixed. They slid around, as if someone was in the process of redrawing the Map..

'What's happening?' Pencil asked. 'Roads don't move. Map, why is everything changing?'

The Map couldn't reply. It was up to Maia to ask the next question. 'Map, what's the quickest way to the inn from here?'

The Map highlighted a road, the same as before, twisting and turning to reach its destination. The direct route through the new territory didn't exist because the entry and exit points had moved.

'I think I know what it is!' Mr Forritt said. 'I may never have left the Library – and I've never looked at a map – but I have listened to travellers who've visited us. The curly roads that don't move, that're fixed, they're the corridors. But the

137

doors, the way you get into the different places, the countries, the lands, call them what you want, they aren't fixed. The same doorway can lead to different places on different days.' He stopped, proud with his analysis.

'It's like,' Maia said, 'you find a door and open it and it leads to, let's say, Berlin. You close it, without going through, open it again, and you find Buenos Aires on the other side. Or Beijing. Or anywhere.'

'That sounds logical,' Tom said, 'in a sort of crazy illogical way. That would be why it's useless trying to copy the Map. Everything's changing, all the time.'

'Except when you're inside a door. But an exit could lead anywhere.' Ten was becoming angry again. 'So it's meaningless looking for a specific place because that place could be a ten minute walk away or halfway across this crazy world! What on earth is the point?'

'What's the point of doing anything in that case?' Tom was squaring up to Ten. 'I'm sick of your pessimism, you're always finding fault, always insulting people. If you don't want to come then curl up here on the floor and wait for the Bazhka to find you.' He jabbed a finger in Ten's chest. 'We'd be better off without you.'

Ten wasn't about to back down. 'If it wasn't for me you'd already be a Bazhka's breakfast, remember?' He pushed Tom back, yelled at him.' It was me who got you out of the book room into the Library!'

'Stop it!' Maia screamed.

The jostling and shoving ceased.

Maia lowered her voice. 'There's got to be a point!' Her fists were clenched, she was in control of herself, but the others weren't used to her fury being on display. 'The inn doesn't move, remember, it's at a crossroads in the corridors. And the exit from the Library isn't moving either.'

'Perhaps some doorways are more volatile than others,' Slip suggested.

'We don't know. There's so much we don't know. But that's no reason for giving in. So we take things a step at a time.' She glared at each of them in turn. 'One, we get out of the Library, over the roof.' Mr Forritt nodded his relief. 'Two, we find our way to O'Carolan's Terpsichory. While we're doing that we can look at the Map in more detail, find out what it can and can't tell us. Three, we decide where we need to go, then we can see about getting a guide. Because I'm going to find my father, we're going to catch and punish those Bazhka for what they did to Tom's mother and Ten's father, and we're going to fix things so we can get out again. But we won't do any of those if we're squabbling and whinging! Now let's go! Mr Forritt, lead the way!'

As they shouldered their bags and sacks Friz leaned close to Slip. 'I like it when she takes charge like that. She impresses me.'

Slip shook his head. 'She terrifies me!'

Mr Forritt took them to the base of the tower supporting the green-arched bridge they'd seen earlier. 'We use lifts where we can, staircases where we can't, ladders if there are any. And if there are no ladders, we climb the shelves themselves.'

Mistress Unthank had accompanied them for the short distance to the bridge towers. She sighed deeply. 'You make sure you look after everyone,' she instructed her husband, then turned her attention to the rest of the group. 'And you all look after Mr Forritt too. Send him back safely and in one piece.' The giant woman and the small, insect bodied man looked at each other. She held out a long arm close to the ground. He scuttled across and, lowering his mouth to the tip of her index finger, kissed her gently. Then he looked up and the adoration in his eyes was evident. Mistress Unthank blushed.

'Until we meet again, my treasure,' he said, 'you are constantly in my mind.'

'As you are in mine, my sweetheart.' She dabbed at the corner of her eye with a handkerchief the size of a bed-sheet, blew a kiss, then turned away and disappeared quickly into the darkness.

The wide doors into the tower opened easily. Inside a tumult of sound assaulted their ears. Wood creaked and groaned, ratchets turned, cogs complained, water tumbled and fell and a misty spray hung in the air. The first thing Mr Forritt did was to open his backpack and take out a harness which he fastened carefully around his upper body. Attached to it were six leather sheaths, each containing a large knife. He took one of them out and balanced it in his hand, examined its long, sharp blade. 'Mistress Unthank doesn't like me wearing these,' he yelled to overcome the noise, 'makes her nervous. But when you're up in the stacks you never know when a quick blade might come in handy.' He hid the knives by buttoning up his waistcoat, then pointed at the wooden platforms climbing upwards from an elevated podium in front of them. 'These lifts are powered by a waterwheel,' he shouted. 'Water is channelled from the rooftops into reservoirs. When released, the water falls into buckets on a wheel which turns gears which turn a rope to which are fixed these platforms. The platforms rise to the top of the tower then descend again. The platforms are large enough for three or four but there are no safety barriers. I'll go first, with Maia and Pencil, the rest of you follow, join us at the top.'

The journey was noisy but uneventful. Maia was pleased that Tom and Ten had decided not to push each other off on the way up.

When everyone was together again on the top floor Mr Forritt pushed at a door and they found themselves on the deserted roadway of the bridge. 'No-one about at this time,' he said,' we should make good progress.' He marched them to a ladder at the foot of the bridge's arch. 'Up there,' he pointed, 'when we get to the top there's a walkway leads to the shelves. Then a spiral staircase winds its way upwards. We'll stop for a rest at the top of that one.'

The green metal of the bridge's arch was dry and easy to walk on as it flattened out at the bridge's apex, but they were all glad of the handrail to help and protect them. Friz, close behind Mr Forritt, kept pointing out books flying past in the gloom, or distant shelves decked with what might have been mist, clouds only a little higher than they were. Slip kept his eyes firmly on the metal beneath his feet, not looking up, not looking to either side. Ten came next, breathing heavily, pleased that his new clothes didn't show how much he was sweating; every muscle in his arms and legs ached. Maia followed Ten, a buffer between him and Tom. One moment she was amazed at what she was experiencing; the next she was in despair at the journey ahead. At least Pencil was happy, close behind Maia, her tuneless whistling and singing keeping them both company; the Map in its satchel was hung tight and proud over her shoulder. Tom brought up the rear and his mood was black. He didn't like Maia shouting at him, he didn't like being told what to do, but he had no ideas of his own about how they should progress. Confusion hung about him like a small, dark cloud.

When Mr Forritt had said there was a walkway at the top of the bridge arch, Maia had expected something solid, something strong, like the bridge they were climbing. What came slowly into view was, in comparison, as insubstantial as a spider's web. Three long stretches of rope were tied to the

141

girders of the bridge; they must have been anchored at the other side, but that was the top of a pale precipice so distant there was only a possibility that it might have been book shelves. Thinner cords tied the three ropes to each other in a V-shape; those crossing were required to use the bottom rope for their feet, the top two ropes for their hands. To access the ropes it was necessary to drop about two metres from the bridge's arch.

Friz stood beside Mr Forritt at the edge of the arch, peered down into the gloom. 'Wow,' she said, 'we are seriously high. Not that I can make out much detail, just the glow of lights on librarians' desks.' She looked up. 'And there's no sign of a roof up there. This is a huge building.'

'You're not really helping,' Slip said, lowering himself to the bridge's warm metal. 'I'm not sure if I can go across that.'

'Best not look down,' Mr Forritt said.

'If I don't look down I won't be able to see where to put my feet.'

Friz didn't seem concerned by her friend's distress. 'In that case you need to cross first, before it gets too light. 'Cos when it gets light you'll be able to see all the way down. And that's a long way.'

'You're only making things worse,' Slip complained.

'I'll go across first,' Mr Forritt said, 'make sure there are no problems at the other side. I won't be long.' Given his excesses of arms and legs, his size and his lightness it was easy for him to move swiftly across the rope bridge, but those watching noticed that the bridge still swung alarmingly as soon as he stepped onto it. It took him five minutes to get to the other side where his diminutive form could just be seen checking knots and fixing points. His journey back was swifter, more confident.

'We should be alright. It's a good job Mistress Unthank didn't come along, though, the ropes are a little thin in places.'

'I really can't do this.' Slip's head was in his hands.

'Yes you can,' Maia said, 'the same as the rest of us. Are you going first?'

'Definitely not!'

'Mr Forritt, will the bridge stand your weight as well as mine?'

'Oh yes. As long as we don't stop in the middle and jump up and down.'

'Then I'd suggest you accompany each of us in turn. For moral support.'

Tom disagreed. 'I think I can manage alone.'

Ten didn't seem so sure. 'I should be okay,' he said, his bravado a thin veneer.

'I'm not too heavy,' Pencil said to Slip, 'I don't mind coming across with you.'

'That's it, then.' Maia had decided to be decisive. 'Mr Forritt and I go first, then he comes back.' She looked at the drop to the rope bridge. 'The most awkward bit, though Mr Forritt makes it look easy, is getting down onto the rope bridge itself, so I'd like him to help each of us down. Slip and Pencil to follow me. Ten next. Then Friz. Then Tom, and Mr Forritt last. Any objections?'

In the absence of any further comments Mr Forritt eased Maia's descent to the rope bridge then led her slowly across.

'Have you noticed,' Friz said, 'that Maia's stopped asking what we should do and started telling us what we're going to do?'

'Yes,' Ten said, 'I've noticed. I think I'd like to be consulted, though. Has she always been this bossy?'

Tom shook his head. 'Not bossy. Confident. Assertive, even. Sure of herself.'

'In other words, bossy.

'No! You clearly weren't listening. Or perhaps you were confused because I was using words of more than one syllable. I thought you might know what they meant, but I'm sure I could find simpler ones if you want me to.'

'No, they'll do. They've got the touch of admiration I would have expected from you.'

'What do you mean by that?'

'I thought you might know! It's obvious what you think of her, the way you look at her all moon eyes . . .'

Pencil cut across them. 'Have you noticed,' she asked Friz, 'how much boys are like apes? Always, arguing, showing off, swaggering, beating their chests?'

'Yes,' Friz replied. 'Except for Slip.'

'What?' said Slip.

'Well, you're sort of an honorary girl, aren't you?' She reached across and ruffled Slip's hair. 'Least, that's the way I've always thought of you.'

'That's a very good thing to be,' Pencil added. She looked at Tom and Ten. 'Do you really have problems with a girl being in charge?' The question itself silenced them.

It took them almost an hour to cross the rope bridge, and each traverse passed without incident. Even Slip managed the passage without protest, though that was largely because he was too occupied in expressing his fear with moans and groans.

The shelves on the other side were full of books, silent, sleeping. Mr Forritt led the way round the towering stacks on a path that was wide enough for two to walk side by side, though there was no handrail. The track spiralled steeply into high darkness, the shelves glowing with a strange phosphorescence that provided warmth and comfort.

'It must be difficult to get books down from here,' Maia said to Mr Forritt, 'given how high the stacks are.'

'We've come the direct route,' Mr Forritt pointed out, 'there are easier paths, but it would have taken us days to follow them. And the books up here, they're all classics, or popular, or both. Dickens, Blyton, Goscinny and Uderzo, all constantly read. People don't need to borrow them. Rare books usually live near the bottom of the stacks, they're the ones that need constant reading and re-reading by the librarians.'

'Wouldn't it be easier to just let them die?' Ten asked. 'Or put them out of their misery? After all, perhaps there's a reason they aren't read enough. Perhaps they aren't any good?'

'Ten,' Maia said, 'do you always say things just to offend?'

'No,' Mr Forritt said, 'He has a good point. There are many librarians - though still a substantial minority - who believe that books should be allowed to fade away naturally.'

'And you, Mr Forritt,' Maia asked, 'what do you think?'

'Thank you for asking,' Mr Forritt said, 'it's not very often people seek my opinion.' He took a deep breath. 'As you know, I was once a hunter, when my form was more human. I'd search the high shelves, the ones we'll travel through shortly, for special books. Renegades. One or two that had started questioning their own purpose, analysed themselves too deeply. And I thought, like Ten here, that books had a natural life span and we shouldn't keep them alive when their time was over. I think I was looking for a copy of Isaac Newton's *Philosophiæ Naturalis Principia Mathematica*, but one in which the printer had added some vulgar comment; it escaped destruction, though the printer may not have been so lucky. It was fit and healthy because its main text was often read and referred to, there were many copies in existence. The hunt for this one was long and arduous, I spent almost a fortnight up here, alone. One night when I was longing for home and for Mistress Unthank, a small volume crept into my company. It was faded, clearly suffering, so I began to read it. It was a book of short stories called "Songs from the Heart", set in South America, told by a Mayan slave girl to a Spanish priest. I'm sure they'd been embellished in their telling and printing and publishing in different languages. But they were full of longing and sadness and joy, and I read them all through the night, and the next night, and every night while I was in the high stacks. When I returned I gave the little book to Mistress Unthank, and each time I went away she'd hide it somewhere in my sack to remind me of her. We still read them to each other. They're a source of great solace when our changing bodies conspire to separate us.' He brushed his eyes with his sleeve. 'And so I changed my mind. Books, all books, should be preserved.'

'I hope you don't mind me asking,' Maia said, 'and please tell me if I'm intruding, but what's Changing like?'

There was a long silence.

'I'm sorry,' Maia said, 'It's a private matter. I shouldn't have said anything.'

'No, I don't mind at all. I was simply trying to gather my thoughts. You see, no-one knows why we Change. It's like a disease. It began for Mistress Unthank and me on the same day, not long after we were married. She was a promising senior librarian, I was a book hunter. I came home from work and found her in tears, her clothes had split while she was at work and her shoes were suddenly too tight. I reassured her that she was still in proportion just . . . larger. Then she noticed that I had strange lumps on my body. Overnight they grew into arms and hands.

'A few days later the Changes grew more marked. Mistress Unthank woke covered with a pelt of rich red hair; I had some vestigial wings. Each time she grew larger and I became more like an insect. Sometimes the Change would make us, for a while, closer to normal, but that was never for long. It's as if someone is playing with us. The Changes are irregular, sometimes years apart, sometimes days. Sometimes we can stand in front of each other and watch the metamorphosis happening. I hate seeing the distress it causes to my wife. And yet . . . it also binds us together. There are, as far as we know, no other Changers in existence.' He sighed. 'Though I do so miss the intimate touch of her.'

They walked on in silence as the sky far above them changed from black to grey, from grey to light blue, and then drew in shades of pink and peach from the approaching dawn. The path narrowed and became even steeper: at one point they had to crawl the slope on hands and knees. For a short stretch it was necessary to climb a vertical surface, unadorned by shelves or bookcases, where handholds had been carved into the hard stone surface. There were more bridges as well, of rope and wood, one of cantilevered metal where they'd had to leap the last few feet to safety.

'We should make the top an hour or two before the Library opens,' Mr Forritt judged. They'd stopped to rest and drink, to eat some of the food that Mistress Unthank had prepared.

'We may need to stop more often,' Maia said, 'we haven't slept for almost a day now.'

'Longer for me,' Tom said. 'Twenty-four hours ago I was in the bakery, getting the day's bread made. And now . . .'

'Now we're in a different world.' Maia looked around her. The air was fresh and clear and cool. She could look back the way they'd come and see, not a Library with high shelves and a multitude of desks, but a distant land. Above her thin struts had appeared that would, she was sure, become the supports for the Library roof.

Mr Forritt pushed them on as fast as he dared. Although the way had become easier, often wide (though still on top of precipitous stacks of shelves) and not as steep as it had been, they moved more slowly. Ahead was a broad stand of cliffs made up of misshapen bookcases with angled shelves piled unevenly and treacherously on top of each other, fragile and occupied (so Mr Forritt said) only by a small colony of Roget's Thesauruses. 'They forage for unusual words,' he explained, 'one or two escape up here from the shelves below.'

They had to sit down to shuffle across a sharp ridge, and a strong wind tried hard to unseat them. 'Not far now,' Mr Forritt kept saying, 'not far now.' But each repetition was weaker, less reassuring.

'There's an outcrop at the top where one of the roof beams is fixed. And there's a window, a big window. You can get out of it onto the roof. I think it was put there so the roof glass could be cleaned, so the roof could be checked and maintained. But no-one goes there now.' He chuckled. 'In fact, the last person to come up here was probably me!' He led the way along a rough path that clung to the face of the stack. Just before a corner Mr Forritt held up his hand. 'As far as I can remember,' he whispered, 'this is the top. I want to check the way's clear. Wait here.'

'If there's anything there it must be stupid,' Ten said, shivering. 'Only the most stupid creatures in the world would want to be up here.'

'But we're up here,' Pencil said.

'Duh! Exactly!'

'Mr Forritt asked us to be quiet!' Maia hissed in time to see their guide returning, shaking his head. He held a finger to his lips

'This is not good,' he said quietly, 'not good at all. This is the right place. But there's a Bazhka outside the window. It looks asleep, but if we try to get past . . .'

'Is there no other way?' Maia asked.

Mr Forritt waved several of his arms in the direction of distant peaks. 'Over there, wherever you can see a high point, there's a place where the roof is fixed. And there'll be a window that opens. But there'll also probably be a Bazhka guarding it. And even if there isn't, it would take us a day to get back down to the Library floor and a day to climb out again. The Library will be opening in two hours time. There'll be hundreds of Bazhka down there.' He slumped against a bookcase. 'Let me think.'

'What type of Bazhka is it?' Tom asked.

'What type of . . ? I don't know! It's big, it's blue, it eats people! What more is there to know?'

'Begging your pardon,' Tom answered, 'but most creatures are big from your viewpoint. I was wondering if we could attack it, but that depends on how big it is. I'm going to take a look.'

'Be careful,' Maia whispered after him as he crawled along the path and round the corner. He returned quickly.

'It's big,' he said, 'same size as the ones that were in Madame Klein's. Head looks a bit like a wolf's, but far more teeth. I think it's got claws on the end of its hind legs, a bit like on a bird's feet, but it's difficult to tell, it was hunched down. At first I thought it had a cloak on, but it's probably wings. I suppose that's how it got up here.'

'Could we attack it? Friz asked.

'I doubt it,' Tom replied. 'There's only enough room for one of us to get through the window at a time, it could easily deal with that. If it was looking the other way, if the window didn't make a noise when it opened, if we all had weapons, if we knew where to strike, then we might stand a chance.'

'In other words,' Ten said resignedly, 'no chance.'

'We could wait, see if it left . . . to go to the toilet?' Slip said. 'You never know, it might have a weak bladder.'

Slip's suggestion was ignored and no-one else felt able to add anything. They huddled together for warmth, lost in their thoughts. Eventually Mr Forritt spoke. 'I've got it,' he said. 'Listen carefully. When you get out, go right, directly across the slope. The glass is strong, it'll take your weight. You'll see a huge stone buttress below you, it's one of the eight that supports the roof. Head straight down the slope towards its top, but not too fast, the angle increases quickly. Go too far, too fast and you won't be able to stop yourself. It's a long way down.'

'But how are we going to get out without the Bazhka seeing us?' Maia asked.

'Leave that to me,' Mr Forritt said impatiently, 'just make sure you follow the directions! Down the slope until you get to the top of the buttress, then look to the left. There's a rusty metal pole, a little taller than me, sticking up in the air. Head for it. It's the remains of a ladder, but the ladder's long since gone. The stonework is sound but the mortar's crumbling, there are lots of footholds and ledges. Go down about ten, fifteen metres, you'll find an entrance. Go in. There's a staircase, it leads down.'

'Down to where?' Tom asked.

'I don't know, I never went that far. I assume it goes down the inside of the buttress. You'll be on your own from there.'

'What are you going to do? How are you going to make the Bazhka move?'

'I could attack it with these,' Mr Forritt said, feeling the knives hidden reassuringly inside his waistcoat. 'Or I could do what my lovely Mistress Unthank would suggest.'

'What's that?'

'Engage the creature in pleasant conversation and ask it politely to move on.' He pushed past them. 'Make way for a good little un. Tom, you keep your eyes open, as soon as the way's clear you get everybody out. Maia goes first, you bring up the rear, the rest of you go fast. Got it?'

'Got it,' Tom said, saluted and immediately felt stupid for having done so.

'Mr Forritt.' Maia tugged gently on his sleeve. 'Thank you so much for all you've done. Please give our love to your wonderful wife.'

Mr Forritt grinned. 'I'm pleased you said that. It means I don't have to ask you to do the same. Here we go!'

He began singing as he sauntered around the corner. 'I know a maid in Banbury town, a fair maid and a dandy-o, she'll lift her petticoats for half-a-crown, with a tickle em high and a tickle em low and giggle em goggle em handy-o.' He disappeared from view.

'This maid and I we danced all day, she's a fair maid and a dandy-o . . .' There was a pause, then the sound of knocking on glass. 'Hello! Hello there! If you don't mind me asking, what are you doing out there all alone, crouched against the wind and looking very cold. Who are you?'

The Bazhka turned its head slowly. It stared at Mr Forritt through the glass. It licked its lips and drooled. Its ears pricked up and began to twitch, its raised it snout and inhaled deeply.

Its voice was high pitched, chittering, like a manic hyena. 'What you? Not human. Smell like,' it inhaled again, 'male. Part human. Not fresh. But . . . not human. Who you? What you?'

'Not human? Takes one to know one,' Mr Forritt said under his breath. 'And at least I speak in sentences.'

The creature's ears revolved. 'What you say?'

'I said do you mind if I come through? I hate talking through panes of glass. But you'll have to shift, you're blocking the doorway.'

The Bazhka stood up reluctantly on long, raw pink ostrich legs. It stretched out leathery wings to steady itself then lowered itself once again, settled its ruffled dark blue feathers. Its wolfish muzzle rippled and dribbled. Its jaws could still easily reach the window to snatch at anyone coming through. Mr Forritt pulled at the handle, opened the window and stepped outside. The wind was strong, he had to crouch low to prevent himself being blown away.

'I'm a bookworm,' he said loudly, 'call me Reddy. And if I smell human, it's because I've spent all my life eating human books.' He spat, making sure he wasn't facing into the wind. 'Very restrictive diet, let me tell you. What do you eat?'

'Everything,' the Bazhka said. 'Humans.' It appeared to be thinking. 'Never bookworm.'

'Me neither. Very bitter, I would imagine. Most unpleasant. What are you doing up here, so high above the world? I don't see many creatures up here at all.'

'Waiting. Waiting bell say opening in Library. Open window fly in. Look for humans.'

'I see. Most people come to the Library to look for books. Are you looking for particular humans or is it just a general love of humanity? For culinary and digestive reasons, of course.'

'Why want know?' The Bazhka leaned closer to Mr Forritt, suspicious.

'Oh, curiosity. You see, I spend all my time up here in the high stacks. Humans don't like me very much because . . . well, because I eat their books. So I have to hide from them when I see them. Perhaps I could help you, if you tell me who you're looking for, describe them, I could tell you whether I've seen them or not.'

The Bazhka tilted its head on one side, a gesture that would have been almost puppyish if not for the lolling tongue and huge teeth. It pondered Mr Forritt's statement.

Then the words tumbled from its jaws. 'Five humans. Young. Three male, two female. One girl very important. Maker want her. Reward.'

'Do you know her name?'

'No name.'

'Then I'm pleased to say I might just be able to help you.'

The Bazhka snapped to attention. It swivelled its long neck down to Mr Forritt's level. 'You see 'em?'

Mr Forritt resisted the temptation to back away from the Bazhka's fetid breath. 'I may have.'

'Where? When?' The Bazhka's eyes widened. 'Think careful, bookworm. Think truthful.'

'Do I get a reward?'

The Bazhka's jaw opened wide in a high-pitched, baying laugh which ended as swiftly as it began. 'Reward not being eaten!'

'Well in that case I'll be very accurate indeed. I saw them a few hours ago, they were heading up the ridge to this very window. Then I saw them again, coming down. I suspect they must have noticed you waiting here and decided to try a different way out.'

'Different way? Where?'

'They probably took the high shelf ridgeway, it leads over there,' Mr Forritt pointed into the distance, 'there's a secret window no-one knows about, except me and a few others. But it's very well hidden, I don't expect you'd be able to see it. Not without some help, that is.'

The Bazhka eyed Mr Forritt suspiciously.

'Oh well, it's rather chilly out here. I'll head back in, if you don't mind, see if I can find a nice nineteenth century periodical for breakfast. Good luck in your search.' He made his way back towards the window. A large claw slammed the window shut before he got there.

'Show,' the Bazhka said.

'I already did,' Mr Forritt replied, pointing vaguely across the broad glinting plain of glass, 'it's somewhere over there.'

The Bazhka lowered its long neck and head to the ground, sank down until it was lying flat. 'Show,' it snapped again, 'now!'

Mr Forritt climbed gingerly onto the Bazhka's back, undoing the buttons on his waistcoat. Two of his hands and all his legs gripped the Bazhka's soft feathery down. 'I'm aboard,' he said.

The Bazhka leaped into the air, unfurled its wings and flapped them strongly, lazily, and they were skyborne. Mr Forritt glanced over his shoulder, the window was open and Tom was already out, helping the others, pushing them towards the descending buttress.

'Where?' the Bazhka demanded.

'Straight ahead,' Mr Forritt yelled. The Bazhka was flying too fast, too low, it would reach the next real window too quickly and there would probably be another Bazhka there. But he couldn't get the creature to turn now, it would easily see Maia and the rest of them, it would be onto them in a few seconds.

'Too far,' The Bazhka cried, 'humans not travel fast.'

'We must have missed it, go higher.'

'Go round, you watch also.' The Bazhka began to bank, a fast turn which almost threw Mr Forritt from its back. And then it pulled its wings back and began to dive. 'See them!' it bayed, 'they hiding!' It brought its long legs and claws forward, howling as it did so. Mr Forritt reached for his daggers, without hesitation plunged one of them into the Bazhka's left shoulder. The Bazhka screamed, turned its head to dislodge Mr Forritt, but he was too far back for it to reach. It veered to the left, high above the buttress, and Mr Forritt glimpsed the worried faces of his friends below.

'I'll explain the new rules,' Mr Forritt shouted. 'When I do this with my dagger,' he plunged his blade again into the Bazhka's left shoulder, 'you go left. When I do this,' he did the same thing with the blade in the Bazhka's right shoulder, 'you go right.'

'You cut!' the Bazhka screamed its reply, 'I bleed, not die! I EAT YOUR HEART LIVE!'

'Really? I've heard your kind can come back to life, but it's hard to do that when your insides are scattered all over the countryside! You're getting too close to my friends! Go right!' The knife rose and fell and the Bazhka veered involuntarily to the right. It banked again, so close to the glass roof that Mr Forritt could see his own reflection, then soared high into the sky. And then the Bazhka stooped. It folded back its wings and plummeted downwards. Mr Forritt felt the wind tear at him, it tried to rip his hands from his knives, open his fingers' fragile grip, throw him from the Bazhka's back. He held on grimly. And then the Bazhka flipped over, both sideways and forwards, and Mr Forritt flew over the creature's head and into the empty sky.

Maia and Tom stood in the entrance Mr Forritt had told them would be there. Pencil and Ten, Slip and Friz were already descending the long staircase deep within the buttress's stone walls. The two watched the Bazhka dive. They saw Mr Forritt lose his grip, they gasped as he was hurled over the creature's back. And then they stared with horror as the Bazhka whirled again and caught Mr Forritt's body in its long taloned claws. They heard a cackling laugh of triumph as the Bazhka climbed higher and higher, then opened its claws to let Mr Forritt's body tumble and fall out of their sight to the ground far, far below, the Bazhka in close pursuit.

EIGHT

It was dark inside the buttress. The staircase was made of narrow steps of crumbling sandstone projecting from the wall with no rail to cling to, nothing to prevent a fall into the echoing depths. Every fourth turn, when they were on stairs embedded in the outer wall, a little light entered through thin openings. Nothing could be seen through these; they were too high and too narrow for any creature to enter save a small bird or insect. The dim light served only to amplify the length of the weary descent. They were all tired, their legs ached with each even, measured, downwards step. Maia and Tom had agreed that they wouldn't tell the others about the loss of Mr Forritt; it was bad enough that someone else had perished while helping them; the group's morale was already low and nothing would be gained by telling them the news.

Even Pencil's cheerful chatter ceased when the smell of smoke filtered through from outside. 'What do you think is happening?' she asked; no-one answered her.

They stopped every hour or so to drink and to eat, though none of them was hungry.

At several points the staircase had eroded and they had to press themselves against the wall to navigate the stumps of the decayed steps, fingers digging into cracks in the mortar as they shuffled one-at-a-time across the gaps, roped up in case they slipped. It added hours to their descent, and when the faint light from outside began itself to weaken Maia told those who had brought torches to switch them on. Pencil was delighted when Slip let her hold his torch. She examined it closely in an attempt to find out how the flame could be switched on and off so easily but, failing in that endeavour, shone it around her, lit up everyone's face in turn.

'Keep them pointing down,' Maia warned, 'not at the openings. We don't want anyone to know we're here.'

'They'll already know,' Tom whispered to her, 'that Bazhka who saw us will have passed the message on.'

Maia said nothing, added that fear to the others fighting to occupy her mind.

Many turns later, just as Maia was considering ordering them to stop for the night, Pencil noticed that the echoes of their steps sounded different. 'And the air feels cooler,' she said, 'and it doesn't smell so much of smoke.' They shone their torches directly down the shaft and saw, only three turns of the staircase below, a pile of rubble that showed they'd reached the bottom. They increased their pace, stepped warily onto the broken steps and shattered pieces of stone, and looked around them.

'There's no door,' Slip said.

'No way out,' Ten added.

'Stating the obvious,' Tom commented. If either he or Ten had been any less tired they might have come to blows.

They sank down wearily, finding flat pieces of broken rock or piles of shattered brick to rest on. 'So what do we do now?' Friz asked.

'Sleep, if we can,' Maia said. 'It's a long climb back to the top. Best put your torches out, save the batteries.

The torches flicked out to a chorus of groans.

'I don't like the dark,' Pencil said a moment later, a tremor in her voice. 'I've never been in the dark, the real dark, before. There was always some light in the Library.'

'I brought a candle and some matches,' Tom said. 'I can light that if you want.'

'I don't suppose that would do any harm,' Maia conceded.

The candle's glow was more comforting than the light from the torches. It was warm and reassuring as it danced and flickered before them. Each of them found their least uncomfortable place to lie, their sacks providing only a little cushioning. Soon their breathing became more even as, one by one, they fell into restless sleep.

Ten's voice abruptly broke the silence. 'Listen,' he said excitedly, waited for the groans to show that everyone was awake. 'We're at the bottom of a deep shaft. There's no way in or out. But look, the candle flame's moving!'

They sat up in unison. 'The nearest window's too high to make it do that,' Tom said, 'that means . . .'

'. . .air's getting in from somewhere!' Maia finished for him.

They all scrambled to their feet and, in doing so, disturbed the flame with the draught of their movement.

'All sit down again!' Maia ordered. 'I'm going to pick the candle up and see if I can find out where the draught's coming from. Just keep still and watch.' She took the candle carefully in one hand, cradled its flame with the other, and moved to the bottom of the staircase.

'It'll probably be in the outer wall,' Ten said, 'that's where a door or an entrance should be.'

'We don't know that for certain,' Tom said, 'there could be an entrance from inside the Library. There could be a tunnel through the buttress itself.'

'Please shut up!' Maia scolded. 'Talking affects the flame!'

'Pardon me for breathing,' Ten muttered.

'If you stop doing that as well,' Tom said, 'we'd all benefit.'

Maia moved cautiously around the space, stopping every few feet to see if the flame moved. 'It seems to be coming from over here,' she said, 'right in the middle. But there can't be a door in the middle of the base, where would it lead to?' She handed the candle to Friz and lay down on the rubble and dirt, her face just above the ground. 'I'm sure I can feel a draught,' she said and began scrabbling at the fallen debris with her fingers. 'Give me a hand, then!' she complained, 'and let's have some more light.'

Friz handed the candle to Pencil. 'I've got a shovel in my bag, one of those that folds up. For digging latrines and such.' She retrieved it quickly and shoved Maia and Tom to one side. 'Best keep out of the way if you want to keep all your fingers.' She used the shovel like a pick-axe first, digging into the dust and earth, then joined the others in pulling it to one side. There was a loud clang as she hit a piece of stone, the remnants of a long-fallen stair; it took all of them to move that out of the way, and there was more rubble beneath. Every few minutes Maia ordered a stop and, while they stood back and regained their breath, she held the candle out to see if the flame moved: it did.

After about an hour, after they'd heaved five large pieces of stair from the hole, after they'd pulled and shoved huge amounts of smaller bricks and mortar and sandy rubble away, Friz brought the shovel down heavily and was rewarded with the dull thud of the metal blade hitting solid wood. She ploughed the dirt aside, the rest of them joined in to reveal a trapdoor, at one side a stout metal handle. 'Don't let it be bolted on the other side,' Maia whispered under her breath, 'please let it open.'

At first it didn't. Only when Friz threaded two lengths of rope through the handle, only when all of them heaved together, only with a rusty warped complaint did the trapdoor judder and twist and then fly open, throwing them all to the ground. Tom was the first to find his feet and grab a torch, to lie on his stomach and peer downwards. 'Wow,' he said, 'very impressive.'

'What is it?' Slip asked.

'The trapdoor's at the top of an arched ceiling, it's about ten metres vertically to the ground but the ceiling curves down to touch the floor.' He pulled his head back up again. 'Whoever built this must have guessed that, over the years, there would have been falls of brick and masonry. Anything that came down would have bounced to the side, filled up the space above the roof but below the level of the trapdoor.'

'Shows how old the Library is,' Slip said.

'There's a ladder on the floor, in one piece. And the floor seems dry, the ladder doesn't look rotten. If you lower me I can get the ladder, then we can all climb down.'

'Is there a door?' Ten asked impatiently. 'There's no point in going down unless there's a door.'

Tom looked down again, twisted his head around. When he raised it there was a broad smile on his face. 'There's a door.'

Using Friz's ropes Tom was lowered to the floor where he raised the ladder which rested, at its full height, on a lip just below the trapdoor. There was a sense of accomplishment, even of joy, as each of them carefully descended to stand on the threshold of escape from the Library. They found themselves in a dry, dusty room beneath a high, vaulted ceiling that reached to the floor, entirely as Tom had told them. There was no decoration. There were no windows. In one wall was the door. That was when Maia looked across at Tom.

'Listen everyone,' she said, 'Just a warning. The Bazhka on the roof saw us running across to the entrance to the buttress. It might have flown down and it could be waiting for us. It might have got word to other Bazhka. We might have a welcoming party.'

Friz sighed wearily. 'It couldn't be easy, could it?'

'Not worth doing if it's easy,' Slip said, draped his arm over Friz's shoulders.

'The door's locked anyway,' Tom said, 'I've already tried it. I think this bit's up to you, Maia. No sense putting it off.'

Maia stepped forward and reached for the key, the one that Madame Klein had given to her, the one that opened every door in the Emperorium, the one that she'd been wearing on a string hung around her neck since they'd begun their journey. The door ahead of her was arched, made of seasoned oak, its keyhole seemed far too large for the small key. But when she pushed it into place, it was as if the key enlarged and engaged perfectly with the tumblers. She turned it easily and pulled on the door handle.

Dawn flooded into the room.

Tom pushed past her, knife in one hand. After a few moments he stepped back into the room and nodded. 'Nothing there.'

The rest of them followed him out into a cool morning. The long grass which ran right up to the door they'd just come through was wet, drenched with dew. Beyond the grass, a short distance down a shallow slope, was a copse of trees. The sky was changing colour, from blue to peach to pink, as the sun escaped the horizon; but none of them appreciated the beauty. It had been a full day since they'd entered the buttress, a day and night of descending the staircase and then clearing away the rubble. They'd smelled the smoke coming through the vents but still weren't prepared for what they saw before them.

The Library's high roof was shattered, plumes of black gathered above it; distant flames crackled and spat at broken windows. Books fluttered to the ground with smoke trailing from their pages, groups of Librarians were visible, tiny figures crouching or sitting or lying on the steps and lawns, hands raised to their heads, guarded by the tall silhouettes of Bazhka strutting and whirling. A small party of Librarians seemed to be fighting back, driving several Bazhka away from an open window, but even as Maia and her friends watched, larger, heavier Bazhka joined the fight and overwhelmed the Librarians. When the slavering, baying pack had dispersed there were no survivors. There were not even any bodies.

'Ms Inkwadi,' Pencil whispered. 'Mistress Unthank. All my friends.' Her tears began to fall.

'Shh,' said Maia, pulling Pencil towards her, 'shh. We'll make them pay for this. We'll make them pay, I promise you.'

Ten brought them back. 'We need to move,' he said, 'now! Into the trees! There are flying Bazhka!' He was pushing them towards the copse even as they looked up to see dark arrow shapes high above them. Tom, Slip and Friz were close behind, they blundered through wiry bushes and dense undergrowth until the leafy canopy above them seemed to offer some protection. Their ragged, panicked breathing steadied.

'I don't think they saw us,' Ten whispered.

'If they did, they'd be down here already,' Tom said.

'Then we're safe?' Slip's question pleaded for someone to answer 'Yes'.

'We don't know for certain,' Maia warned. 'Like I said before, the Bazhka on the roof may have sent word to others. They could be down here looking for us. We need to be careful, we need to watch out.'

'If this here is the crittur you're talkin' 'bout', a voice spoke from the depths of the copse, 'then I c'n reassure you that you need have no fears in that direction.' The man walking towards them was dressed in faded jeans, a checked shirt tucked into his waistband. On his head was a broad brimmed, high peaked hat. And from one outstretched hand hung a Bazhka's head. 'My name is Zeke. This here,' he waved a second figure forward, 'is my wife Esther. And this,' he threw the Bazhka's head onto the ground in front of them, 'is very dead.'

He dusted his hands together then wiped them on his jeans.

'They's difficult animals to kill,' the woman said, 'but gen'rally speakin', if'n they's heads is removed, they don't spring back to life too quick.'

Pencil was the first to find her voice. 'Are you cowboys?'

The man grinned. 'I do believe we's dressed like you might see cowboys in old time books. But they's no cows near here, Esther 'n' me's jest traders.' He gestured towards the Library. ''Cept'n we din't 'spect to see the likes of Bazhka warrin' on the Library. Sad day. Very sad day.'

Pencil turned to Maia. 'They're cowboys! I've heard stories about cowboys!'

'Zeke,' Esther said, 'you's forgettin' your manners.' She looked at them all. 'We's got breakfast cookin', addin' a little more'll do us no harm, coffee's near brewed, if'n you'd care to join us we'd be pleased to have your comp'ny.'

Maia looked at her companions. Tom shrugged. Ten shook his head wearily and looked to the skies. Friz patted her stomach, Slip licked his lips, and Pencil simply muttered 'Cowboys'.

'My name's Maia, and I'd like to thank you kindly for your courtesy. We'd love to join you.'

'Then foller me.' Esther turned and lead them through the trees. Zeke brought up the rear after kicking the Bazhka's head under a bush.

'We were on the roof trying to escape,' Maia began, 'the Bazhka saw us and . . .'

'Hush, child, not now,' Zeke said. 'We c'n talk later. Y'see, although I have no claim to fame in any field myself, I c'n swear that Esther's cookin' is without a doubt miraculous 'n' as soon as you start eatin' you'll find you cain't say a word 'til you've finished. 'N it looks as though y'all need t'set 'n' eat 'n' rest 'fore y'all do any talkin'.'

They soon found themselves in a large clearing mostly taken up by two covered wagons. Eight horses were hobbled and tethered beneath the trees.

'See, I told you,' Pencil grinned, 'cowboys!'

In the centre of the clearing some logs had been dragged around a fire. To one side a pan was set, in it rashers of bacon and fried eggs were already sizzling. A second pan contained slabs of crusty biscuit, while a third was filled with beans.

Maia stopped abruptly. 'Hold on,' she said, 'something's not right. There's too much here for two of you. Who else is here?'

'You is without doubt a smart young lady,' Zeke said. 'Come on out, everyone,' he shouted.

Two more people stepped slowly forward and Zeke introduced them. 'This is Jed, and Matthew.' Each raised a hand in greeting. Jed was older than the others, mostly bald but with a grey moustache. Matthew was perhaps in his early twenties, red haired and bearded.

'Matthew's my son,' Zeke explained. 'Jed's my Paw. We din't want to frighten y'all by appearin' together at first.'

'No more?' asked Maia.

'This is my whole family,' Zeke replied. 'Esther, we need more food. Paw, Matthew, the horses need feedin' 'n' waterin'.' His face broke into a huge grin. 'We have guests!'

When everyone had eaten their fill, when they'd laughed at the faces of Ten and Tom as they tried the strong, thick coffee, when all the plates and mugs had been washed and left to dry, when the fire had been put out, Zeke spoke up.

'At the risk of bein' accused of unfriendliness, y'all look in need of a rest, a wash, a change of clothes 'n' then another rest. After you've done that we'll be pleased to hear your stories if'n you wish to tell 'em. Until then, me 'n' my fam'ly is at your service. I assure you, y'all come to no harm while we's lookin' out for you. We was on a tradin' trip to the Library offerin' fine hides for backin' books when them critturs appeared. We have no love for 'em, but we ain't afraid of 'em. We pulled over to wait 'em out, then we saw 'n' heard what they'd done. That was when the crittur landed nearby, injured, knife wounds in 'is back, but beginnin' to heal. So we finished 'im off, separated 'is head from 'is body. Body might grow 'nother head yet, head might grow 'nother body, but it'll take time 'n' we'll be gone by then.'

'How did you manage to kill the Bazhka?' Tom asked.

'We has axes 'n' saws, knives 'n' swords, 'n' we knows how t' use 'em. But mostly we has these.' He strolled across to the nearest wagon and reached under the seat, brought out a longbow and a quiver of arrows. 'I see you got a little bow 'f your own,' he said to Tom, 'you figurin' on tradin' up sometime, jest have a word with me. You wanna try it?' He held out the bow to Tom who took it gently in both hands. It was light but tense, full of pent-up energy. He plucked the string.

'Can I try?' Tom asked.

'If'n you want. You done much with bows?'

'Not much,' Tom said. He stood up and held the bow in his left hand, tried pulling the bowstring with his right.

'Is that "not much" as in "not at all"?' Zeke smiled.

'Yes,' Tom confessed.

'Then after you've rested I'll be honoured to give you your first lesson. But now, y'all need to rest.' He stood up, took his bow from Tom, addressed his family. 'We look after our guests. Take your weapons, make yourselves scarce.' As Esther, Jed and Matthew found their own bows and faded into the dense green undergrowth, Zeke turned to Maia.

165

'You will come to no harm while you're under my protection,' he said. 'This is my word, and my word is my honour, I swear to God.'

'I believe you,' Maia replied. Within minutes she was asleep.

The sun was already in the west when Maia woke. The dappled canopy of leaves above her was shielding her eyes, the warmth surrounding her and the drone of insects made her feel happy. When she looked around, none of her companions were there. She was on her feet in an instant, hand reaching for the dagger at her waist. But then she heard Pencil laughing, and she saw that she was helping Esther mix ingredients in a large metal bowl. Pencil looked up, saw Maia looking at her. 'Esther's showing me how to make those biscuity things we had for breakfast,' she called, 'I'm going to be so useful to you.'

'Where's everyone else?' Maia said nervously. She'd become accustomed to company.

Pencil was pleased to respond in detail. 'Zeke is showing Tom and Ten how to use a bow. Friz's at the stream having a wash. Slip's washing his clothes, and Friz's and everyone else's. Except yours, that is.'

'They's all safe, young lady,' Esther said. 'Jed 'n' Matthew's still on watch. 'N' I'm havin' such a good time with your sister.'

'My sister?'

'I've been telling Esther how I look after you,' Pencil said, nodding vigorously, 'because you sometimes get into trouble. And people sometimes think we're twins because we look like each other. I've told her how you pulled my hair when we were young, and told tales, and blamed me for things. But she knows I still love you.'

Maia blinked. She felt she ought to tell Esther the truth, explain why Pencil had come along, that they weren't sisters. But this, her new world, was already so strange that it suddenly didn't seem important to correct Pencil's imagination. 'And I love you too,' she said. 'Now where's this stream? I really do need a wash.'

'Excubitor,' the voice whispered. 'Excubitor, are you there? Are you asleep?'

'I am awake, Master.'

'Oh, that's good. That's very good. Are you wondering why I'm asking?'

'No, Master. I have been involved in the search for the female human. I had not given thought to sleeping.'

'I see. And your response worries me. Because I have a recollection of you telling me that you would find her for me. You implied that this would be an easy job. Straightforward. And yet the hours passed, day rolled into night, and I heard nothing from you. And now you tell me, but only when I have initiated the conversation, that you are still searching for her. Has she escaped you?'

'The Library is large, Master, there are many possible places for her to hide. And resistance has been greater than I would have expected. It has been put down, of course, but my army . . .'

'Your army,' the voice interrupted, 'has behaved exactly as you and I knew it would. It has indulged itself in murder, destruction and feeding. Yes?'

'I have had to make examples of Bazhka who have transgressed my instructions, Master. And the Librarians have been most reluctant to succumb to interrogation. The Head Librarian in particular, who I feel knew exactly how the humans made their escape, did not . . .'

'Past tense, Excubitor? "Knew"? She died before you could get information from her?'

Excubitor's reply was barely audible. 'Yes, Master.'

'And you have no idea where the humans are? Inside or outside the Library? In the corridors or in another land altogether?'

'No, Master.'

'YOU WILL FIND HER!' The message was so strong, so urgent, so venomous, that Excubitor fell to her knees. The Bazhka around her, many engaged in their own slaughter of innocents, felt the Maker's anger as a sharp pain deep inside their brains and held up misshapen hands to anguished, blood-soaked heads.

'If you don't find her,' the Maker's voice continued, though calm and measured, 'I will eviscerate you. I will extract your heart from your body and feed it to you a morsel at a time. I will torture you with a pain so great you will beg for death, but I will keep you alive for eternity. Do you understand?'

Excubitor rose to her feet. 'Yes, Master.'

'Good. I'm pleased we've sorted out that little misunderstanding. I will inform you of any eventualities. I trust you will do the same for me.'

'Yes, Master.' Excubitor breathed in deeply, exhaled slowly. The voice and pain in her head had ceased. Three Bazhka stood before her, waiting for her command. In one swift movement she unsheathed her battlesword and swung it before her. Three Bazhka heads hit the ground.

'Find the humans!' she bellowed, and the smoking ruins of the Library echoed with the sound of her anger.

It was dusk when they sat round the campfire again. Zeke reported that some of the Bazhka had moved on, suddenly, without any warning, taking with them the bodies of those injured in the fighting. Others remained in the burnt-out

Library. He said that he and his family felt it would be safe enough to travel next morning. Without any prompting from Zeke or his family Maia felt encouraged to tell her story, explain why they'd been attempting to escape from the Library, and even ask advice on what to do next.

'My friends and I are travelling together to seek answers to questions that may, unfortunately, have no answers. That may be an unfortunate and unusual way to begin, but I can think of no other. We are, as I imagine you've gathered, not from this world.'

'Your accents, your manners, your appearance, your demeanour, all point in that direction,' Zeke said. 'Though I would not be so impolite as to mention those unless you had intimated that in your statement.'

'We entered through a door into the Library, escaping from Bazhka. They had entered our world and killed Tom's mother. They injured Ten's father. They attacked us. I believe they had something to do with the disappearance of my father, and I suspect that he's still in your world. He may be a captive. He may be unable to find his way home.' She had to summon her courage to continue. 'He may even be dead. The Head Librarian helped us escape and suggested we seek help, that we hire a guide, a bodyguard, from O'Carolan's Terpsichory. We need to make our way there. Even when we get there, we don't know what we need to do or where we need to go. That's our story in short.'

Zeke nodded, held up his hand to show he was thinking and wouldn't welcome interruption. Eventually he asked, 'And do y' know the way to the Terpsichory?'

'The Head Librarian, Ms Inkwadi, told us she'd once ventured out of the Library and hired a guide at the Terpsichory. She could remember . . .'

'And the Map,' Pencil interrupted, 'she gave us the Map!'

Maia wasn't sure if her glare would silence Pencil's enthusiasm, but she was sure Pencil caught the glance and the message: she was to be quiet. 'As I was about to say, she could remember little of the route, so she gave us a map to help us find our way.'

Esther nodded her approval. 'Pencil mentioned the map to me this aft'noon, I weren't sure if it might be an exaggeration, I knows they doesn't like books to leave the Library. I's pleased to hear that 'er story be acc'rate.'

'A map?' Jed said, his moustache quivering. 'I'd sure like to see a map someday. I's never been one much for readin' or writin', but folks say a map be like pictures, 'n' I c'n sure un'stand pictures.'

'I'd be pleased to show you all the mapbook,' Maia said.

Zeke spoke up. ''N' we'd sure be pleased if'n you'd allow us to 'company you to the Terpsichory. You see, that's pretty near where we live. It's a place for hirin', it's a place for tradin' . . .'

'It's a place for gittin' t'gither,' Jed joined in, 'it's a place for dancin' 'n' music playin' 'n' singin'.'

'It's on a import'nt crossroads,' Zeke continued, 'they's houses 'n' a general store, a church, a toothpull. Soon be a town, I reckon.'

'How does all that fit in a corridor?' Ten asked. 'I mean, I know things seem to change in size, but . . . well, we've seen the corridor near to where we came into the Library and it's not exactly big.'

'Ah, the corridors. Some places,' Esther explained, 'the corridors is as wide as counties. They's rivers run through 'em, trees 'n' hills 'n' varmints . . .'

'Varmints?' Slip asked, looking round at his friends. 'What's a varmint?'

'A varmint,' Matthew said shyly 'is like a crittur but no good to eat or hunt.'

'Vermin, I think,' Maia explained. 'Rats and mice and such.'

'Tha's right! 'N' little Bazhka, sometimes, they's varmints.'

'Matthew's right good at huntin' varmints,' Zeke said with pride, 'since he were a little 'un.' He stood up. 'Will you be comin' with us tomorrer?' he asked Maia. 'We c'n offer good company 'n' protection.'

'We'd be pleased to come with you,' she replied, not even consulting the others, 'and thank you for your kind invitation.'

'Then we ought to turn in, make a start at sunrise so's we c'n see the road ahead.' They all rose to their feet and began to prepare for sleep, except Maia who drew her host to one side.

'Zeke, you and your family are very kind, but I have to tell you that we have no money. We can't pay you for the food we've eaten, or for the protection you've offered, or for the advice you've given.'

Zeke shook his head. 'Young lady, food an' company that has been freely offered is, by definition, free. But if'n you do want to pay us, tell us stories. Sing us songs. Entertain us. That'll be a payment far more valuable than any money you might have.' He doffed his hat. 'Sleep well.'

They settled for the night, Zeke taking the first watch. Maia lay down beside Pencil on blankets provided by their hosts. 'Pencil,' she whispered. There was no response, only the heavy sound of breathing on the verge of a snore. 'Pencil,' Maia said again, a little louder, 'I know you're only pretending to be asleep. Why did you tell Esther we were sisters?'

Pencil turned over and looked straight at Maia. 'Because I feel as if we *are* sisters. Because I don't have any relatives.' She reached out a hand and touched Maia on the forehead. 'Because I want to be your sister?'

'Pencil, you can't always have exactly what you want.'

'I know.' She turned onto her back, stared at a dark sky filled with leaves and stars. 'But sometimes if you wish it hard enough . . .'

They were soon asleep, lost in their own dreams, their own wishes for someone to be there for them.

Early next morning Maia kept her word and showed Zeke and his family the Map. They seemed interested at first, but Jed soon admitted that he didn't see the point and the pictures weren't real enough; he went off to get the horses ready. Esther, after admiring the leather and the quality of the book's construction, said she needed to pack up the cooking utensils. Matthew decided to find Slip and Friz, see if they wanted a game of pitch and toss. That left only Zeke to ask questions about how the Map worked and he watched with interest as Maia demonstrated the fact that the Map interacted with its users. After a while he too started looking around, pointed at the lightening sky and hurried away to prepare for their journey.

The two wagons were filled with the hides that Zeke and his family had hoped to sell to the Library. Esther explained that they would take them back and hope to find another buyer somewhere. 'Leather's always useful. Shoes, bags, coats, hats; we'll find someone who wants 'em.' She was driving one of the wagons, Zeke the other, each wagon with two horses in the yoke, one hitched to the rear. Jed and Matthew were going to ride as outliers.

'Best stay hidden 'til we hit the corridors,' Zeke told them, 'once we's there, they's not gonna be too many Bazhka 'n' other critturs around.' The wagons were draped with oiled tarpaulins fitted over a frame, a little like a ridge tent, tied at front and rear. They'd all decided to occupy the same wagon and sat with their backs against its frame, cushioned from the bumps and ruts of the road by the hides they were sitting on.

'Zeke told me that, if I practise, I might get to be pretty good with a bow,' Tom said. 'He's going to give me one of his old bows when we get to the Terpsichory.'

'Esther's going to let me help with the cooking,' Pencil said proudly.

'They seem very nice people,' Maia said, 'we were lucky to find them.'

Ten's eyes were closed, though he wasn't trying to sleep. 'They're a bit stereotypical, aren't they?' he suggested. 'The way they talk, the way they dress. The only thing they don't have is guns.' His eyes flicked open. 'I mean, I'm not complaining but . . .'

'Yes you are,' Slip said, 'you always complain. It's what makes you the person you are, the person we know so well and love so much.'

'Matthew was saying that they hunt Bazhka.' Friz seemed impressed with the fact. 'I'd like to see that. They can run fast - the Bazhka, that is - so they do it from horseback, using their knees to control the horse. But you've got to be really strong to use a bow that would injure a Bazhka.'

The wagon lurched as they joined the road. 'Now you needs to stay hidden in there,' Zeke called through the canvas, 'we don't want nobody knowin' you's aroun'. An', to be honest, they's sights I wouldn't want y'all to see neither.'

There was an acrid smell of burned timber in the air, one that was quickly joined by the sweet sickening odour of decay. Pencil was sitting at the rear of the wagon; as it jolted over the track the rear canopy parted and she reached out to close it. Her mouth fell open and she inhaled sharply, stared wide-eyed.

'What is it?' asked Ten.

Pencil snapped the canopy shut, fumbled with its ties. 'Nothing. At least . . . The Bazhka must have burned a building down. And there's bodies too.' Her awkward fingers succeeded in tying a knot in the cords and she sat back in her seat. 'Not nice,' she muttered, 'not nice.' Ten put his arm around her and she leaned into him, wiped her face with her sleeve.

Subdued, they said little for an hour or so until Zeke spoke up again. 'We's close to the doorway. Should be okay for y'all to see as we go through. Sorta plays tricks on your mind, though, makes you dizzy. If'n you feels that way, jest close your eyes.' He pulled back the end of the canopy and they all crowded forward. Ahead of them was a pair of hinged gates, wide open and large enough to allow the wagon through with room to spare. They were attached to a stone wall beyond which they could see only blue sky, as if they were approaching the crest of a hill. But as they grew closer the sky seemed to close in on them, the walls moved closer and drew in around them, it was as if they were heading into a long tunnel. The opening at the end seemed to get smaller, the sky and the walls and the ground less realistic, as if they'd been painted onto a pliable, crumbling surface.

The archway itself looked as if it had lost its battle with time. All the original stones holding up the arch had broken or been removed, and their replacements didn't fit quite as well. The ground on both sides was littered with what looked like fragments of white glass, Maia pointed them out to Tom. 'Looks like this is a fixed doorway,' she whispered, 'it doesn't move.'

Tom nodded his agreement.

They all ducked as they passed through the gates and beneath the archway, then suffered the same feeling of disorientation on the other side. This time the receding walls were painted with scrub trees and prickly shrubs, the roof above them was grey, and the air began to get hotter. A dusty breeze whipped around them.

'Where are we now?' Maia asked.

'We's outa the Library and into the corridor,' Zeke replied. 'But if'n y' look close, y' can see in some places they's a door or a gate, sometimes just an openin', sorta shimmers in your eyes unless y' look real close.'

'And where do the doors lead?' Tom asked.

'Ah, well, that's a good question. Doors, y' see, come in diff'rent types. They's doors that stay open and mostly stay in the same place all the time, like the Library gates. If'n we go lookin' for 'em they's always close by where we last left 'em. Some doors is locked, y' cain't get in at all, no use hittin' 'em with a axe or tryin' to knock the wall down. They jest won't give way. Some doors open easy 'nough from outside but not from inside. Some doors open both ways nice 'n' simple. Trouble is, y' cain't tell 'fore it closes if'n a door'll open again. Some folks is brave enough t' not care if'n a door closes behind 'em, they jest likes t' look around, they likes t' travel. We gets 'em at the Terpsichory every now 'n' then, they don't stay long, always got a wide, open look in they eyes.'

Zeke suggested they get down and walk; he did the same, controlled the horses with a flick of the traces he held in his gloved hand. Their pace was slow but measured; the corridor seemed to have opened out on all sides and the track they were following was only mildly rutted. They could see Jed ahead of them, he would occasionally ride back and doff his hat, mumble to Zeke then ride off again. 'He's lookin' out for other traders,' Zeke explained, 'If'n they's headin' for the Library it's best they know what's been happenin' 'N' we c'n also get news from where they's been.'

'Are all the corridors like this?' Maia asked.

'Like this?'

'Yes. It reminds me of films I've seen on TV, westerns.'

'I'm sure I don't unstan' a word you's sayin', lil lady.'

Maia laughed and felt good for doing so. 'No, I don't suppose you would. What I meant was, is it all like a grassy plain with some small stands of trees? Or does it change to, I don't know, a forest?'

'The corridors is mostly easy to travel. 'Tween here and the Terpsichory it's like this. A day or two beyond, they's a desert, with waterin' holes if'n y' know where t' find 'em. Beyond that the land gets steep, climbs up into snow. But still they's a path across. I's bin up t' the top with my Paw many years ago, looks like a wide forest on the far side, but we din't go down.'

Tom spoke next. 'And how many doors have you been through?'

It was Zeke's turn to laugh. 'You's reg'lar curious young 'uns, isn't ya! Lemee see. No more 'n seven, ten p'rhaps. Course, that's not countin' the ones me 'n my buddies would go through when we was young. That was different, we'd find a door that opened 'n one of us'd stay by the door, keepin' it open, while the others went in 'n explored. We never went far in. One time we was lookin at pictures 'f buildin's so tall y'd fall over backwards to see the top, so we went in a bit further 'n further 'n there was machines 'n noise, 'n the paths was wide 'n black 'n smooth but so many people. Som 'f 'em saw us 'n started runnin' after us, so we high-tailed it outa there 'n back through the door. No-one follered us out so I guess that door wouldn't open from the inside.

'Some places was just wild, or too cold, or too hot. We stopped goin' through doors that time when Ruthie din't come back.'

'Was Ruthie a friend?' Tom asked.

'Nah. Ruthie was my sister.'

They walked in silence for a while. Pencil decided that Tom would be her new best friend, she sidled up to him with a smile in her voice. 'Are you good at bows and arrows?' she asked. 'Do you know all about them?'

'No to both questions, I'm afraid,' Tom replied.

'But Zeke was showing you what to do.'

'Yes, but it was only for a short while. I think you need to practise for a very long time to be good at it. Same as with anything, really.'

'Do you like his bow? And his arrows?'

'Well . . . yes, I suppose so. Why are you asking?'

Pencil screwed her face up. 'I'm not sure. My brain's telling me to do things, so I just do them. Ask questions, that is. Do you mind me asking you questions?'

'No, Pencil, you can ask me anything you want.'

'That's good.' She looked down and seemed to take great delight in watching the soft prints her feet made. She looked back and waved at Maia who was admiring the horses; Zeke had allowed her to hold the reins.

'Maia's nice,' Pencil said, 'she gave me shoes and clothes and she said I could come along with you.'

'Yes, Maia's very kind.'

'I asked if she would be my sister and she said yes.'

'Did she?' Tom tried not to smile. 'Do you like having her as a sister?'

'Oh yes. Sometimes I look at her and I see me.' Pencil shook her head. 'No, wrong words. I look at her and see the way I'd *like* to be. If my head was working properly. Which it isn't. But sometimes I think it does. Or it might. Does that sound confused?'

'No, Pencil, I think it sounds quite sensible.'

'That's good. Because it sounds very confused to me!' She giggled. 'Do you think I'm older than Maia?'

Tom turned his head to look at Pencil. She was very similar to Maia in build and in height, but her face was definitely that of a young adult, not a teenager. 'I think you're older than her, but not by much. A few years, perhaps? Don't you know how old you are?'

'No. I was at the Library for about thirteen years, they said, so I must have been quite young when they took me in. About six or seven? But I can't remember being six or seven. I can't remember being little. All I can remember is being like this.' She held out her hands. 'All I can remember is being me.'

'That's quite a good thing to be, Pencil.'

'Thank you.' She skipped round in front of him, walked backwards up the trail. 'Tom, do you think I'm beautiful?'

Tom's eyes widened. 'I don't think a girl has ever asked me that before.'

'First time for everything. Well? I'm going to keep walking backwards till you answer. If I fall over and break my neck and die it'll be all your fault.'

'Alright then! Yes! Yes, I think you're beautiful. Though I've no idea why you'd want to ask me, it's not as if I have much experience in the matter.'

'Ah, but you do!' Pencil joined him, walked alongside him. 'You see, I look a bit like Maia, and you think Maia's beautiful, I've seen the way you look at her, so it's good that you think I'm beautiful. Makes things balanced.'

Tom found himself blushing. 'Now listen, Pencil, I hope you don't go saying things to Maia about the way I look at her. Or rather, the way you think I look at her. Because . . .'

'Your secret is safe with me!' Pencil tapped the side of her nose. 'I won't say anything.' She skipped a few paces so that she was in step with Tom. 'Have you loved her for a long time?'

Tom would have screamed if the noise wouldn't have drawn attention to him. 'Pencil! Stop it!'

'What do you mean? Stop what?'

Tom said nothing at first. He looked away, examined the sky, then glanced over his shoulder at Maia. 'You said the secret would be safe?' Pencil nodded enthusiastically. 'In that case, yes. Yes, I think I've loved Maia for a long time.'

'That's good,' Pencil danced away, called over her shoulder 'I want someone special for my new sister. For my *family*.'

'What you don't understand, Pencil,' Tom said to himself, 'is that everyone loves Maia. And Maia loves everyone in return. So I'm really nothing special at all.'

The night passed much like the previous one. They ate a hearty meal round the campfire then Zeke and Esther talked about life on the trader trail. Slip and Friz coaxed Ten into joining Matthew in games involving throwing things accurately, and seemed surprised when Ten won more than his share. Tom had another archery lesson with Zeke while Maia persuaded Esther to tell her a little about Zeke's sister Ruthie. It was apparently not uncommon for young people to go missing like that. Life in the corridors was very restrictive, the horizons were limited. There were a few settlements not too far distant, trading opportunities with some open-door communities, but they were mostly agricultural, rural. Life passed too slowly for some people. Youngsters in particular simply walked away. Some stayed in the corridors, others tried the nearest open door. 'Me 'n' Zeke, we got Paw 'n' Matthew, they's a boon sent by . . .' She paused. 'Sent by fate.' She stood up hurriedly, bustled about doing jobs that had already been done. 'Jed!' she called. 'Jed, I know our guests'd like to hear some music 'n' you's the only one who c'n help in that direction. Where are y'all? Paw?'

Jed appeared, his face decked in smiles, carrying a battered fiddle. He drew his bow across the strings, gently tuned them, then began to play. He knew what he was doing. As the melody rose and fell and told of loneliness and longing, Slip, Friz, Matthew and Ten were drawn back to the campfire. A vibrant, exciting jig encouraged Tom and Zeke out of the gloom. Even Esther stopped pretending to be busy and joined in the clapping. A joyful reel enticed Zeke into performing a shuffling head-down dance of sorts, and the polka that followed saw Zeke drag Esther with him round the fire to whoops of approval from the captivated audience. Jed played a waltz; Zeke pulled Maia to her feet, Esther did the same with Tom, and soon they were joined by Slip and Friz stepping awkwardly on each other's toes, and Matthew and Pencil embarrassed to be enjoying themselves in the dance. When Ten rose, tapped Zeke on the shoulder to take his place, and showed Maia that the dance lessons he'd hated had actually been worthwhile, the evening seemed perfect.

'Sing us a song, Paw,' Zeke said. 'Something old-timey.'

Jed nodded. 'Okay. This here's a love song 'bout as old as they come. 'Minds me 'f my dear departed wife Mary, rest her soul in heaven.'

'You sure, Paw?' Zeke asked.

'I think I c'n manage it, son.' He retuned his fiddle, and began to accompany a low, sad song pulled deep from his heart.

'Once I was a man of sorrow,
all I did was sad and wrong,
Till you showed me how you loved me,
taught me how to sing your song,
Then I found the joy of caring,
safe in your sweet company,
Living, laughing, giving, sharing,

loving you as you loved me.'

He drew the bow across several strings at the same time, the chords sombre yet filled with hope, before beginning the chorus.

'Life is hard and life is tiresome,
life is full of hurt and pain,
When I'm feelin' most alone,
then I turn to you again,
You're the one who loves me dearly,
you're the one who heals my woe,
I'll be with you soon forever,
 deepest love that I could know.'

There were more verses telling of love lost and found, but each time the chorus returned and the melody seemed so familiar that they all joined in, harmonising and swaying together. At the end Jed lowered his fiddle and bowed slightly, arms crossed over his chest.

'Thank you, Paw,' Zeke said, returning the gesture, 'a good choice of song, jest right.'

'Thank you, son. But time's gettin' on, so I think I'll hit the hay. You watchin' first?'

'I'm first,' Matthew said. 'Don't 'spect t' hear much, though.' He waited for his grandfather to move a little further away. 'Singin'll 've scared off near ever'thin' for miles around.'

'Why you . . .'

Matthew disappeared into the darkness chuckling softly.

The next day was colder, a thin rain had begun to fall during the night and it became heavier as the morning gave way to afternoon. Zeke suggested that everyone should ride under cover, but Maia declined, took her place beside Zeke, pacing the horses.

'You like gettin' wet?' he asked.

'Sometimes,' she replied. 'Nature can be good in all its guises.' She was wearing a bright red waterproof and Zeke looked at it with a mixture of admiration and horror.

'If'n you's ever hopin' t' hide, I'd suggest y' don't choose that there coat.'

'Hide? Is there anything to hide from here?'

'Not while we's travellin' together, lil lady. But the corridors ain't always a peaceful place to be. Used to be that they was a code, ever'body in the corridors treats ever'body else with respect. But lately, bad things start to happen. So take care,'

'Bad things? Like Bazhka?'

'They's the worst. Never met a good un'.' He spat his contempt on the ground. 'But others too. Y'all see 'em when we get t' the Terpsichory, they's all types 'f low life. But they's a man I know, a guide, a good fighter too, he sees the world in the right way. I 'spect he'll be there, 'n' I need to have some words with 'im too, so I'll tell 'im your tale 'n' ask if'n he c'n help you. If'n y' want me too, that is.'

'I'm sure if you trust him, that he's an honourable man, Zeke. The truth is, I don't know yet where we should be going. There's so much I don't know, so much I need help with . . .'

Zeke put his hand on Maia's shoulder. 'This man,' he reassured her, 'he might be able to help you in all sorts of ways. He is wise beyond his years an' . . . Well, I hope you'll see what I mean when we git t' the Terpsichory.'

'Thank you, Zeke. I don't know what we'd have done if you hadn't . . .'

'No, lil lady. No need for more thanks.' He fished in his pocket. 'I've somethin' for you. It was on the ground near where that Bazhka fell. I 'spect you'll find better use for it 'n I will.' He brought out a small oilskin package that he passed to Maia. She unfolded it, holding it close to protect it from the rain. Inside was a book, tattered, dog-eared, its spine almost broken She read the title. 'Songs from the Heart.' It was Mr Forritt's book, the one he'd brought back from the stacks, the one he shared with Mistress Unthank, the book she used to sneak into his pack when he went away. She must have done the same this time.

'You know it?' Zeke asked.

'I know of it. And I knew the man who owned it.' She folded the leather round the book again, slid it into her pocket.

'Was he a good man?' The way he spoke was unusual, with the word 'man' stressed rather than the word 'good', but he looked at her with real curiosity, as if the question meant a lot to him, as if her answer was important.

'He was one of the best.'

He seemed to approve of her response. 'Then I am reassured that my course of action has been the right one.' He took a deep breath. 'I do believe that I shall share your enjoyment in this inclement weather.' He took off his hat and let the rain fall on his upturned face.

There was no gathering round the campfire that night. The rain persisted, food was cooked under an angled wooden framed shelter and eaten on the wagons. They also provided a dry sleeping place, while Jed and Matthew kept the first outlying watch.

It was still dark when Maia woke. Everyone else was asleep, or so she guessed from the snuffles and deep breathing surrounding her. Wrapped in her red coat and a blanket, she climbed out of the wagon. The rain had departed and the night sky was black, pin-pricked with stars, the moon a pale crescent low in the sky.

'It's a beautiful night,' Esther's voice whispered from the wagon's seat. 'Best not wander too far from the wagon, though. Jed says he mighta seen somethin'.'

'Something dangerous?'

'He weren't sure. Too big to be a jumbuck or one o' them alpaca critturs. Too quiet to be an auroch. So possibly a lion or Bazhka. Lions is rare in these parts, so most likely a rogue Bazhka. They's difficult to find at night, tha's why I's got the crossbow here, ready 'n' loaded. Not as acc'rate as a longbow, but a lot quicker.'

'Will Zeke and Jed be alright? Maia couldn't hide her concern.

'Hush, child, they's experts at huntin' Bazhka. Was a time when them hides you's lyin' on woulda been Bazhka skins. Taken in self-defence, o' course,' she added without irony.

Maia climbed up beside Esther. 'Has nobody ever tried talking to the Bazhka? I mean, if you hunt them because they hunt you, and they kill you because you kill them, wouldn't it make sense to just stop?'

''T would be like a rabbit askin' a cougar politely not to kill it. Or tryin' t' talk to a scorpion, tellin' it not to sting. It's in their nature. They's critturs, not people.' She stiffened, hissed for silence, raised her crossbow.

'Best not shoot that thing, Esther, 'nless y' wanna go home a widder.'

'Zeke! You shoulda whistled!'

Zeke appeared out of the gloom. 'More fun t' see if'n I c'n sneak up on you. 'N' Maia too. Swear I could see that coat down the deepest mine.'

'Maia's been wonderin' if anyone's tried talkin' t' Bazhka. Tried askin' 'em t' stop their killin' 'n' murderin' ways. I telt 'er it's real hard t' try reasonin' with vicious critturs.'

'I tried once,' Zeke said. 'Catched me a live one. Asked it that very same question. Damn thing spat in my face.'

'What did you do?' Maia asked. 'Did you let it go?'

'Sure did. It'd stole a horse, but I set it on that horse's back 'n' told it t' get clear outa my sight.' His pause was theatrical. 'Mind you, it was hog-tied with its neck - or what passed for a neck - in a noose when I whipped the horse away. Damn crittur cursed 'n' swore for ten minutes 'fore it was still enough t' call dead.' He and Esther stifled their laughter.

'No sign 'f anythin'?' Esther asked when she'd begun to control herself.

'Nothin'. But it don't feel right.'

'I think I'll try to get some sleep,' Maia said. She too felt that something wasn't right.

NINE

It was late afternoon on the third day of their travels when Zeke halted his wagon and stood up in the seat. He pointed to the distant horizon. 'O'Carolan's is no more'n an hour away, folks. Like I sez to Maia, they's a man I know who could possibly help y'all, if'n 'e's there 'n' if'n 'e wants to. Esther 'n' Paw's gonna see y'all into the Terpsichory 'n' make sure yer looked after, I'm gonna ride on ahead 'n' see if'n I c'n find 'im.'

'This man,' Tom asked, 'what's his name?'

'I ain't telled y'all 'is name? I am so sorry. He is called Jean. Jean Baptiste.' He rode off on Jed's horse while Jed climbed up alongside Matthew and the slow-moving wagons approached O'Carolan's Terpsichory.

They were expecting a village with a few buildings. Zeke had mentioned a store and a church, houses and even a dentist's surgery, but what they found was less compact than his description had suggested. The houses were more like smallholdings, and they straggled alongside two streams that joined to become a river. They were all built of wood, like the grey-stained church that squatted on a slight rise, its tower crowned not with a cross but with a strange 'Y' shape, a small circle in the notch of the Y. The wagons pulled up in front of the three storey building which gave the community its name. O'Carolan's Terpsichory was undoubtedly, as its name suggested, a dance hall: a sign painted on the wall invited customers to try 'the latest dance fashions from . . . everywhere!' On a blackboard was a list of activities that would take place that day: games of chance, card games, mime classes, foreign language instruction, crochet and knitting. The smell wafting through the open doors suggested a restaurant. The barrels beside the doors promised beer. Another sign, high up on the first floor, proclaimed that there were 'Clean Rooms and Hot Baths', but perhaps the large, long, handwritten notice above the door was most illuminating. It decreed, 'All welcome regardless of colour, shape, size, sex, number of arms and legs, or ANY OTHER VARIABLE. If you hurt someone or something, you will be killed and disposed of. By my order, Turlough O'Carolan.'

Esther led them all into a large hall in which were scattered mismatched tables (a glass vase of fresh flowers on each) and chipped wooden chairs. U-shaped booths made up three sides of the room, there were healthy green plants on every windowsill, and a staircase straddled the bar to climb high to the rooms above. In front of the bar a man with long, curly grey hair and a frock coat was sitting, playing a small harp while, scattered around the room, people sat politely and listened or talked in gentle whispers. The tune was Irish with a complicated rhythm and what seemed, to Maia, like too many notes for the fingers and strings available. She was captivated.

When he finished the man acknowledged the applause with a gentle wave. 'Esther,' he called out, 'and some young people I don't recognise. Come closer, let me sense you.'

'He's blind,' Esther said, 'uses his other senses instead.'

'Indeed I do. So if you'd like to step forward one at a time and tell me your name, I'll add you to my memory.'

They approached the bar one at a time. Pencil went first, said her name clearly, then stood still as the man reached forward and gently touched her hair and her forehead. He inhaled and smiled. 'I'm pleased to meet you, Pencil, both younger and older than you seem. I hope you'll enjoy your stay here.'

Pencil curtsied; Tom took her place. 'A strong man, in heart and body,' the man said as Tom retreated and Ten stepped forward. To each of them he made a short comment. Ten was 'a thinker dressed in the thin coat of the cynic.' To Slip he whispered, 'you are the tree of life.' He grinned broadly at a puzzled Friz and said, 'the lakes and the seas will be yours, and you theirs.' Only when Maia was standing in front of him did he seem confused. 'You will, I think, lead your companions to safety and redemption. Although . . .' He shook his head, as if dispelling troubling thoughts. 'My name is Turlough O'Carolan, welcome to my Terpsichory. In exchange for the information you have given me, I offer you refreshment. Mead if you wish? Cordial made from sweet flowers and berries? Fresh water, cool milk, juice of oranges?' He clapped his hands and was joined by two waiters and a waitress, clearly members of his family given their resemblance to him, who proceeded to hold out bottles and jugs for his customers' approval.

'Mr O'Carolan,' Maia said, 'we haven't really given you any information other than our names. I must tell you that we have no money to pay for anything you're offering us.'

'My name, Maia, is Turlough. And we don't accept money. Money of any type is worthless here. Information, however . . .' He leaned towards her. 'Information is the only currency of value. And sometimes you don't even know what information you give, let alone its value.' He took a jug and poured a slightly oily liquid into a glass in front of her. 'Elderflower cordial, I can recommend it. Please, drink.'

Maia sipped the liquid, found it delicious, so quickly drained the glass only to have it refilled immediately.

'Where was I?' O'Carolan asked. 'Oh yes, information. I pride myself in being the hub around which information flows. I gather it, consider it, mix it up, watch it with my blind eyes, and hold it until it makes a completely new piece of information. Then I can do what I want with it. I can exchange it for new information, or for goods, or services. Or

I can store it away to see if it increases in value.' He tapped his head. 'This, Maia, is my bank. This is what makes me a wealthy man.'

'And is knowing our names of value?'

O'Carolan considered the question for a long time, so long that Maia thought he'd fallen asleep. Around her she could hear Slip and Friz discussing what O'Carolan had said to them. Ten and Tom were daring each other to cross the room and find out what three or four giggling girls were giggling about. Pencil was looking around, singing under her breath, while Esther was talking softly with Matthew and Jed, their eyes roving the room.

'Yes,' O'Carolan said. 'Your names are valuable, though not only in themselves. They are, taken together, as a whole, an interesting mix. Add to them to the way you speak, the accents you own, your ages, your genders, the clothes you wear, the smells of your bodies - please don't take offense at that, all odours are interesting - and the combination suggests the degree to which you are strangers in this place.' He leaned closer. 'In this world.'

O'Carolan's head turned to pick up whispers of conversation, words stressed, tones and pitches employed. 'It is no secret that above every table in this building there is a cone, a funnel, which amplifies the conversations of those sitting there and sends it, through a series of pipes and tubes, to a member of my family sitting somewhere upstairs. I have an exceptionally large family: children, grandchildren, great-grandchildren, more than I can remember or count. They write down what they hear and read it to me.' He tasted the air, as a snake might flick its tongue out.

'So you tell me your names,' he continued, 'but you tell me much more. And then I add this new knowledge to that which I heard yesterday: that the Library has been attacked by Bazhka soldiers. There were many casualties. Bad news travels fast, certainly faster than your journey here with Zeke and his family. Was their slowness deliberate? A few hours ago a man appeared here, a man who has never entered this building, a man I don't trust. His name is Jean Baptiste . . .'

'That's the man Zeke said he'd ask to be our guide!'

'Ah. Then I was correct, they knew he wouldn't be here until today so they came slowly. Were they worried you and I might exchange information? Information is a double-edged sword, Maia, and you've given me more information than you ought to have done: you told me you need a guide. But where do you need to go, and why? No, don't tell me, not yet.' His voice became softer, his words tumbled more swiftly from his mouth. 'Some Bazhka passed through here, moving fast, there's a crossroads not far away. They stopped for water but nothing else, yet they were overheard and their words came quickly to me. They had been seeking people in the Library, not books, but young people, outsiders, though only five were mentioned, not six. Pencil is your sixth? She is different to the rest of you. Why has she travelled with you? No need to answer, Maia, I can think the answer out. But you are obviously the source of the Bazhka's interest. There were many of them, I'm not sure how many because they passed in the night, but their trail suggests well in excess of a hundred.' He laughed and then coughed, one of the waiters patted him gently on the back as he slipped past.

'I'm getting old, Maia. There I am, giving *you* information for free.'

Maia ignored what the old man said, more concerned that the Bazhka were still searching for her, that they'd already passed through. 'But I don't know why they were looking for us! And I don't know where we should be going next. Tom wants to get revenge because the Bazhka killed his mother, Ten needs to find out if his father's really dead, I have to find my father, Madame Klein's put up a barrier to protect the outside world, but I don't understand how, though I do know she was a Truthsinger . . .'

'No!' O'Carolan was on his feet and speaking loudly enough to be heard around the room. He smiled. 'The young lady,' he explained to all those who'd raised their heads, 'was asking if I would play some more tunes and I had to explain that I was very tired.' He sat down again, put his head close to Maia's. 'You say too much! I'm not the only one who listens! And some in this room have far better hearing than I do!'

Maia looked around her. 'Esther and Jed and Matthew already know what I've told you,' she said, 'and no-one else is close.'

'Maia, have you not been paying attention? What you say is one thing. Who you say it to, when you say it, how you say it, they are all important as well! Now turn around and look more closely.'

The room had been filling. In a distant corner three tall white-haired men, their eyes wide, were watching everyone over the rims of glasses filled with dark blue liquid. A more animated group was sitting nearer, but a second glance showed they had no mouths, only a scarred gash where their lips should be, and they seemed to be communicating with their hands and their eyes and the whole of their faces. A cloaked and hooded figure was hunched over the bar next to three unnaturally tall and beautiful women taking musical instruments from stout, well-padded cases; a dark-skinned man with plaited black hair reaching almost to the ground was in conversation with two others, one of whose long arms and short legs contrasted with his companion's short arms and long legs. Customers were dressed in finery and rags, embroidered silks and rough-sewn furs, they were tall and short, wide and thin, and although most of them seemed to be human, Maia would have had to move close to them to make sure of that.

Jed nudged Matthew. 'Gonna see where Zeke got to. You comin'?'

They moved to the door, slapping Slip and Friz on the back as they passed, waving at Tom and Ten.

O'Carolan was bending close to Maia again. 'More information, Maia. From me to you. When Zeke left here his wagons were empty.'

Maia sat up straight. 'But he said he was taking hides to the Library. For book covers.'

'And he brought them back. More information? Each of his wagons was pulled by two horses.'

'He had eight when we met him.'

'Use the information, Maia. Use it wisely. Make meaning.'

Esther stood up and tapped Maia on the shoulder. 'Zeke's back,' she said, 'we ought to go.' She began to round up her charges. Zeke, waiting beside the door, waved a hand in greeting at O'Carolan, gestured to Maia to join him.

'Turlough, what do I do?' Maia didn't want to leave, she was suddenly suspicious.

'I don't know, Maia, because I don't know enough. Let me think about what you said. Madame Klein, that seems familiar, why would I know that name? I'll have to check my records. And your father. What's *his* name?'

Esther was back at the bar. 'The rest of 'em's waitin', lil lady, you need to come along.'

Maia climbed down from her seat, picked up her rucksack. 'His name's Argilla Pequena,' she said to O'Carolan. 'He might have said his name was Gill.'

'I know that name! Damn, but I know that name! Though I can't remember why!'

Esther took Maia's arm and pulled her away. 'Y' don't want t' keep Jean Baptiste waitin', Maia. He's a busy man. 'N' yer friends'll be gettin' nervous. Y' need to go.'

Maia allowed herself to be guided away. She looked back over her shoulder, O'Carolan was whispering urgently to the waiters who headed for the stairs even as she watched.

Then she was outside.

'There she is!' Slip called from across the dusty track.

'What kept you?' Tom asked as she drew closer.

'I was talking to Mr O'Carolan. He said . . .'

'Mr Baptiste's waitin',' Zeke interrupted, 'I spoke t' him 'n' I think he's willin' t' help y'all. He's waitin' fer us in the Church.'

There were indeed lights shining through the church windows; they made the building seem warm and safe as dusk darkened the world around them. The church's doors were open and the sound of murmuring voices crept into the night.

'That's our prayer group,' Esther explained, 'normally me 'n' Zeke'd be there but we had more important things t' do, lookin' after y'all. They'll soon be finishin', though. Jean'll be in the room beyond.'

Zeke led them through the church hall, a large bare room with no decoration save a single cross, an echo of that they'd seen on the church tower, standing on a rough wooden table. There were no pews, but around ten people were sitting on straight-backed seats drawn in a protective circle round an inner ring of lanterns set on the floor. They were a mixed group of young and old, men and women; none of them looked up.

At the far end of the hall were two doors. Zeke knocked on one of them and opened it, went through, beckoned to those following him to do the same. Maia felt Esther's presence pushing her, shepherding her.

There were lanterns here too, but they were hung from rafters and placed on window ledges. They lit up a circle of seats on one of which a man was slumped, long legs stretched out, hat pulled down over his eyes. He was wearing a dusty, faded leather overcoat, and the shirt collar beneath was stained with a line of black. His boots were worn down at the heel.

'Jean,' Zeke said softly. There was no response, only the slight rise and fall of the man's chest and the soft sound of his sleeping.

'Jean.' This time he spoke louder; the man didn't move.

Pencil strode forward and stood in front of the man. 'Mr Baptiste,' she shouted, 'you're keeping us waiting!'

The man's head was thrown back, his hat fell off to reveal a sharply angled face and long hair (so black it must have been dyed) tied in a short ponytail. He opened his eyes slowly, looked around and unfolded himself from his seat. He was not only tall. Some tall people are gangly and thin; Jean Baptiste was neither. His shoulders were broad, his chest broader, and the way he moved suggested that his muscles would also be well-developed. He towered over Zeke by at least a foot, and Zeke was over six feet tall. He surveyed the room with blue eyes so dark they were almost black, set in a face that was craggy and weather beaten. His shirt might have once been white. The thin red bow tie at its collar wilted like a rose in need of water.

Pencil took several steps back. 'I'm sorry,' she said, 'I didn't mean to . . .'

'Wake me?' Jean Baptiste lowered his head, bent at the waist so his eyes were level with Pencil's. And he smiled. It was the type of smile that encouraged confession and the telling of secrets, it guaranteed friendship and support and protection. 'I'm pleased you did wake me, Pencil, because we have much to do together.'

'How do you know my name?'

'Because I'm a mind reader?' This time he laughed, and his laughter took away most of the tension in the room. Only Maia, chilled by her misgivings, didn't warm to Baptiste.

'Or it could be,' he continued, 'that Zeke told me your names and described you to me. Please, won't you sit down. I do apologise for the austere surroundings, but this church is designed for worship, not for comfort.' He sank again to his trembling seat and the others did likewise. Maia was the last to sit down.

'We could have talked in the Terpsichory,' she said, 'it's more comfortable there.'

'It is indeed, Maia, or so I've heard, never having crossed the threshold myself. I dislike the place because I prefer my conversations to be private.'

'Mr O'Carolan told me all about the listening devices. He didn't try to hide anything.'

'I'm sure he did tell you, Maia, why would he want to hide such a thing. But if you live beside a stream for a while you soon don't notice the sound it makes. You forget the stream exists. But still it flows and flows.' He mimicked the flowing waters but his hand ended up behind his ear, capping it as if straining to hear something. 'In the Terpsichory you forget you're being listened to. You forget to guard what you say. But I can see you talked at length with Turlough and he made an impression on you. May I ask if he said anything about me?'

'He said he didn't trust you.'

Baptiste shrugged, held his arms wide. 'Yet he is the one who asked you questions, while I am hoping to provide you with answers. Let us leave your mistrust for the moment. I understand from Zeke that you need a guide, though you aren't sure where you wish to go. Am I correct?'

Maia was unwilling to move on. 'Perhaps you don't need to ask questions because Zeke already told you everything he knows about us.'

Tom threw a look of anger at Maia. 'Stop it!' he hissed, 'he might be able to help us.'

'You are being a bit rude,' Ten added.

'Am I? Well answer me this. Mr O'Carolan said that Zeke left a few days ago with an empty wagon and with only four horses. Yet Zeke told us he'd brought the hides to trade at the Library. That's obviously not true.'

This time it was Slip who spoke up. 'Zeke rescued us, Maia. Have you forgotten that?'

'And he fed us and sheltered us,' Friz added.

Baptiste sat up straighter. 'What's this, then, Zeke. Have you been stealing?' His voice was that of a judge, demanding the truth. 'Or do you have some other explanation?'

Zeke looked at Maia, his brow furrowed with pain and hurt. 'We's traders, 's what we do all the time. You seen the land 'tween the Library 'n' here, Maia. Was they any sign 'f beefs? Where d'you think we'd get hides from? They's no beefs round here. But foller the corridor to the crossroads, talk the left fork, 'n' y'all come t' grassland, sweetest prairie there ever was. 'N' beefs. We traded a promise 'f timber fer beef hides 'n' we was gonna trade hides at the Libr'y fer taters 'n' carrots 'n' such like, heavy stuff, so we borrowed some horses t' help on the way back.' He turned to his wife. 'Ain't that right Esther?'

'I swear tha's the truth, Zeke.'

Baptiste stood up and addressed Maia directly. 'Could that fit the facts?' he asked.

'I . . . I suppose so.'

'Mr O'Carolan gives you a fact or two, wraps them up in suppositions and opinions, then leads you to focus on the one incontrovertible truth he has built. Except that his 'truth' is only a hypothesis which can be, ought to be, tested until it is proved correct or found wanting.' He sat down again. 'And in this instance it was found wanting.'

Maia hung her head in her hands. 'I'm sorry, I'm so sorry. You see, I thought . . . It's been so difficult . . . I wanted so much to believe . . .'

Pencil got up, crouched at Maia's side. 'It's alright,' she whispered, 'it's alright to be wrong. I'm wrong all the time. Sometimes I'm so wrong I meet myself coming out of the wrong being completely right.'

Baptiste's voice was at its most reassuring. 'Apologies are not required, Maia. You've been under considerable pressure. And no-one here will take offence. We'll say no more of it.' He crossed his hands over his chest then spread them wide, as if banishing all possibilities of negativity. 'Now then, to the business in hand. I doubt that Zeke has told you much of me. You know my name but little more, so allow me to explain and to introduce myself. I am a traveller, as are all of you judging by the bags you carry with you. I am an explorer in this world of strange pathways, I seek the truth and I sing it loud when I find it.'

Maia was listening carefully. That juxtaposition of the words 'truth' and 'singing' couldn't have been an accident. Was Baptiste trying to tell her something without letting anyone else know. She looked around, no-one had shown any sign of recognising what she had. Was it her imagination? Or had Baptiste been looking directly at her when he'd spoken those words?

'Throughout my years of wandering I have met many people and many creatures. Some have become my friends, they've offered me help in times of need and I hope I have given them help and guidance in return. Others have been less kind. Some have even sought my death.' He grinned broadly. 'They haven't succeeded yet.

197

'Zeke has told me that you need a guide and a protector. He has told me of your adventures so far, the hurt you've suffered at the hands of the Fallen, those you call Bazhka. He has told me that you have secured the Map from the Library but that you are not yet sure where you ought to be going. I wish, therefore, to offer my services. With the Map and my experiences I am sure I can help you achieve that which you desire most of all.'

Maia looked at her friends' faces. All had a look of triumph on them, as if they'd succeeded in moving further along the road to their destination, though they weren't quite sure what that destination was. And so she gave way. Her own suspicions were as nothing compared to Tom's wish for revenge of some type, Ten's desire to find out if his father was, somehow, still alive. Slip and Friz were having the adventure they'd said they wanted. And Pencil? Pencil was thinking, or doing what passed in her mind as thinking. Her face was screwed up, head on one side. Maia couldn't yet understand how to understand her.

'What happens next, then?'

Baptiste smiled his satisfaction at Maia's words. 'Behind the church, built into its walls, is a doorway. It opens from the outside. We need to go through it and open the Map, see if it can show us the quickest way to your destination.'

'But we don't have a destination yet,' Maia pointed out.

'I think we do. I think the answer lies in finding the creator of all this.' He held his arms wide and the gesture was meant to signify more than the church, or the township, or the area surrounding it. 'We need to find the Maker.'

Ten snorted. 'Isn't that a myth? I mean, I've picked up bits and pieces from what people have said, but . . . A godlike figure responsible for all this? Really?'

'But you've seen the Fallen. One of them took your father's soul. Don't you trust your own senses?'

Tom joined in. 'Why do you call them the Fallen?'

''Cos that's what they is,' Zeke said, 'Fallen from grace, from the grace of our Maker.' He crossed his arms and bowed his head.

Baptiste inhaled deeply. 'As you will no doubt be able to tell, my young guests, these people are guided by their faith. I can explain more, but I feel that we must hurry. I examined the world beyond the doorway just before you arrived. It was, how shall I put it, docile. But as you may have gathered, these things change swiftly. I would rather be in a friendly place to discover the degree to which the Map is trustworthy.' He rose to his feet. 'May I lead the way?' He snapped his fingers at Zeke and his family. 'Would you be so good as to provide us with some cover? In case of hostilities?'

Zeke retreated to the main hall and reappeared a moment later with several bows and quivers full of arrows which he distributed to Jed, Matthew and Esther, as well as offering the longest bow to Baptiste.

'These are for our protection,' the big man explained, 'I want no harm to come to anything precious.' He led the way to what Maia had assumed was the rear door and opened it. Zeke, close behind him, held it wide for Baptiste to pass through. He motioned to Maia to follow.

Pencil was beside Maia. 'I don't like this,' she whispered, 'they have arrows.'

'I don't like it either,' Maia said, 'but the arrows are there to protect us.'

'But they're black arrows, Maia!'

Maia would have liked to ask Pencil why the colour of the arrows was so important, but the pace of their movement forced them apart. She looked over her shoulder. Jed and Matthew were pressing the others while, at the entrance to the small room, the prayer meeting from the main hall seemed to have gathered. They were all armed with bows or axes, knives or clubs.

'I think we need to talk about this, Mr Baptiste,' Maia called after the massive figure ahead of her.

Baptiste didn't look back. 'So we shall, my dear, but in a place where we may talk freely without fear of interruption and without any misunderstanding. Please follow me.'

The door had led them into a room where the walls seemed to be white-stained panes of glass; the air was cool and moist and smelled of rain and leaves, of mould and moss. Maia could feel herself being pushed from behind.

'Esther,' Baptiste yelled, 'please make sure the door doesn't close.' His voice, formerly so reassuring and friendly, was now threatening. 'Zeke,' he shouted, 'you have some words to say?'

Zeke hurried closer. 'I swore y'all would come to no harm while y'all were under my protection. I now hand you into the protection of Jean Baptiste.'

'Thank you for the formality of your statement, Zeke. My guests, you are now in my hands.'

The room was opening out. There were tree trunks covered in lichen rising straight for hundreds of metres, their branches climbing up and out in a blue-green canopy. There were no shrubs or flowers; the cathedral gloom was filled with shades of celadon and viridian and towering cerulean. The ground felt damp and slippery beneath Maia's feet. There was no birdsong. Save for the sound of footsteps and breathing, all was silent.

The path opened out into a natural clearing. Grey rocks broke the surface of lush green, and small verdant hummocks were scattered around like seats.

Baptiste held up his hand. 'This is as far as we need go,' he said as he turned to face Maia and her companions. 'Let's talk business. First of all, I need to see this Map book of yours.'

No-one moved.

'Children, do not be silly. I can have your packs taken from you and searched. You are outnumbered.' He waved his hands and the figures who had followed them into the forest stepped forward. There were at least six of them, as well as Zeke, Matthew and Jed, and each had a longbow, arrows notched and ready to fire.

'Black arrows,' Pencil whispered to herself, her face contorted as if she was trying to remember something important.

'I thought you wanted to help us,' Slip said.

'I do. But in this situation only one person may lead, only one may give orders. That person is me. And I wish to see the Map.' He pointed a finger at Pencil. 'I believe you are normally the bearer of this miraculous book. Please let me see it.'

Pencil looked up, glanced at Maia; Maia nodded. Pencil took her pack from her back and undid the fasteners, brought out the Map wrapped in folded leather. She laid it reverently on the ground in front of Baptiste. He kneeled down and opened it, turned the pages slowly. 'I can see the corridors, they wind and turn more than I would have expected. This area here I recognise as the Library, and here,' he pointed with his finger, 'is the Terpsichory. The doorway is marked, but the area within, the place we're standing, lacks any detail whatsoever. Why is that?'

Again there was silence until Maia spoke up. 'I don't know. Because it hasn't been mapped?'

'Which would mean no-one who has entered has escaped to tell of the experience.' Baptiste looked around. 'And yet this place seems so peaceful. So safe. And I've been here before, as far as this clearing at least, and never been threatened, never felt in danger. Perhaps it would be wise not to explore further.' He flicked the pages. 'These blank areas are all unexplored, then. But where doors are open it appears that the territory within has been mapped.' He closed the book, wrapped it in its leather and motioned to Pencil to pick it up. 'Place it in your bag but leave the bag in front of me. I have further questions.'

Baptiste held out his hands and motioned to his followers to lower their bows. 'I have no wish to make you unnecessarily nervous. But I do need to know where the Fallen gather. I need to find the Maker. And your Map tells me nothing.' His impatience showed in his voice, in the urgency and speed of his speaking.

'Then we can't help either,' Maia answered. 'We're strangers, you've been exploring these corridors for many years. What makes you think we know something you don't?'

'Precisely because you're strangers?' Baptiste stared at Maia. 'Because you see things in a different way.'

'And why,' Maia hurried on, 'would you want to find the place the Bazhka come from? And the Maker? If such a creature exists . . .'

'He exists, have no doubt about that. And be aware that your doubts about his existence have already been recognised.'

'Why does that sound like a threat?' Tom said.

'Because,' Baptiste snapped back, 'my people themselves feel threatened by your attitude to their faith.'

'Their faith?' Maia was angry. 'We've offended their faith? And so you have us surrounded by people with bows and arrows? And you threaten us? What kind of faith is that?'

'That faith,' Baptiste thundered, 'is one that you should strive to understand!' He took a step closer to her. 'We are Vanjelists. We believe that this world was created by the

Maker.' He crossed his arms in front of him, bowed his head. 'He made us in his image, and all who are not like us are not human. They are the Fallen, led from the path of righteousness, parodies of mankind. We seek to destroy the Fallen and we desire to free the Maker.'

'How long,' Ten asked, attempting to calm the situation, 'has your faith existed?'

'Many years.'

'And how does the Maker, if he's held in captivity, let you know what he wants?'

'He cannot move about like his followers; he has been imprisoned. But he speaks to me and others like me. He tells me what he wants. He tells me what to do. He told me I should seek out the strangers in our midst. He told me I should offer my services. He told me that, in return, these strangers might be able to help me. But now I am unsure that you can do any of this.'

'Black arrows,' Pencil muttered once more, 'black arrows.' Her eyes lit up. '*Now* I remember! When we came out of the Library Zeke told us to stay in the wagons, but I looked out. I saw dead people, Librarians, lying on the ground. They had black arrows in them. And somebody had put them like this,' she crossed her arms in front of her, as Baptiste had done.

'They's not people,' Zeke said. 'They's not like us.'

Maia's voice mirrored the look of disgust on her face. 'Did you *kill* them because they didn't look like you?'

'Like my son said,' Jed answered, 'they's not people. They's critturs. Spawn of the Fallen.'

'But the Bazhka attacked them,' Maia said, 'you can't say they're the same as the Bazhka.'

Baptiste tried to calm matters. 'The Fallen were looking for you and for the Map to stop us, his people, setting him free; they do not want us to find salvation.' He sounded like a patient teacher explaining a straightforward point to a child

203

who hadn't been listening. 'Sometimes animals fight amongst each other, that's what was happening in the Library. I had sent Zeke to observe. He did so. He destroyed a flying Fallen and saved you from capture. Is this not a good thing?'

'Why did you kill the Librarians?' Maia asked Zeke.

'They's not people. 'N' they had hides we coulda used, 'n' horses, things we needed. So we took 'em. Ain't nothin' wrong in takin' from critturs. We ain't done nothin' wrong.'

'And you agree with this, Baptiste?' Maia spat out the words.

'It is a guiding factor of our Faith. I adhere to the same Faith.'

'So you'd kill some of those people we saw in O'Carolan's, the ones who don't look the same as we do? The men with white hair and pink eyes, those with no mouths that I could see. You'd kill them?'

Baptiste shrugged. 'If I felt it would help our Faith prosper, yes. If it would help us move closer to the Maker, yes.' He pointed at the mossy hummocks around him. 'Zeke and I, Jed and Matthew, we've already done so.'

Maia felt sickness overwhelming her but she forced the bile back down her throat. 'Is that why you brought us here? To steal the Map and kill us?'

Baptiste smiled. 'Ah, that is a little more problematical, my dear. You see, you're all perfectly human in your form. You aren't, as Zeke put it, "critturs". But you are most definitely not adherents to the Faith. Indeed, it could be said that your beliefs are completely opposing ours, that your existence is preventing our search for the Maker. Perhaps the end justifies the means. And yet . . .'

A soft sighing sound came from across the glade, from the direction of the entrance door, and nervous heads turned that way. Pencil took the opportunity to dive forwards and scoop up her bag from Baptiste's feet, she threw it onto her back and sprinted away down the track deep into the woods. Several bows swivelled in her direction.

'She should not have done that,' Baptiste snarled, 'Zeke, my bow.' Zeke handed him a bow so tall, its willow so thick, that a normal person shouldn't have been able to draw it. But Baptiste managed it with ease. He pulled on the bowstring.

'Pencil!' Maia screamed, 'swerve!'

Tom and the others were shouting too, 'Get down!', 'Get off the track!', but in her panic Pencil could only keep to the straight and narrow path. Baptiste let his arrow fly. It arced only a little before hitting Pencil between the shoulder blades. She fell forward and didn't move.

In the same instant the world exploded. Maia dived at Baptiste's legs in a vain attempt to knock him over. Tom, standing close to Zeke, whirled on him and punched him in the face as hard as he could. Ten spun round and kicked Matthew's legs away from him. Friz lowered her shoulders and ran at the bowman closest to her, knocked him to the ground and leaped on top of him, rained blows down on him. Slip barged into Jed, knocking him off balance as he was lowering his bow to aim at Friz.

'Stop!' Baptiste's voice cut through the yells and screams, the moans and grunts of pain. He was holding Maia in front of him, one arm across her chest, pinning her arms to her side, the other holding a knife at her throat. Zeke elbowed Tom in the ribs and knocked him to the ground. He wiped blood from his nose. 'Unfinished business, boy,' he muttered. Ten was kneeling on Matthew's chest, he climbed slowly to his feet when he saw Maia's plight. The bowman Friz had been pummeling was unconscious but two others ran up to her and hauled her upright. Jed easily pushed Slip to one side and stood over him, one foot on his chest, daring him to push back.

'You are NOTHING!' Baptiste yelled again. 'I've killed one of you already! Why would I hesitate to do the same again?' He was breathing heavily. 'Bring them forward.'

There were more hands to push and shove and carry. Tom was dragged across to Baptiste, gasping for breath, body curled into a curve. Ten and Friz were forced to their knees, Jed lugged Slip after him and pulled his hair so that he too was kneeling. And still Baptiste held Maia pinned to him, eyes wide, afraid to move.

'It should not have been like this,' Baptiste growled. 'You could have made it so easy.'

'You would still have killed us,' Ten muttered.

'But it would have been less painful for you.' He gestured to his followers. 'On the ground with them, on their backs. I want them to see how they're going to die.' He jerked his head towards Zeke who took his place holding Maia, his own knife ready.

'This is our sacrament,' Baptiste began, reaching for his bow. 'The arrow driven through the heart of the unbeliever, or the Fallen; or any and all of those who oppose us.'

'That's how I finished off them Librarians,' Zeke whispered to Maia, 'Standin' over 'em. Sorta like a sacrifice.'

'You're evil,' she managed to gasp.

''N' the lil varmint who had that book I gave yer. Said his name was "Mr Forritt" or sump'n like that. I speared 'im too.'

Zeke wasn't as strong as Baptiste, he wasn't as careful. His grip was a little looser, the knife he held was a little further away from Maia. She pictured Mr Forritt struggling with the Bazhka and somehow surviving the fall only to meet his end at the hands of Zeke. She opened her mouth and bit hard into the flesh at the base of Zeke's thumb. His grip loosened entirely, then he swung round and lifted his knife hand high above his head. 'You'll pay . . .'

He didn't finish his sentence. He tumbled to the ground, a crossbow bolt in the back of his neck.

'Please step back from the children,' said a sonorous voice, smooth and sweet as treacle. A hunched figure stood at the edge of the clearing. It was clad in a dark grey hood and cloak, pulled back so that its arms were free. At the end of each arm a six fingered hand was clutching a multi-stringed crossbow.

Jed released his hold on Slip's hair and in one smooth movement began to raise his bow. It required barely a twitch from the cloaked figure to reward Jed with a bolt in his shoulder. Jed fell screaming to the ground

'I could have killed him.' The stranger announced in a voice that dripped authority. 'If you do as you're told he may not bleed to death. Someone's body is holding the door open, she may even still be alive. You can take this wounded man with you. But you should leave. Now.'

Baptiste was motionless above Tom, fingers ready to pull on the bowstring, to release his arrow into Tom's chest. Instead he lowered the bow, unstrung the arrow. 'There are still ten of us standing. There's only one of you. That seems like good odds to me.' He held out his hands in weary supplication then screamed 'Kill him!'

Baptiste's followers were obedient to the end, and their end came swiftly. Four more were despatched with crossbow bolts; the stranger dropped the bows and reached to his waistband for throwing knives, as he strode forward their silver blades flashed across the clearing and two further Vanjelists dropped to the ground.

There were four bowmen left standing. One of them was Matthew and he dropped his bow, brought out a sword and threw himself at the stranger.

'You killed my Paw,' he spat, 'you hurt my Gran'paw 'n' my maw!'

'Then stupidity runs in your family,' the stranger replied. The knives in his hands seemed small in comparison to the curved blade of Matthew's sword, but each blow of the sword was blocked effortlessly or turned aside.

Baptiste was making the most of the fighting, creeping slowly towards the edge of the clearing nearest to where the door was. Two of the other Vanjelists had noticed, moved towards him either to protect him or join in the retreat. The stranger's eyes flicked to one side and saw Baptiste moving; one of his hands diverted from the sword fight and a knife flew in Baptiste's direction. It hit one of the Vanjelists passing in front of the big man. Baptiste's mouth opened wide in horror but he kept moving, increased his pace to a crouching run.

'This is becoming tiresome,' the stranger said. At the next blow from Matthew he turned the blade aside and ducked under it, sliced at the man's hand and two of his fingers fell to the ground. The stranger reached up and snatched at the falling sword, seized the grip and rotated the sword swiftly so that its point rested against Matthew's throat. 'Do not faint,' the stranger said, 'do not collapse unless you wish to impale yourself on your own sword.' The stranger's head turned within its hood to reveal a flash of amber eyes. They saw that Baptiste, at the edge of the clearing, had just raised his bow and sent an arrow flying; it was aimed, not at the stranger, but at Maia. The stranger dropped the sword he was holding and leaped into the air, cloak streaming. Maia knew that the arrow would hit her. She heard the mosquito wine of its flight feathers, saw its inexorable descent towards her, yet she couldn't move quickly enough to avoid it. But the stranger was fast. He fell towards Maia, hand outstretched, and plucked the arrow from the air, rolled neatly to his feet in front of her.

Baptiste disappeared into the shade of the tall trees. The stranger reached into a pocket deep within his coat and brought out a scrap of rag, handed it to Matthew. 'Wrap that round the finger stumps,' he said, 'then get out. Take your grandfather with you. Be quick, the door doesn't open from the inside.' He watched as Matthew half-lifted, half-dragged Jed's body away.

Tom was climbing painfully to his feet. The others were staring at the bodies around them. Maia turned longingly towards Pencil. The stranger moved around them without comment, stopped to pull the crossbow quarrel from each of the Vanjelist corpses, wiped the blood from the arrowheads on the victims' clothes.

'You need to go and pick your friend up,' the stranger said to Maia. 'She's not dead.'

Maia was already running along the track to where Pencil still lay, motionless. She bent down. The arrow was sticking vertically, not from Pencil's back, but from the bag containing the Map which she'd thrown over her shoulders when she ran away from Baptiste. Maia pulled the bag away, turned Pencil over. She had a large swelling on her forehead, red and raw, where she'd hit herself on what Maia could see was a mossy rock in the middle of the path. But she was breathing, and her eyes were fluttering.

'She's alive!' Maia shouted. The stranger was strolling towards her. 'How did you know she hadn't been killed?'

'I smelled her life.'

If Maia found the statement strange then she didn't show it. 'Thank you. Thank you for saving us.'

The others joined them, moving slowly, still shocked by the treachery of Baptiste and the Vanjelists, not daring to look at the bodies surrounding them.

'Here,' Ten said, 'let me give her some water.' He kneeled down and took a bottle from his pack, dribbled a few drops of liquid onto Pencil's lips. She groaned.

Tom was looking at the bag containing the Map. He snapped the arrow shaft away and brought out the book, turned it carefully in his hands, then held it up for them all to see. 'The arrow went all the way through, the point's sticking out. She was lucky.'

Maia stood up and faced the stranger. 'Were you at the bar in O'Carolan's?'

The stranger nodded. 'You talk too much. You talk too loudly.'

'You heard, and you came to rescue us?'

'I heard, but that's not why I followed you. This is why I followed you.' The figure reached out a hand, gloved in pale brown leather, and extended one finger towards Maia's neck. Maia flinched nervously but didn't move away, didn't ask the stranger to stop. The stranger gently caressed the necklace round Maia's neck. 'I recognised this,' the velvet voice declared.

'How could you? My father made this for me.'

The cowl of the stranger's hooded cloak moved slowly; the head within must have been nodding. 'I knew that had to be so. You have his look about you. His friendliness. His generosity of character. And, of course, you mentioned his name.'

'You know him?'

The figure nodded.

'How do you know him? When did you meet him?' Maia's hands darted out and grasped the stranger's arms, felt the muscles and sinews beneath the torn sleeves. 'Have you seen him recently? Was he well? Please, you must tell me!'

'I'll tell you. But the light is falling. I'm not familiar with this place, yet the ground and the trees and the smell of the air

210

suggest high rainfall. We need to build a fire. Somewhere to shelter. And you need to help your friend. We need to eat and drink and rest, we have a long journey ahead of us.' The stranger's long pause was deliberate, it was clear he had something else to say. Maia waited. 'And I'll guide you, if you wish me to do so. But it must be agreed by all. And there will be conditions.'

Maia tried to take in everything the stranger said; the more she found out, the more complicated her life seemed to become. But she gathered her thoughts and priorities. She raised her voice. 'Listen, everyone, our new friend has a lot to tell us, but it's getting dark and we need to make camp. Light a fire, eat and drink.' Pencil was sitting up, shaking her head, taking in her surroundings. 'We need to make sure Pencil's okay as well.'

The stranger moved away to the nearest of the bodies, removed its bow and a quiver of arrows, found a knife attached to a belt and laid that to one side. He dragged the corpse out of the clearing and into the undergrowth.

'Should we bury them?' Maia called after him.

'They wouldn't have buried you,' the stranger replied, continued his task.

Tom came to join Maia. 'Who is he?' he whispered. 'What did he say to you?' Can we trust him?'

'He hasn't mentioned his name. He said he'd met my father. And he rescued us and put himself at risk while he was doing so. So I think we can trust him.' She looked at the rest of them, helping Pencil to her feet. 'Is she okay?'

Slip nodded at Maia. 'Yeah, she's more concerned that the Map's alright than with her own injuries. She's scraped her forehead, she'll have a bruise and a bump for a few days. No signs of concussion.'

'Can you start getting tents up? I don't even know what we have, Friz has one, and I think you do too, but we have Ten and Pencil with us, we weren't counting on that. And we need to light a fire. Food, what do we have? And . . .'

Tom raised a finger to Maia's lips. 'I'll sort it out. We've two tents, each big enough for three. Loads of food. There's a stream not far away, I'll get some water. Leave it to me. You need to relax.'

'Relax? Tom, people have tried to kill us, they've ended up dead. We've been rescued by a stranger who says he's met my father. We're in a strange forest, night's almost on us. And you tell me to relax?'

'Yeah, it's ridiculous, I know. But someone has to stay calm and sensible, someone has to take decisions, someone has to think about what to do next. And that's you.'

'No it isn't! I'm no leader, I don't want to . . .'

'You're already doing the job, Maia, no sense arguing about the title.' Tom moved away, started giving instructions to the others. Even Pencil was helping. Maia felt she ought to assist in some way, but she felt so tired she could barely move. She wasn't aware she'd taken charge or that she'd been giving instructions, and leadership certainly wasn't something she'd sought. She sat down, her back against a tall mossy rock. The trouble was, she didn't really want the lives of her companions in her hands. But if Tom was right, if the others saw her as their leader, then she'd have to accept that. But she'd continue to ask their opinions. She wouldn't dictate to them.

Maia wasn't sure how long she'd slept. But when Tom nudged her awake with a bowl of warm food, the others were already sitting round a bright campfire, ladling pasta and vegetables into hungry mouths, tents erected close by. The stranger had strung an oilcloth between two tree branches but was crouched opposite them, only slight movements of his hood showing that he hadn't fallen asleep.

He declined their offers to share their food, yet seemed to enjoy their company.

When they were full and had begun talking about their misadventures, when Pencil started yawning and Friz had to stretch her aching legs, when it looked as if Tom and Ten would find something new to argue about, Maia cleared her throat and there was immediate silence. She smiled, enjoyed the heat of the fire on her face, luxuriated in the slow awareness that the quiet was actually full of the noise of the night. The fire was crackling and spitting, the breeze stirred the embers and carried them up to sighing leaves and branches. The nearby steam burbled an accompaniment, the air smelled crisp and clean. And Maia was surprised that she'd done exactly as Tom had told her: she was calm and relaxed.

'I can't believe how much we've done over the past few days. We've seen terrible things. Some of us have suffered more than others.' Her glance at Tom and Ten showed, she hoped, her sorrow and sympathy. 'But we're warm, we're well-fed and we're safe. We can continue our journey with hope and a little more confidence. And we have our new friend to thank for this. He's told me that he knows my father and has seen him recently. And he said that he'd tell me - tell us - more as soon as we were settled for the night. So here we are. And I don't even know his name.' Maia held out her hand to the stranger.

The stranger stood, nodded, and began to speak. 'Thank you for your kind words.' The voice soothed with its richness. 'My name is Mephita.'

'That sounds like a Bazhka name,' Ten said.

'That's because I *am* a Bazhka.'

This time the silence was deep and real and unbreakable.

'There is no need to fear me. No need,' the hood moved so that its cowl pointed at Tom who was reaching for his bow, 'to consider attacking me. If I'd wanted to harm you I could have done so easily. If I'd wanted to kill you, you'd be dead by now.' The figure pulled back its hood. Its face was baboon-like with a long, broad hairless snout set below gold-flecked eyes whose lids flicked restlessly sideways; the creature's tongue licked scaly lips to reveal double rows of serrated teeth, the cuspids hanging long and low. Most of the head was covered with luxurious blue-white hair, long at the jowls, shorter towards the top of the head, and through it protruded three pairs of horns: just above the eyes were the remains of two thin, pointed black daggers, their broken stubs capped with plugs of finely carved wood; behind them the second pair were longer, ivory-white, slightly curved back, twisted like corkscrews; the third pair, much further back on the head, were massive and purple, curling out and down to protect two wine-dark twitching ears.

'I'm aware that humans find us - find me - horrific. Disgusting. Ugly. Threatening. That is why I kept myself hidden. But if we are to travel together . . .'

'I'm going nowhere with a Bazhka!' Ten rose to his feet, it seemed he would stomp off into the undergrowth, until Maia spoke.

'Sit down and stop being childish,' she hissed. 'Mephita rescued us.'

Ten did exactly as he was told; none of the others said anything.

'It doesn't matter to me,' Maia went on, 'what you look like. Your actions were those of a friend. So thank you again.' She looked at Tom and at Pencil, at Slip and Friz, then - last and longest - at Ten. 'On behalf of all of us, thank you.'

Tom sucked his lips into his mouth as if he couldn't trust them not to say something offensive, but he nodded his agreement. Slip and Friz mumbled their own thanks. Ten's eyes flared with anger and he refused to look at Maia or

Mephita, but he remained where he was, didn't walk away. Only Pencil moved. She took several steps forward and stood in front of the Bazhka who was twice her height, examined the creature carefully. 'I don't think you're ugly,' she said, 'and you certainly don't disgust me. In fact you're rather beautiful in a way.'

'The same way an axe can be called beautiful?' Tom asked, his words dripping irony.

Pencil didn't recognise sarcasm. 'Sort of,' she replied, 'but more beautiful like Maia.'

'But I'm not . . .' Maia began.

'You are,' said Tom and Pencil together.

'Indeed you are,' Mephita nodded. 'But courtesy demands I explain myself. May I do so?'

'I think you should do exactly that,' Tom said.

'Please sit down,' Maia said. The Bazhka folded neatly to the ground, pulled at the cloak so that it fell away from broad shoulders. The body revealed, though muscular and clad in leather, was not male: it swelled in the wrong places, its hips were broad.

It took Pencil to state the obvious. 'You're a lady Bazhka!' she exclaimed.

'I am definitely female,' Mephita said. 'And although my name is Mephita, your father, Maia, felt it was inappropriate. Apparently, in one of your people's ancient languages, it's the name given to an animal called a skunk. And since I don't, so far as I'm aware, have an unpleasant or offensive odour, he chose another name for me, a name I prefer. He called me Shard.'

'Oh, I like that name,' Pencil said, rubbing her hands together, 'that's a lovely name.'

'I must start with the history of my people. It is a short history, but it is important. And then I must speak a little of

215

your father, Maia.' She looked around at faces pink with fireglow. 'If you're sitting comfortably, then I'll begin.'

TEN

Shard settled herself. She closed her eyes as if drawing up memories from some deep hidden place. Maia and Pencil were sitting close together; Slip and Friz were beside them, Friz's back against an upright stone, Slip lying across Friz; Tom and Ten were as far away from each other as they could be, on opposite sides of the fire. Their faces were a circle of expectancy lit by the fire's crackling, scented flames (some of the kindling they'd gathered was a little damp; larger, drier logs were infused with spits of resin), and by the embers' warm, red, reassuring gleam in the dark cathedral of the night.

'You will have questions,' Shard said, 'and I will try to answer them. You will have doubts; I will do all I can to help you put them behind you. I will tell you the truth as I know it. But it will be my truth.'

'Whatever that means,' Ten mumbled.

'Why do Bazhka want to kill humans?' Tom jumped in, clearly unwilling to let Shard tell her story slowly; he wanted answers to *his* questions. 'Why did they kill my mother?'

Shard's voice remained calm, patient. 'Bazhka are made creatures, Tom. They were created by the Maker who has no love of humans because they imprisoned him. So when he built his first creations he made certain that *he* would retain control of *them*. Their desire to destroy is his desire. He may be imprisoned, but he lives in their minds. He is their conscience, their guidance; he controls their morality.'

Ten spoke again from his sullen seat, slightly further from the fire than the others, almost in the dark. 'So he controls you.'

'No, he doesn't control me. I belong to no-one save myself.'

'How?'

'Perhaps,' Maia said softly, 'Shard was going to tell us all this. Should we save our questions until she's finished?'

'I think we should let her speak,' Pencil added. 'I like a good story.'

The silence was a suitable response and Shard nodded her thanks. 'This is a story from many sources. In my travels I have listened more than I have spoken, questioned more than I have answered. This is not the truth, nor is it all the facts. This is my truth and my facts.

'Many years ago - I don't know how long - the Truthsingers, humans who denied the existence of any deity of any type, heard rumours of miracles in a land far from their own civilisation. Such was their desire to explain the miraculous by scientific means, they found their way to this land and discovered that a being was indeed making miracles. He was making water flow in the desert. He kept flames alight when there was nothing to burn. He helped crops grow. He showed his followers how to build safely, how to care for their young and their sick. And so they worshipped him.'

'Yeah,' Slip said, 'gods usually want to be worshipped.'

'Or to have churches or temples or other such buildings erected.' Friz added. 'And there's usually a demand for exclusivity. "Worship me and no-one else. Oh, and by the way, if you find anyone worshipping a different god, kill them."'

'And then,' Slip continued, 'there's the carrot and the stick. "Do as I say and you'll go to heaven. Don't do as I say? Eternal punishment in hell!"'

'Let her go on,' Maia whispered.

'The Truthsingers found a creature unlike them, not human at all. He – and I use that word because others have done before me, but the Maker is neither male nor female – was powerful, Godlike, but disinterested. It was as if the humans

218

around him were ants: he had a certain curiosity in their existence. Sometimes he seemed inclined to protect them; at other times he treated them cruelly, he experimented on them, tortured them; but otherwise . . . he ignored them.'

'Is this a myth?' Maia asked. 'A creation story?'

'In a way,' Shard replied, turning large eyes that were suddenly old and wise in her direction. 'It is, in large parts, the story your father told me. And I will come to him, I promise.' She closed her eyes, paused, gathered her thoughts. 'The Truthsingers sought the Maker out. They visited his temple, they asked his followers questions, they asked *him* questions. Loudly. Repeatedly. The Maker became interested in them, they were so unlike the humans he was familiar with. They argued with him. They demanded he justify his actions, his beliefs. His ideology. He could only give them answers in words they couldn't understand, but still they persisted. And he was captivated.

'Remember, as I've told you, he wasn't human. He had no physical existence unless and until it was necessary to interact with humans. So he appeared before his followers, and the Truthsingers, in human form; he transformed himself into a man.'

'Was he a good man?' Pencil asked.

Ten raised his eyes in exasperation. Tom shook his head impatiently. But Shard considered the question, then drew back her lips in what might have been a smile that was friendly, not condescending. 'I'm not sure he would have understood what "good" meant, Pencil. But he was powerful, even in his human form, and he enjoyed demonstrating his power. He made snow fall in the desert; he flew through the air and took Truthsingers with him; he lifted great weights. And the Truthsingers could not explain how he did these things. They could find no rational

219

explanations. He was God-like. But they didn't believe in gods.'

'He sounds like a show-off to me,' Ten snorted.

'He sounds like a teenager,' Maia countered.

'I think he sounds like someone who just wanted to be loved,' Pencil added.

'He may have been all these things,' Shard continued, 'but he wasn't a god. There were limitations to his power. The Truthsingers asked him directly if he had any weaknesses and he - naively - said that he found it difficult to function fully in certain places: he was at his weakest when in a cave he'd discovered whose walls were made primarily of clay. They lured him there one day. In the guise of experimentation they asked him to break bonds of different materials. They found that nothing could restrain him except for manacles made of pure, fine porcelain. When the Truthsingers found this, they refused to release him. Instead, in a deep cave where his power was at his lowest anyway, they shackled him in porcelain chains and built a prison of porcelain bricks around him. Then they left him, imprisoned forever.'

'But they hadn't, of course,' Ten yawned, 'there's always a weakness to the weakness. Green kryptonite in a lead container. I bet he found a way out.'

'No, his body is still there, imprisoned. But his mind is free. Weakened by his cage, of course. Lacking the ability to function as it used to, but still with incredible power. And, because of the evil that he felt was done to him, completely insane. This is the story your father told me, Maia.'

'But there's more, isn't there.'

'There is much more. The Maker wanted to have revenge on the Truthsingers. So he created Bazhka. He made them in the image of all that would strike fear into humans. He made them of flesh and bone, and he gave them his own focused hatred of mankind. And he ordered them to seek out the Truthsingers and destroy them. The Truthsingers had learned much during their time with the Maker, so they sought to imprison him further. They built more walls, they sought to enclose the Maker in a prison within a prison within a prison.'

'That's a sad story,' Pencil said, 'I feel sorry for him.'

'The Maker's mind was free, remember that, and his mind could make new creatures; but it could also make new worlds. These worlds were imaginary until you entered them, then they became real. This,' Shard gestured with long, strong arms, 'is one of his worlds. The corridors, the paths between and around the worlds, are the Truthsingers' walls. And the doors? They are points of entry. Weaknesses.'

'I'm lost,' Slip said wearily. 'Is anyone else lost?'

'What about the Emperorium?' Maia asked, 'the shop where we came into the Library?'

'The Emperorium is the name of the Maker's world, Maia. It belongs to him. There were twelve places, Gateways, where the Maker's Emperorium touched your world. Each of them was fortified, guarded by a Truthsinger; but the Truthsingers grew old. Truthsingers would choose and train their successor when they found a suitable candidate, but few had the potential to keep the Maker's creatures at bay. If a Truthsinger died without a successor, the remaining Truthsingers would destroy the Gateway. Now only one Gateway and one Truthsinger remain. That Truthsinger is Madame Klein. But she is old and weak, if she dies there is no-one left to defend or destroy her Gateway. The Maker's creatures will have access to your world; the Maker will be freed. He feels his time is approaching. He seeks to bring about the destruction of humanity.'

The fire was dwindling to red and amber ashes. Shard bent forward and threw some twigs into their midst, waited for

221

them to burn, then added several logs. None of her audience said anything. The mood was sombre.

'The Maker continued to make Bazhka, but he also, with his later creations, gave them the ability to reproduce. This is a slow and long process whose mechanics you need not know. Only when a Bazhka matures can it be influenced by the Maker. Most Bazhka are aware of this only as a desire to hurt humans. But individual Bazhka can be used, controlled even. The Maker sees his many worlds through the eyes of his Bazhka.'

'Including you?' It was Maia's quiet voice that spoke, but the words could have come from any of her companions.

'I met your father before I came to maturity. I was . . . weak. I had suffered from an illness which stunted my growth. I was left in the corridors to be hunted and killed by humans. But your father found me, Maia, and he fed me and nurtured me and he gave me this.' Shard pulled at the hair around her neck to reveal a necklace almost identical to Maia's. 'It's made of porcelain. As long as I wear it I can't be controlled by the Maker. He can't see through my eyes. And I have free will. I choose what to do with my own life. I can't say this is a gift. At times it feels like a curse, I'm lost to my own people, they're together and I'm alone. But there are others like me.

'Thank you, Shard, for telling us all this. I think we owe . . .'

'There is more, Maia. More that you should know, more that you must know. When the Maker created Bazhka, he gave us a hatred for humans. And some Bazhka, the oldest, survive by draining humans, not of blood, but of their life essence, Ten. Does that seem familiar?'

'My father.'

'If that essence is not taken in its entirety then the human lives on. If the Bazhka is destroyed - and the oldest Bazhka are not easily destroyed - then the essence returns to the human. But that type of Bazhka is now rare. Most Bazhka hate humans because they've been conditioned to do so. I am a Bazhka. But this,' she touched her necklace again, 'has freed me from the need to hurt humans. It's more common for humans to wish to hurt me. And when they do, when they fail to kill me and if I kill them in self-defence - though I am often merciful – I feel no joy in my actions. And I have never killed an innocent human.'

Maia had been listening but her mind was elsewhere. 'When did you last see my father?'

'The word "when" has little meaning here, Maia. Time twists and turns and loops back on itself. But when I last met him he was healthy. He was weary. But he was in hiding. He has many enemies, Maia. The Vanjelists and the Bazhka, even though they hate each other, want him for the same purpose: he can free the Maker. He knows clay. He has the knowledge, the ability, to destroy the Maker's manacles and set the Maker free. The Truthsingers needed him to fortify the prison they built so long ago. Perhaps that is why you too are being hunted, Maia. You have a key. That is a valuable thing in the Emperorium.'

Maia fingered the chain around her neck. 'I need to find my father. He never even hinted that he knew about this other world. I thought he travelled abroad to lecture, to teach people how to make pottery and beautiful things. And all the time he was fighting this war against the Maker and Bazhka and Vanjelists.' She looked at Shard with weary eyes. 'He lied to me. Do you know where he is?'

'I know where he was. I can show you on the Map if you wish.'

Pencil was already reaching for the book, she brought it from her pack and laid it fearlessly on Shard's knees. The Bazhka turned the pages reverently. 'The key, the Map. These are riches indeed.' She flicked her eyes at Tom who

223

was resting a hand on the dagger sheathed at his waist. Tom took his hand away immediately.

'Have you looked in the book?' Shard asked, her voice directed at all the travellers. There was a chorus of silence. 'It means little to those who haven't travelled the corridors. I've seen copies of individual pages, of Lands beyond the doorways; doorways exist within the Emperorium, Gateways are the means of travelling from the Emperorium to your world.' Shard paused to ensure that everyone understood. 'The doorways themselves move. Better observers than I have tried to determine whether that movement is random or if, perhaps, there is a complex pattern to the changes. But if there is a pattern, it remains hidden.'

She turned some of the pages until she found something recognisable. 'Here, right in the middle of the book, this is the whole of the Emperorium. Each of the twelve Gateways that once led to your world is marked with a red glyph; most have a cross through them. This one here,' a long, sharp-nailed finger pointed at the Map, 'nearest to the Library where you entered, is the only remaining Gateway. It was, until recently, locked and in good repair. But now . . ?'

'I think that only Madame Klein's strength is keeping the Gateway closed,' Maia said.

'As I have already said, Madame Klein is old and weak,' Shard added.

'And injured,' Slip said.

They returned their worried eyes to the Map lying open before them. The page was decorated with a network of pale blue lines which seemed to be the corridors, twisting and snaking and doubling back on themselves like meandering rivers on an open plain.

'There's no scale,' said Friz, ever practical. 'How do you know distances from one place to another?'

'You don't. Think of when you passed through the doorway into this land.' Shard gestured around her at the dark forest. 'Did it seem natural?'

Friz shook her head.

'The entrance to the Library was the same,' Ten pointed out, 'and going from the Library into the corridors felt strange.'

'There is no constant scale from one land to another. The Emperorium is unnatural. The Emperorium is unusual. Don't expect to find normality anywhere within its borders.'

Ten poked the fire's embers with a stick. He didn't look up as he spoke. 'You mentioned earlier that some Bazhka could absorb the essence of people rather than killing them. What did you mean by that?'

'The first Bazhka - the Old Ones, there are few of them now - have that ability. They consume the life force of their victims. If an Old One is prevented from taking all that life force – perhaps by being attacked – then some of the essence remains with the victim who continues to live. Perhaps that's what happened to your father, Ten.'

'Maia butted in, 'And remember, your father's being protected by Madame Klein in her shell or whatever it is. We'll find a way of rescuing him.'

Ten seemed unconvinced, his voice a dull monotone. 'Can I get his life force back?'

Shard raised a six-fingered hand to her forehead, rubbed gently at the base of her broken front horns. 'There are legends . . .'

'Fairy tales, you mean.'

'Legends. The Old Ones sometimes fight amongst each other, they can steal the life force from one another. There are stories that humans can also do that by killing the Old One. Do you know the name of the Bazhka who attacked your father, Ten?'

'Seflapod. There were two of them, the other was called Atraxa. But Seflapod was the one who . . . It seemed to absorb . . . It would have been me but my father . . .'

Maia rose quickly to her feet and hurried to Ten's side, crouched down beside him, reached out to embrace him but, at the last moment, withdrew her arms. 'We'll find him. We'll do what we can. We'll get him back.'

'Seflapod is known to me,' Shard said softly, menacingly. 'She is powerful. She and Atraxa often work together. They did this,' she reached up and fingered the stubs of her broken horns, 'and this,' she stood up, turned around and pulled her cloak and shirt aside: a series of livid purple scars ran diagonally from one shoulder down to her waist. She covered herself again and sat down. 'There are more wounds. I was lucky to survive. I will find them for you.'

'They killed my mother,' Tom added.

'I *will* find them for you.' Shard rotated her broad shoulders. 'There *will* be a reckoning. But that will not be tonight. It's late. You're all tired. We need to sleep.'

'The Map,' Pencil protested, 'you were showing us the Map! And we have special lights.' She looked at Slip and Friz, encouraging them to bring out their torches.

'I'm curious about the Map as well,' Maia added. 'A few more minutes won't harm us.'

They reconvened around Shard, Slip and Friz shining their torches over her shoulders, Maia and Pencil kneeling at her sides, Tom and Ten peering in from a distance, pretending not to be interested.

'Each of the lands on the main map has a separate page. Here is the map of the Library and its surrounding area.' Shard flicked the pages to find a detailed plan of the Library itself and, beyond it, a network of roads, villages and towns. 'This is the corridor from the Library to the Terpsichory. And here is the land we occupy at the moment. As you can see, there's no detail. It hasn't been explored or mapped. But there are other lands which have been.' She turned more pages. 'This land is called Plains. It's mostly grassland, some crops, and areas where animals roam freely in huge herds. There are humans and a few Bazhka, Giants and Walkers, they live peacefully enough together.'

'Walkers?' Maia asked.

'There were some in the Terpsichory. Tall, white-haired, pale, pink eyes. They won't use other creatures as food or beasts of burden. They teach, heal. The Giants are huge and strong. They cooperate in the Plains. There are few places like that.' She turned the pages again. 'Snowtops, very cold and wintry, mountainous, but there are places where people can live. Clans of Bazhka, mostly, in remote villages.' Shard closed the Map. 'I've visited some Lands in my travels. Acma is a sandy desert, Walkers live there too. And Bazhka, though not together. Gaelle has permanent storms, its inhabitants communicate by gestures and hand signals and they have no mouths, they can only eat gruel through pores in their fingertips. Sarens are unusual people, dark skinned, taller than me, but very thin. The females travel from Land to Land entertaining with their singing and dancing while the males stay at home and raise their offspring.'

'When you say "people" you don't mean just humans, do you?' Slip asked.

'No. Why should I? Humans are only one type of people in the Emperorium. Can you recall, Maia, the man in the Terpsichory with plaited black hair reaching almost to the ground? He is Tschagen, one part of a group mind; even alone Tschagen is never alone. Each of these creatures I've mentioned believes they are normal and that all others are different.

'There are many other lands I've only heard about, inhabited by all types of creature. Most of my life has been

227

spent in the corridors, giving me the chance to meet others who, like me, are wanderers. Some choose this life. Some are forced into it. Once they take this path they don't usually return.' There was a longing in Shard's voice that they all recognised because it reflected their own thoughts. She idly turned the pages of the Map. 'There are so many places I don't recognise. I know so little.'

'Seems to me you know a lot,' Ten said.

Shard nodded. 'That's only because you know less than me.'

'Do you know where to find Seflapod?'

'And Atraxa?' Tom added.

Shard sighed. 'No.'

'But you said you'd find them!' For once Tom's anger perfectly matched that of Ten. 'You *said* you'd *find* them!' he shouted.

'I will. We will,' Shard said evenly, calmly. Then she raised her head to stare for a moment into Tom's eyes, did the same with Ten. 'But you asked if I knew where they were, and I don't. It would seem that your command of language and your memory are even poorer than your knowledge.'

Ten ground out the words through gritted teeth. 'So how will you find them?'

Shard opened the Map again. 'As I told you, I know few of these lands. But this one is familiar to me.' She tapped an open page, its territory bordered in purple. 'This is Home. This is the land of the Bazhka.' She turned the pages again and found a series of more detailed maps. They showed fields and rivers, hills and mountains, roads passing through villages leading to a central town. 'This is our capital, Arx. Legend states that the Maker is imprisoned there, but the jail has many cells and many doorways. Only one cell hides the Maker. Only one path through many doorways leads to that cell. And so I propose this: we use Maia's key and the Map to find the doors that lead to the Maker.'

'What? You're completely insane!' Ten was on his feet in an instant. 'You're telling us we have to confront a mad god whose only interest is gaining revenge on humans?'

Tom joined in, jabbing a finger at Shard. 'Not only that, we have to go through the Bazhkas' own territory to get there? What do we do, carry a big sign saying "Hello, we're breakfast!".'

'It does seem rather a stupid thing to do,' Maia added.

Slip clearly agreed. 'Takes adventure to the boundaries of suicide,' he said.

'There are indeed risks,' Shard replied, her voice still calm and level. 'But consider the following. You want to find Atraxa and Seflapod,' she glanced at Tom and Ten, 'the best opportunity to do so is in Arx, in Home. And even if they aren't there, when we attack the Maker he will summon them. And so you will find them. Or they will find you. Perhaps your bravery and determination are in words only?'

'That's not true!' Tom spat out.

'What he said!' Ten added.

'Then we need have no worries. Maia, I told you your father was healthy though weary and in hiding, but I didn't tell you where. Let me show you now.' She pointed at the Map again, finding what appeared to be a village close to Arx. 'Your father and his friends decided that the best place to hide would be in open view. To Bazhka most humans look alike. So he's hiding on a farm where humans are used as slaves. We will enter Home with you all pretending to be my captives. In that guise we will be able to move safely through Home to find your father, Maia. Then we head for Arx and beyond, to the citadel where we will confront the Maker. In doing so Atraxa and Seflapod will appear and you, Tom and

Ten, will have the opportunity to revenge your parents. Does that seem reasonable?'

'What do you get from this, Shard?' Maia asked.

Shard stared at each of them in turn. 'I shall destroy the Maker,' she said, 'as he - or his disciples - destroyed my love, my Akwila. And killed my daughter before she could be named. Killed her and forced me to watch.' She closed the Map gently. 'Do any of you have any questions?'

Shard's revelation silenced them all until Pencil raised a hand. 'Do you need a hug?'

Maia smiled. 'I'm sure Shard would like to get some rest, Pencil.' Even as she spoke Maia realised how condescending she sounded, and Pencil's face showed her disappointment. Shard saw this too and, without any hesitation, nodded to Pencil, whispered 'Thank you,' as Pencil tried to wrap her arms around Shard's wide, hard body. 'Thank you,' she whispered again as Pencil, blushing, retreated, 'from one mother to another.'

Only Maia heard. When Pencil, still beaming, took her seat again, while Ten stoked the fire and Tom fetched more wood, while Slip and Friz excused themselves to fetch water, Maia moved close to Shard. 'Did you say Pencil was a mother?' Maia asked.

Shard nodded slowly. 'You have eyes, Maia, you see, but sometimes you are blind. You have ears, you can hear, but you are deaf to some sounds. You have a nose, you can smell, but . . .' She shrugged. 'You are young, and you experience your world in such a limited way. I tell you, Pencil has borne at least one child.' She looked at Pencil. 'I know this.'

As the mist which had formed around them mingled with the last of the campfire's smoke and became a wash of rain, they headed for their shelters. Tom and Ten, with Slip as a buffer, all silenced by fatigue and worry, took one of the tents; Maia, Friz and Pencil crawled into the other. Within minutes Friz was asleep in the pattering darkness.

Maia chose her words carefully. 'Pencil, have you looked after a baby before?' At first she thought that Pencil must have fallen asleep, there was no response at all. But then Pencil replied.

'No. At least, if I have, I can't remember it. But I have dreams of looking after my own baby, Maia,' she said, her voice trembling. 'I dream of holding her. Feeding her. Loving her.' She began to cry, shuddering, gasping, but otherwise silent, and Maia could do nothing but reach out to her and comfort her, soothe her. And so, entwined in each other's arms, they fell into their own troubled dreams.

The tent flysheets were a dull orange; they filtered the dawn light in similar hues, so their occupants were surprised when they emerged to find all around them was misty grey-green. The treetops were shrouded in low cloud, the grass and moss were damp. Shard was already awake, re-fletching the arrows she'd used so effectively the day before. Maia sleepwalked towards the Bazhka's dull brown tarpaulin, stretching and yawning as she did so. Shard gestured to one side where a pile of kindling and logs remained dry. Maia picked them up and looked for the charred earth and the circle of stones that should have identified the place where last night's fire had burned, but found only a raised patch of new moss. She looked up to see Tom returning from the stream he'd found the previous day after a perfunctory wash. 'Is this where the fire was last night?' she asked.

Tom looked around him. 'Can't be. It was quite a big fire. Hang on though.' He scraped at the moss with his heel; beneath it was black ash. He did the same with two of the mounds close to the ash and revealed the stones that had kept the wood and ash in place. 'Strange. This is the place, but the moss has grown over it in the night. Must be some fast-spreading variety.'

Maia nodded as she bent to place the kindling and logs. 'Did you sleep well?' she asked.

'Slip snores. Ten mumbles in his sleep. So no, I had rather a bad night.'

'Did you dream?'

'I don't think so. I can't normally remember dreams. But I woke up with a headache, I felt as if I couldn't breathe properly. Why?'

'Would you mind lighting the fire? I don't really feel hungry but I think we ought to eat, have a hot drink. Shard says it could be a long journey to the next doorway.'

Tom went away, returned with his matches and managed to encourage a few flames. They watched them catch and dance. 'I dreamed I was drowning,' Maia said. 'Pencil was tossing and turning, Friz was gasping for breath. And *my* head hurts too.'

'Like a hangover?'

'I don't know, I've never had one.'

Tom opened his eyes wide. 'Maia, how old are you? Fifteen and you've never had too much to drink?'

'Never had any alcohol at all, Tom. You know me, Miss pure and Innocent.'

Tom wasn't sure if Maia was joking, but he didn't really want to investigate further. 'I'll get the kettle, make some tea. The dreams and the headaches are probably just a reaction to what's happened to us. And worries about what's to come as well.' He lowered his voice. 'Do you think we can trust the Bazhka?'

'She has a name, Tom. And yes, I trust her. She's wearing a necklace given to her by my father. She saved our lives several times over. And she's the only one who's thought of a way to help us.'

Tom dug the toe of his boot into the ground, refusing to look directly at Maia. 'She could have taken the necklace from someone else. She could be hoping to take the key from you, and the Map, and that's why she rescued us from the Vanjelists. And her plan might just deliver us to the Bazhka and the Maker.' He sounded like a sullen teenager. 'Ten and I don't get on with each other, we don't like each other, but we agree that we should all watch Shard carefully.'

'That's alright Tom, I'm sure she'll be watching you too.' Maia hurried away. She felt she had to trust Shard because there was no alternative. But she was still worried.

It took them longer than they anticipated to clear up and pack away the tents. The ground, so soft the night before, seemed unwilling to release the pegs holding the groundsheets and guy ropes. The ropes themselves were covered in grass where they touched the ground. Even Shard had difficulty in untying her tarpaulin cords from the branches where she'd knotted them. But eventually they were on their way as the sun struggled to break through the clouds and the damp turned to muggy mist.

'We seem to have no choice in which way to go,' Shard announced. 'Since we can't go back through the doorway to the church, we follow the track.' She led the way, Pencil followed close behind. Next came Tom, bow in hand, ready for action. Slip and Friz walked together, whispering about the silence and the possibility of monsters hiding behind trees. Ten and Maia brought up the rear.

'Have you noticed,' Ten said, 'there are no birds. Not even birdsong. Just the sound of the wind in the branches and the leaves.'

'It's too quiet,' Maia agreed, began humming a tune. She stopped after a few bars when no-one joined in.

They trudged in silence as the day grew hotter. There were, thankfully, no insects to annoy them. Maia tried to identify different types of trees and shrubs, but when she thought she recognised a leaf, she found it didn't match the tree's bark or its size and shape.

After a few hours Shard called a halt and asked to see the Map. The blue dot signifying their position showed that they seemed to be making good progress towards the far edge of the territory. When they set off again Ten and Tom changed places.

'Ten mentioned that there were no birds,' Maia said to Tom.

'No birds, no insects, no flowers, no fruit. No sign of any life other than trees and moss. No paths running off to the side showing there've been deer or rabbits or other animals. Just this well-worn track with nothing to actually make it well-worn. And has our guide spotted these peculiarities? No, she just marches on without a word. She has no idea where we are.'

'I'll speak to her,' Maia said, 'see what she thinks.'

'Good luck,' Tom said, his voice implying that he wasn't really offering any luck at all.

Maia made her way forward, smiling at Ten, winking at Slip and Friz, touching Pencil gently on the shoulder. She was sure that Shard would be able to deal with her worries. Their guide was moving at a suitable pace, far slower than she would have been capable of if travelling alone; she was stopping regularly to give them time to drink and rest; she often looked back to make sure they were all keeping up; and every ten minutes or so she asked Pencil to open the Map, to check their progress. And yet Maia felt a sense of oppression, of the world leaning heavily on her. Her head was still aching and she was weary. When she caught up with Shard she walked alongside her, not saying anything. It felt strange to see the unoccupied track ahead of her, twisting and turning gently with only an occasional rise or fall. All around was green and peaceful and silent and . . . threatening, that was the word. She looked up at Shard's impassive face. 'Shard, I don't know why, but I think there's something wrong.'

'I agree,' the Bazhka replied, 'I don't think the forest wants us here. And I suspect we're being watched.'

Maia looked round. 'I haven't seen or heard anyone following.'

'That's because we aren't being followed. There's no reason to follow us, we have no choice in where we go. But I can feel eyes upon me. I feel nervous. I can sense danger. You and the others feel the same?'

Maia nodded.

'Then we should do something about it.' She held up her hand and stopped, waited for the others to catch up. When they did so, when they'd all drunk from their water bottles and flexed their aching shoulders, when their whispered conversations ceased, she spoke.

'I'm sure you agree that there's something wrong here,' she said. 'Our path is too easy, too broad, yet we've seen no signs of other users. And we're being watched, I'm certain of that. But there's a greater problem.' She summoned Pencil who opened the Map wordlessly. 'What direction are we heading?' Shard asked.

Ten looked up at the trees and the hot grey sky beyond. 'Feels as if we're going north? Sometimes, when the sun tries to come out, it's at our backs.'

'I'd agree with that,' Friz said. There was a chorus of 'Me too'.

'And the Map showed the same thing at first. Yet although our path has been reasonably straight, the Map has shown

235

us heading round to the east, then south. We're heading into the middle of the forest.'

'That doesn't make sense,' Ten said, 'I think I'd know if I was going in completely the wrong direction.'

'So would I,' Shard said, 'which is why I called a halt. I think we need to try something different.' She reached into her pack and brought out a leather sheath from which she drew a long-bladed machete. 'Let's try going this way,' she said grimly, turned to her right. There was a wall of dense greenery, leaves and thick stems, twigs and thorns, yet the machete cut through them easily. Shard's strokes were easy and regular, economical yet effective. Within moments she'd made a tunnel into the forest and she led the way into the green gloom.

'Why are we going this way?' Maia asked.

'Why not?' Shard grunted between swings. 'It's as good a way as any.' The machete rose and fell effortlessly. 'Let's see what happens.'

Maia felt the others crowding behind her, eager to see what was happening. They soon emerged into a small clearing, a patch of cloudy sky was visible above them. Shard strode straight across, began cutting again on the other side, but managed no more than a few strokes before Tom, bringing up the rear, yelled 'Wait!'

Shard turned quickly. 'What's the matter?'

'Look, behind us.' Where there should have been a tunnel through the greenery there was only a wall of leafy branches, the same as on all sides of the clearing. 'It's grown back,' Tom said, amazement his voice. 'And watch!' He held his hand out so that it was almost touching the foliage. Within seconds two or three tendrils had whipped out and curled themselves around his fingers. He pulled his hand away. 'There's no strength in them,' he said, 'but if I stood still, if I let them grow, if others joined them . . .'

Slip spoke up. 'I don't think the forest wants us to do this.'

'We go back,' Shard said, 'now.' She marched back across the clearing, began the metronome slashing that would find their way back to the path.

'I think the clearing's getting smaller,' Tom said to Maia. She looked around, it was certainly darker than a few moments before. She looked up: there was no sky visible, only interlocked branches and the dark shadows of leaves. She hurried after Shard.

It took only a few minutes for them to return to their starting place. The track was still there. They stood and looked around them. The forest filled the gap behind them but made no attempt to do the same with the path in either direction. They sank wearily though warily to the ground.

'Now what?' Friz asked.

Slip looked nervously around. 'We don't have any choice. The forest doesn't want us to cut through it. It wants us to follow the track. And I don't think it matters which direction we go, we'll find ourselves heading into the middle anyway.'

'You make the forest sound like a person,' Friz said.

'Sort of. Have you ever seen plants grow as fast as that? And with so much purpose?'

'But if you're right,' Maia said, 'why is it keeping us on the path, moving us into the middle? What's its purpose?'

Ten cleared his throat. 'Have you noticed how few species there are? I mean, I'm no expert, but it looks to me like the moss is only one variety. Where there's no moss there's grass, but only one type. And all the trees have the same colour bark on their trunks, the same shape leaves. There are no birds, no insects. Look.' There was a moss covered branch on the ground, he pushed it over with one foot; there was no scurrying of ants or woodlice, no centipedes, no film of spider-web or coating of termite dust. 'Slip said the forest

237

was like a person. I think it is. And it's in charge, it can do what it wants with us.'

Shard lifted her head and inhaled deeply. 'I know forests and woods. This is different to all others, but I wasn't sure why until you mentioned it.' She acknowledged Slip and Ten with a nod. 'It's like going into a room full of people and finding they're all the same. Different ages, different sizes, different clothes and hair, doing different things. But still the same person. Multiplied.'

'So what do we do?' Maia asked.

'Since we have no choice, perhaps we should go where the forest wants us to go,' Pencil announced suddenly, 'and we should go now. Then, when we get to wherever we're going, at least we'll be ready for whatever is in store for us. It'll still be something bad, but at least we won't be tired with trying to find a way of escaping.' She was tracing the pattern on the cover of the Map with her fingertip, following its maze of curves and whorls. 'Is that sensible?'

'That's very sensible,' Shard said.

'Really?' Pencil looked up, delighted at the compliment. 'That makes a change. I'm not used to saying sensible things.' She unfolded her crossed legs and rose to her feet. 'Should we go, then?'

They walked again in single file, Shard leading. Now that they knew they were being shepherded, now that they could see the monotony of the scenery around them, now that they could hear the silence, they said little. The track seemed to skirt hills, to move around the natural swell of the landscape on level ground. Sometimes they could hear water flowing, sometimes a breeze tossed the leaves into a whispering susurration, sometimes the clouds broke to reveal a brief flag of distant blue sky; but mostly they heard only each other's footsteps, saw only the back of the person walking ahead. They didn't look to either side, firstly because there was nothing different to see, but mostly from fear of seeing something different. Without telling each other how they felt, they knew they were feeling the same sense of oppression, of suffocation, of moving inexorably towards something dangerous. But they kept walking because they had no alternative.

The hours passed. Twilight gathered. Shard held up her hand to halt the group, told them where they should erect their tents - this time in the middle of the path - and gave them tasks. They collected firewood and water in threes, one doing the work while the other two guarded the first. Shard would take first watch, she said, the others would do the same in pairs. The fire wouldn't be allowed to die down. No-one should leave the area alone. 'There's no such thing as being embarrassed,' she said. 'Washing, calls of nature - whatever the need, someone goes with you.'

They forced themselves to eat and drink. Even Pencil seemed subdued. And though they were all tired, none of them wanted to sleep; the dreams of the previous night had frightened them, not with any specific memories, but with a creeping claustrophobia which deterred them from crawling into the narrow confines of their sleeping bags and tents.

'Does anyone know any jokes?' Maia asked, aware that they needed something to cheer them. 'Or songs? Anything to cheer us up?'

No-one volunteered.

'I'm hopeless at jokes,' Maia continued, 'can't remember them, can't tell them. But this is one my father liked to tell.' She licked her lips. 'A man goes into a baker's shop - you should like this, Tom - and points to some cakes in the window. He says to the lady behind the counter, "Is that a doughnut or a meringue?" And she replies . . . Oh, hang on,

I've missed a bit. I forgot to say it's in Scotland, the baker's shop's in Scotland.'

'Where's Scotland?' Pencil asked.

'Oh. Of course, you don't know. Nor you, Shard. That makes things difficult.'

'Just tell the rest of us,' Ten said.

'But if some of us don't understand then . . . Oh, alright then. Where was I?'

'The Scottish baker's shop?' Tom prompted.

'Oh yes. The man goes in and says . . .'

'What's his name?' Pencil asked.

'I don't think it matters, Pencil. And you won't really understand because you don't know about Scotland or the way people talk in Scotland. I'm sorry, it'll all seem a little pointless to you and Shard.'

'Names always matter,' Pencil said. 'My name, Pencil, isn't really a name, not a *real* name, so I must be called something else. Isn't that right?'

'His name was Donald,' Ten said, 'that's as good or bad a name as any. Can we get on?'

'Alright!' Maia was trying not to show her exasperation. 'Donald goes into a Scottish baker's shop and asks, "Is that a doughnut or a meringue?" and the lady replies . . .'

'What's a doughnut?' Pencil asked.

'And the other item,' Shard said, 'I've not heard of that either.' She rolled the word around her mouth. '"Murrang". Unusual. Can you explain?'

Slip and Friz were nudging each other. Tom was grinning, Maia suspected he knew the joke already. Ten was smiling at the serious expression on Pencil's face.

'Agh!' Maia screamed, 'I give in! The lady says "Ach, you're nay wrang, it's a doughnut".'

Tom burst out laughing, Slip and Friz sniggered, Ten tried to make his face serious. Shard shook her head as if the whole thing was beneath her, while Pencil muttered 'I don't understand. Why are you laughing? It isn't funny at all!'

'I'm sorry,' Maia apologised to Pencil and Shard, 'that wasn't a good choice. Do *you* know any jokes?'

'You would understand mine even less than I understand yours,' Shard said.

'I don't do jokes,' Pencil said. 'But I can sing you a song!'

'That would be good.' Maia shushed the others, her look telling them that they should approve of Pencil's song, no matter how bad it was.

'I don't know how I know this,' Pencil said, 'because I used to sing it in the Library and everyone who heard it said they'd never heard it before. I hope you like it.' Pencil cleared her throat and began to sing, quietly but with confidence. Her words carried clearly in the cool night air.

> *'My lover's smile is like the sun,*
> *So smile for me, my love, my own,*
> *And fill my day with light and love*
> *That I may never be alone*
> *So smile for me, my love, my own.*
>
> *My lover's eyes are like the night,*
> *So dark and deep and wide and high,*
> *I care not for the coming dawn*
> *When 'neath my lover's gaze I lie,*
> *My lover, and the night, and I.*
>
> *My lover's touch is like the breeze,*
> *A summer's breeze that's warm and calm,*
> *With fingertips that dance and slide,*
> *A touch that never can do harm,*
> *A touch that heals with soothing balm.*

My lover's kiss is like a fire
That burns and roars with heat and flame . . .'

Pencil came to a halt. She looked around her. 'I can't remember any more. I wish I could, because I want to know how it ends, but . . .' she shrugged, 'that's it.'

'That was beautiful,' Tom said.

'You're a really good singer,' Ten added. He reached out a hand to touch her then thought better of it.

'I wish I could sing like that,' Friz smiled.

'So do I,' Slip agreed, 'my ears are still hurting from the last time you sang.'

Shard put her head on one side, looked directly at Pencil. 'How can it be that a few simple words put to music can say so much? How can it be that a song is both happy and sad at the same time?' She lowered her head. 'Humans are such complex creatures.'

Maia wiped her eyes. 'So good,' she said, 'so very good.' She took a deep breath. 'I think we might be able to sleep now?'

Later, when the tents were quiet and drowsy, Maia whispered to Pencil. 'Can you remember nothing about who taught you that song?'

'Nothing. Sometimes I see pictures in my head. A man. With his back to me. But I don't know if he sang to me or I sang to him. Perhaps we sang to each other? I don't know.'

'I think you do know, it's just that you can't remember. One day you will remember, I'm sure of that.'

'I think . . . I think I'm getting better at thinking, Maia. And that's a step closer to getting better at remembering. That's good, isn't it?'

'That's very good, Pencil.'

'I might even remember my own name. My real name.'

'What's in a name. Pencil? "That which we call a rose by any other name would smell as sweet."'

'Mmm,' Pencil whispered, already half asleep. Maia closed her eyes and felt fatigue begin to claim her. But she thought she heard Pencil say something from a world far away from the dreams that were already gathering around her like dark, suffocating clouds. Pencil's distant voice sang to her, 'Then for that name which is no part of thee, take all myself.'

The morning was dark with rain and premonitions. Maia was pleased when Friz nudged her awake, her troubled dreams replaced with a familiar dull headache. 'You need to see this,' Friz said, hurried Maia out into the cold air. She pointed at the flysheets of the tents. They were covered with green tendrils, as were the tent walls. Thin filaments of green seemed to have threaded their way into the zips and airvents.

Ten and Slip were propping each other up, back to back, in front of the circle of rocks where the fire had been. They were asleep. Moss seemed to be covering their boots and their trouser cuffs. Maia strode over to them, shook their shoulders. Their eyes opened slowly. 'Weren't you meant to be on watch?' she asked angrily. 'I assume Shard woke you. You were meant to keep the fire burning! If you'd done that you would have seen the moss and the grass! Look! Look!'

They could barely move, it was as if they'd been given some sleeping potion.

'We did watch,' Ten protested, 'Shard woke us, we sat here and . . .'

'And you fell asleep! If you were tired you should have woken someone else!'

'I didn't think I was tired,' Slip said, 'but . . .'

'Don't blame them,' Shard said, appearing at Maia's side. 'I too feel slow, lethargic.' She raised her head and inhaled. 'I think there's something in the air, something that affects us all. And there's no sign of the others waking, despite the noise we're making. The forest is . . . doing things to us.'

Maia looked warily around her. 'But why?'

'We may find out later today. I think we're close to the centre of the forest and that's where the track seems to be leading us. Wake the others, I'll light the fire.'

'We're sorry,' Slip said, struggling to his feet, 'We didn't realise how tired we must have been.'

'It's alright,' Maia patted him on the shoulder, 'I shouldn't have shouted. We're all feeling strange at the moment. Tired and bad-tempered.' She wandered away to wake Pencil and Friz.

No-one spoke while they ate breakfast. They sat with their heads low, trying to ignore the oppressive green crowding in around them. They packed slowly, even Shard seemed to have difficulty in preparing for the journey: she rolled and folded her tarpaulin several times before being satisfied that it would fit into its carefully stitched bag.

Her troubles were mirrored by the others. Tom stared at the laces on his boots as if uncertain of their purpose and then unsure how to tie them. Friz put on her T-shirt and fleece inside out, then struggled to pull her coat on, unable to thread her arms into the sleeves. Maia tripped over the same guy-rope three times when trying to dismantle her tent. Pencil spent ten minutes searching frantically for the Map which was in the pack already on her back. Ten, ready before the others, began counting the trees surrounding the glade in which they'd camped and, no matter how many times he tried, always arrived at a different total. Slip, head in hands, sat immobile beside the path, deep in thought and concentration.

When it seemed as if they were ready Shard held up a hand to gain their attention. 'I'm not sure what's happening,' she said, 'but I know you're all feeling the same way this morning. We need to focus our minds on . . .'

She was interrupted by Slip falling forward onto his knees and spreading his fingers wide, combing the grass, crawling away from the path and into the thick undergrowth. 'Spores,' he muttered to himself, 'spores. Perhaps spores might do it. But what type?'

Friz marched over to him. 'Come on, Slip, you're making me even more nervous.' She tried to haul him to his feet but he fought her off.

'Can't you see? Spores might do it.' He parted some fronds of fern and cried out 'Yes!' He motioned to the others. 'Come and look!' They gathered around him. 'Down there, close to the ground. Some type of mushroom or fungus.' He stood back so they could all see. 'Or here,' he pointed at the ferns, turned a leaf over to reveal dark pods beneath.

'And?' Friz asked, 'why is this suddenly important?'

'I had to really think, my mind's not working properly. We did it in Biology class, can't you remember?'

'No,' Friz said, 'I can hardly remember going to Biology classes, let alone what happened in them.'

'Asexual reproduction. Spores. Fungi and ferns reproduce by releasing spores.'

'I can remember doing that,' Maia said, 'but why is it important?'

'Some spores are so small they can enter the lungs and get into the bloodstream. See, I was listening, I actually did some research.' He seemed proud of his knowledge. 'They can cause hallucinations. And they can cause illnesses. Perhaps the spores are making us tired?'

'That's nonsense,' Ten said.

Slip whirled on him. 'No it's not! Think! It all points in the same direction. A track that's easy to follow but there's no way of getting off it. Plenty of water to sustain us. No

245

dangerous creatures, no attacks. But we're being softened up for something, we're being weakened so we can't fight back. It's the forest, it's got a reason for doing this. It's trying to get us somewhere in a fit and healthy state, but weak so we can't fight it.'

'Sounds like paranoia to me,' Ten said, 'a whole forest that's able to think?'

'Perhaps there's something in it,' Maia said. 'We should cover our mouths and noses, just in case Slip's right.'

'Pointless,' Slip said, 'spores are so tiny they'll get through any fabric.'

'Then we move on quickly,' Shard announced, 'bring this matter to a close. Let's go.'

The urgency seemed to help. Knowing that there might be a reason for their tiredness seemed to help. And fear helped, having an enemy who was trying to harm them forced adrenaline into their bloodstream and helped banish their fatigue. And so they marched on with purpose.

Just before midday the path ended. It ran through a tunnel of trees forming an archway over their heads then stopped in a meadow of long waving grass. Where the meadow narrowed there were some standing stones, about a dozen spaced regularly in front of an old, gnarled tree. It wasn't the tallest tree; others behind it towered forward, bent over it as if protecting it, deferring to it. Its trunk was wide and thick, its branches were twisted with time, it dominated the meadow. A breeze rippled the grass and the tree seemed to beckon them forwards.

'I think we've arrived,' Shard said softly. 'We have nowhere else to go.'

ELEVEN

Shard looked around suspiciously. 'There's no other path out of this clearing, we have to go forward. But go slowly. Be careful.'

'I'm not frightened of a plant,' Ten said as he stepped forward.

'I am,' Pencil whispered. 'I once fell into a patch of stinging nettles.' A look of puzzlement spread across her face. 'But there are no nettles in the Library. When did that happen?'

'Talk about it later,' Maia said kindly, 'after we find out whether this tree has anything special about it.'

They approached the tree, staying out of reach of its branches which tossed and shook in the breeze. They were surrounded by tranquillity: the grass whispered, the leaves sang like a soft applause, a hidden stream murmured to itself. The clouds, their permanent companions for days, drew open like curtains and sunlight filled the air.

'It feels so peaceful,' Friz said.

'Look at the haze,' Slip warned, 'a cloud of pollen or spores or something like that. And it's all around us, most of the time we can't see it.'

'What do we do now?' Tom asked.

Ten had been looking around. 'Whatever it is,' he said, 'we'd better do it soon. That avenue of trees seems to have closed up.'

They all turned round; the tunnel of leaves and branches they'd passed through only a few minutes before was now choked with interwoven creepers and dense foliage. Maia glanced at Shard, seeking advice, but the Bazhka simply shrugged. Maia took a deep breath. 'Look everyone, I know this will sound silly,' she said, 'but I have to do it.' She raised her voice, aimed her words directly at the tree. 'Why have you brought us here? What do you want from us?'

There was no change. No new movement. No response.

'Can you communicate? We know you've led us here. Why have you done that? Why are you keeping us prisoner?'

Again, nothing.

'We aren't without weapons. We don't want to hurt you. But we need to leave this place.'

This time there was a new sound, a clicking as if twigs were being tapped together. Beyond one of the stones there was movement and Shard raised a ready crossbow to point in that direction. A thin, bony hand appeared, wrapped in grass and leaves, gripping the stone as if it was heaving itself from the earth beneath. Another joined the first, together they dragged a figure upwards. It stepped unsteadily from behind the stone.

'It's a skeleton!' Maia whispered; even Shard took a step back. But as they watched, the bare bones began to disappear beneath a covering of green. Thin stems threaded their way through the bones of the legs and the pelvis, worked their way upwards. They curled their way around the spine, wove themselves in and out of the ribs to form a skin. Tendrils as strong as watch springs anchored themselves on joints, long shoots grew between them to form muscles and tendons, and these too were encased in wide leaves that wrapped themselves around the growing body.

The head was completed last of all. Vines grew up through the chest cavity and around the neck, swirled around the loose, drooping jawbone until it began to move and close. Small hard seeds of pearly white were carried upwards by buds and leaves, fixed in place to form teeth. Lips and a tongue were made of fleshy pink-skinned mushrooms; the ears were pale flowers; the nose and eye cavities were packed with leaves; and long strands of grass grew down from the head. The body filled out at the hips and chest.

'It looks like a woman,' Tom pointed out the obvious.

The body began to sway as an unseen puppeteer pulled at new, unfamiliar strings. It seemed as if the skeleton would fall and break, it bent at the waist and its hands groped for something on the ground, scuttling like frightened spiders. But it found what it wanted and stood straight again, pushed a polished brown nut into each eye socket.

'It doesn't have a brain,' Ten said, 'it's nothing more than a mannequin.'

'Mannequins don't move,' Slip said.

'Alright then, it's a wind-up doll.'

The creature's head moved slowly up and down, then from left to right. The end of its tongue slipped from its mouth and seemed to lick its lips. It opened its mouth wide and from within came a harsh sound, as if two pieces of wood were being rubbed together. The creature closed then opened its mouth and the sound changed, not only its volume and resonance, but the quality; it was no longer rasping, it was smoother, like drum skins being stretched and released.

The creature made no attempt to move any other part of its body but it was growing stronger, firmer, it no longer needed to rest against the stone it had first used as a support.

It played with the sound it was making by using its tongue, by opening and closing its mouth. And suddenly the sounds became near words. 'Eugh . . . eychum . . . oye . . . oo . . . hurgh . . . vurs.'

'It's trying to speak to us,' Pencil said, hiding behind Shard's huge legs.

'"It" can't be speaking because "it" has no brain,' Ten said harshly.

'Then what's it trying to do? Maia asked. 'We've been brought here by something sentient, that much is obvious. Perhaps the "it" you're talking about is the forest itself.'

Shard agreed. 'Strange things happen in the Emperorium. Am I not strange to you, Ten? Yet you had no objection to me saving your life.'

The creature spoke again. 'Vurst,' it said again, and raised one awkward arm to describe a quarter circle.

'"Forest"?' Slip asked, 'do you mean "forest"?'

The creature nodded slowly. 'Vurst,' it said again, then modified the word. 'Vur-est. Vor-est. Vee . . . veycum . . . yoe . . . oo . . . vhe . . . vorest.'

Slip nodded. 'We - something something, I can't tell the next two words - to the forest? Yes?'

'We weycum yoe to the forest.'

'Yes! Got it! "We welcome you to the forest"! Is that right?'

'We . . . welcome . . . you . . . to the . . . forest.'

Slip grinned at Ten. 'It seems you don't need a brain to communicate after all.'

'I knew that much from listening to you,' Ten answered back.

'Behave,' Maia warned them both, went on to speak directly to the creature. 'Who are you?'

The creature was learning how to control its speech quickly. 'We . . . are . . . the Forest,' it replied, slowly but accurately, and the voice was that of a woman.

'What do you mean by "we"?' Shard asked.

'We. We are . . . the Forest. We are . . . all things. We are trees. We are grass. We are flowers. We are plants. We are all things, as we are, as we were.' This time the creature raised two arms and held them wide. 'We are . . . everything.'

Shard took a step closer. 'You're built around a skeleton. A human skeleton. Do you know who she was?'

The creature nodded. 'I was Ruthie. Before I was the Forest I was Ruthie.' The creature seemed puzzled. 'I *am* still Ruthie.'

Maia jumped in. 'Do you have a brother called Zeke?'

'Zeke? A brother?' The creature lowered its head. Green eyelids closed over black-brown eyes. The leaves and foliage of its face rippled with unpleasant memories, but when it spoke its voice was flat and unemotional. 'Zeke left me. No. Zeke gave me to . . . 'nother man.' The creature that had been Ruthie, that was Ruthie, was seeking deeper memories. 'A man called . . . Baptiste. Tha's right. Jean Baptiste.'

'Is it a ghost?' Friz asked softly.

'I don't know. A ghost that forms around its own body? I don't know.' Maia pressed on. 'Zeke, your brother, gave you to Jean Baptiste. Then what happened?'

'He did things. He did things he shun't a' done. An' he knew it. I said I'd tell. So he hurt me. An' he left me here. Alone. I w's thirteen years old.' The creature's eyes opened again. 'An' the Forest took me. The Forest cared for me. I'm part o' the Forest. I am the Forest. I *am* the Forest'

Another voice, deeper than Ruthie's, echoed her words, 'I am the Forest!' It came from a figure that appeared from behind the most distant stone. 'I am the Forest,' it said again. 'I am Tobias Aloysius Procter, farm hand, wandered into the woods looking for a short cut home. Never found it.'

'We are the Forest.' Two figures appeared together, spoke together, their arms entwined, red flowers blooming in their hair. 'We are Soraya and Ibrahim Khawam, we sought time alone together and found time forever in each other's arms.'

'I am the Forest.' This figure was tall and thin, breeze-tossed. 'Arnalo Sweetgood, Walker. Walked too far.'

Other voices joined the chorus.

'Anders Boij, woodsman, fell into the Forest drunk, never need drink again.'

'Ndawe Sephola. Singer of songs, poet. Now part of my own story.'

'Ochar Steel, mercenary. Attacked by my own men, left to die. Resurrected.'

'Annie Wellbeloved, spinster. Never found love till the Forest took me.'

'Parsifal Sadonis.'

'Knut Bladesinger.'

'Emily Prettygirl.'

'Angry Simon.'

'Peg the Scissors, cut off in my prime.'

'Sideways Thompson. Should have gone straight on.'

The speaking diminished to a soothing sibilance, a low harmonious humming. When more than twenty of the green people had appeared, when they seemed to be doing nothing but sway and sing softly, waiting and watching with sightless eyes, Maia felt a sense of peace and contentment. They'd travelled far but they'd reached their destination and they were now safe. This was actually a good place to be. There was no danger, no-one was trying to chase them or kill them. The others clearly felt the same, they too were standing still, mimicking the green people, swaying slightly from side to side. Even Shard's face was calm. But . . .

Pencil was whimpering softly to herself. The rollcall of the dead had disturbed her, reminded her of her dreams of loss though she couldn't recall exactly who or what she'd lost. The ghosts in her head teased and tormented Pencil; her eyes snapped open. She reached out a tired hand and touched Maia on her back, the gentlest of butterfly touches, and said 'I'm frightened.'

In the same way that her own fragmented dreams had woken Pencil - stealthily, almost by accident - so Pencil woke Maia. Her words broke the lethargy that was stealing through Maia's mind. She saw Pencil's startled expression, saw the others in their dreamlike state, saw the green people swaying gently, hypnotically; and when she looked down she saw tendrils of green, creepers and vines and stalks of grass, entwined around everyone's legs, moving slowly upwards.

She pulled her feet away from the ground, called everyone's name to wake them, saw them all snap out of their collective torpor. 'Move your feet,' she ordered, 'stamp them!'

They all did so, though slowly, still not fully conscious of what was going on.

'It's the spores,' Maia shouted, 'sending us to sleep. And then the creepers. Wake up!' She shook Tom and then Ten, Slip and Friz. Pencil was already doing the same to Shard but with little effect, the Bazhka's eyes were closed. Maia reached up, drew back her arm and slapped Shard across her muzzle. One of the Bazhka's arms shot up and grabbed Maia's wrist. Her eyes flew open.

'Thank you,' Shard whispered. 'But best not strike a Bazhka. Under any circumstances.'

Maia glanced down. Shard's other hand was holding a knife. It was resting gently against Maia's abdomen. She stepped away.

'What do we do now?' Tom asked, trying to overcome his panic. He and the others were awake, looking around at the green people who were still moving in time with each other, rippling in some private breeze, swimming in a sea of lush tranquillity, singing wordless, soothing, siren songs. Sunlight filtered through the high canopy of endless green to reveal a golden haze in the still air.

'It's the Forest,' Slip said, 'I told you, it doesn't want us to go. The air's filled with spores or pollen that's sending us to sleep. The grass is trying to hold us in place. The . . . whatever these things are that are pretending to be people,

253

their singing is, oh, I don't know, trying to calm us, that's sending us to sleep as well. It's the Forest itself!' He stared wildly around. 'And there's nowhere else to go!'

'It's okay,' Friz said, placed a tender hand on her friend's shoulder, 'calm down. We'll find a way out.'

'No!' Ten's angry voice filled the glade. 'Don't calm down! If we calm down it'll happen again, we'll fall asleep, the grass will grow, soon we won't be able to move. We need to keep our adrenaline flowing. We need to be anxious. We need to be worried. We need to be frightened!'

'I already am frightened,' Pencil said.

'But how do we fight back?' Tom had taken Ten's words to heart, he was marching to and fro, knife in hand. 'What can we do?'

Maia turned to Shard. 'Any suggestions?'

'Listen to me!' Shard's voice bristled with authority, it commanded immediate attention. 'All you can do is stay alert. Don't jump around, that will make you breathe more heavily. Think. I believe Slip is right. The Forest is an entity and these creatures are simply extensions of the Forest. They are part of it. I have questions. Why won't the Forest let us go? What will happen to us if we can't get away? What use are we to the Forest? Think. Use your brains.'

'It needs us for something?' Maia suggested.

Tom had stopped his marching but was moving his feet, determined not to let the grass twine itself around his legs. 'It can think. It can communicate. Could it be lonely?'

'Possible.' Shard sought involvement from the others. 'Friz?'

'I don't know. I can't seem to think straight.'

'Double numbers,' Ten suggested, 'it's a thinking game. One, two, four, eight, sixteen and so on. Keep it going.'

'Thirty-two? Sixty . . . sixty . . . Yes, sixty-four!'

'Next? Come on, work it out.'

'I can't do mental maths!'

'Yes you can! Double six is?'

'Twelve.'

'Good. So double sixty is?'

'Two times sixty is two times six times ten, that's . . . a hundred and twenty.'

'But it was two times sixty-four! Add two times four!'

'A hundred and . . . a hundred and twenty-eight!'

'Keep it going. I'll help you.'

The slow multiplication fought against the green people's singing.

Shard turned her attention to the others. 'Maia, if we stay here we fall asleep and we die. Then we're no use to the Forest as company. I don't think it wants us to be its friends. What else could it be?'

Maia's eyes were wide open. 'The green people seem to have their own identities,' she said, realising she was talking too fast but unable to slow the words. 'They talk about "us" and "we". But they're actually just bones padded out with twigs and leaves. So they can't have their own identities. A contradiction. I don't know, Shard, I don't know!'

'I'm so tired,' Pencil said, 'I just want to lie down and go to sleep. But if I do the grass will crawl into my mouth and up my nose and I'll never get up again, and I don't want that to happen. Maia, don't let that happen.'

'That's exactly what it wants!' Slip was agitated again. 'It wants us to fall asleep. Then it can, oh, I don't know how, but it wants to absorb us. Absorb our minds, it wants us to become part of the Forest, just like the skeletons of these lot.' He gestured at the green people. 'It's like Pencil said, the tendrils will crawl inside us, connect with our brains, suck us dry.' He turned to the green person who'd identified herself as Ruthie. 'Is that right? Is that what you want to do?'

The green people stopped singing. Ten and Friz were working their way through powers of two, 'Four thousand and ninety six, yes, that's right. What's next? Break it down, Friz.'

All the green people spoke at once, different voices, the same words.

'We mean you no harm. We want you to enjoy eternal life. We want you to join us.' They all turned to look at Maia as one, unblinking, staring, focused. 'We want you to share your minds with us, to give us your thoughts, to keep us new, to fill us with fresh knowledge.' More than twenty heads twisted in Slip's direction. 'But you can give us more. You have already given us more. Each of you has already left something of yourselves in our earth, something that nourishes us, that feeds us. We thank you for your gifts. But we need more.'

'What do they mean?' Ten asked. 'What have we given them?'

Shard shrugged. 'We've left nothing behind.'

'Oh yes we have,' Slip said. His words rushed from his mouth. 'Useless facts, Friz always tells me I remember useless facts, we saw a TV programme on plants and propagation and they were talking about fertiliser and . . . We've been fertilising the Forest every time we've been to the loo. We've even dug it in when we've made latrine trenches.'

'You speak truly, boy,' the green people said, and it was as if the Forest was speaking with its own voice. 'Your wastes contain much that is rare and nutritious, save that of the monster who travels with you.'

'I think they mean you, Shard,' Slip said.

'Then I am pleased to be a monster, to be rejected.'

The green people continued to speak together in a single voice. 'We thank you for your gifts. But we need more. You will sleep, you must sleep, and when you do I will invite your minds, your thoughts, your memories to join me. No-one declines the invitation to join the Forest. And then, when your body is no longer necessary to your existence, the Forest will absorb your body, take its nutrients, leave only your frame.'

'The skeletons,' Shard said. 'Only the skeletons remain.'

'Tha's a lie,' Ruthie said. 'Thoughts an' mem'ries remain. I'm the Forest. But I'm also Ruthie. I c'n speak with ma own mind. I c'n think. I c'n even move.'

Until that moment the green people had remained where they'd grown, rooted to the spot. But then, in a parody of a walk, Ruthie lifted one foot from the ground and placed it delicately a short distance ahead of her. Then she moved her other foot, taking a small step towards Slip. Another step moved her a little closer to him. 'Join me, boy Slip,' she said, holding out bone framed leafy arms to him, 'I'll welcome you.'

All the green people followed Ruthie's example, took faltering steps forward, arms outstretched. Shard reacted first. A single stroke from her sword easily removed the head of the nearest figure. It halted briefly, then continued to stagger forward.

'They don't move fast enough to do any harm,' Tom called out.'

'Unless they surround you,' Ten added. 'And haven't you heard of poisonous plants? Or stinging nettles? I wouldn't let them get too close if I was you.'

'We're being blocked in,' Shard said, 'look behind.'

The path through the trees had already been blocked. Now a fence of tall saplings growing close together prevented any retreat to the meadow.

'I can cut my way through,' Shard yelled, 'get ready to follow.'

'There's no point,' Maia shouted back, 'there'll be more beyond that. It got us here, It's not going to let us go.'

The saplings were now more like a wall than a fence, a circular wall that was tightening, constricting, pushing them closer and closer to the old tree. Its worn, ribbed bark seemed suddenly threatening, hard and sharp ridged. Its branches were like claws, reaching out for them, trying to drag them into its grasp.

'The old tree,' Slip cried, 'we're being herded towards the tree.'

'Pencil,' Maia said, 'let me look at the Map again.' Pencil shuffled closer, took the book from her pack and opened it for Maia. Their position was marked, as usual, by a faint blue circle. 'As near as I can tell we're in the middle of the Forest,' Maia said, 'and this tree marks its centre. Is it the original tree? Is it the first tree in the Forest? If it is, it's very old.'

Pencil stared at the Map. 'Maia,' she said, 'I think I can see . . .'

'Not now, Pencil, I have to think. We've found only one way into the forest, the way we came in, and the Map shows no other doorways. That doesn't make sense, Shard, surely every land in the Emperorium has more than one way in or out?'

'Every land I've entered has many doorways, Maia. But we're being pushed closer to the tree. I think I ought to cut our way out. Make some of this wood deadwood.' Shard raised her sword again, stepped forward and easily cut down several of the saplings coming closest to them. But beyond was a solid wall of other similar growth; the trees hadn't been moving towards them, they'd been sending up new, rapidly growing shoots.

'The tree,' Slip yelled, 'attack the tree! It's the heart of the Forest.'

'It's too big,' Shard said, 'I'll only be able to cut through its bark.'

'Maia,' Pencil said again, tugged at Maia's sleeve, 'you should look at the Map.'

'Sixty five thousand, five hundred and thirty six!'

'The bark! That's it! That's how trees get nutrients from the ground, through the bark.' Slip took out his own knife, began digging at the tree trunk. 'Cut away the bark all the way round the trunk, a thin band is all we need, and the tree can't survive. Everyone! Do it!'

No-one moved. Even the green people ceased their swaying, even the sapling wall stopped its advance for a moment.

'Do it!' Maia said.

As knives and swords rose and fell, as the thick fibrous bark was slowly cut away, as the wall began moving and the green people slipped forward, Pencil grabbed Maia's arm. 'Look,' she hissed, 'I need you to look at the Map! Not later! Now!' She was still holding it open to show the faint blue circle in the centre of the Forest. But flickering into existence, touching the blue with faint red, was another circle. 'I think it's a doorway,' Pencil said.

'But where is it?' Maia asked. 'Why can't we see it?'

Pencil glanced up at the canopy of the tree. 'It must be up there! It's not real, Maia, it's like a room with a high ceiling. There's nothing says a gateway has to be in a wall. I can climb up and look if you want.'

Pencil was the smallest of them and the nimblest. Maia nodded urgently. 'Be careful, though,' she said. 'Shout down, let me know what you find.' She yelled to the others, 'The Map says there's a gateway right here, Pencil's gone to check out the upper branches of the tree!'

Pencil seemed to find it easy to climb the rough bark, and there were many branches to make her passage easy. She was soon hidden by the leaves and branches.

The green people were prompted by Maia's words, or by seeing Pencil climb, or perhaps the tree had felt her movement through its branches and was communicating with them; they looked upwards as one. Then they retreated, their backs pressed against the wall of saplings, save for Ruthie, still standing as close to Slip as she could. 'The Forest don't wanna lose ya,' she said, 'I don't wanna lose ya.'

'Can't you see,' Slip shouted, 'we don't want to be part of your great commune of vegetables! Let us go!'

'I want . . . I want . . . '

'It doesn't matter what you want.'

'He hurt me. The Forest saved me.'

'You owe the Forest nothing,' Maia interjected, 'the Forest kept you here, took your thoughts and memories. You've given it more than it's given you.'

Ruthie swayed from side to side, lowered her arms. 'If the forest cain't have yer minds, it'll have yer bodies.' She swayed again. 'I wish ya no harm.' Her head turned to look at the other green people who had been absorbed by the wall except for their arms, now whip thin. 'The Forest wishes to harm y'all. Beware.'

Maia followed Ruthie's gaze. The green people no longer existed. Their bones had fallen to the ground, the remnants of their arms, flexed branches, had been pulled back and were covered in black thorns. 'Watch out, looks like darts heading our way!' Maia warned. Shard was the first to look up, the first to react. One sweep of her sword cut down most of the armed branches. She spun around, pulled her comrades roughly to her, held out her leather coat like a shield to protect them. The remaining branches hurled their thorns in the direction of the Bazhka; their accuracy was poor but there were many of them, a handful struck the tree trunk above their heads, some fell to the ground, the majority embedded themselves in Shard's leather coat. One or two hit Shard's exposed hands.

Tom picked up one of the thorns from the ground. 'It's tipped with something,' he said, 'a liquid of some type. Do you think it's poisonous?'

'I know it,' Shard replied. 'But the Forest isn't interested in killing me, after all, I'm a monster and my body can't feed it, so I doubt it can make any poison that would affect me. But it would be lethal if any of you were hit.'

The wall was moving closer again, growing more thorns. Shard shrugged herself out of her coat. 'If they fire again, get under this,' she said before attacking the wall again, trying to remove the thorn-bearing branches. But the Forest was learning. Each sweep of the Bazhka's sword revealed thorns growing well behind the front of the wall, beyond even her reach.

'There's a door!' came Pencil's scream from above, 'I can see a door!'

'Your turn,' Shard said to Maia, picked her up and pushed her as high into the branches of the tree as possible. 'Go!'

Maia did as she was told, hurried into the heights of the tree. It was taller than she'd imagined, the branches old and twisted, at times helping her on her way, at times hindering her. She could hear the yells and shouts from below, Shard urging the others to shelter when she felt a flight of thorns might be unleashed, Slip encouraging them to cut away more bark. From above Pencil tried to hurry her, impatience in her voice. But Maia didn't want to fall and the dizzying glimpses she had of the tops of the trees around her showed her that any slip might be fatal.

'I can see you,' Pencil cried, 'not far to go.' Maia pushed her way past a tangle of thin branches and she was there, beside Pencil in the rocking canopy of the tree. 'Up there,' Pencil pointed, 'there's a door in the sky.'

There were a few large branches to stand on or hold onto, but still she felt insecure and anxious. She tried looking up but the very action made her feel sick and lightheaded. 'I need you to hold on to me,' she said to Pencil, 'just to hold me still.'

Pencil reached out. 'I'm sitting on quite a big branch,' she said, 'it'll hold both our weights.' She pulled Maia towards her, held her closely round the waist. Maia still felt uneasy but managed to look up. Directly above her head the sky was grey-blue and faded into the far distance. 'I can't see anything,' she said, 'no door, no handle.'

'There,' Pencil pointed again, 'a keyhole.'

Maia focused once more. A small dot of darkness resolved into something larger that was most definitely a keyhole. And once her eyes were fixed on that, the door itself became apparent, a square of painted wooden boards, and next to it a handle. But she was sure they were too high above her head to reach. 'I don't think my arms are long enough,' she said, 'even if I stretch. Even if I could stand up with you holding my ankles I couldn't reach.'

Pencil leaned forward. 'Shard,' she screamed, 'we need your help!'

At the base of the trunk Shard heard Pencil call out. She was trying to keep the thorns at bay and her skin was peppered with the ineffectual pinpricks of the spines, darkening her white hair. Slip, who had taken charge of the attack on the tree, had heard Pencil shout too. 'Just go,' he yelled, 'Ten and Friz can hold your coat, Tom and I will keep cutting.' He was so focused on his task he didn't see the ease with which Shard leaped for the lower branches, he didn't see how quickly she moved on and up.

'We're not going to do this,' Tom said, 'we're going too slowly.' He was dripping with sweat and his hands were cut and bleeding where his knife had slipped, or where sharp fragments of wood or bark had cut his skin. Slip checked their progress; they'd removed a narrow layer of bark about six inches wide, but only from around a third of the circumference of the tree.

'At the moment we're trying to gain time for Maia,' Slip said. 'If there's a doorway up above she needs to get through it.'

'So we're collateral damage?'

'We're pawns in the game, Tom, pawns in the game.' Slip laughed. 'But we always have been.'

'Yeah. Suppose you're right.'

'Swap after the next incoming?' Ten asked, Shard's coat held high to protect them all.

'I'm okay for the moment,' Slip said. 'I just need to . . .' He stopped, then began again, excitedly. 'Something strange here, Tom. Bark's off but the wood beneath sounds hollow. If I can just push hard . . .' He sat down, making sure he was still in the shadow of Shard's coat, braced his legs against the tree trunk and shoved hard. There was some movement so he kicked and kicked again, was rewarded by the wood cracking and breaking. He swivelled round, stared at the hole he'd just made. 'Tom, look at this.'

Tom crawled to join him.

'Listen you two,' he said to Friz and Ten, 'it looks to me as if the whole tree's hollow.'

'Can't be,' said Ten, 'it's too big.'

'It was being supported from the inside. Can you see what's happening, Tom?'

Tom peered into the inside of the tree-trunk. 'Slip's right,' he said, 'the tree's hollow. But there were roots holding everything up, making a sort of internal cylinder, just like the saplings used in the wall.'

'The wall's coming closer,' Friz shouted. 'The wall and the tree and us will soon be incredibly good friends!'

'But the inner support is going! The roots or whatever they are, they're disappearing back into the earth! There'll be nothing left to hold the tree up!'

The tree groaned and creaked, shuddered heavily.

'But why?' Ten and Friz were backing towards Tom and Slip. Friz almost fell over Slip's outstretched foot. 'The tree's where the Forest started,' Friz said, 'it's the oldest part. The tree was the Forest to start with.'

'But now the tree is only a small part of the Forest. And the Forest knows what's happening, it knows Maia and Pencil and Shard are escaping, it's doing the only thing it can do to bring them down. It's collapsing the tree.' Slip looked up. 'The only question now is, which way will it fall?'

Shard reached the top of the tree far more quickly than Pencil or Maia. She looked skyward, immediately made out the gateway. 'I'll lift you,' she said to Maia, 'then you can use the key to open the door. I'll pass Pencil up to you as soon as it's open.'

The tree shook and trembled.

'What's happening?' Maia asked.

'I don't know, but we don't have much time.' Shard reached out to lift Maia.

'No! No, Shard, I'll fall. The tree's moving and jolting, you'll have to stand on the branch here and you won't be able to keep your balance. We should go down, be with the others.'

Shard grinned. 'We'd be no use to the others, this is what they'd want. And you won't fall because I won't fall. Look.'

From around her waist she unwound a long piece of what looked like thick leather which wrapped itself around the branch.

'A tail?' Pencil exclaimed. 'Oh, I'd love one of those.'

Shard winked at Pencil, judged the distance to the door. 'I don't think even I can jump that far.' She quickly braced her feet against the branch. 'Let's do it,' she said. Maia climbed up Shard's knees and legs, up her body until she was standing on her shoulders, Shard's hands gripping her ankles. She took the key from around her neck and raised it upwards. It was still some distance from the lock.

'I can't do it,' Maia said. 'It's no good, I just can't reach.'

'You can if I help,' Pencil yelled. The tree was lurching from side to side, but that didn't prevent Pencil from following Maia, crawling carefully up Shard's body, hands entwined in fabric and hair. 'Can you do this?' she whispered in the Bazhka's ear. Shard nodded once. 'You are my lovely Bazhka,' Pencil said, rose higher to sit on Shard's broad shoulder. 'I'll take your place,' she said to Maia, 'then you climb up me just as you climbed up Shard. I'm stronger than you think, I can hold you. Then you can reach the lock.'

Despite Maia's doubts she found herself giving way, letting Pencil stand on Shard's shoulders, her hands gripping the Bazhka's horns. She judged that, with Pencil's extra height, she should be able to reach the lock and open the door. Pencil made a stirrup with her hands but, just as Maia put her foot in them, there was a loud crack and the tree staggered to one side, paused, then began to swing back in the other direction like a pendulum.

'This is it,' Shard yelled, 'only one chance. Don't miss!'

'Up!' Pencil grunted. 'Now!'

Maia climbed, stood on Pencil's shoulders, felt the girl's hands grip her ankles, watched as the door swung dizzily toward her. She held up the key, felt the surge of strength as it passed close to and, even if it didn't touch, engage with the lock. And the door fell open, downwards, knocked Maia's clutching hand to one side, knocked her sideways so that Pencil's hands lost their grip, and Maia could feel herself falling.

She fell only as far as Shard allowed her to fall. The Bazhka's outstretched outsized hand caught her ankle and she hung upside down, the world twisting and turning beneath her as the tree began its death throes, gyrating to one side and the other. In one dizzy, sickening spin Maia could see that the doorway was there, it was open, but it was now beyond their reach. 'We can't do it,' Maia yelled, 'we'll have to go back down!'

'Not yet!' Shard shouted as the tree spun back. They approached the gateway again, too far to reach, too far to jump, Maia felt Shard's muscles tense then suddenly relax. 'No,' she said, 'no, you can't. You . . .' The Bazhka flexed one huge, strong arm, drew it back, and hurled Maia skywards. She felt herself spin in the air, the gateway revolved around her, growing larger, getting closer. Maia's head and shoulders were through the opening before she knew it, her knees and then her back slammed against the sky-painted surround, but she scrabbled and pulled herself through the opening. She turned quickly, looked down on Shard doing the same with Pencil, but this time, as the Bazhka let go of her human slingshot, the tree fell again. It was Maia's turn to take drastic action. There was a handle on the inside of the door, she leaped out of the opening, both hands grabbing the cold metal arch, spread her legs to make herself as big a target as possible. Pencil hit her rather than caught her, knocked Maia's breath from her body, almost made her lose her grip. Almost, but not quite.

'Crawl up me,' Maia said, and Pencil did so quickly, without looking down. Then she hung over the opening to pull Maia up.

'Quick,' Pencil said, 'get ready.'

The treetop was drawing jagged shapes against the background of the Forest floor far below, Shard holding grimly to the topmost branch. 'I don't think she'll be able to do it,' Pencil said, 'it's too far.'

'Then we do it the easy way,' Maia said, 'look.' Pencil scuttled backwards to see Maia pointing at a rope ladder coiled neatly behind her. She kicked it through the open trapdoor and watched it unfurl, saw the look of incredulous relief on Shard's face, watched the Bazhka judge the distance as the ladder flew towards her, saw her leap and find the last, the bottom rung even as the tree beneath her toppled and fell to the Forest floor.

Pencil and Maia helped Shard through the door. She clambered to safety, sat back and let out a low moan of pain.

'We made it,' Maia whispered.

'Thank you, lovely Bazhka,' Pencil added, her hands stroking the fur around Shard's muzzle.

'We made it,' Shard agreed. 'But others didn't.'

They looked down. Amongst the shattered debris of the fallen tree, the fractured limbs and broken branches, the litter of leaves and cloud of dust, several figures were visible. They lay on the ground. None of them moved.

'Ropes,' Maia said, 'surely we have ropes? We can go down the ropes and . . .'

'Our ropes are down there,' Shard said. 'Even if they were up here, they wouldn't reach the ground. Even if they're alive down there, we can't help them.'

'No!' Maia said, 'I won't leave them! They bought us time, we can't just let them die!' She reached for the top of the rope ladder, tried to climb down it, but Shard pulled her back and threw her to one side. Her lips were pulled back, teeth barred in an angry snarl. Maia scrambled away from her. Shard pulled up the rope ladder, drew the trapdoor closed. A square of light appeared high above them, as if they were at the bottom of a steep stairway.

'We owe it to them to go on. There's no point in staying here.' Shard climbed to her feet. 'Are you ready?'

Maia began to weep, tears fell copiously from her red-rimmed eyes and Pencil hugged her close, murmured meaningless sounds to her. When Maia stopped shuddering and shaking, when she was once more in control of her breathing, Pencil used her sleeve to wipe Maia's eyes. 'Shard's right,' she whispered, 'we need to move. We have a job to do. Come on.' She helped Maia stand, smiled grimly. Together they followed Shard, began the long climb to the fragment of daylight high above them.

Tom blinked. He was confused, unsure where he was, unable to recall why he was lying down. But his arms and legs ached, his neck was stiff and sore, and his skin was alive with a faint touch of softness, of gentle electricity. He could see little above him, he appeared to be caged in by twisted, broken branches. He tried to lift his head but there was an elastic resistance, as if he was being held down. That was when he remembered that the tree had collapsed, its hollow core unable to sustain its own weight; and that was when he panicked. He was being held down, that was what the Forest did, and it intended insinuating itself into his mouth, his eyes, his ears, his nose . . . His head cleared suddenly and he thrust himself upwards, tore strands of grass and fibrous creepers from his body as he did so. 'Wake up!' he shouted. 'Where are you? Wake up!'

Slip was already conscious, confused like Tom, but climbing to his feet. 'What happened?' he asked. His face was scratched and bleeding.

'The tree came down.'

'The Forest brought the tree down, you mean.' Slip looked around at the ruins of the fallen tree. 'At least the poisoned darts have gone. But . . . Where's Ten? And Friz?'

'I don't know. You look for them. I need to find out if Maia and Pencil and Shard came down too.' He climbed up onto the trunk, headed to where the tree's crown ought to have been. The way was treacherous. Boughs had been snapped by the fall, torn from the trunk leaving stubs of sharp timber projecting at awkward angles. Thinner branches had been bent and twisted around each other, slowing Tom's progress. He made his way carefully using hands as well as feet, looking out and around as he did so, hoping that he wouldn't see Maia lying broken on the ground, Pencil tangled in the wreckage, Shard twisted in the undergrowth.

The tree's descent had crushed part of the wall of saplings that had surrounded them, penned them in, but they were already recovering and creeping onto and over the trunk. Tom kicked them away as he passed though he was aware that this was more to vent his anger and helplessness than to hold back the vegetation's spread. If Maia and the others had passed through a doorway at the top of the tree then it was now inaccessible to those left behind; if Maia, Pencil and Shard were safe, then the Forest would be even more determined to claim those remaining on the ground.

The trunk grew thinner as Tom moved along it. Long grass and tendrils of creeper were climbing over it, threading themselves into the fibrous bare wood where bark had been scraped away. 'Maia!' Tom shouted, 'Pencil! Are you there? Shard! Are you okay?' There was no reply. Tom climbed hand over hand up a branch that remained attached to the main trunk. From his vantage point he could see, a long distance behind him, the tree's roots clawing at the sky. The clearing which had greeted them only a few short hours before was smaller, the vegetation crowding in on the dead tree.

Tom looked up at the sky. It seemed like any other sky, blue flecked with grey and white, clouds fighting each other at the horizon, bad weather on the way. There was no sign of a doorway, but Tom had to assume that Maia, Pencil and Shard had escaped.

'Tom! We need you!'

Tom saw Slip where he himself had climbed near the roots, perched on the trunk, waving. 'Ten's hurt,' Slip yelled, 'broken leg, I think. Friz's got cuts.'

'No sign of the girls,' Tom shouted back, 'I'm on my way!' He hurried as fast as he could, frightened now; the grey trunk was being invaded by a carpet of aggressive verdant green. He found Slip crouched beside a pale faced Ten covered by Shard's coat. Friz was on her feet, trudging a slow square around the borders of the coat to prevent it being invaded. She was bleeding from a large gash on her forehead, but when Tom twitched aside the coat he could see that Ten was in far greater need. His leg just below the knee was bent at a peculiar angle, the bone had pierced the flesh, and Ten was barely conscious.

'What do we do?' Slip asked.

'To be honest I'm not sure it matters. We're under attack, there's nowhere to escape to.' Tom sat down with his back against the tree trunk, idly watched leaves beginning to grow over his legs. 'I don't know what to do, Slip. Maia seems to have escaped, but I can't see any way out for us. Perhaps we should just lie down and wait for the inevitable.'

Slip was aghast. 'You don't really mean that?'

'Why not? Can you think of anything?'

'Fight till the end?'

'I think the end's already here.'

There was a movement from Shard's coat, Ten's hand appeared from beneath it an beckoned Tom closer. Tom bent down to hear Ten's whispered word, one word only. 'Coward.'

It was enough. Tom fought off his lethargy, took out his sword and began hacking at the new growth around him. 'Friz,' he said, 'do what you can to one side. Slip, take the rear. We go down fighting.'

After a few minutes it became clear that the wall of new saplings was being reformed. It would only be a matter of time until they grew thorns again, and while the survivors were sheltering from that onslaught beneath Shard's coat, they couldn't continue to cut away at the insidious creepers crawling around their feet.

A familiar shape rose from the ground in front of Slip. 'I know how t' git out, boy Slip.'

Slip's machete was already falling as the words entered his brain. He tried to stop the blow but it was too late; the machete cut deeply into the wood and bone of Ruthie's shoulder, lodged there. The shock of the blow numbed his hand, he let go of the handle. Ruthie reached round with her other hand and grasped the machete, levered it to and fro until her shoulder blade was almost cut in two, but the machete came free. She raised it high above her head, then brought it down, slowly, reversed the grip, handed it back to Slip. 'I'll show ya how t' git out. But ya hev t' take me with ya.'

'Slip,' Tom yelled,' what are you doing?'

'Ruthie says she knows a way out.'

'What? And you trust her? She's part of the Forest!'

'Why would you help us escape?' Slip asked, cutting at the saplings growing towards him. His arms were tired, he could barely move.

'The tree was th'oldest part o' the Forest, but th' Forest killed th' tree. I cain't feel the tree no more. The Forest killed th' tree an' it'd do the same t' me. I c'n . . . free myself. I have . . . free will. But I cain't survive by myself. I need you. You need me.'

Slip looked around him. Tom was tiring, Friz was barely able to move and Ten had lapsed into a sweating, head-tossing unconsciousness. 'My friend is hurt.'

'Y'r friend'll die. You too'll die.' Ruthie's head turned towards the wall just behind Tom, a branch of thorns was arming itself, pulling back to fire. 'Tom!' Slip yelled, 'Drop!' Tom dropped to the ground and the thorns flew over his head. But Slip hadn't noticed another row of thorns aimed directly at him, even as he turned and saw them he realised it would be too late to avoid them. He lifted an arm to stop them hitting his eyes and head and felt . . . only the slight touch of leaves. Ruthie had moved in front of him; all the thorns had hit her, harmlessly.

'Where do we go?' he barked.

''Neath th' roots.'

'Show me!'

Ruthie slid behind him and ducked easily beneath the fibrous white roots of the tree. 'Tom, Friz, this way!' Slip shouted, grabbed the edge of Shard's coat and tugged Ten after Ruthie. Friz did as she was told; Tom was more reluctant, but when he saw another regiment of thorns appearing he lost no time and slid into the gap beneath the roots.

As soon as he saw Ruthie's green form he lifted his blade. 'I think something needs pruning,' he said.

'No!' Slip's voice was assertive, Tom had no choice but to lower his axe. 'She saved me,' Slip said.

'She's a bunch of greenery and human bones, and she's part of the Forest.'

'And she said she'd help us escape.'

'Where to? Look, Slip, the weeds are already following us.'

Leaves were covering the gaps between the roots. Grass was sliding after them as if it could sense them. Coiled spring tendrils beckoned with curled come-here fingers.

'Boy-Slip, boy-Tom. Here's y'r way out.' Ruthie had moved further into the shadow of the tree's tap-root and was pointing downwards. Slip moved closer; he could smell the leaves and fresh-earth aroma of Ruthie's body. Beyond her outstretched arm a tunnel lead down to an old round-topped wooden door.

'She was right,' Slip cried excitedly, 'it's a doorway.' He grabbed Tom's sleeve, shoved him down the tunnel. 'There's only room for one at a time, you take the front, pull Ten after you. Friz, you follow, keep your eye on Ten, make sure he doesn't fall off. Then me.' He looked back the way he'd come, there was no retreat now, the space beneath the roots was filling with new grown shoots and branches and, beyond them, shadowy, re-formed green people. 'Come on, Ruthie,' he said, 'you're part of a different team now.'

Friz was forced to hold onto the rear of Shard's coat as Tom slid down the steep tunnel, and Ten's moaning intensified each time he was dragged over a lump of earth or knotted root. When Tom reached the door he hurled himself at it, it swung open immediately and he tumbled into a windowless room with a hard-packed earth floor. He found his feet and went back, pulled Ten after him, helped Friz who collapsed onto the floor beside Ten, then hurried back again. He could see Slip at the top of the tunnel, still cutting and chopping at branches, Ruthie's shadow close behind him.

'It opened,' he shouted, 'we're through! Come on!'

He watched as Slip and Ruthie negotiated the slope, saw the green people beyond. He pulled them through the door and slammed it shut behind them, heard the rapid repetitive

273

snicking of thorns burying themselves in the wood. 'There's no way of locking it,' he warned, 'we need to move on quickly.'

'They daren't foller,' Ruthie said, 'the Forest fears what it don't know.'

'Does anyone have a torch?' Slip asked.

'In my pack,' Tom said, 'which is glued to my back by layers of sweat.' He groaned as he manoeuvred it to the ground, felt for the torch inside, then switched it on. A warm glow lit up their dirty faces. It shone on the walls and ceiling around the door, though its beam didn't reveal anything of the way ahead.

'Oh dear,' Slip said.

Tom smiled. 'Don't worry, we'll find someone to help Ten. Nothing can be worse than being back there.'

'Oh dear,' Slip said again. He held up his hand. Embedded in the flesh between his knuckle and his wrist was a single thorn, and the veins on the back of his hand and running up his arm were already turning black.

TWELVE

'Oh dear,' cried Pawquine. His eyes darted to and fro beneath furrowed brows, his shoulders twitched spasmodically, his hands squeezed each other so tightly they turned pale as his ashen face. 'What do we do now, Grovelle?' His voice was trembling.

Grovelle was in a similar state of panic. If it hadn't felt so unseemly, so embarrassing, so very wrong, he would have clung to Pawquine for both company and safety. 'I'm not sure, Pawquine,' he whispered. 'I'm not even sure what happened.'

They were standing in front of the Emperorium. The door was open and clouds of dust billowed out. On the far side of the square the bakery was roofless, flames dancing in the bones of its charred rafters and blackened joists. Bricks and rubble littered the street. The statues were lying on their sides, broken and shattered.

'There was a creature,' Pawquine whimpered. 'I recall a creature. Do tell me I remember correctly, Grovelle.'

'Two creatures, Pawquine. Blue. They wanted to . . .' he gulped and swallowed, 'they wanted to . . . to kill us. And eat us.'

Pawquine sucked his bottom lip into his mouth. His neck disappeared beneath his grubby suit collar as he tried to make himself look smaller. 'Have they gone?' He sniffed and wiped his eyes with the sleeve of his jacket.

Grovelle took a step towards his larger companion; if anything wanted to eat them he would seem a less tasty morsel if the bulkier, fatter Pawquine was close by for comparison. He looked around nervously. 'I think they've gone. I can't see them.' His slicked hair had fallen over his pale face but he made no move to pull it away. 'I think,' he added, his voice trembling, 'that if they'd still been here . . . we wouldn't be alive.'

'I think that too,' Pawquine concurred. 'Oh, Grovelle . . .' He began to cry. Grovelle gave in to the inevitable, stepped closer, held out his arms, and the large, blubbering frame of Pawquine collapsed into them.

They comforted each other.

They were interrupted by the sound of distant sirens.

'Police,' said Pawquine.

'And fire engines,' Grovelle added, nodding in the direction of the bakery.

'No doubt there'll be ambulances too.'

'And television reporters. Perhaps it would be best if we weren't here when they arrived.'

'I think it's too late for that,' Pawquine said. They both looked up as the unmistakeable sound of a helicopter announced its own imminent arrival. They turned their backs and closed their eyes as the clattering dragonfly-blue machine landed in the centre of the square. A hunched figure leaped from its open door and hurried towards them, straightening as it came nearer. It became a thin middle-aged man dressed in a creased T-shirt, a sleeveless padded jacket whose pockets were bulging with hidden treasures, and sagging jogger bottoms which he hitched up around his waist every few steps. He wore a knitted hat pulled down over his ears, almost covering his black-rimmed, thick-lensed glasses. Around his neck at least three identity cards dangled from tangled lanyards. He stopped a few feet in front of Grovelle and Pawquine who wilted under his disapproving gaze. He put his hands on his hips.

'Well? he said. 'Care to explain?'

They began to speak together, their voices overlapping.

'It's not our fault, Nic . . .'

'Strange blue creatures, Nic . . . Frightening!'

'Terrifying!'

'Horrifying!'

'Klein, we went to see Klein . . .'

'Said they'd eat us!'

'We didn't do anything!'

The man called Nic lost his patience. 'Shut up!' he said firmly, not shouting, but with authority and aggravation combined which silenced the two older men. 'I *saw* what happened,' he said, pointing at each corner of the square. 'CCTV. So I don't want a *description*. I want an *explanation*.'

'Oh no,' Grovelle said, 'CCTV? Has anyone else . . ?'

'Even as we speak,' Nic said, 'the evidence is being wiped.'

'Wiped?' Pawquine asked.

'Yes, wiped. Completely. No record.' There was a pause, long enough for Pawquine and Grovelle to hear each of the carefully chosen words that followed. 'That is, gentlemen, no record save for the single copy which I will retain for the purposes of . . . shall we say, security.' Nic smiled. He didn't smile very often but, when he did, he resembled a hyena. And neither Pawquine nor Grovelle were left with any doubt that the security he spoke of was his, not theirs.

A police car sped into the far side of the square, lights flashing. It screeched to a halt in front of the shattered bakery. Nic pulled a mobile from one of his pockets, selected one of his identity cards and held it close to the phone. 'Police Commissioner here,' he said, 'I'm outside the Emperorium, minor damage here but the bakery's suffered. Set up cordons, keep the public away. There may be casualties.'

The police car was followed by two fire engines. Nic took out another mobile from a different pocket, swapped identity cards. 'Honorary Acting Chief Fire Officer here,' he said, 'priority is the bakery, normal procedures. Fire control, check for injuries and fatalities, suspected gas explosion.' He glared at Pawquine and Grovelle, raised his eyebrows so they disappeared under his hat, reinforcing the fact that he was in charge and that they should remember what he was saying.

Nic changed phones and cards again as an ambulance swept into the square. 'Senior Public Health Officer here, at least one fatality suspected. Move with caution under police guard, possibility of terrorism event.'

He switched back to the police phone. 'New information, lads, high probability of terrorism event, news blackout until we have further information, code red, I say again, code red.' He repeated the same information, with small variations, into each of his phones, then took out a fourth. 'Briony, code red emergency, set up a news conference for,' he checked his watch, 'two hours time in City Hall. Have each of my Deputies of Police, Fire and Health attend my office in 90 minutes for a briefing so they can run the conference. Mayor Pawquine will not attend, nor will Deputy Mayor Grovelle, they're with me at the scene of the incident. They've acted as first responders, they're shaken, some minor injuries, they can't appear in front of the cameras yet. Unattributed comments say they're heroes. I'll be in touch. Thank you.'

Pawquine felt his arms and head, looked at his legs. 'My suit's a little battered,' he said, 'but I don't think either of us, *de facto*, has any injuries, minor or otherwise.'

Nic inhaled deeply. Then he launched a kick at Pawquine's shin. 'You have now,' he muttered.

'I think I've found a very bruised arm,' Grovelle announced, taking a step back, watching Pawquine hop up and down in pain.

'Good. Think what I would've had to do if I'd told Briony you were seriously hurt.' He took a deep breath; his smile returned. 'The bakery and its explosion are being managed. Now, should we see what's been happening in the Emperorium?' He looked at Pawquine. 'And stop complaining,' he growled, 'or I'll kick you again, harder and higher!'

Grovelle led the way into the Emperorium, hesitantly, eyes shifting rapidly from one side to the other. Pawquine minced painfully after him. Nic pushed them both forward, peering over their shoulders.

'No fires,' Nic said, 'only superficial damage. But we can still claim the building's in danger of complete collapse.'

'Why would we do that?' Pawquine asked.

Nic sighed, a patient teacher admonishing a naughty child. 'Did you inherit your stupidity, Mr Pawquine, or did you learn it at that ridiculously expensive school you went to? No, don't answer! It was probably both. Grovelle, you're as devious as a sack of weasels, tell him what's happening.'

'Safety?' Grovelle suggested. 'If the building's in danger of collapse then we demolish it for safety's sake?'

'Give the Grovelle a lollipop.'

A smile illuminated Pawquine's face. 'I see! Then it's all *pro bono publico*! Cripes, Nic, I don't know how we'd manage without you.'

'You wouldn't.' He looked past Pawquine, surveyed what had once been the general sales area of the Emperorium. 'We might have a problem here. Any comments, gentlemen?'

They stopped in their tracks. Inside a glowing sarcophagus of shimmering, translucent green light sat Madame Klein in a leather armchair, at her feet the body of a man. Neither of them was moving.

'Mayor Pawquine,' Nic said, 'please would you furnish yourself with a piece of wood. Deputy Mayor Grovelle, you'll need a small stone. A piece of brick will do.'

Pawquine cast around for a length of broken timber; Grovelle didn't have to look far to find half a brick.

279

'You first, Mr Grovelle. Please throw your missile at the green object.'

Grovelle tossed the brick underarm. It arced onto the top of its target and disintegrated in a shower of sparks.

'Hmm,' Nic said, 'this will be rather expensive. Your turn, Mayor Pawquine. If you wouldn't mind stepping a little closer, then try to poke the green barrier with your piece of wood.'

'What?' Pawquine jabbed his wood in the direction of Grovelle. 'He just had to throw his rock. Why do I have to get close to the thing? Why do I have to touch it with this very short piece of wood?'

'Because you're expendable,' Nic said. 'If anything happens to you then I can replace you with a pig in a suit and no-one will know the difference.'

Grovelle sniggered.

'Whereas, if Mr Grovelle here suffers an early demise, I would find it far more difficult to secure the services of a venal baboon newly rescued from an oil-slick. Now please, just do it.'

Pawquine held out the piece of wood at arm's length and slowly moved it forward. When it met the green haze its tip blackened and flamed. Pawquine, entranced, kept pushing. When only a few inches of wood remained Nic pulled him back. 'Very expensive,' he whispered. He brought out yet another phone.

'Gyorgi! Nic here. I need your advice. Are you still running that concrete shuttering business? Yes? Good, I need a job doing quickly and confidentially. It's for our mutual friends Pawquine and Grovelle. No, it's not for free, they'll pay the going rate plus a sizeable amount for the aforementioned confidentiality. Steel framework, concrete shutters, you'll need to build a sort of room, a box about six feet square. A door? Why would I need a door? No, I wouldn't need to put bodies inside it, Gyorgi, they're already there.' He sighed. 'Yes Gyorgi, I do appreciate the irony of it, we'll both know where the other has buried the bodies.' He closed his eyes, held the phone away from his ear until the loud laughter had ceased. 'On more thing, Gyorgi. It could be dangerous, you need men who are experienced in decommissioning and entirely trustworthy. Or replaceable. I'll give you the information later. Yes, give my love to Katyusha. Cheers.'

Grovelle had been listening while Pawquine sought a longer piece of wood with which to explore the green barrier. 'Decommissioning?' Grovelle moved behind Pawquine.' Do you think that green thingy might be radioactive?'

'No,' Nic said, 'I got the helicopter to fly over it with a geiger spot meter just before I landed. If there'd been any danger like that I would have sent you two in and waited a safe distance away.' He turned on his heels. 'Come on, I need you to check some visuals.'

He took them outside. A police cordon had been erected all around the square but a large black truck without number plates had been allowed through and waited for them, squat and threatening. A door opened as they approached and three steps snaked down to the ground.

'Does the Municipality pay for this? 'Pawquine asked as he peered inside at the banks of monitors and computers. Four black-clothed operators, earpieces and microphones fixed to their heads, murmured gently.

'Indirectly,' Nic said. 'I believe a government grant for school computers bought the contents. The vehicle was donated by friends in the arms trade. Ongoing costs are met by investment interest. Best you don't know the businesses providing the rather excellent returns on the very reasonable capital.' He climbed in after Pawquine and Grovelle and snapped his fingers. 'Fatalities,' he said, and pointed at one of the monitors where a picture of Tom's mother appeared. 'Mrs Vogt. Bakery owner. No problem dealing with deaths, all we need do is find a plausible explanation.'

'You're very good at that,' Pawquine said.

'And you're a slimy sycophant. A larger problem might be those missing. No bodies, you see. Dead bodies are good.' He snapped his fingers again. 'Any idea who this is?'

A fuzzy video of Maia appeared on the screen, walking across the square from the bakery. The image froze.

'Madame Klein's helper,' Grovelle said, 'rather an unpleasant young lady. Her first name's Maia, that's all I know.'

'Maia? Spelling? No, you won't know, it doesn't matter.' Nic turned to one of the operatives. 'Check different spellings, please. An address would be useful. Next of kin and so on.'

'She was most disrespectful,' Pawquine said, 'if you do find her I'd recommend burying her with the Klein woman. Preferably alive.' He giggled unpleasantly. '*Quid pro quo* and all that.'

Nic ignored him. 'Maia spoke to these two,' he said, and blurred photographs of Slip and Friz were suddenly brought into focus. 'They disappeared into the Emperorium with her. Any ideas?'

'Never seen them before,' Pawquine said.

'Me neither,' Grovelle added.

The operative who'd been given the task of finding out more information about Maia raised her hand. 'The girl is Maiolica Pequena, daughter of Argilla Pequena. He's a ceramicist, expert in his field, worldwide reputation, but . . . we're not coming up with any information on his current whereabouts. Search still underway.'

Nic tapped another of the black-clad operatives on the shoulder. 'The other two kids?'

'Just checking local schools. And . . . here we are. Classmates of Maia. Both from the same address which is . . . Saint Anthony's Home for Needy Children.'

'That's good,' Nic said, 'that's very good. Two orphans and a girl whose father's gone missing.'

'This other boy,' the third operative interrupted as Tom's face appeared, 'is Thomas Vogt.'

'Son of the baker?' Nic laughed aloud. 'This is getting better and better. Come on people, keep feeding me good news.' He squinted at the nearest monitor. 'Run me the video of everyone who entered the Emperorium this morning but didn't leave.' The operator did so, froze the screen when Ten and his father entered, when Yves Chavanel sauntered through the door. 'I know Chavanel,' Nic said, 'he can be linked to Klein. But the other two? Trace them back, see what you can find.'

'Sir,' the first operator said, 'According to Border Agency records, Argilla Pequena was in Argentina six months ago, then Nigeria. He flew to Russia, Japan, then home again. Last visual is three months ago.' An image flashed onto the screen. 'He entered the Emperorium very early one morning. But there's no record of him coming out.'

Nic's grin almost split his head in two. He performed an awkward, shuffling three-step dance and raised his arms in triumph. 'It all falls into place,' he said.

'The customer in the video,' the fourth operative said, 'is Mr Yingjie Li, known as Tony, American, Accountant, widower, and his son Ten.'

'Why's he visiting our glorious country? Come on, come on, check visa applications!'

There was a pause, no more than a few seconds. 'Tourism, sir. His wife died . . . six months ago. He works for a chemical company, he's been on long term sick leave. His son has been away from school since his mother died. No siblings. No other close relatives.'

'Good work, everyone. This is the story we run with.'

There was a knock on the door and it was opened to reveal a tall black-haired woman carrying a briefcase. She looked to be a stereotypical businesswoman wearing a white blouse, severe dark blue skirt and jacket, black shoes with heels that were only just sensible; but when her jacket fell open it revealed two holsters, each containing a glinting, black handled pistol.

'Briony!' Nic said. 'Just in time! I was about to explain to Mr Pawquine and Mr Grovelle exactly what they've been doing. If you wouldn't mind filling in any gaps?'

'Of course, Nic,' the woman said as she curled into his arms and kissed him softly on the lips. 'Everything else you asked for is set up.' Pawquine and Grovelle looked at each other with envy in their eyes.

'You are so good!' He glared at Pawquine and Grovelle. 'If only I could say the same for our two figureheads. But we can only use what we've been given. Pay attention you two!'

Grovelle stood up straight, though even at his straightest he was slightly hunched as if he was bowing obsequiously. Pawquine saluted. '*Dulce et decorum . . .*' he began, then tailed off into silence because he couldn't remember what followed.

'That can be arranged,' Nic said. 'Now listen carefully. This is what happened. Klein and Chavanel are the leaders of a child smuggling ring. No, no, that won't explain the explosion. Got it! They're part of an international terrorist ring. Drug trafficking, child smuggling, robbery, larceny, working for foreign powers . . . Briony, see if there are any unsolved crimes we can pin on them?'

'Got it, Nic.'

'Good. Maia's father . . .'

'Argilla,' one of the operatives filled in.

'Argilla uncovered this and was imprisoned. His daughter was blackmailed into working for Klein, if she didn't then her father's disposed of. Klein and Chavanel were about to, I don't know, blow something up, something or someone important. Any ideas, Briony?'

'I'll find something. Royal family opening something? Research laboratory?' She winked at Pawquine. 'The Mayor's residence?'

'Nah, not important enough. Work on it. Anyway, they're stockpiling explosives. Not in the Emperorium, too risky, they put some in the outhouses they've rented at Vogt's Bakery.'

'I'll draw up a lease, make that bit above board. Do you want Mrs Vogt to be implicated?' Briony asked.

'No, she can be the innocent bystander when the explosives go up!'

'And her son?'

'Oh, I don't know. He can be in love with Maia, something like that. The two orphans and Maia are about to be sent into slavery, he follows Maia. There's an explosion, half the square goes up, Klein and Chavanel escape with their drugged captives. Get some video of a panel van, plates obscured, for the plods to put out. That'll give them something to do. Anything else?'

Grovelle cleared his throat. 'You mentioned us being heroes?'

'We'd make damn good heroes,' Pawquine said, *'per ardua addendum.* My father's regimental motto,' he explained.

Nic sighed. 'They were on their way to talk to Klein, heard screams, went to investigate. They were attacked by Chavanel . . .'

'We were!' Pawquine exclaimed. 'But we fought back and . . .'

'But they were overpowered by him and a henchman.'

'Could we make that "henchmen"?' Grovelle said meekly. 'It would make it more plausible.'

'It would be plausible to say you were attacked and overcome by a single one-armed fluffy bunny with arthritis,' Nic said, 'so don't push it!'

'I'll write up a press release,' Briony said, 'base it on what Dumb and Dumber here are supposed to remember. And I'll make them repeat it until it really is a memory.'

Nic nodded absently. 'I'll get someone to plant a small amount of explosives of some type in the bakery ruins, something for the soldiers to find. And I need to show you this green apparition thing in the Emperorium, Gyorgi's going to encase it in concrete so that won't be a problem. I think it's a force field of some type.'

'You want me to push through the approval for the demolition of the Emperorium?'

'Yes, no point in waiting.'

'Okay then, I can't see too much of a problem with that.' Briony stroked Nic's shoulder. 'I sent the car away. Any chance of a lift?'

Nic smiled. 'For you, my dear, anything.'

'Could we have a lift?' Pawquine asked. 'After all, we are heroes.'

'No,' Nic and Briony said together.

Pawquine and Grovelle watched the helicopter leave. 'Nic's story,' Pawquine said, 'it didn't mention the blue monstery things.'

'What blue monstery things?' Grovelle replied.

'You know! You said before that we really did see them. They threatened to kill us and eat us. You must remember.'

Grovelle shook his head. 'No recollection of any such thing, I'm afraid.'

'But we saw . . .' Pawquine's eyes suddenly opened wide. 'Ah! Yes! I remember now what really happened. We're heroes.'

Grovelle nodded. 'We're heroes. But without . . .'

'. . . without the blue monstery things!' Pawquine tapped the side of his nose. 'I get it!'

They trudged away together, out of the square, looked back once at the police cordon and the flashing blue lights, the dust and the debris.

'I don't think I'll sleep well tonight,' Grovelle said.

'Me neither.'

Grovelle rubbed tired eyes. 'I don't think I want to sleep anyway. I might dream.' He dusted down his trousers and his jacket. 'And I don't think I can persuade myself, when something comes for me in my sleep, that it never really existed.'

Pawquine shuddered. 'I know what you mean. The problem is, *In somnis veritas*, old bean.'

'What does that one mean?'

'No idea. But it sounds good.'

'Mmm. Should we go?'

'We should go.'

THIRTEEN

The climb to the light was steep. Shard led the way up the narrow tunnel, halting at regular intervals to let Pencil and Maia catch up. None of them spoke. Despite their exertions they were feeling cold.

The ground beneath their feet was dry and had the hard give of old wood, though it wasn't carved into steps. The light which drew them on was bright and vibrant, it appeared at first to be a small window but, as they drew closer, it was obvious that its frame was actually the end of the tunnel itself. When they reached it they found themselves standing in a long gallery on a floor made of wooden planks. There should probably have been a cover of some sort above their heads (there were joists visible and a roof was in place not far away to their left) but most of the supporting walls had rotted away, and to their right the whole gallery had disappeared. Beyond this gap the structure reformed, but the distance was too far even for Shard to leap. And in the gaps was cold blue sky.

Immediately opposite them a second tunnel descended, a third wasn't far away. Shadows in the gallery walls showed where other tunnels descended. Shard held out her arms to hold Pencil and Maia back, pointed to places where the floor was missing. A bitter wind swirled and shrieked around them; conversation was impossible.

Shard guided them into the comparative shelter of the tunnel adjacent to theirs, sat down with her back to the wall and motioned to the others to do the same. 'What do you have with you in your packs?' she asked.

Pencil had with her the Map and a change of clothing, a flask of water and a packet of oats, a little dried fruit. Maia simply shook her head. She'd either taken off her pack when she climbed the tree or lost it in the climb itself. She searched her jacket pockets, found a few cubes of chocolate-coated sugar. Two knives were still in their sheaths at her belt. But she'd brought nothing else with her.

'I have my own provisions,' Shard said. 'Some dry tinder. But I fear the floor beneath us would burn if I tried to light a fire.'

'So what do we do?' Pencil asked. Her breath was misting as she spoke.

'We have to find a way down.'

Pencil looked around her. 'Which way do we go?'

'Perhaps we should look at the Map.'

Pencil took the battered book from her pack and handed it to Shard, shuffled round to sit beside her. 'Do you want to look?' she asked Maia.

Maia shook her head, fastened her coat tight around he and closed her eyes. Pencil looked as if she would move across to Maia, comfort her, encourage her to join in, but a glance from Shard warned her not to do so.

'I think Maia needs to rest,' the Bazhka said, 'sleep for a little while. You and I can look at the Map together, Pencil, consider which path we ought to choose. I confess that all this is new to me.'

'New? Aren't these just high up corridors?'

'The corridors *I* know, Pencil, feel as wide and tall as the lands they lead to. I've never seen anything like these.' She gestured at the tunnels leading from the platform. 'They're narrow with lots of branches leading off them, like wormholes. So that's what I'll call them. Wormholes.' She opened the Map at the page they'd last used, where the unexplored Forest had almost killed them, but there was no sign of the small blue circle which normally showed their position. Shard frowned. 'In leaving the Forest we climbed through a doorway, that much is clear. But we ought to be at a point adjacent to, or even directly above, the Forest. Yet I see no trace of us.'

'Perhaps we died,' Maia said without opening her eyes. 'Perhaps we don't exist any more, that's why we don't appear on the Map.'

Pencil held out her hand in front of her face. 'I don't feel dead,' she said.

'I do,' said Maia.

'I probably look a little bit dead, though.'

Shard ignored them. She found the page showing the whole of the Emperorium. 'According to this we're above the desert land I spoke of, Acama.' She flicked through the pages until she found Acama. 'But Acama isn't close to the Forest. I don't understand.' She unfurled her long legs and stood up, took a few steps across the platform to the Forest tunnel. 'Now I'm above the Forest again.' She stepped back to rejoin the others. 'Once more, Acama. Can the Map be wrong?'

'The Map's right,' Maia said, her voice a monotone. 'And if the Map's right, then the way we've been looking at it's wrong.'

'Explain,' Shard said, puzzled.

'Isn't it obvious? Let's face it, the Map is almost useless by itself. Doorways move. Some places, like the Forest, have no detail, others have too much. Think of the Library. If you're in the Library it's great, but as soon as you leave, as soon as you get into the corridors, you're lost. A doorway might move or it might not. Go through it one day and it leads to, let's say this desert land, Acama. On another day the same doorway leads to the Plains, or Snowtops, or any of the other places you know, or even some you don't know. It doesn't make sense. But this,' she waved her hand around, 'makes sense.'

'Go on,' Shard encouraged her.

'The place we're in now, there's probably a better word, but let's assume it's above all the lands in the Emperorium, we'll call it the Attic. The Attic doesn't move. The doorways from the attic, or at least the paths to the doorways, are fixed.'

'Wormholes,' Pencil said, 'Shard and I decided to call them wormholes.'

Maia ignored Pencil's interruption. 'Shard, you said yourself that time in the Emperorium was out of phase. If time's like that, so is space. The Attic is real time and real space.'

'Please tell me what you're talking about,' Pencil said.

Maia disregarded Pencil. 'Who built this?' she asked. 'The Maker?'

Shard looked around. She tapped the walls, scratched the floor with her nail. 'I don't know,' she admitted.

'Make a guess, then. Everything the Maker does is designed to cause turmoil. Moving doorways, Bazhka programmed to kill humans. All the different lands with their different climates and different people. It's chaotic. Yet this, despite its rotting floors and missing ceilings, is logical. Man made. But it hasn't been used much recently, it's fallen into disrepair. No-one's been up here for a very long time. How could they get here? The Maker's probably got the doorways into the Attic hidden, like in the Forest.'

'I suppose it's a possibility,' Shard said.

'More than that, it's a probability. A likelihood. Look on the wall behind you.' Maia climbed wearily to her feet, reached out and wiped away the dust from a piece of wood close to her head. Several wavy lines were scratched into it. 'Could that be sand dunes?' Maia asked.

Pencil stood up, examined the lines closely. 'It looks like it could be water to me.'

'This one, then.' Maia pointed to what was clearly an image on the wall at the top of the Forest wormhole.

'That's a tree,' Pencil said, 'definitely a tree.'

Shard sounded disappointed. 'I should have noticed that,' she said.

'Wrong height,' Maia pointed out, 'they're mounted at human eye level. You're probably too tall to notice them, they're worn away and hidden by dust. There's probably one at the top of every wormhole, we just need to work out what they mean.'

'You do realise,' Shard said, 'that if you're right, we should be able to find our way directly into Home. My Home. The Bazhka land.'

'It had occurred to me.'

'You don't seem pleased at the prospect.'

Maia stared wildly back at Shard. 'Why should I be? Everywhere I go, everything I do, I find that I lose my friends, people who are important to me.' Her anger made her spit out her fears. 'No, these are the wrong words. I don't *lose* them. They *die*. Chavanel, Mr Forritt, Tom and Peter, Slip and Friz, all dead. My mother, probably my father. Madame Klein, she's probably dead as well. So why should I feel pleased about taking you and Pencil into the most dangerous place I can imagine? So I can see both of you killed? No, I've had enough of dying. I've had enough of death. I just want this all to end.' Maia sank again to the floor, not crying, beyond tears, her head buried in her arms.

'Perhaps you're right,' Pencil said. 'I mean, if people close to you keep dying, that's a bad thing. But what do you mean by wanting it all to end?'

'Just stop. Stay here. Wait for the next monster to come along. Just wait to die.'

'You can't do that.'

'Why not?'

'Because if you sat and did nothing then I'd do the same. I wouldn't go on without you, and Shard wouldn't either. So you'd die, but we would too, and that *would* be your fault. So we can't stay here.'

Shard listened attentively, head tilted to one side, but said nothing.

'Wherever you go,' Pencil continued, 'I go too. If you decided to jump through one of those holes in the floor, I'd race you to the ground.'

Maia looked up. 'Why?'

'Because of what you've done *for* me. Because of what you've done *to* me. You've helped me be someone different.' Pencil laughed, a deep-throated, happy, joyous laugh. 'Look at me, Maia.'

'I am looking at you.'

'No you're not. You're looking in my direction, but you're not looking *at* me. Look at me properly and tell me what you see.'

'I don't know, Pencil. I'm too tired to play silly games.'

'Alright, am I the person I was in the Library. Have I changed?'

Maia sniffed, forced her mouth into a false grin. 'Yes, you've changed.'

'For the better?'

Maia considered the question, then nodded.

'Tell me, then. I need to know. You see, nobody ever said anything nice about me until I met you. I was good for sharpening pencils, that's all.'

Maia stared at the wall ahead of her, thinking. 'You're kind,' she said eventually. 'You're helpful. You always see the best in anyone.' She began to talk a little faster. 'You never complain about anything, no matter what happens to you. You cheer people up just by being there. You're actually very pretty, though I never really noticed that until now, but I did notice that Ten liked being with you. And you're good at getting people talking, you ask good questions, you're not

293

easily embarrassed. And you weren't like that at all when we first met. I think . . .' Maia paused, then hurried on. 'Yes, I think you're clever. You keep saying you aren't, but that's because you don't know a lot, and you don't know a lot because no-one's ever taught you things. But you learn quickly, and you're curious. I know there are bits of your life you can't remember, but that doesn't hold you back. And . . .' She came to a halt.

Shard spoke up. 'The word "and" normally means you have something else to say, Maia.'

Maia nodded eagerly, as if some important fact had suddenly dawned on her. 'And you managed to get me talking when I didn't want to talk. You got me to stop thinking about myself. That's really clever. Thank you for that.'

'Clever?' Pencil said, delighted. 'Clever? Well I never, I'm so clever.' She giggled at the rhyme. 'No-one's ever said I'm clever!'

'All because of your endeavour,' Maia added.

'Yes! More rhymes!' Pencil's smile quickly became a wrinkle of confusion. 'What does it mean?'

'It means you try hard at things.'

'I do! At least I try hard to try hard.' After a moment's thought she added, 'Does that make sense?'

'I think so,' Maia said.

'I like listening to this playing with words,' Shard said, 'however . . .'

'You can do it too!' Pencil shouted.

'Do what?' the Bazhka said. 'I don't know what I'm doing. Whatever . . .'

'You did it again!'

'Did I?' Shard seemed genuinely bemused.

'You could knock me down wiv a fevva,' Maia continued.

'No,' Pencil judged, her face serious again, 'that doesn't work. That's not a real rhyme. That's cheating.'

'Sorry.'

'That's alright. But you're feeling a little better, aren't you? We can play the rhyming game another time, can't we?'

'Of course we can,' Maia said. 'Any time you want.' She sighed, adopted her serious face again. 'Whenever.'

Pencil looked at Maia. 'Did you . . ? Was that deliberate?'

'I think we ought to explore these wormholes now, see if there's a way down to Shard's Home. That's what the others would have wanted, isn't it?'

Shard agreed. 'That's what they would have wanted.'

Some of the signs at the top of the wormholes (they'd decided to adopt that name, it seemed more accurate than 'corridors') were easy to decipher and could be confirmed by referring to the blue indicator circle showing their position in the Map. Although the Map showed no detail in the Land at the bottom of the tunnel where they were resting, Shard had judged by its position that it was probably Acama with its sandy deserts. The next wormhole had a jagged electric zig-zag of mountain peaks at its top, that was Snowtops. The Map showed only a few tracks leading between small towns and villages; the knowledge that these were probably inhabited by Bazhka who kept humans as slaves ensured they didn't descend that way. Maia had to push that thought to the back of her mind.

She found herself eying Shard warily, and then Shard was looking directly at Maia, as if she'd known what Maia was thinking. But there was no antagonism in that glance, only a wistful hope that Maia could overcome her sadness, her sense of loss. When Maia looked back and smiled, Shard winked; that was when Maia knew that she could manage, that she would press on with her desperate quest to find her father, to do whatever she could to defeat the Maker and the Bazhka and the Vanjelists.

She stood up and looked again at the sign on the wall behind her. It had been scratched there, written, inscribed, by an unknown hand, a human hand, she was sure of that. How long ago had that been? Had the hand belonged to a man or a woman? How many others had passed that way since? She reached out and touched the rough surface with her fingertips. Her nails were broken and cracked, dirty and worn. Her jacket sleeves were grubby and torn, as were her trousers. When she looked at Pencil she could see an echo of her own condition: hair blown awry and knotted with twigs, clothes stained, face streaked with grime; they'd been able to wash only quickly and briefly since they'd left the Library. But she felt fit, the aches in her muscles that had dogged her in the long climb out of the Library had disappeared.

'Should we rest before we go down?' she asked Shard.

'We need to sleep,' the Bazhka replied, 'but there's no water up here and it's cold. We don't know if anyone else comes this way either.'

'I don't think anyone's been here for ages,' Pencil said. 'There's dust on the floor but no footprints. And there are holes in the floor too, you'd think someone would've repaired them.'

'It would be dangerous to be up here at night,' Maia said.

'Then that answers your question,' Shard said. 'But I don't want to go down into Home, even if we can discover the way. We should find somewhere else, somewhere safer. Spend a day or two recovering.'

'I need to recover,' Pencil said. 'I need hot food and a hot drink, but most of all I need a hot bath.' She lifted her arms in the air and sniffed beneath them. 'Because I stink.'

'It looks like we're searching for specifics now,' Shard said. 'We should explore a little. At least going down a wormhole should be easier than going up.'

They decided that a horizontal line with several vertical lines climbing from it was probably an indication that the land beneath was Plains. Shard had already mentioned that the people there lived in comparative harmony, so they descended carefully until the floor levelled beneath them and they came to the end of their pathway. A wooden trapdoor, similar to the one they'd come through to climb into the attic, rattled and jumped as if something was trying to get through. Shard knelt carefully in front of it and sniffed, declared that there was nothing there, that the movement was probably due to the wind. She grasped the handle and pulled but the trapdoor wouldn't move. She searched for a latch in case the door opened downwards but there was nothing. Only when Maia moved closer, felt for her key but didn't actually take it from round her neck, did the door fly open.

The noisy, angry wind threatened to blow them off their feet, they shuffled back up the wormhole to escape it. Shard crawled slowly down the passage until she could peer over the edge. She reversed the journey and reported back.

'It's a long way down,' she said. 'It looks as if there might have been a platform of some type just below the trapdoor, but if there was, all that's left is a few planks of wood. We have to go back up.'

She managed to pull the trapdoor closed again and they began their long walk back to the gallery above. Maia estimated that the whole journey down and back had taken about two hours, and there was only a dim blue light to lead them back to the heights.

The next wormhole seemed to suggest that it lead to somewhere with waves, though they might have been hills.

The Map showed a featureless expanse of blue and they decided it was probably not worth descending to find out what was below.

'It's getting too dark to explore any more,' Shard said, 'I think we should go a little way back down one of the tunnels, spend the night out of the wind where it isn't quite as cold. No fire, though.'

They ate Maia's chocolate sugar cubes and drank a little water, huddled together for warmth and tried to sleep. Shard seemed to manage that task quickly while Pencil and Maia attempted - with little success - to absorb some of the Bazhka's warmth. The wind howled and whistled around them, a counterpoint to the creaks and groans of the gallery above and the wormhole below. At some time, when the night was at its darkest and coldest, when Maia still hadn't fallen asleep and was huddled with her legs drawn up, arms around her knees, she felt a touch of feathery chill on her face. She flicked on her torch and noticed a few flakes of snow drift down the tunnel and settle on her feet. They didn't melt; indeed, their presence seemed to invite others to join them. Before long a snowstorm was swirling around them, over them, past them. Pencil was disappearing beneath a blanket of white. A thought occurred to Maia: Pencil had grown up in the Library, she'd probably never seen snow before. She leaned across Shard and nudged Pencil. 'It's snowing,' she whispered.

Pencil didn't stir.

In the torch's dim light Maia could see her breath clouding in front of her. She tried to touch the vapour, saw that her fingers were almost transparently blue. 'I'm turning into a Bazhka,' she said to herself and laughed. This time she tried to wake Shard to tell her about the transformation. She shook her, then shook her again, harder. The Bazhka didn't wake.

Maia was shivering, her teeth chattering. 'Shard!' she said, 'wake up!' She'd forgotten why she was trying to wake the Bazhka, she had to fight the cold and the overwhelming tiredness that was threatening to engulf her. 'Shard!' she yelled.

Shard's eyes blinked open. In the fading light of the torch she took in what was happening. She shrugged herself out of the snow, took the collar of Pencil's coat in one hand, grabbed Maia with the other and dragged them down the tunnel. In places the snow was deep, Shard barged her way through the first of these drifts and the second, then stopped abruptly. She threw Pencil and Maia behind her and started to rebuild the wall of snow she'd just destroyed. When it was solid she built another wall further down the tunnel. They were encased in their own snow capsule.

'We should be safe now,' Shard said, 'I'm sorry I fell asleep. Thank you for waking me.' She shook Pencil roughly awake. 'We share warmth!' she announced, her voice cutting through Pencil's drowsiness. 'We stay awake until I say you can sleep! Come here!' She sat down and held her arms wide, gathered Maia and Pencil close.

'I feel so tired,' Pencil shivered, 'so cold.'

'You'll soon warm up. Don't fall asleep. Think of things to keep you awake. Make up those things I don't understand, rhymes. Sing a song. Anything.'

'I can't remember any songs,' Pencil said.

'I'll try,' Maia said. 'This is one my father used to sing to me when I couldn't sleep.' She took a deep breath, smelled Shard's warm, damp fur. She hugged the Bazhka closer, heard - to her surprise - the metronome beat of her heart, slow and steady, like the ticking of an old clock. She sang to that rhythm. Her voice was quiet because she couldn't find the strength to sing loudly. But somewhere there was a tune, and the words fitted together.

> *'Hush, little baby, don't say a word,*
> *Momma's gonna buy you a mockingbird.*
> *If that mockingbird don't sing,*
> *Momma's gonna buy you a diamond ring.*
> *And if that diamond ring turns brass,*
> *Mama's gonna buy you a looking glass.*
> *If that . . .'*

She broke off. 'I'm sorry,' she said, 'I can't remember the next line. I can start again at the beginning if it helps you stay awake.

Pencil's voice was perhaps more tuneful than Maia's, but it was no louder.

> *'If that looking glass gets broke,*
> *Momma's gonna buy you a billy goat.*
> *And if that billy goat won't pull,*
> *Momma's gonna buy you a cart and bull.'*

'Oh yes,' Maia said, 'I remember it now.' She joined with Pencil and they sang together.

> *'And if that cart and bull turn over,*
> *Momma's gonna buy you a dog named Rover.*
> *And if that dog named Rover won't bark*
> *Momma's gonna buy you a horse and cart.*
> *And if that horse and cart fall down,*
> *You'll still be the sweetest little baby in town.'*

When they finished it was left to Shard to break the silence. 'That was beautiful,' she said. 'even though I've no idea what it was about.'

'How do you know the words?' Maia asked Pencil.

'I don't know. Someone must have sung them to me, I don't know who, but it must have been in the Library. Perhaps when I was young?'

'That must have been it.' Maia reached across Shard and pulled Pencil's hair away from her forehead. Pencil smiled at her, felt for Maia's hand and stroked it gently.

'I do believe,' Shard said, 'it's getting warmer in here. Would you mind singing the song again?'

They sang the whole song through together, twice. Although their breath was still fogging, the temperature was definitely rising. 'I think it should be safe to sleep now, if you want,' Shard said.

'I think I'd like to sleep,' Pencil said.

'We all need to sleep,' Maia added.

Shard watched them close their eyes, listened to their breathing become synchronised. She allowed her eyelids to droop and listened to the night, but this time stayed awake. Maia and Pencil needed her to remain vigilant.

The snow wall nearest the top of the wormhole was beginning to glow when Shard woke Maia and Pencil. 'Daylight is showing through,' she said as they stretched, 'because the wall is becoming thinner. The snow is melting.'

The evidence was at their feet, a rivulet of melt-water running down the centre of the tunnel.

'Drink the melting snow,' Shard told them, 'and use the run-off to wash. You won't notice how cold it is after a while.' She was setting an example, splashing her fur with water and combing it with long clawed fingers. When she'd finished she pulled the remnants of the snow wall down and climbed the slope of the wormhole, leaving Maia and Pencil some privacy. They took off their outer clothes and came fully awake when the cold water touched their skin. Maia even plunged her head into the lower snow wall to wash away the grime from her hair that had built up over many days.

It was a pleasure to pull on their clothes again, the chilling wind was still sharp as a blade; but they felt clean, even though Pencil mentioned that she still smelled of Bazhka.

'There are worse things to smell of,' Maia said. 'Shard kept us alive last night. She built the snow walls and gave us her warmth. We owe her.'

'We do,' Pencil agreed. 'Again. Or more. Or both.'

They rejoined Shard who was looking anxiously where the attic stretched away into the distance. There were wormholes at irregular intervals on both sides but some were inaccessible because the floor close to them was broken or missing. There were places further along the attic where holes were visible in the floor or walls or ceiling. Immediately behind them was the huge gap close to where the Forest wormhole met the Attic.

'We need to find a way down,' Shard said. 'We're almost out of food and I don't want to spend another night up here.'

'Then it would be best to find a suitable land quickly.' Maia looked to her right. 'We can't go that way, not unless we've learned to fly.' She pointed at each of the wormholes close by. 'That one's Forest, no going back. Plains? We know there's no way down. Snowtops? We end up freezing or captured and eaten by Bazhkas. Acama? Not much chance of finding food or water in a desert. I say we move further along, see what the options are.'

'We could even go down a wormhole each and then report back to the others,' Pencil said. 'Is that a good suggestion? I mean, it sounds like a good suggestion to me, but in the past that's usually meant it was silly. Is it silly?'

Maia raised her eyebrows at Shard.

Shard nodded. 'That sounds like a good idea to me, as long as we don't fall through an open trapdoor. If the door won't open, come straight back. If there's a way down, don't take it, come straight back. No exploring. Any questions?'

'I'll go down this one, 'Pencil pointed to a wormhole with four diagonal lines inscribed at the top of it. The Map showed an empty land with no name. 'We don't know what to expect,' Maia said, 'so be careful.'

The next wormhole sign consisted of several rectangles on their shortest edges, all of different heights. The Map told them that this was simply Nuam, and the detail showed a regular grid of what looked like streets with green spaces, rivers crossed by bridges, a blue area that could be a lake or part of a sea.

'Looks like an American city,' Maia said, 'if it is, then the trapdoor might open direct onto the roof of a skyscraper. I'll try that one.'

'I've no idea what "American" means, or "skyscraper",' Shard said, 'but it sounds as if you know what you're talking about. I'll take this one, then.' The sign at the top of the wormhole opposite was missing, but the Map told them that the land below was Gaelle. 'The people there have no mouths, 'Shard said, 'they speak with their hands and eat through their fingers.'

'Because of the permanent strong winds, or so you told us.'

'So it's said, Maia. I have met some Gaelleans but haven't visited their land.'

'Can I go now?' Pencil asked.

'Let's all go,' Maia said.

'Let's all take care,' Shard added.

Shard was the first back, her long legs made her journey feel short. Pencil was the next to appear. 'I couldn't open the trapdoor,' she said excitedly, 'but there were gaps in the wood so I lay down with my eye close to one of the gaps and, guess what?'

'I think you should wait until Maia returns,' Shard warned her, 'or you'll have to tell your story all over again.'

'Oh, I don't mind doing that, I like stories, and anyway, there's not a lot to tell . . .'

'No, you wait.'

It was almost an hour before Maia returned. She looked tired.

'Unsuitable, I take it?' Shard asked.

Maia slid down beside her. 'You go first,' she said.

'Can I go first?' Pencil continued before the others could say no, 'It got very narrow and twisty, then it opened out a bit, and then I found the trapdoor, but it wouldn't open. There was a crack where two bits of wood didn't quite join together, so I lay down and I could see through.' She stopped, waited awhile. 'Go on, then, ask me what I saw!'

'What did you see, Pencil?' Shard asked dutifully.

'Nothing. It was all grey, like clouds, and there was damp air, like it was raining.'

'No sign of a way down?'

'No way at all. I could see sideways a little bit, there were some bits of wood sticking out from where the trapdoor should have opened, but they were black at the ends, like they'd been burned a long time ago.'

'No luck for me either,' Shard said. 'The wind grew stronger and then the wormhole opened out so I could see the end of it. Either the trapdoor was open or it had blown away entirely. I had to crawl until I could see down the opening, it was definitely Gaelle. Nothing but sky and strong winds. But there were black scorch marks on the walls beside the opening.'

'Looks like someone or something's been attacking the trapdoors,' Maia said.

Shard looked thoughtful. 'Not just the trapdoors,' she said, 'it looks as if there were platforms of some type suspended below the open doors. But they've been destroyed. An attempt to stop anyone getting into the attic?'

'Or to stop people getting out,' Pencil said, 'a bit like us. What did you find, Maia?'

'Nuam looked just as I expected, a city,' Maia said wearily, 'a huge city. Full of tall buildings, tall as cliffs, tall as mountains,' she added, to help Shard and Pencil understand. 'There's no platform under the trapdoor, but there's a long coil of rope, and the door's directly above the top of the tallest building.'

'So we could get down?' Pencil asked. 'That's good! Should we go?'

'It was like a city in my world, it's called New York. I just lay down and stared at it; it was beautiful. I could see busy roads and the lights shone in the buildings, there were ships on the river. I thought I could hear the sound of traffic drifting up from the streets, and I could smell food cooking. I was sure I could see the shadows of people moving in the windows. That was when I realised I could just let the rope down and slide down it onto the roof and I'd be safe. Free. Back in my own world.'

'So why didn't you do that?' Shard asked.

'I wanted to. It would have been so easy.'

'But you didn't,' Pencil said, 'you came back for us.'

Maia shook her head. 'No, that's not why I came back. I was tempted to go down into that world. Then I began thinking. My first thought was that it would solve nothing: every problem I'd come across in the Emperorium would still be there. The Maker, rampaging Bazhkas, Vanjelists trying to kill me, my father lost somewhere, Madame Klein and Ten's father in limbo. Going back now wouldn't help me find an answer to any of these. And what if I couldn't get back into the Emperorium? Who'd believe my story? Who'd be able to help?

'Then I thought I'd come back for you two, take you down into my world with me. But the people down there would treat you like a circus creature, Shard, a curiosity to be locked up and investigated. And they'd listen to you, Pencil, and they'd think you were insane, and you'd be locked up too.

'So I just lay there, not knowing what to do. Part of me wanted to escape. Another part of me said that it wouldn't actually be an escape. I looked down and the world looked back at me, and held its arms wide, and welcomed me into it.'

'What happened?' Shard asked. She placed a hand on Maia's shoulder, and Maia looked up and slid her own hand beneath the Bazhka's massive paw. Pencil moved close and curled her arm round Maia's waist.

'I looked more closely,' Maia said, tried to swallow the lump of sorrow in her throat, 'I had such a longing, such a need to climb down, and I wanted to know what it was that I desired so much. And I opened my eyes and my heart. I saw that the whole thing was false. The buildings were a facade, the lights weren't real, everything was painted onto a moving backdrop. The city smells were suddenly the aroma of decay, the sounds I heard were groaning. I was frightened and I stood up, I accidentally kicked the rope and it fell down so that it touched the top of the building. And quickly, faster than I could have imagined possible, tentacles whipped round and grabbed the rope, pulled at it. The top of the building became a mouth full of sharp, grinding teeth, the lights were eyes, the movements were patterns on the skin of a huge monster.

'The first tentacle actually got through the trapdoor, it was looking for me. I managed to cut it off. I cut the rope too, I hacked at the other tentacles that had managed to grip the frame of the trapdoor. The creature fell, and it screamed as it fell.

'It was its own lure. It knew what I wanted and it became what I wanted. And if I'd gone down that rope it would have caught me and killed me, then it would have come after you two as well.'

The three huddled close for a while. Maia leaned across to Pencil and kissed her on the cheek; she had to stand up to do the same with Shard.

'Should we keep exploring?' Shard asked.

'We have to,' Maia replied, 'we have a job to do. A quest to fulfil. We have a ring to throw into the fires of Mount Doom.'

'No,' said Shard, 'I don't know that one either.'

'Does that make me Frodo or Sam?' Pencil asked as she dusted herself off. She frowned. 'Did I say that? What does it mean?'

It was Maia's turn to put her arm round her friend. 'It means you've remembered something else, probably from a book in the Library. It means you know more than you think you know. You'll soon remember other things as well. Like your real name? And details about your past?'

'That *would* be good! I might be someone really important.'

'You are important,' Shard said.

Each of the wormholes brought the same result. A laborious descent down a steep slope, a trapdoor that opened onto the blackened stumps of a burned platform, and open sky. Sometimes there was a strong wind, sometimes no wind at all. There were rainclouds and snowstorms, land visible far below or vast expanses of water, distant hills or mountains, towns or villages, the shimmer of a heat haze or the sharp clarity of cold air. But there was never any way down, always a laborious climb back up. They stopped looking at the Map to identify the land below; if there had been a staircase or a ladder they would have taken it regardless of their destination.

They spent the time wondering why the platforms that had once been below every trapdoor had been destroyed and came to two opposing possibilities. The first was that they'd been demolished to prevent access to the Attic; the alternative was that they'd been torn down to stop the Attic being used as an easy passage between lands.

'So who would know about the Attic?' Maia asked Shard. 'You didn't, and it doesn't appear on the Map.'

'If it was built by humans, as you suggest, then it can only have been the Truthsingers.'

'Then what's its purpose?'

'Easy movement from one land to another?'

'Why would the Truthsingers want to travel at all inside the Emperorium?' Maia asked. 'It's the Maker's creation. They imprisoned him, he fought back by using his will to make all these different lands, so the Truthsingers made a bigger prison round the Emperorium itself, guarded by people like Madame Klein. So why, once they'd done that, would they ever want to go back inside?'

They were about to edge their way across a narrow strip of wood where the floor of the attic had almost disappeared. They were able to make use of the attic wall to protect them from the blasts of wind that were becoming more frequent, and to provide them with occasional handholds.

'Because the Maker was becoming more powerful,' Shard suggested, 'and was finding ways to threaten your world. So the Truthsingers had to find a way to fight him inside the Emperorium.'

'They didn't do very well,' Pencil said, 'this place is in danger of falling down completely.'

Maia was the first to venture across, slowly, carefully, not looking down at all. Pencil followed her, more surefooted, more confident; Shard brought up the rear, stepping warily, her greater size and weight making the timbers bend and bow beneath her.

'Who might have destroyed the platforms, then?' Maia asked. 'Certainly not the Trusthsingers.'

'If the attic was a secret from the Maker,' Shard pointed out, 'then the Truthsingers would have kept it open. But if they were discovered, if the Maker or the Vanjelists or Bazhkas found them, then suddenly it and the platforms are a liability.'

'How would anyone get down from the platforms?' Pencil asked. 'You'd have to have wings and be able to fly.' She flapped her arms as if hoping she might rise from the ground.

'It's all an illusion,' Maia said, 'the sky in the Forest looked miles above the trees when we were on the ground, but once we got high up . . . it wasn't that high. There must have been a way down.'

'Rope, ladders, who knows what was attached to the platforms?' Shard was looking ahead at the attic disappearing into the distance. 'We need to keep going, it's getting late.' The attic soon seemed in better repair: there were no holes in the walls or ceiling, the floor was intact. There was still, they noticed, no sign of the dust on the floor being disturbed; it was a long time since anyone had passed this way. But the frequency of wormholes was decreasing. When they saw a light ahead of them they slowed their pace, it became clear that there was a section of the attic entirely missing. Where the walls, floor and ceiling should have been there was nothing.

Shard held the others back. 'We don't know what caused this. We don't know how fragile the floor is, it may give way beneath our feet.'

'I can see across,' Pencil said, squinting into the distance, 'it starts again.'

They paused. From her pack Shard drew a battered telescope. She passed it to Maia. 'Tell me what you see.'

Maia extended the telescope, rested it on Pencil's shoulder to look across the gap. The lenses were a little out of true and grimy at the edge, and the magnification wasn't huge, but she could confirm what Pencil had seen. 'The attic does start again on the other side of the gap.' She lowered the telescope. 'It's resting on the top of a pinnacle of rock. I can't tell how high it is until we get closer, but if it's the same on this side we might be able to climb down, then climb up the other side. There might even be a place down there where we can get food and shelter.'

They edged closer to the broken floor at the end of the attic, ignored the remaining wormholes to both left and right. Pencil went first, she was the lightest, and she tested each step by rolling her weight forward and back. Maia followed, her hand grasping Pencil's belt. The floor seemed to remain solid, it made no creaking or groaning sounds, and so they inched forward, motioning Shard after them once they were sure it was safe.

Floor, ceiling and walls had been sheared as if giant scissors had simply cut away a whole section. This left a frame, not perfectly smooth, but less jagged than the other cuts and holes they'd passed earlier. As they approached the edge the vista opened before them.

Directly opposite them the attic opening rested on an apex of shining smooth grey rock. That pinnacle itself was the end of a long, narrow ridge which curved away into the misty distance, undulating gracefully, neither descending nor ascending more than a few metres. No visible path or track left the ridge, and its slope was precipitous; there was no way down from it.

The attic went on its long, straight way, its artificial flatness jarring with the natural formations of the rocks around it. There was no way across. The gap which had looked, from a distance, as if it might be crossed with only a long leap could only be bridged by flight.

A few steps more revealed that the needle of rock opposite was the summit of a cliff, a wall of vitreous stone which fell sheer to a steely blue-grey expanse of white-frothed sea. Small specks of seabirds sailed across the cliff's vastness, using its whirling thermals to glide, stiff-winged, over the water. None of them found a resting place on the cliff; it was too sheer, there were no ledges, nowhere at all to rest.

'I'm pleased there's no way down,' Maia said, 'it would have been so annoying to find a path down the cliff when we have no way of crossing.'

Mingling with the shriek and wail of the wind came a deeper, booming sound of waves tearing at a sea cavern, or the echoing of powerful cannons.

'We should go back,' Shard said, 'explore some of the wormholes, find somewhere to shelter for the night.'

Just one more thing to do,' Maia said. She sank to her knees and shuffled forwards. 'Perhaps this side of the gap is manageable. Perhaps we're actually on a cliff with a way down.' She lowered herself onto her stomach and stretched her arms out so that her hands could reach the edge of the floor, dragged herself forward. Soon her head was level with the floor's end and she could look up and down, left and right.

'Can you see anything?' Shard yelled.

'It's as if the Attic's the mouth of a cave,' she called back, 'in a cliff rather than on top of one, like it is opposite us. I can't see how high it goes above us. It's not as smooth as the other one, it looks like there are crags and overhangs, but nothing much to hold onto. There are plants growing in the cracks in the rock face. And . . .'

Maia scuttled quickly back from the edge. 'We need to move, we need to go back,' she yelled as she rose to her feet. There was no need to say anything else because, as she stood up, a pair of long, flickering antennae appeared over the rim of the attic floor. The rest of the creature followed, a ripple of legs tapping the wooden floor, a pointed, malevolent head turning from one side to the other, seeking, sensing. The creature was as large as Maia's hand, and it was followed by a second, a third, then many others. Like the first, they raised their heads and the front segments of their bodies, flicked their antennae to and fro.

'What are they?' Pencil asked, her voice dripping disgust. At the first sound the creatures' heads swerved towards her and they moved swiftly in her direction. As she backed away from them Shard stamped her foot once, sharply. The creatures ceased their movement, turned their heads towards the Bazhka, swayed hypnotically.

Maia's voice was a whisper. 'They're like centipedes. And centipedes are poisonous.' The creatures closest to her turned their heads in her direction, moving their antennae gracefully, tasting the air. 'Go slowly back the way we came.'

'Too late,' Shard's voice husked. 'These ones are small compared to those behind us.'

Maia turned her head slowly. More of the creatures had emerged from the wormholes behind them, and these were almost half her height. They behaved just as the others had, lifted their heads to reveal sharp pincer-legs dripping with dark liquid, antennae searching the air like radar.'

'Don't . . . move,' Maia's voice was barely audible. 'They . . . sense . . . vibrations.'

Pencil was close to panic. Some of the creatures had climbed the walls and were scuttling across the ceiling above her head. The floor was a mass of quivering, patient legs and oily brown bodies. They were crawling over their shoes, tugging at the fabric of their trousers. Maia gasped as one of the creatures dropped onto her shoulder, she closed her eyes and mouth as its delicate antennae explored her face.

The same must have happened to Pencil, there was a scream and Maia opened her eyes to see her friend only a few feet away, dancing on the spot, brushing creatures from her hair and her clothes, trying to stamp on them. But those she shook off were replaced by even more, and two of the larger creatures were already moving rapidly towards her.

Shard's knives despatched them, sliced them in two, and as the twitching bodies fell to the floor they were engulfed by others in a feeding frenzy. Heads rose and fell, there was a snare-drum clatter of excited feet, but still more of the creatures appeared, large and small.

'There are too many,' Shard yelled, and was immediately clothed in a coat of centipedes, 'I'll kill the big ones, you two retreat!'

There was no hope of retreating, Maia could see that. More centipedes were emerging from the wormholes, more were climbing into the Attic from the cliff outside.

'I can't stand this,' Pencil screamed, and in her terror staggered towards the mouth of the Attic.

'No!' Maia shrieked back at her, 'you'll fall!'

Her words, once spoken, became a prediction. Hands and arms striking out at the centipedes, wailing and moaning, Pencil slid and tripped towards then away from the edge, repeated the movement, but each step took her inexorably closer to the precipice. In a moment of slow clarity Maia saw Shard's mouth open in anger and warning; both of them dived towards Pencil; neither of them was able to stop her tumbling over the edge.

Maia whirled and spun, pulled centipedes from her and dashed them to the floor. Shard did the same, roaring with anger. Both of them had their knives in their hands, cutting and thrusting. Many of the centipedes attacked the fallen, others clambered over the bodies in pursuit of their attackers.

The thought crossed Maia's mind that a fall to a quick death was preferable to being overcome by centipedes. There was water at the base of the cliff; perhaps she might survive and swim to safety.

She could feel the tiredness of her exertions wash over her. It was time to decide, so she began her slow move to the opening of the Attic.

FOURTEEN

The edge came closer. Maia, cloaked in wriggling, squirming, stinging centipedes, every nerve in her body an agony of electric pain, felt a sudden calm relief that it would soon all be over. One more step, a long descent, a quick release.

And that was when she heard Pencil's voice.

'I'm alright! Maia, I'm alright! I'm flying!'

Maia clawed the centipedes from her face and looked up. Pencil wasn't flying. But a winged man or bird or bat was holding her, flapping laboriously, while others clustered behind her. Three of them landed in the mouth of the attic, Maia caught a glimpse of pale skin before she was knocked to the ground by a powerful wing which proceeded to sweep and beat the centipedes from her. She covered her head with her hands. It couldn't have been a man, not a flying man, because it had been holding Pencil with its feet. A bird, then, or a bat. But it hadn't had feathers, she was sure of that, so it wasn't a bird. A bat, then? But it had been shaped like a man. She looked up again. Pencil had been deposited on the floor of the attic and four - no five - of the man-bats were using the claws on their feet to spear the centipedes and throw them from the mouth of the attic. Their wings were mostly furled and folded, but at the point of each wing were spurs which they used like sabres to slash at the centipedes. Their torsos were almost human, broad-chested and clad in a tight, woven material; each had huge eyes set in a hairless head decorated with bright whorls of paint, blues and greens and reds; below their eyes were sharp, savage beaks. This was too confusing, Maia decided; man-bird-bats?

Three of their rescuers stalked past Maia, past Shard who was slumped, exhausted, at the centre of a pile of dead centipede bodies, and ruthlessly killed the remaining centipedes. Even the largest of the monsters scuttled away down the nearest wormholes.

Maia rolled over, sat up slowly. The remains of centipede legs still pierced her clothes, and now that she was calmer she could feel tiny pin-pricks where they'd punctured her skin.

One of the man-bats strutted across to Maia. It walked on its knuckles, the claws on its feet temporarily sheathed, like a cat's. Its wings were folded but they were entirely like a bat's wings, thin and leathery, formed over the elongated bones of the creature's hands. It stood over her, seemed to be examining her closely, turned its bird head from one side to another. It shook its head, raised the sabre-like blade of its middle finger high above her, and brought it down rapidly. Maia closed her eyes and felt the breeze of its passing, heard it whistle past her ear. When she blinked her eyes open she saw a wriggling centipede impaled on the blade. The man-bat held it close to her eyes.

'These legs are venomous,' it said in a sing-song voice, pointed just behind the centipede's jaw. 'The poison doesn't kill, it paralyses. Your attackers were mostly young, you'll hurt a lot very soon, you'll throw up, but that will be it. But if they'd overcome you, or if one of the adults had stung you . . .' it pointed down the tunnel of the attic '. . . or if you'd tried to climb down the cliff, then the second pair of legs would come into play. They use these to glue you down, or attach you to the rock so even if you wake up, you can't move. And then they eat you alive if you're lucky. If you're unlucky, they lay their eggs in your flesh.'

Maia felt sick at the thought, then felt sick to her stomach, and threw up. She heard Pencil doing the same. The bile burned in her throat, she longed for some water.

The second man-bat, standing close to Pencil, had a deeper voice. 'Are they humans?'

'These two are,' the first replied, 'though they do appear small. They may be young. They may be female; I understand that females of the species are smaller than males. Perhaps they're young females.'

'My name is Maia, this is Pencil.' Her voice was faint, creeping from a sandpapered throat. 'You're right, we're females. Girls.'

'And your goat?' the second said, pointing at Shard.

'Her name is Shard and she isn't a goat, she's a Bazhka.' The long speech exhausted Maia; she sank back to the ground, her body a mass of painful needle pricks.

'A Bazhka? I've heard of them, they have a reputation as fighters. Do you know who we are?' the first man-bat asked.

Maia signalled her ignorance with a weak shake of her head. Pencil seemed to have recovered her strength more quickly. 'We don't know who you are but thank you for saving us. We don't know where we are either.'

'My name is Vesper. This is Muis. Behind you are Fladder, Shish, Lepako. We are the Malakhai. Our land is called Kaldera.'

'I join my friends in thanking the Malakhai,' Shard said.

'The goat can speak!' Muis said.

Vesper made a chuckling sound. Maia noticed that the creature's beak didn't move, the sound seemed to come from behind it. 'Are you,' she managed to say, 'wearing masks?'

Vesper reached behind her head. 'Of course we are. Do you really think we look like this?' She pulled the mask forward, revealed a face framed by bright yellow short hair, eyes far larger than a human's eyes, and shot with gold.

'Are you a girl too?' Pencil asked. 'Your hair's a lovely colour.'

'I am female,' Vesper confirmed. Her nose was small, nothing more than a fleshy swelling above a wide-lipped mouth that seemed to contain many large, sharp teeth. She motioned to the other Malakhai to remove their masks as well. 'Does the way we look frighten you?' she asked.

Maia considered her response while looking round at the other faces. They seemed similar to Vesper's, differing only in the colour and length of their hair; Muis had long blue plaits, Fladder's scalp was shaved to a dark green fuzz, while Shish had a rope of orange wrapped around and framing a scowling face; Lepako's hair was short, like Vesper's, but striped red and blue.

'I haven't seen people like you before,' Maia said, 'so you appear unusual to me. But not frightening. It's impolite to be frightened of people who save you from being eaten alive.' She bowed her head in thanks.

'You call us "people"?'

'Of course.'

Vesper nodded approvingly. 'We must find a way to move you safely from here, because you will not survive the night if you remain. I can carry you, and Muis has already shown that he's able to take your friend Pencil.' She looked worriedly at Shard. 'The Bazhka, however, is far heavier than one of us can manage. The other three will be able manage her, but she will have to be supported in a rope cradle. It will not be easy. It will not be comfortable.'

Shard spoke up. 'Is there an alternative? Could I climb down? Could you summon more of your friends?'

'If you try climbing then you will be taken by the centipedes. It will be dark soon, too late for me to summon other Malakhai. You have no choice.'

Shard nodded. 'You all look strong. I place myself in your care.'

Muis seemed pleased with the compliment. 'The goat is a good judge of strength and character.' From far below came the deep rumble Maia had heard before. At first it had sounded like the sea, now it was like rolling thunder. Muis noticed it too. 'We should go,' he said, 'we may be needed. These humans might be able to give us valuable information. Their talking goat could also be of use.'

'Where are you taking us?' Maia asked.

Despite the stated urgency of moving, Vesper thought long and carefully before replying. 'You should not be here. You are human. So you will be taken to a safe place to be interrogated in our court,' she said, flexing her wings. 'To be judged. And, if found guilty of being human spies, you will suffer the will of the court. You will be executed.'

'What? Spies?' Maia couldn't believe what she was hearing. They'd been rescued from almost certain death at the hands - or pincers - of the centipedes to find themselves facing death again at the hands - or claws - of their rescuers. 'That's ridiculous! Who would we be spies for?'

'Our enemies. Humans. Those who are attacking our land and killing our people. The Vanjelists.'

'The Vanjelists?' Maia hissed, 'They tried to kill us! They're our enemies as well!'

'Then I advise you to tell the inquisitor everything. Be helpful. Prove that you are our enemies' enemy. Show that you want to be our friends.' She motioned Maia towards the edge of the attic. 'You have an air of honesty about you. But what do I know? I'm a fighter, not a politician.'

Fladder, Shish and Lepako, the three Malakhai who were to carry Shard, were uncoiling long ropes from around their waists. 'Wherever they take us,' Shard said to Maia and Pencil, not lowering her voice, 'will be safer than spending the night up here.'

'Unless I lose my grip,' Muis grinned.

'You lost your grip with that human you pulled from the ship,' Fladder said.

'He was trying to cut my leg off,' Muis protested.

'You could have dropped him in the sea,' Fladder reminded him.

'But you didn't,' Lepako joined in, 'you shook him until he dropped the knife and then you dropped him.'

'In the lava baths,' Fladder added.

Vesper bent close to Maia. 'They joke a lot. My squadron numbered thirty at the start of this war. We five are all that remain. Humour helps them. You and your friends will be carried safely to the court where you will be handed over for questioning. You will be treated fairly, you have my word. And unlike humans, I keep my word.' She tore a piece of wood from the roof above her head, trimmed it to size with her sabre finger. 'I will hold this firmly with my claws, you must sit on it and reach up, hold my legs with your hands. The flight will be short.' She looked at the others. 'Muis?'

Muis nodded, he had given Pencil the same instructions. His mask was pulled over his head. He was ready to go.

'Fladder?'

'Ready,' Fladder answered. Shard's seat was a single rope, one end held by Fladder, the other by Shish. A second rope was tied to the first in two places and Lepako held both ends of that. It seemed that Fladder and Shish would fly on the flanks, Lepako would be directly above Shard. It would require coordination and strength to keep them flying without dropping Shard, and Maia was obviously worried that the task was beyond the Malakhais' abilities.

'I wouldn't have asked them to do this unless I trusted them,' Vesper explained. 'You will be reunited before too long. You are valuable to us.'

Muis was the first to leap into the sky, to hover with flapping wings, to grab his cargo and dive. Vesper nodded the other three Malakhai on their way. Their take-off was more awkward; they paused on the brink of launching before Lepako gave the word, and their descent was so rapid that Maia thought they'd fallen. But after a few moments she saw the Malakhai beating their wings in synchronised motion, fast and firm, with Shard swinging beneath them.

'Our turn,' Vesper said. Maia sat on her wooden seat, Vesper straddled it, grasped it, and leaned forward with outstretched wings.

They were flying.

Maia saw the massive cliff ahead of her bank swiftly to one side to be revealed as an isolated ridge of a huge sea stack, tall and wide, but surrounded by other stacks that were even taller. The air was full of life: some of the cliffs were dotted with nests, and all around Maia was the shrieking screech and salty tang of vast numbers of seabirds.

Vesper swooped down over a flight of pure white arrow-heads plunging into the sea, rising to the surface with beaks full of fish which they gulped down whole, then flapping laboriously into the sky to repeat the process. Other smaller birds, fat and black and white, thrummed past like bees; long-necked snake-like birds dived from the surface; birds as stiff as crucifixes glided past without moving their wings; raucous mobs bullied and fought for food while others pleaded and cajoled for scraps.

The air was cold and sharp as Vesper wheeled left and right. Maia had to keep her eyes pinched, almost closed, to stop them from watering, but she managed a glimpse of Muis and Pencil flying a similar course to her own; only once did she see Shard, far below and behind.

They plunged towards a rock face bathed in silvery sunlight only to climb the escalator of a thermal over a high escarpment. Animals - the size of large rabbits or small sheep - grazing on the lush green plateau, scattered and ran as

Vesper's shadow rushed onward. There was a series of islands with grassy rather than mountainous tops, and Vesper rode the updrafts on each, rising higher and higher until Maia saw, in the distance, the largest of the archipelago. Vesper looked back at her, mouthed a single word that Maia understood immediately: 'Kaldera'.

Kaldera was the shattered rim of an ancient volcano. It formed a crescent, a giant mouth, and in its jaws lay four or five islands, small in comparison, each cone-shaped, each crowned with a column of smoke and steam.

Vesper had to flap her wings vigorously to make progress across the wide channel leading to Kaldera. Maia thought that, like the stacks and columns they'd left behind, the cliffs ahead of her were inhabited by nesting seabirds. But as they drew closer the dots of white, the specks of red and blue and green, resolved into buildings. The whole cliff face was filled with them, they could only be houses and shops, stores and taverns and meeting places, a vertical city towering into the sky. There were ropes and ladders linking buildings, walkways and staircases. Each building had a platform in front of it, a landing space for a Malakhai, the doorways were wide and high, the windows small, and although Maia knew that the whole city must have been built into and from the cliff, it seemed as though it was constructed with uneven blocks, one on top of the other, in a crazy competition to reach the sky.

Vesper banked again, flew parallel to the city, and Maia saw that it was deserted. There was no sense of the busy metropolis, it was a ghost town. The only Malakhai Maia saw were in the air.

'Why is it empty?' Maia shouted, and in response Vesper turned, hung in the air, and Maia saw for the first time, anchored in the middle of the volcanic islands, a black, slug-like ship. It was no galleon, no sailing ship, it wasn't made of wood. It was an ironclad battleship, smoke rising from its chimneys, four huge paddle wheels on each side of its hull, six tall masts climbing from its deck; at the top of each mast was a white flag bearing a Y shaped cross, a circle resting between its outstretched arms. Even as she watched, numb hands gripping Vesper tightly, one of its six gun turrets fired. First came the flash of igniting gunpowder, then the boom of the explosion, and then the shell landed.

It was aimed at the lower levels of the city, and Maia saw the destruction its blast and detonation caused. A whole block of buildings fell away down a cliff of rubble where other shells had already landed, slid into the white-foamed sea beneath. This was no random destruction. The city was being destroyed a little at a time.

A second turret turned and fired. The shell landed a little further along from the first, and again many buildings were destroyed, taking others on the cliff above with them into the sea.

'Vanjelists!' Vesper shouted. 'Humans!' Both words sounded like a curse. There was nothing Maia could say in response.

Vesper was finding it difficult to remain in position, she turned again, flew once more along the face of the city-cliff right to its end then swung abruptly round a pinnacle into the shelter of Kaldera's lea side.

Here the walls of rock were smooth, glassy and black with only an occasional launching platform and small rough building, but they fell to an undulating fertile land which sloped down to coves and beaches before meeting the sea. And this was where the Malakhai were hiding. Tents and shelters were scattered over the land, together with wooden ramps giving fliers the opportunity to take off. This was the tragedy of the Malakhai: they couldn't live on the plain; they didn't have the strength to launch themselves into the air from flat ground. They needed to fall from the heights, and the destruction of their city was taking that away from them.

Vesper headed for the furthest edge of Kaldera where the buildings from the city followed the curve of land round for a little way, seeking softer rock, avoiding the glossy, vitreous obsidian. Bridging the highest pinnacles, perched on the highest corner, was a broad irregular plateau of wood, a stone fortress at its heart. It was generally wider at its apex than its base, an inverted pyramid, but decks and platforms, stages and podia jutted out at all angles from the hollowed granite of the tower. Maia guessed that this design allowed the largest possible number of Malakhai to take off simultaneously. There were no barriers or rails to prevent falling, no decoration or artifice, no bright colours; there were no stairs or ladders. The only way into the keep was through the air; the only way out was by flying or falling.

Maia could hear that Vesper's breathing was deeper than before, more laboured. The day was dimming and there were no ladders of warm air for the Malakhai to use to gain height. Instead she hugged the land then turned out to sea, glided for a while, climbed for a while with beating wings. When she turned again they were still not high enough to fly into the fortress, and Maia thought Vesper would repeat her journey out to sea and back. Instead she flew faster and harder directly at the cliff, then fixed her wings in a slight bow. At first Maia thought there might be a hidden entrance, but as they drew closer all she could see was black, lava-slicked rock. She would have screamed if the speed of their approach hadn't already taken her breath away. Instead she closed her eyes and so felt rather than saw Vesper find a crosswind, roll into it, use its strength and force to climb, wingtips brushing the cliff face. Maia opened her eyes again to find Vesper landing gently on one of ledges.

'You're heavier than you look,' Vesper gasped, one wing urging her towards the stone building. 'Muis has already landed, your friend is waiting.'

Pencil was alone; there was, of course, no need for guards, no way of escaping. 'I like flying,' Pencil said. 'Do you think, if I ask Muis nicely, he might take me out again?'

Maia looked around her, saw Vesper fall into a steep dive and head out across the sea. 'I think they might be a little busy,' she said.

'Muis said he was going to help the others with the goat. Why do they call Shard a goat?'

'I think it's a joke.'

'Is it?' Pencil thought for a while. 'I don't understand. We told them she was a Bazhka.'

'It's because they're young - at least I think they're young - and they're living in dangerous times, and they have to find something to make them laugh, even if it isn't funny, because if they didn't laugh they'd probably cry.'

'So they're like us?' Pencil shook her head in puzzlement. 'I still don't understand.'

Maia tried to explain. 'The Malakhai's city is being attacked by a big ship using terrible weapons. Vesper and Muis and the others, they're trying to fight back. But as far as I can tell they have no weapons. Their homes and their people are being destroyed.'

Pencil's face fell.

'The people in the ship are humans. We're humans. That's why they don't trust us. That's why they're worried about us.'

'But we wouldn't hurt anyone,' Pencil protested.

'They don't know that.' Maia looked around. 'Have you seen what's inside the building?'

Pencil was subdued. 'Muis told me to wait here, not to move. I thought I'd better do as he said in case he decided to drop me in the volcano. Or is that his sense of humour as well?'

'I'm not sure,' Maia admitted. 'We don't actually know much about them and the way they think. But because they're under attack, because they're suspicious about strangers, it would be best not to do anything that might offend them or surprise them. And when they ask us questions, well, we just tell the truth.'

'Do they think we're bad people? They said the Vanjelists were their enemies, but the Vanjelists are our enemies as well, they tried to kill us. So if we're their enemies' enemies, doesn't that make us their friends?'

Maia sighed. 'In theory, yes. But things don't always work out according to theory.'

Pencil's eyes widened. 'Look! Shard's coming!'

The Bazhka was looped around with more rope than when they'd last seen her; Vesper and Muis had joined Fladder, Lepako and Shish to haul Shard up to the fortress, and all five of them were struggling with their load. But a burst of effort from all of then bought them extra height, and they managed to deposit Shard in an ungainly heap on the platform in front of Maia before joining her, breathing heavily, exhausted.

'I think,' Fladder gasped, 'that the goat . . . was eating . . . on the journey.'

'It seems heavy . . . for its . . . size,' Shish added.

'Or perhaps you three,' Muis suggested, 'aren't as strong as you boasted?'

'Thank you for helping,' Lepako said. 'The winds were against us,' she explained, 'otherwise we would have managed.'

Shard unwound herself from her ropes and cords. 'Thank you all for the experience of flying,' she said, 'I confess that I can't see its attraction at all.'

'Shard,' Pencil admonished, 'it was wonderful! And Muis is such a good flier, I felt safe all the time.' She looked at the big Malakhai. 'Even when he flew close to the lava beds.'

'Enough,' Vesper said, 'we need to take you before the court.' The gravity in her voice required obedience; when she stood immediately in front of Maia, Pencil and Shard, the other Malakhai fell in behind them to shepherd them on their way. They walked stiffly on the front of their toes, their claws drawn up in uncomfortable curves, wings furled awkwardly at their sides. Vesper led them through a tall doorway into an echoing rectangular hall. On one side the original basalt of the mountain intruded in tall cathedral columns; on the others there were tall doorways. The air was already chilled and cold winds stalked the gloom; this was not a place for comfort.

A fire burned brightly in a chimney breast against one of the outer walls and, in its glow, Maia could see five stone seats, carved to fit Malakhai bodies, arranged in a semi-circle around a stout wooden table. One of the seats was occupied by a shadowy form. Two other shadows stood over the table, staring intently at scrolls of paper strewn across its surface, talking in high-pitched whispers.

'Come, Vesper, approach with your bad news.' The deep voice appeared to be that of the sitting figure; the two others raised their heads to see what had disturbed their conversation. 'You never bring good news,' the voice continued. 'Unless you're here to inform me that the Black Ship has sailed away? Or sunk?'

'I have brought you humans, Lady Yarasa. We found them on the High Cliff where we were hunting centipedes. We thought they might be spies but . . .'

'How could they be other than spies? Why else would humans be on the High Cliff?'

'They say that the Vanjelists are their enemies and tried to kill them. I thought it best to bring them to you and the court so you could question them.'

'They're spies, Vesper. You've wasted time bringing them here, you should have brought bags of centipedes to drop on the human ship as you were instructed. Or do you propose dropping these spies on the ship instead?' Yarasa's long fingers tapped together irritably like duelling rapiers.

'I've already informed you and the court that attacking the Vanjelist ship with centipedes is pointless,' Vesper continued. 'We need to explore alternatives. These humans, spies or not, may provide us with alternatives.'

Lady Yarasa stopped tapping. 'Very well, Vesper, I will indulge you, providing the other members of the court agree.'

The other two Malakhai whispered to each other again. 'Let the prisoners approach,' one of them said.

'Yes, Lord Jaranat.' Vesper ushered her charges forward. 'This is Maia, she seems to be their leader. Pencil. And Shard, a non-human.'

'The one at the rear looks to me like a Bazhka,' Jaranat said. 'I have seen a Bazhka once before. They are fighters. Though how one Bazhka might fare in combat against a gigantic metal ship is a moot point.' He addressed Shard directly. 'What are you doing here, Bazhka?'

'I guide these humans,' Shard replied. 'I am their guardian.'

'And where are you taking them, Bazhka?' The third Malakhai had a voice as soft and quiet as a dagger.

Maia interrupted. 'Her name is Shard and I'm Maia. She's taking us to find my father who's lost somewhere in the Emperorium. We think he's been captured by the Maker. We think he may be held prisoner in Home, the Bazhka's land. That's where we're going.' As her eyes became used to the dim firelight Maia could make out the faces of her inquisitors. Lady Yarasa was wrapped in her wings, she had short grey hair, her eyes stared at Maia with a mixture of curiosity and malice. Lord Jaranat was standing with his weight distributed on his feet and his knuckles; he seemed to be missing the scimitar claws that Vesper and the other fliers possessed. The third Malakhai seemed more intent on the charts and papers on the table until he looked up and grinned at Maia; it wasn't a particularly pleasant sight; it was as if he was about to devour her.

'Thank you, Maia,' he said, 'my name is Schlager, neither lady nor lord at present.'

'Your task is hopeless, girl,' Yarasa muttered. 'You might as well attack the Black Ship with centipedes.'

'May I ask a question?' Schlager requested in a voice that gave no prospect of opposition. 'How did you come to be on the High Cliff, Maia?'

Maia left nothing out of her story. And when there was nothing else to say, when she was silent, then everyone around her was also silent. But through the floors and walls of the fortress came the hollow boom of the Black Ship's guns tearing at the heart of Kaldera.

'Thank you for your tale, Maia,' Schlager said eventually, 'it would entertain a gullible audience for many nights.'

'It would become a saga worthy of a warrior,' Jaranat added, taking his cue from Schlager, 'and its outlandishness would benefit from even more fabrication. Add some music and actions, a dance perhaps, and you would never go penniless in the halls and mansions of any world.'

'In other words,' Schlager continued, 'your story is precisely that, a story. A fabrication. You are spies and, as such, will be sentenced to death.' The Malakhai looked around. 'With the consent of the other judges present, of course. Lord Jaranat?'

'Guilty.'

'Lady Yarasa?'

'Schlager, I fear we proceed too quickly in this. There may be some truth in what the girl is saying, and Bazhka do not normally aid humans. If what they say is untrue, why is the Bazhka here?'

'You are too forgiving, Lady Yarasa, too gentle. And even if you dissent, in the lack of other judges, Jaranat and I form a majority. We have other matters to consider. Vesper, take them and drop them in the lava ponds. Darkness is near, give them the night together. Do it tomorrow at dawn.'

From somewhere above their heads came a wheezy cough, and slow dust fell onto the table. 'And if I too think you are being a little hasty, Schlager?' The voice was slow, hesitant.

'Lord Morcego. I hadn't realised you were . . . with us. I believed that your injuries would prevent you from . . .'

'Schlager, you thought I was dead or so near dying that I was insensible. Neither is the case.' High in the roof above them the hidden Malakhai, Lord Morcego, breathed in and out noisily. 'You think you know everything and therefore you know nothing.' There was another rattling cough. Maia strained her eyes to see Lord Morcego.

'Vesper, bring a light. The human needs to see me.' Vesper tottered quickly to the fire and returned with a burning brand held between two pincer fingers. She held it high above her head, showing Maia a figure resting in the high rafters of the hall. At first it appeared to be simply a pair of huge eyes in a wrinkled face, but with no body beneath. Then, as she became accustomed to the gloom, she realised that the Malakhai she was seeing was suspended from the rafters, was hanging upside down. Lord Morcego stretched one groaning, painful wing and then the other, but his unblinking gaze never left Maia. He looked old. His wings looked parchment thin, almost white but patched with spots of livid grey. His large eyes had allowed him to see Maia despite the gloom, but they were cloudy and rheumy. He seemed to be held in great reverence by the other Malakhai, even Schlager didn't contradict him, treated him with respect.

'Do I frighten you, girl?' As Lord Morcego spoke he rotated his head so that it appeared the right way up. 'Does my face fill you with loathing?'

'No, Lord Morcego. No to both your questions.'

'You should certainly be frightened. I hold your life, and the lives of your companions in my hands. And those humans on the Black Ship loathe the Malakhai. Do you know why?'

'I don't know for certain, Lord Morcego, but I have met other Vanjelists. They hate people who are different to themselves, or who believe different things.'

'And you say that they hate you as well? Yet you are similar to them. You look the same as them. What is the difference between you and a Vanjelist?' Morcego coughed, a loud, hacking sound that suggested illness or injury.

Maia considered her response carefully. 'Vanjelists see their beliefs as the only true beliefs. They kill those who disagree with them.' Maia thought of Mr Forritt, murdered by Zeke all those days and weeks and years ago. 'And they kill those who look different to them. Perhaps that's why they seek to kill your people.'

'This may be true, girl, but there is more. We have captured a Vanjelist who is still alive, who has told us that we look like "the Devil". This "Devil" is some part of their mythology. So we are being systematically murdered because we look like an imaginary being in their value system.' Morcego coughed again, louder and more rasping than before.

Pencil had been quiet for a while but obviously felt that the conversation required a contribution from her. 'Mr Morcego, It's very smoky up there and you're coughing badly. Wouldn't you be better down here with the rest of us? It's quite breezy down here.'

'Your concern is noted, second girl.'

'Pencil. My name is Pencil.'

'Then I shall join you, Pencil.'

'Would you like some assistance, Lord Morcego?' Schlager asked ingratiatingly.

'I would not,' Morcego replied. He slid slowly along the rafter until he reached the wall and transferred his weight to another, lower beam, then another parallel to the wall. He hooked one long finger around a piece of projecting timber and lowered one leg, then another until he was able to slide down the wall. He managed to move across the floor in a half-crouching, half-sliding manner until he found an empty chair, then raised his body painfully into it. He closed his eyes.

'Lord Morcego?'

'Have no fear, Lady Yarasa, I am not dead yet.' He beckoned Pencil closer with one long finger. 'What should I do with you? How can you help me?'

Maia stepped forward to join Pencil. 'I see you're wounded,' she said.' You're bleeding. You have holes in your wings. How can we help you?'

Lord Morcego laughed, then coughed, and flecks of blood showed around his mouth. 'Destroy the Black Ship for me?'

'I doubt that we can do that,' Shard said, 'but I have healing herbs and poultices with me, I may be able to stop your pain. I may be able to treat your wounds. I have some skill . . .'

'Do the Vanjelists wish to kill you, Bazhka? You are even less human-looking than we Malakhai.'

Shard nodded. 'All Vanjelists and most humans wish to kill Bazhka. There are complex reasons for this. But I believe that Vanjelists and Bazhkas both wish to find Maia, for reasons we aren't sure of.'

'You say "we", Bazhka. Is the plural signifying all Bazhkas?'

'No, Lord Morcego. It signifies myself, Maia and Pencil.'

'Ah. A small group, are you not? It is obvious to me that you, Maia, are of value to your enemies. You, Pencil, less so. And you, Bazhka, not at all.'

'But I might be of use to you, Lord Morcego. Allow me to treat your wounds.'

Morcego drew himself up in his chair. 'Do you have enough medicine and bandages to treat all my injured and dying people? They number in their thousands. Many tens of thousands will die through hunger or lack of shelter unless I can find a way to halt this attack. I have no doubt that some, like Vesper and Muis here, will take to the cliffs and survive. Or they might gather enough warriors to attack the Black Ship in one great effort. Using centipedes and sabre claws and spears and scatterpods, eh Vesper?'

'As you did, Lord Morcego,' Vesper replied.

'As I did. And I survived!' He sighed, and a bubbling sound threatened from his throat. 'Though not for long, I fear. And so many of my friends and my people didn't survive.'

Schlager was growing impatient. 'Lord Morcego, we were about to pass judgement on these humans and their pet. Lady Yarasa was the only dissenting voice when I proposed their death, therefore our judgement is carried by a two-to-one majority. Do you concur with our decision? With respect, we have wasted enough time in deliberating the matter. We have a war to plan. Your opinion is, of course, paramount, but we are aware of your wounds, your pain, your steadfastness in the face of your suffering . . .'

'Schlager! If you had a brain you might be dangerous!'

'Yes, Lord Morcego.' Schlager had, while delivering his rhetoric, inched forwards to stand directly before Morcego. He quickly shuffled back.

'I believe what this girl has just told me. She and her friends are not spies. They are, like the Malakhai, victims. And we cannot, we will not, judge them simply because they are humans,' Morcego glanced at Shard. 'Or assisting humans. To do so would make us as bad as our enemies.'

'Thank you, Lord Morcego,' Maia said, 'but will you please allow Shard to treat you? She is wise in many ways and . . .'

'I haven't finished yet, girl,' Morcego dismissed Maia's intervention. 'I wished to say that I do not agree with Schlager and Jaranat. And since I am Elder, my voice carries the greater weight if a proposal is tied. And so our prisoners will not be taken to the lava ponds. They will be released.'

Maia smiled at Pencil and Shard. They would now be able to ask for help to seek an exit gateway that would take them close to the Home where, whatever fate might befall them, they would at least be nearer her father. And nearer the Maker. She was certain that finding the Maker was important, that was why the Vanjelists and the Bazhkas were searching for her. But she would rather meet him on her terms, not as a captive. She climbed to her feet. 'Thank you again . . .'

'I still haven't finished, girl. And I am not as kind nor as merciful as you might believe.'

Shard too was on her feet, and Maia could tell by her stance, by the play of muscles beneath her skin, that she was prepared to fight. Morcego too had noticed this. 'There are no guards here,' he went on, 'because there is no way you can escape. Attacking us will serve no purpose; we are already as good as dead. So please do not think of attempting to harm us. Your Bazhka would no doubt injure or kill some of us, but you, Maia, and you, Pencil would be killed in the process.'

Maia shook her head at Shard; Shard forced herself to relax. 'What's going to happen to us?' Maia asked.

'You will be kept safe and warm. You will be fed. In the morning I will send fliers to the Black Ship in the shelter of a flag of truce. They will inform the leader of the Vanjelists that you are our guests. They will inform them that we will hand you over to them if they stop destroying our city, if they stop killing us, if they give their word that they will leave us in peace.' Morcego coughed blood. 'This is my proposal, Schlager, Lady Yarasa, Lord Jaranat. Do I have your support?'

'Yes, Lord Morcego,' Yarasa said.

'Of course, my Lord Morcego,' Jaranat bowed his head.

'An excellent plan, gracious Lord,' Schlager said, 'how I wish I had your foresight, your ability to see solutions in . . .'

'Be quiet, Schlager. Leave me now. Go on! All of you, save Vesper.'

They shuffled out of the room and onto the platform, dived into the quickening night. Only Vesper, Maia, Pencil and Shard remained.

'Vesper?' The effort of speaking seemed too great for Morcego, his voice was nothing more than a whisper.

'Yes, father?'

'I sense that you . . . do not approve of my judgement.'

'I don't trust the Vanjelists, father. I believe they will take the girl and continue to attack our city and its people. Maia is innocent of any crime against us. How can we justify delivering her to those who would kill her? Surely a punishment must fit a crime, and here no crime has been committed.'

'Your argument is valid, daughter. I have taught you well.'

'Then why will you sacrifice them?'

Morcego was slumped in his seat, eyes closed, breathing shallow. He forced his eyes to open, looked at Vesper, summoned up the remains of his strength. 'I will sacrifice them for the greatest good of the largest number of people, daughter. They are four lives; we Malakhai are many hundreds of thousands. Don't you see? I have no choice.'

'And what about the others who might die if we are killed?' Maia could barely control her anger. 'What happens when Bazhkas are unleashed on my world? What happens when the Vanjelists spread their doctrine throughout the Emperorium? How many lives will be lost? Vanjelists can't be trusted, we know that. Would you trust people who attack you and your people because of the way they look? You're wrong, Lord Morcego, you're wrong!'

Morcego shook his head. 'I will not be lectured by a human.'

'Then you're as prejudiced as the Vanjelists!'

A brief spark of defiance appeared in the old Malakhai's eyes. 'Take them away, Vesper. Put them with the other human, the captive. Have them fed. I must rest.'

'Yes father,' Vesper said, reached out a long finger and stroked her father's weary head. 'Sleep. I will carry out your wishes.' She beckoned to Maia. 'You and your friends will be found rooms in the lower floors. I will bring you food. Follow me.' She led them down a wide ramp descending the outer wall of the fortress, doubling back on itself two or three times.

'Morcego is your father?' Shard asked. 'This isn't a name given to him because he's your leader?'

'He is my father.'

'He's also wrong. The Vanjelists will agree to your terms. They'll take Maia and they'll kill her. Then they'll continue to bombard Kaldera.'

'I suspect you're right. But the judges have given their decision. I have been given my orders. I can't change either of these.'

'Vesper,' Maia asked, 'how do you fight the Black Ship?'

Vesper seemed embarrassed in her response. 'We drop centipedes on the Ship, in the hope that they will attack those on board. At first we tried fighting the soldiers and sailors. I may have killed one with my own sabre claw, but now they shoot us out of the sky before we can get near. We've tried using spears but they aren't accurate, we have to throw them from too far away. Or we drop scatterpods on them.'

'What's a scatterpod?' Pencil asked.

'It's the fruit of a tree that grows only on islands with a volcano. The husk grows hard in the heat and, when it fractures, the seeds burst out. We drop them from above the Black Ship. When they hit the deck they burst, just like in a fire, and if the seeds hit a human then the human will be injured or die. But if we fly high to launch the scatterpod then we can't be accurate, we often miss our target. If we fly low they shoot us.'

'So you don't really have a chance,' Maia said.

'That is why Morcego chose to hand you to the Vanjelists. We have no other options.'

'Have you thought,' Shard asked, 'of attacking from the water? Have you no boats?'

Vesper looked at Shard disdainfully. 'We have wings, Bazhka. Why would we ever need to use a boat?'

'But you have trees. You could float to the Ship and . . .'

'Bazhka, can you fly?' Vesper unfurled one wing. 'You appear to lack the necessary attachments. Without them you would fly in one direction only, straight down. I would never be so stupid as to suggest you even attempt flight. So accept the fact that the Malakhai cannot, will not and do not use boats!'

Pencil smiled. 'I think you've been told, Shard. No boats!'

Vesper didn't want to linger. 'You will find our human captive from the Black Ship here. We questioned him but he was unwilling to answer us. Schlager wanted to dispose of him but I felt that he might react well to a combination of kindness and confinement. I was wrong.'

'What were you trying to find out from him?' Shard's question was straightforward enough, but Vesper's reply showed her impatience.

'How to destroy the Black Ship, of course.' Vesper turned quickly. 'I must go now. You may recall that my father is dying.' She ducked out of the room but Maia followed her.

'If we can find out how to destroy the Ship, will you let us go?'

'I'll do more than that, I'll fly you to your destination, wherever that may be.' She leaped from the platform and out into the dark night.

Maia tried to follow Vesper's flight. She thought she saw her, wide-winged, eclipsing unfamiliar stars, but then she disappeared into the silence. The new constellations were mirrored by the pinpricks of light dotting the plains below the fortress, each a marker of dispossession, desperation and despair. Maia knew that there were families clustered round fires, facing a future that was at best uncertain, at worst, hopeless. The Black Ship would destroy the city of Kaldera and the Vanjelists would then hunt down the Malakhai. She could understand why Morcego had made his decision; she suspected that she would have done the same if she'd been in his position. And Morcego had himself attacked the Black Ship, an act of bravery and stupidity given his age and the laughable weapons at his disposal.

Between the sky and the plain, each shimmering with its own light, lay the sea. It was black and cold and threatening, and Maia shivered at the thought of its unforgiving inhumanity. She pulled her coat around her and went back into the stone fortress to join the others.

They were clustered round a heavy wooden table on which fruit and raw vegetables had been laid, as well as cold cooked fish and carved meat. None of it had been taken; there was no sign of the captive Vesper had mentioned.

'Should we eat?' Pencil asked, guilty that she should be thinking of food when they were in such an awkward situation.

'Of course,' Maia said, 'we need to stay strong.'

While Pencil experimented with the unusual tastes and strange textures of the food, Maia sat close to Shard. 'I'm worried,' she admitted.

'As am I. I can see no way out of this.'

'Put that aside for a moment. What really concerns me is the Black Ship. Vesper flew me near it, it's powered by steam, it uses sophisticated weapons. Not as advanced as in my land and time, but far superior to anything else I've seen in the Emperorium. It's the sign of an industrial society, and I thought the Emperorium was rural and agricultural.'

'When you say "sophisticated" and "advanced",' Shard asked thoughtfully, 'do you mean capable of killing a lot of people?'

Maia's face sank. 'Yes, I suppose I do.'

'And the Vanjelists call Bazhka "monsters".' Shard sighed. 'I haven't seen anything like the Black Ship you describe. Nor have I heard of this land of Kaldera, which must be large beyond our immediate surroundings if it holds both humans and Malakhai. Yet they met for the first time when the Black Ship arrived. What does the Map say?'

Pencil brought the Map from its pouch and opened it.

'It shows that we're in another unexplored land,' Shard said, 'though no larger than many others.'

'When we first came to the Emperorium,' Maia said, 'we thought there were corridors and gateways to move between lands. Then we found the attic and wormholes,

339

which seem to be a sort of shortcut between lands. Do you think there could be another way of moving around, on water? So that a sea in one land might lead directly to a sea in another?'

Shard pondered the question. 'Such a thing might be possible in the Emperorium.'

'So the Black Ship might have come from a part of the Emperorium we've never seen or heard of, somewhere the Map doesn't know about.'

Shard rotated the muscles in her neck. 'Anything is possible in the Emperorium.'

'The food's good,' Pencil said. 'You should try some.'

Once they'd eaten a few morsels they attacked the rest with relish. Maia and Pencil competed in describing each new taste in terms of something more familiar, while Shard picked daintily at everything. After a while she leaned across to Maia. 'I know that you know we're being watched, I saw you glancing up at the balcony where he's hiding. Do you want me to go and fetch him? I won't hurt him, unless he struggles too much.'

'No,' Maia whispered, 'let's be open with him. But . . . I've an idea. Follow my lead. Don't say anything at all.' She signalled to Pencil to come closer. 'There's a man watching us. Can you pretend to be someone you aren't? Can you pretend to be my servant?'

Pencil nodded. 'I think I'm someone who isn't really me all the time, so being a different someone won't be a problem.' She nodded deferentially. 'Milady.'

Maia looked up at the balcony. 'I know you're there,' she shouted. 'You might as well come down and eat before we take it all. We're captives, like you. And we're humans.' She giggled, and the sound belonged to someone who wasn't Maia. 'Except for my pet, and she won't harm you.'

There was a long silence before a gruff voice asked, 'Who are you?'

'I was going to ask you the same question. But since you asked first, my name is Maria and my maid here is Penelope. And you are?'

'Where are you from?' The man asked suspiciously, though he appeared to be moving closer.

'The same place as you, I'd imagine. From the Ship.'

'The Susquehanna? I ain't seen you on board.'

'I doubt I've seen you either. But that's difficult to be certain of, since I don't know what you look like. Come now, are you frightened of two girls and a pet goat?'

The figure that shuffled out of the shadows wore an untidy black naval uniform. He was middle-aged, the top of his head pale, the grey hair growing long at the sides. He had several days of bristle growing beneath a hooked nose, and his eyes shifted rapidly as he slowly approached the table.

'I ain't seen no girls on the Susquehanna. No women neither.'

Maia motioned him to a chair. 'The Captain didn't want our presence to be widely known.'

'The Captain? Persimmon?' The sailor reached for a fruit that looked like an apple but tasted almost savoury. He took a large bite. 'There was a rumour,' he said through uneven teeth, 'that 'e 'ad a woman on board. 'S that you?' He leered at Maia. 'You 'is doxy, then?'

'I am Captain Persimmon's niece, and I will inform him when I see him of your rude and inappropriate assumption.'

The man blanched. He put down the remains of his fruit on the table and stood up, bowed his head. 'Beggin' your pardon, Miss, I didn't mean no offence. I've been here alone with those devil bats, they've tortured me an' hurt me an' I ain't told them nothin' 'bout anythin', but I'm so tired an' starvin', I ain't eaten their food 'n case it's poisoned, but I

341

seen you here an' . . .' He began to sniffle. 'Say you won't tell the Captain, Miss, 'e'd 'ave me keel-hauled.'

Maia felt sorry for the man, he was clearly terrified of the Captain. But she had a role to play. 'Oh, do stop whinging, man,' she said haughtily. 'And tell me your name.'

'Langhorne, Miss. Sam Langhorne.'

'And your rank? Clearly you haven't risen highly.'

'No, Miss. Seaman.'

'As I thought.' She drummed her fingers on the table. 'Very well, Seaman Samuel Langhorne, I'd suggest you eat heartily. I intend escaping from this place and I'll need your help to do so, this will require you to answer some rather detailed questions. If you do so fully and accurately then I will refrain from telling my uncle of your insulting language. Do you understand?'

'Yes, Miss.'

'Then eat. You have five minutes, after that time my questions will begin.'

'Yes, Miss.'

Maia was surprised how readily she was able to deceive Langhorne, and even how much she enjoyed doing so. It felt good to be in charge. She was pleased that Shard and Pencil had said nothing, their silence reinforced her own acting skills. But they had roles to play as well.

'Penelope, I want you to listen to everything this man has to say.'

'Yes, Miss,' Pencil said, bobbing her head, no trace of a smile on her face.

'I suspect you've seen more of the ship than I have, if there is any inaccuracy in what he says, do not hesitate to inform me.'

'Yes, Miss. I'll be all ears for you.'

'Shard!' The Bazhka's ears flicked up. 'Come here, that's a good girl.'

Shard stood up to her full height and glared at Langhorne, pulled back her lips to reveal her teeth. Langhorne and his chair slid rapidly away from the table.

'Shard, behave! Here, girl, sit by me.'

Shard sat down at Maia's feet and began to emit a low, contented cat-like growl as Maia scratched at the base of her horns.

'You have two minutes, Langhorne, two minutes eating time. But don't worry, Shard will only tear you to pieces and devour you if I tell her to.'

'I, uh, I don't feel 'ungry n more,' Langhorne said.

'Very well. Then I'll begin. Whereabouts in the Susquehanna do you normally work?'

'Boiler room, Miss.'

'And where in the ship is that situated?'

Langhorne was about to reply, but decided to hold his tongue. After a few moments deliberation he began to speak 'Part of me,' he said slowly, 'is wantin' to answer your question. But another part of me is suspicious and is askin' why you needs to know this. If you don't mind explainin' this to me then I'll be forthcomin' with the answer to your question.'

Maia was surprised that the sailor seemed to have recovered some of his confidence. She could feel Shard tense under her fingertips. 'I am asking, Mr Langhorne, because I was not aware that any seaman had been taken from the Susquehanna. I am asking because I suspect that you may actually be a spy, working for the devil bats. I am asking because the accuracy of your response determines whether or not you will be alive in five minutes time. Because that's how long it will take Shard to disembowel you if I find that you are lying. Now then, do you wish me to repeat my question?'

Langhorne swallowed. 'The boiler room's aft of midships, fourth staircase from bows, port 'n' starboard access. Down five decks.'

Maia looked at Pencil. 'Does that sound right to you, Penelope?'

'I think so, Miss. Though I'm not sure about the number of decks, I've never been that far down.'

'No, I'm sure you haven't,' Maia said, her tone suggesting that her maid had probably visited most of the ship for some nefarious purpose. She turned her gaze once again on the frightened, shivering seaman. 'Thank you, Langhorne. Your truthfulness has saved your life.'

Langhorne sat back in his seat and sighed.

'Tell me, Langhorne,' Maia said, 'how does a seaman, a boilerman who works five decks below main deck, get taken by a devil bat? Because I can't imagine my uncle permitting someone like you access to the main decks, and I can't imagine a devil bat travelling through the bowels of the ship solely to take away a lowly boilerman. So please, do elucidate.'

Langhorne looked puzzled. 'Do what, Miss?'

Maia looked up in exasperation. 'Explain, Langhorne! Clarify! Give details! Put into plain words? For goodness' sake, just tell me what happened!'

Langhorne was beginning to think that being eaten alive by Shard might be preferable to enduring Maia's continued withering wrath. 'Yes, Miss! Me 'n' Josh, Josh Perkins, we was both stoakin' boiler eight when the sergeant at arms comes down 'n' says one of us is to go on deck, they needs extra shooters. Well, I used to be handy with a rifle, but Josh ain't handled such a thing before, so up I goes. There's lots of us bein' given guns 'n' rounds, it's near sunset, 'n' the devils 're comin' out of the sun at us. So we're lined up at the rails, 'n' it's like shootin' chickens in a barn, there's so many 'f 'em. I reckon I must've got five or six when I feel a rope wrap around me, like a whip, 'n' suddenly I'm in the air! It was gettin' dark, I couldn't see too much, but at first I was down near the water 'n' then I was bein' taken up, higher 'n' higher. I thought I might untangle myself but then I figured the drop might kill me, 'n' I didn't really want to be dead. So I hung on, 'n' then the devils brought me here.' He spat on the ground. 'It was like we was told, they're devil bats! They don't deserve to live!'

'But they didn't kill you,' Maia said.

'They tortured me! But I didn't say nothin'!'

'Excuse me, Miss, may I ask a question?' Pencil bowed her head towards Maia.

'If it's sensible, Penelope. But do be quick.'

'Yes Miss.' She turned towards Langhorne. 'You said before that these creatures tortured you, that they hurt you. Do you need any assistance with your wounds?'

Langhorne stared at Pencil, unsure what reply he should give. 'When I said they tortured me, it wasn't with nothin' physical, Miss. It wasn't like they tied me up 'n' beat me. But they wanted to know why we was shellin' them, 'n' I knew if I told the truth, if I said it was 'cos they was the spawn of the devil, 'cos they wasn't human, then they'd drop me in the volcano. I heard 'em talkin' 'bout doin' it! So I said nothin'.'

'So they didn't really harm you?'

'Oh, they harmed me, Miss! Not in the body, perhaps, but here!' He tapped his head. 'They were playin' with me.'

Maia waved Pencil back to her seat. 'Did they give you food?'

'They left food out for me, but I didn't eat any 'cos I thought it'd be poisoned. Then they took it away 'n' left more next day.'

'And a bed? Blankets?'

'A straw mattress, Miss. 'N' yes, some blankets.'

'What would have happened if one of them had been captured? What would you have done to them?'

Langhorne was dismissive. 'Oh, some 'f them was wounded, landed on the deck. They was lyin' there with their wings all torn, 'n I seen the Captain himself amongst them, 'n he put a bullet in 'em. But they're animals, they ain't people like us.'

Maia nodded. 'Yes, I see. You've been very helpful, Langhorne. I'll make sure my uncle knows all about your assistance and your honesty. But,' she stretched and yawned, 'I feel it's time to retire. I have a great deal to think about.'

'Yes, Miss. There's rooms aplenty to choose from.' He looked at the table in front of him. 'Would it be possible to take a little food away with me?'

'Yes, I'm sure it hasn't been poisoned.'

''N' I'd like the chance, if it's possible, if you can think of a way, to get back onto the Susquehanna.'

'We'll see, Langhorne. We'll see.'

She waited until the seaman had taken more than his share of food and retreated to the room he'd been using. She motioned Shard and Pencil close to her. 'Well, what do you think?' She said softly.

'It was a good game,' Pencil said, 'but I'd like to have a bigger part to play next time.'

'I enjoyed having my horns scratched,' Shard said, 'but I can't see what your purpose was.'

'To find out more about the Black Ship. To see if I could persuade that sailor I was someone I wasn't. To discover what the people on the Ship were like; are they like the Vanjelists we've already met?'

'Worse, by the sound of it,' Shard said.

'I agree. So I have no qualms about destroying their ship.'

'And how might we do that?'

346

'That's what we need to talk about as soon as Langhorne's asleep. A way to destroy the Black Ship, so Vesper can take us on the next stage of our journey.'

'Oh,' said Pencil, 'is that all?'

'What do you want me to do?' Shard asked. 'I trust there'll be a role for me.'

Maia grinned. 'Well, I have one or two ideas.'

FIFTEEN

Friz was the first to react. She pulled the thorn out of Slip's flesh and threw it away, ripped a length of fabric from the bottom of her shirt and tied it tightly around Slip's arm above the encroaching blackness. She looked wildly about her. 'What do we do? Where do we go?' Her gaze fell on Ruthie. 'This is all your fault,' she hissed, advancing on the figure of twigs and bones, 'I've a good mind to tear you apart right here and now!'

'That won't do no good,' Ruthie replied, 'I guess I'd jus' grow somewhere else and y'r friend boy-Slip, well, he'd die.' She glanced at Ten. 'And y'r friend boy-Ten'd also suffer an' prob'ly die.' She stared at Friz with nut-brown eyes. 'And *you'd* be lost, and y'r friend boy-Tom'd be lost, and y'd both die, or p'raps be killed. But I c'n help y' all.'

Friz turned her attention to Slip. 'Sit down,' she ordered him, 'don't panic. Relax.' She helped him to the ground. He put up no resistance. His eyes were closing.

'No!' Friz shouted. 'Stay awake! Don't close your eyes!'

'How can you help?' Tom demanded. 'You're not even alive!'

'I'm *Ruthie*, I'm human, 'neath this parcel 'f branches an' bones.' She held up her arm. 'But I'm also 'f th' *Forest*, I'm 'f a world you cain't never un'stand. I'm one with *trees* an' *plants*, with *flowers* an' *grasses*. An' I *know* things. I know what *poison* the Forest's thorns use. I know how t' *help* boy-Slip. I know how t' help boy-Ten.' She stopped speaking. She reached out her arms to the tunnel walls and, even in the dim torchlight, Tom and Friz could see a thin filament of pale tendrils escape from her fingertips into the packed earth. 'I know where y'all *are*. I c'n guide you to where you want t' *go*. I c'n do *all* this. But I need y'r help.'

Slip's eyes closed. His head fell forward. Friz looked at his arm, the blackness was spreading beyond the tourniquet. 'Do it,' she said to Ruthie, 'do what you can, do what you have to.'

'But you don't know . . .' Tom began.

'He's dying!' Friz yelled. 'Are *you* going to cure him?'

Ruthie stepped close to Slip. She extended her right arm, and from the tip of one finger a needle thin thorn grew. She spread the fingers of her left hand over Slip's upper arm.

'What are you doing?' Friz whispered.

Ruthie ignored her. She slid the thorn over Slip's arm until it was above the blackest vein and pushed the thorn into it.

'Look at her feet,' Tom said. Ruthie's feet appeared to be spreading wider, growing out into the ground, rooting deeply and firmly. She was becoming less like a woman, more like a small tree.

'What's happening?' Friz whispered.

The leaves along Ruthie's hand, the one with the sliver of thorn in Slip's arm, slowly turned red, then brown, then withered to black and fell to the ground. The change continued, moved along Ruthie's arm; summery leaves became autumnal brown then shrivelled to skeletal ash.

'I think she's drawing out the poison,' Friz said. 'Look at Slip's arm.'

The darkness was slowly waning. Friz untied the cloth from above his elbow and, after a momentary surge, the black veins lost their funereal shade. Slip's eyes flickered, then opened.

'But look at her.' Tom said. 'It looks as if she's dying instead.'

As Slip returned to life, so Ruthie's leaves turned and fell. She became thin and gaunt, all colour drained from her except the pale white of her human bones and, wrapped around them, slender limbs of black-barked bough. Her leaves lay at her feet like old, bleached confetti. The polished acorns that had been her eyes rattled to the ground.

Slip sat up. 'What's going on?' he said, 'I can remember . . .' He looked at Ruthie's dead twig fingers, didn't resist when Friz pulled the thorn from his arm. 'Is that Ruthie?' he asked.

Tom nodded. 'You were poisoned, a thorn got you. Ruthie drew the venom out but . . . She can't have known how bad it was. She took it away and . . .'

Friz shook her head. 'No, she didn't just take it away.' She laughed, and at first Tom thought she'd gone mad. 'Look,' Friz said, 'she dispersed it into the ground. Look at her. Look at her!'

Green shoots were appearing at the crown of Ruthie's head. They unfurled, spread around each other, linked into a fresh, new skin that spread rapidly over her whole body. She pulled the roots of her feet out of the ground and, unsteadily but deliberately, moved them away from the earth that had become black, stained with poison.

Ruthie rippled with green life, and then burst into flower. She grew a dress of tiny white hibiscus blossoms with dark purple centres, her hair was cascades of golden laburnum, and her eyes two bright blooms of periwinkle. There was no breeze, but she moved and danced as if there was one. 'I wan't sure I c'd do that,' she said, and her rose red lips smiled.

'I think,' Slip said, 'I owe you my life.'

'I'll 'mind ya o' that,' Ruthie replied. She looked round at Ten. He was slumped against the wall of the tunnel, almost unconscious. Sweat clung to his fevered forehead, his eyes and mouth were pinched, his face grey. He tossed his head, groaned and whimpered. 'Y'r other friend's in great pain. The poison I took from boy-Slip's body'll, in small doses, take th' pain away, he'll rest, he'll lose his senses.'

'I think she means,' Tom said, 'it's an anaesthetic.'

'I c'n take his pain. Ya must then reset his leg an' sew up th' wound. Ya must bind it. Ya must keep it firm an' straight while the bone heals. I knows this 'cause I has the knowledge of all who once were an' are an' always will be th' Forest. But I,' she said with pleasure in her voice, 'am stronger than the Forest.' She looked at Friz. 'Do ya want me t' do this?

Friz in turn looked at Tom and Slip. The latter flexed his wounded arm. 'If she can do this then I think we can trust her, don't you?'

Ruthie extended another thorn and inserted it into a vein in Ten's arm. Within moments his fists unclenched, his body relaxed. Ruthie produced other thorns to be used as needles, and strong threads made of fibrous leaves. She gave instructions on how to mash up special leaves into a calming poultice, she even guided Tom and Friz (by placing her hands on Ten's leg and covering the wound with a thin film of what might have been sap, which seemed to allow her to sense the bone's position) when they reset Ten's broken leg. She then produced extra-large leaves to use as bandages, and guided them to the walls of the tunnel where long thin roots could be found to use as splints.

They rested when the operation was finished. 'Y'all need t' sleep,' Ruthie said. 'Y'll be safe here, but we mus' move quick when daylight comes.'

'Will the Forest try to attack us?' Slip asked.

'No. I c'n sense that th' Forest won't attack. It feels, for th' first time in centuries, unsafe. The need t' move is mine. I've done things I din't know I c'd do, and I've used up energy. I need t' rest an' I need t' feed. I need sunlight. We're below ground; we mus' move up from this tunnel.'

They settled down for the night, Ruthie beside Ten, occasionally brushing her leafed hands over his dirty face. He appeared to be sleeping naturally, though Ruthie said she was making sure his pain wouldn't return.

Tom and Friz discussed how they might move Ten next day until their voices became deep breating sleep. Slip couldn't join them, despite feeling warm and comfortable.

'Are you there, Ruthie?' he said.

'I'm close, boy-Slip.'

Slip gathered his jumbled thoughts. 'Ruthie, why did you help us?'

Ruthie's voice was the whisper of a breeze over new leaves. "Cause I knew that th' Forest was selfish. It wished t' keep y' there t' feed itself with y'r bodies an' y'r thoughts. The part 'f me that was once human knew this was wrong. An' so I sought to help y' escape.'

'But the Ruthie part of you is so small compared to the Forest.'

'Small, yes. But powerful.'

There was something in Ruthie's reasoning that didn't quite fit, but Slip couldn't think what it was. And then it came to him. 'Powerful? Why more powerful than any of the other humans that the Forest had absorbed?'

'Some'f 'em was old when th' Forest took 'em, boy-Slip. Others was tired'f life. Some wanted t' die. I was none o' those.'

Slip waited, was about to continue his questioning when Ruthie spoke again.

'Until I felt ya, heard ya, saw ya, Ruthie din't exist. Ruthie was asleep, dreamin'. Ruthie could no more think than a tree or a blade'f grass c'd think. Then the Forest woke Ruthie an' made 'er speak, made 'er move, an' at first she din't want t'. But the Forest was strong. It forced 'er. An' that made Ruthie 'member a day she'd forgot. It made 'er 'member a time when others forced 'er t' do somethin' she din't want t' do. Her brother Zeke was the first. *My* brother. An' I woke t' fully become Ruthie, t' become me. An' my mem'ries made me strong!'

'We met him,' Slip said. 'He was going to harm Maia. Shard killed him.'

'Tha's good. One less t' hunt down. But his was a lesser evil. He just sold me, f'r money or 'cause he wished t' ingratiate hi'self with someone more powerful 'n him, it don't really matter. The man who violated me, who hurt me, who maimed me, who left me f'r dead, was Jean Baptiste. Do ya wish t' know what he did?'

'I've met him too. No, please don't tell me what he did. I can imagine.'

'I'm not sure ya can, boy-Slip. But the Forest re-woke my fear an' loathin' 'f him. I fought agin the Forest as I fought agin Baptiste, but this time I won. An' what drove me on was my thirst for revenge.' There was no anger in Ruthie's voice, just a calm determination to tell her story that made the telling even more chilling.

'How did you think we might help you get revenge?' Slip asked.

'By takin' me with ya. I has . . . limitations. But, as ya found out, there's advantages t' havin' me with ya. In this form I move slow. I need sunlight. I need t' touch th' earth. You an' yer friends c'n move fast an' think fast. If'n ya find a way t' help me, I'll find ways t' help you. But 'member, I wish to search for an' kill Baptiste.'

'I don't have any problem with that, Ruthie. But we have our own tasks as well. What happens if the paths we need to take go in different directions?'

Again there was a long silence. Perhaps, Slip thought, Ruthie had entirely run out of energy. Perhaps she needed sunlight now! But then she spoke again.

'You an' me 're bound togither in ways we cain't yet comprehend. Yer blood, boy-Slip, an' my sap've mingled. An' ya 'mind me 'f a boy I knew long ago. I knew him well. I could not've imagined life without him.'

'I hope he was handsome,' Slip joked.

'He was kind, as 're you.'

Slip felt the soft touch of leaves on his forehead. 'I'll do everything I can to help you,' he said.

Ruthie's voice faded into nothingness. 'Y're kind, like him.'

When Tom woke and switched on his torch he found Slip, Friz and Ten still sleeping. Ruthie was standing in the middle of the tunnel, motionless, rooted in place. Her flowers were fading. 'I'm going to see if there's a way out,' he told her, and immediately felt stupid for talking to a plant. Ruthie replied, however, with a 'Stay safe . . . boy-Tom.' But her words were slow and listless.

Tom was surprised to find that the tunnel didn't widen like the corridors, and there were no side tunnels. He soon came to an opening whose wooden frame suggested there might once have been a door there; if so, there was nothing remaining of the door itself save, beyond the opening, a few planks of black-stained wood. He looked gingerly through the entrance. There appeared to be a room beyond, its walls built of stone and supporting thick, twisted beams of wood that bore a ceiling. He could almost touch the beams and the rough-sawn timber boards beyond. The floor was the same packed earth as the tunnel. The room appeared to be empty.

There were other openings in the walls, spaced irregularly; soil spilled from some of them, as if the tunnel beyond had collapsed. Tom switched off his torch; there was no light filtering through the floorboards above his head, nor from any of the tunnels. There was no sound. The air smelled only of damp earth.

Tom decided not to explore further. The torch might fail, and he wasn't sure he'd be able to find his way back in the darkness. And with the light extinguished, the silence and the black emptiness threatened to suffocate him. He hurried back the way he'd just come, stopping only to pick up the pieces of broken door.

He soon heard Slip and Friz talking in the distance.

'The question is,' Slip was saying, 'how do we move the lump in the corner.'

'The lump,' Ten's voice said, sounding slow and tired but not in pain, 'objects to being called a lump.'

Tom grinned. He flicked on the torch beam. 'I never thought you'd hear this from me, Ten,' he said, 'but it's good to hear your whinging voice again.' In the dim light Ten looked as if he'd slept well; although his leg was bound and splinted, he was smiling.

'Likewise, oh mighty leader,' Ten replied, 'Are you keeping the light low so we can't see your ugly face?' He hurried on before Tom could think of further insults. 'Slip's been filling me in on what's happened since I broke my leg. It looks as if Maia and the others got away. That's good. At least, I think it's good. She's got Pencil and the Map, and Shard to help her.' He'd clearly seen the anxiety etched in Tom's grubby face. 'And it seems I owe my life to . . . well, to all of you, for dragging me down here and fixing my leg. But especially Ruthie.'

Tom held up the torch. Everyone blinked in the light except for Ruthie who was standing where Tom had left her. Her flowers had all gone; even her leaves were wilting. She said nothing. The sight forced Tom into action.

'We need to get moving,' he said, looking grimly at Ruthie. 'We need to find our way up into daylight. I've been along the tunnel, there's an opening at the end with a room beyond, stone walls, low ceiling, a bit like a basement. But there's no way through the ceiling, it's solid. There are exits, more tunnels, by the look of them, but I thought it would be better to explore them together.' He moved to stand in front of Ten. 'Would you be able to stand it if we drag you on Shard's coat? We can't stay here and . . .'

'I can stand the discomfort if you can stand the screams,' Ten said.

'What about Ruthie?' Slip asked. 'She doesn't look as if she can move at all.'

'I . . . c'n . . . move . . . boy-Slip,' Ruthie countered. She uprooted one foot and dragged it across the floor, but the movement was slow.

'No you can't,' Slip said, 'but I can carry you.' He moved across to her. 'Uproot both feet,' he said. 'And . . . Wait a minute, I've an idea.' He'd been sleeping with his head on his sack and he picked it up, then turned it upside down to empty it. 'Friz,' he asked, 'have you still got that folding shovel?'

Friz reached for her own sack. 'Yeah. Why?'

'First, can you put as much of my stuff in your own sack as you can carry. Second, let me borrow the shovel.'

Friz passed the shovel to Slip. It was perhaps the best indication of their long friendship that she did as she'd been asked, began loading Slip's spare clothes into her own bag without asking any questions. Slip hacked at the floor of the tunnel with the shovel. The ground was hard, but it soon gave way to his efforts and he began filling his sack with soil. 'Anyone got any water left?' he grunted, digging and shovelling quickly.'

'Not much,' Tom said, 'half a flask.'

'Pour it in the sack,' Slip ordered.

'What? Don't you think . . .' Tom suddenly realised what Slip was doing. He poured all the water into the sack, it mixed rapidly with the earth.

'This,' Slip said, 'is where you, Ruthie, will go to be carried. We might not have sunshine yet, but there's soil and water for you. He picked up Ruthie's frail, trembling body and placed her roots gently in the sack.

'I thank ya,' Ruthie said, then more softly, in a rustle of leaves only Slip could hear, 'I wus right. Y're very kind.'

'There were bits of old door in the room,' Tom added, 'dry wood. We might be able to make a fire from them later. We ought to look out for anything that might be useful. But the torch battery is almost dead, we soon won't be able to see where we're going.'

'I c'n see.' Ruthie's voice was soft but she seemed stronger than she had a few moments before. 'I've no eyes. I c'n sense. I c'n feel. I c'n taste th' air.'

'We'd better lead the way, then,' Slip said. He lifted Ruthie and his bag, slung the straps from the crooks of his elbows so she lay over his shoulders, the fragile twigs and bones of her arms round his neck. It was uncomfortable but she wasn't heavy.

Tom and Friz each grabbed a shoulder and sleeve of Shard's leather coat and dragged it, Ten resting on its back, slowly across the floor. He grimaced at each bump but didn't complain.

It had taken Tom about fifteen minutes to reach the room at the end of the tunnel, and he hadn't been hurrying. This time, with Slip carrying Ruthie and Tom and Friz pulling Ten, the same journey took over an hour. When they stopped just inside the room they were all exhausted.

'You can't go on like this,' Ten said. His face was grey again, he was speaking with his eyes closed. 'I'm holding you back. Just leave me here, find a way out, then come back and get me. There's nothing down here to harm me except my imagination.'

'Not an option,' Tom said. 'We stick together.' He held up the torch. 'Any suggestions?'

As he'd seen earlier, three of the tunnels leading off from the room were blocked with earth. That left two in the wall ahead, two on the right, and one beside the opening they'd just come through.

'Take me t' each,' Ruthie said. 'Let me sense 'em.'

Slip did as he was asked. He knelt at the nearest exit, closest to where they'd just entered. Ruthie's head turned left and then right. She took a hand away from Slip's shoulder, extended it slowly to touch the earth wall of the tunnel.

A lng time passed.

'Are you alright?' Slip asked.

Ruthie said nothing.

'I'll check another exit,' Tom said. 'Friz, can you do the same?' They moved away to different exits and each peered into the darkness. They returned slowly.

'I couldn't see a thing,' Friz said, 'I think it was cooler, but I couldn't be sure. If I had the torch I might be able to go a little way down, but without it . . .'

'Same with me,' Tom said. 'Perhaps we should try lighting the pieces of wood, see if they burn. Then we could get a better idea of what's down each tunnel.'

Even as they finished speaking Ruthie withdrew her hand and sighed. 'Blocked. Fall 'f earth. Too thick. Dangerous. Beyond . . . sunlight. Cool fresh air. Clean waters. Would've been good.' She sighed. 'Take me t' th' next.'

Friz's opening brought a quicker response. 'Not far, deep hole, pit. Bad creatures at bottom. Not go . . . that way.'

'How do you know all this?' Slip asked. 'What do you do?'

Ruthie held out a hand and Slip saw fine white threads extend from her fingertips. They quickly withdrew. 'Taste soil,' Ruthie said slowly, wearily. 'Listen stories. Ask questions worms, beetles, small critters. Smell salts, minerals. Caress roots, they like givin' information. Better 'n seein'.'

The next opening, the one Tom had chosen, provoked another long wait. Friz took the opportunity to examine Ten. Although his leg appeared, beneath the fibrous green bandage and well-tied splints, to be healing (it was neither hot nor swollen) Ten was in pain. He lay with his eyes closed but he wasn't asleep. 'When Ruthie's finished her virtual exploring,' Friz whispered, 'I'll ask her if she can do anything to help you.'

'Don't do that,' Ten said, 'we need her to show us the way out of here. I don't want to weaken her. Look at her. She's not well.'

It was true. Ruthie appeared to be sleeping, at least her human form was sleeping. Her eyes were lidded and she was leaning against the wall. Brown leaves were scattered at her feet.

'Ruthie,' Slip said, 'come back. We'll manage without you, we can stay here until you're stronger or we can move on, find somewhere by chance. You'll kill yourself.'

'No way through,' Ruthie whispered.

'Okay, let's go,' Tom said. 'Straight on.'

'Boy-Tom, take wood. Down tunnel. Not far. Black fire liquid.' Ruthie's words were so soft only Slip heard them.

'Tom,' he called, 'Ruthie says you should go down this tunnel, not far, there's something she called "black fire liquid". Could it be oil? Or tar, pitch? Something to burn, to give us light?'

Tom hurried back. 'I'll try,' he said, 'Friz, come with me? Bring the wood and anything to carry any type of flammable liquid. This torch won't last.' He and Friz hurried down the tunnel.

'Take me,' Ruthie husked, 'next opening.'

'No,' Slip protested, 'you've done enough.'

'Take me, kind boy-Slip.' She moved a finger-branch lightly across his lips.

'Tom's taken the torch. I can't see where to go.'

'Ahead. No excuse.'

'I'm beside the next opening,' Ten called, 'follow my voice.' He began to hum, a tuneless, wordless sound whose only benefit was its volume.

'You can stop now,' Slip said as he grew closer. 'Please, just stop. I think my ears are bleeding.' He felt before him with outstretched arms. 'Is there a draught?' he asked.

'Nothing I can feel at ground level,' Ten said, 'but most of me's trussed up like a parcel at Christmas.'

'I think there's a draught. Ruthie, can you feel a draught?'

Ruthie's reply seemed even slower. 'Nothin'. Blocked.'

'They're on their way back,' Ten said, 'I can see you! Flickering light, and it's not the torch. They must have found something!'

Tom and Friz appeared, Friz carrying one of the lengths of wood with black treacly pitch dripping down its length, smoky flames sputtering from a wad of material tied at its end. 'There was a sort of tar-pool,' Friz explained, 'stretched as far as we could see.'

Tom's hands were stained with the black goo. 'It's not pleasant,' he coughed, the dark smoke swirling around his head, 'but it's better than nothing.'

'We've nowhere to go, though,' Slip said. 'Ruthie says all the tunnels are blocked.'

Tom's optimism disappeared. He opened his mouth to speak but couldn't find any words.

'Go back the way we came?' Friz suggested.

'I don't think the Forest would be very forgiving,' Slip said.

'Do we have any choice?' Ten said. 'I mean, I suffered rather more than anyone else because of the Forest, but . . . At least there's light and air. If I'm going to die I'd rather do it in the open.'

'And be absorbed by the Forest?' Friz said. 'No thanks.'

'Could Ruthie be wrong?' Tom asked. 'She's tired, she doesn't have much strength left. She might have made a mistake.'

'She hasn't been wrong yet,' Slip defended Ruthie, 'I trust her.'

'What's the *point* of it,' Tom growled, 'why have a way out that's useless?' He took his bow from his shoulder and threw it to the ground. 'There are tunnels but they've all collapsed or they're dangerous with bottomless wells, or they descend into tar pits.' His eyes were wide. 'There must be some way to dig our way through one of the earth-falls.' He turned to he first tunnel Ruthie had checked. 'This one, she said there was air and water beyond the blockage in this one. I vote we try digging our way out.'

There was no enthusiastic chorus of agreement, no sound at all save for the spitting, sputtering torch flame.

Tom spoke direct to Ruthie. 'Do you know how far the tunnel's blocked?'

Ruthie's voice was nothing more than a summer breeze: 'Too far.'

'Then what do we do?' Tom shouted. 'You got us in here, you stupid plant, now tell us how we get out!'

'Tom,' Slip said quietly, 'it's no good shouting at Ruthie . . .'

'Ruthie? Slip, Ruthie's dead! Look at it! What is it really? A vague memory of what Ruthie was tied up in a bundle of twigs! Grow up man, this isn't a fairytale!'

Ruthie drew a gentle finger across Slip's ear. 'She wants to say something but she doesn't have much strength left, mainly because she expended her energy saving my life and Ten's life.'

'And mine, and yours, Tom,' Friz pointed out. 'Without her we'd be pushing up the daisies. In fact, we'd probably be talking to them.' She grinned. 'So what does she say, Slip?'

Slip bent his head to the grey-brown leaves that were Ruthie's mouth. He nodded. 'She says, "Up".'

'"Up"?' Tom shook his head angrily. 'And what on earth does that mean?'

'Look up,' Ten said.

'Yes. It's a solid wooden ceiling. It hasn't changed since the last time I looked at it. No opening, no trapdoor. And - oh dear, how stupid of me - I forgot to bring my saw!'

'Burn it?' Ten said.

All of them looked up at the sturdy timber planks supported by strong, thick beams.

'They look dry,' Friz said.

Tom picked up his bow and reluctantly tapped one of the planks. 'Sounds as if there's air beyond. But there's probably another floor above, and another, and . . .'

'Pessimist,' Ten interrupted. 'There might not be.'

'And even if the floor burns through, how do we get up?'

'On Slip's shoulders,' Friz said, 'and he'll be standing on my shoulders, because that's what we do.'

'And me,' Ten said, 'I can be the base of the tower.'

'You're mad,' Tom shouted, 'all of you!' He stalked away to the entrance of the Forest tunnel. 'But what choice do we have?' He waved his hands wildly. 'Come on then! I'm not setting fire to the ceiling while you're all standing underneath it.'

Friz pushed the base of her torch into the ground and dragged Ten, still on Shard's coat, after Tom. Slip, with Ruthie on his back, followed closely.'

'I've never done this before,' Tom said. 'It might be someone's house we're burning down.'

'If it was someone's house,' Slip pointed out, 'they'd be down here finding out what all the noise was about.'

'Where do we light it?' Friz asked.

'Does it matter?' Ten seemed keen to get the job done. 'In the middle. Use both brands at the same time, a few feet apart. Make sure you don't get trapped in a corner.'

'Let's do it, then.' Friz went back for her torch, lit Tom's, and together they stepped into the middle of the room. At a nod from Tom she raised her flame until it was licking the planks between two of the beams. Tom did the same. The flames were drawn upwards by invisible draughts but the wood didn't seem to be burning.

'Perhaps we should have tried wiping them with pitch,' Tom said. 'Is yours catching?'

'No, there's . . . Yes! It's caught!' Friz backed quickly away, burning torch in her hand, closely followed by Tom as the timbers above his head also caught fire. Within minutes the whole floor was ablaze, not with the sooty, smoky flames of the pitch brands, but with an inferno of crackling and roaring, and flares of molten resin. They had to retreat down the tunnel to escape the breath-sapping heat, the eye-watering smoke. They felt the air rushing past them to feed the conflagration.

The flames persisted. After an hour, when the garish light dimmed and there was no sound save the occasional crack of falling timber, Tom and Friz crept forward to examine the damage they'd caused. The floor was carpeted with red-black embers, still glowing hot. The ceiling was gone, but there was another above only part burned away, and another beyond that almost intact.

'There might be more,' Tom explained excitedly, 'it was too dark to see.'

'But what we did see,' Friz added, 'was a ladder a few floors up. And what use is a ladder unless it leads to a trapdoor?'

'I don't think I can manage a ladder,' Ten said glumly.

"No, but I can,' Friz said. 'And you aren't that heavy.'

'Yes I am,' Ten said.

'You were. But you've lost weight over the past few days. Or weeks? I can't actually remember.' Friz shook her head. 'Doesn't matter, we'll get you up there.'

Slip rose to his feet. 'We'd better get going, I'm not sure Ruthie can last much longer.'

'Slow down, Slip,' Tom said, reaching for Slip's arm. 'The fallen timber's still too hot to go near, let alone stand on. We might as well rest for a while, try to sleep, gather our strength. The climb out won't be easy.'

'Anyone got any water for Ruthie?' Slip asked. There was a chorus of muted no's.

'I don't suppose there was any down any of the tunnels?'

'Nothing,' Tom said.

''Fraid not,' Friz added.

Slip moved away from the others. 'We'll soon have you out of here,' he whispered to Ruthie, and was rewarded with a faint breath which might, but only might, have been her whispering 'Thank ya, boy-Slip.'

They slept fitfully. Slip was the last to wake, to dull whispers from the others. The darkness of the tunnel had returned, there was no glow of fire or embers, only a single smudge of light from an oily brand. 'Is it cooler now?' he asked, struggling to his feet. 'Are we ready to go?'

When Tom moved closer Slip could see that his face was dark with ash and soot. 'It's cooled down. Still some hot spots, but we can walk on it. Dirty though, as you can see. Every step you take there's a cloud of ash. Gets in your eyes, up your nose, makes it difficult to breathe.'

'We'll have to be quick, then. Get up and out. If I carry Ruthie can you and Friz manage Ten? If not, I can go first, find somewhere safe to leave her, then come back and help you.'

Tom placed a dirty hand on Slip's shoulder. 'There's a problem.'

'What's that?' Slip was already heading along the tunnel to see for himself, scooping his bag up, not even commenting on the fact that it was so much lighter than it had been. The soil in it had almost dried out. Ruthie's leaves had all fallen. All that remained was a knotted human form of bare bones and twigs.

It took him only a few seconds to reach the room where the fire had destroyed the ceiling. Friz was close behind him, she held her pitch brand high in the air. Slip tilted his head back.

They seemed to be standing at the bottom of a rectangular shaft. Nothing remained of the ceiling, but above it the charred beams of another floor projected into the shaft, and another, less damaged above that, and another, until the light showed a floor blackened but otherwise undamaged.

'There,' Friz moved the flame and pointed, 'can you see a ladder fixed to the wall, about three floors up? And I'm sure I can see the outline of a trapdoor as well.'

Slip nodded. 'But no way up to that ladder.' He lifted his sleeve to his face and stepped gently across the floor, but no matter how slowly, how delicately he moved, he was soon engulfed in a cloud of ash. He reached out his fingers and felt the wall beneath which, high above his head, the ladder stretched upwards. 'I can feel something,' he said, 'there must have been a ladder here at some time as well. And probably a trapdoor above. But it was taken down, the door removed. Why? Who did it?'

'Someone who didn't want us, want anyone, to go up. Which means it's the way we should go.'

'Except we can't.' Slip took off his bag, laid it gently against the wall. 'Wait there,' he said, not expecting a response. There was little of Ruthie left to respond.

'We were talking about what to do while you were asleep,' Tom said. 'We agreed that we go back to the Forest with Shard's coat, that seems to be reasonably thorn-proof. Two of us hold it up, the third cuts lengths of lengths of wood or root or whatever's there. We bring it back, make a ladder out of it. We've some spare clothes we can rip up to tie it together. If we can get up to the bottom of the ladder in the shaft we can climb all the way, take it slowly, haul Ten up after us.'

'Do you really think that'll work?' Slip asked. 'We've no water, no food, the ash in the air's making it difficult to breathe.'

'Any better ideas? I'm always open to suggestions.' There was no antagonism in Tom's voice, just tiredness.

'No,' Slip sighed, 'I can't think of anything. Let's go back then. See what the Forest's got in store for us.'

Ten had already rolled himself out of Shard's coat, accepting that his role would be limited in any action they took. 'Be careful,' he said as they headed along the tunnel. 'Don't forget to come back,' he called after them.

They reached the door quickly. Nothing seemed to have changed, but when Tom pulled at the handle the door refused to open. It needed all three of them, using their combined strength, to move it a few inches, but they could see immediately why the task had proved so difficult. The door had been held closed by suckers that pressed against the timber, embraced it with coiled tendrils that grew back as they watched. Beyond was thick, smooth bark. A new tree had already grown from the grave of the old.

'There's no way we can cut through that,' Slip said.

'We shouldn't have come,' Friz warned, 'it knows we're here now. Look.' She held the brand low, pointed at the floor beside the door. It was moving, rippling with new roots that broke the surface then dived down again. Friz pushed the fiery brand against the bark of the new tree; the flames barely marked the surface.

'It's new wood,' Tom said, 'too wet. It won't catch.'

'All you're doing is annoying it,' Slip said as the roots beneath his feet broke surface and twitched towards them.

'Back the way we came!' Tom yelled urgently.

They ran along the tunnel to find Ten waiting wide-eyed. 'I take it that was a failure,' he said, 'unless you were running because you were desperate to see me again.'

'Let's get him on the coat,' Tom said, 'we go down the furthest rabbit hole, that'll give us most time to figure out what to do.'

'They're all dead ends,' Ten pointed out. 'Why the hurry?'

'The Forest's decided it's worth coming after us! Come on, Ten, roll! Help us here!' He turned his attention to Slip. 'You get the bag with Ruthie.'

Slip picked up the brand Ten had been watching over, hurried past them into the fire-stricken room beyond. He stopped in the doorway. 'Tom. All of you. Change of plan. You need to see this.'

'Now what? We don't have . . .' Tom's words were cut short as he moved to stand beside Slip.

'What is it?' Ten called out. 'Will someone tell me what's happening?'

Friz helped him to his feet, supported him as he hobbled the three steps to the entrance. Directly opposite, in the wall immediately below the trapdoors and ladders, another stairway had formed. What had been the almost human shape of Ruthie had altered. In its stead a scaffold of wooden frames and rungs, natural, uneven but heading inexorably upwards, was still growing. Slip ran across to it, not caring that he was kicking up a dust of dirty ash. 'She's rooted herself to the cracks in the wall!' he shouted. 'But she had no strength, no energy. She'd lost all her leaves. How did she do it?'

'I don't care about the how,' Tom said, 'but that's how we escape. Will it stand our weight?'

Slip took a step onto the bottom rung. It sagged slightly, but there was no danger of it coming away from the wall. 'She'll hold us,' he said, 'she got us this far, she won't let us down now.'

'This is how we do it, then. Slip, you first with one of the brands so we can see where we're going. Anchor it if possible, if not, just hold it. Ten, you put Shard's coat on upside down, arms in the sleeves but the collar down near your backside. Friz pulls you up using the coat, Slip helps where he can. I get the unpleasant job of pushing from below. I'll try not to hurt your leg too much.' He glanced back along the tunnel. Pale rootlets were already creeping in their direction. 'Let's do it.'

Slip climbed first. 'Thank you, Ruthie,' he whispered, 'you're saving us again.' He rose past the burned-out ceiling. 'Don't follow me yet,' he shouted down as he reached the next stage where he had to knock burned and broken timbers out of the way with his elbow, the flaming brand proving more of a hindrance than help. Ruthie's interwoven branches, sneaking through gaps in the remains of the timber floor, seemed thinner here, the roots holding them to the walls less substantial. 'Just hold on as long as you can,' he whispered, 'not long now.'

He managed to clamber around a slight overhang at the next stage, pulled himself gingerly up onto a floor that moved under his weight but didn't break any further. He slid across to the wall. Only the centre of the floor had burned away; he'd reached the level where there was a wooden ladder fixed firmly to the wall, and a trapdoor in the intact floor above. He jammed the bottom of the brand into a gap between the base of the wall and the floor.

'I've found somewhere to leave the torch,' he shouted, 'on my way down to help, you can start climbing.'

'That's good,' Tom shouted back, 'the visitors will soon be here.' He and Friz had already dragged a coughing, spluttering, ash-blackened Ten to the base of Ruthie's ladder. Friz climbed up three rungs then turned, held on with one hand while pulling Shard's coat, Ten wrapped in its folds, after her. Tom kneeled on the ground and slid underneath Ten.

'I'll say sorry now for hurting you, because I will,' Tom said, raising Ten into the air.

'I'll say sorry for swearing at you, because I will,' Ten grimaced.

'Push when I say,' Friz shouted. 'And . . . Push!'

Tom rose from his kneeling position. Ten was straddling his shoulders, his splinted broken leg at an awkward angle. 'We've got company,' Tom shouted. The Forest's snake-like roots were at the entrance; they seemed to pause, sniff the air, before diving back underground.

'And . . . Push!' Friz yelled.

Tom was on the bottom rung. Ten was helping where he could, trying to find a resting place with his good leg, reaching back over his head with one hand to grasp a rung.

'And . . .Push!'

Slip was on his way down, unsure that Ruthie would be able to cope with the weight of all four of them. 'Hold on, Ruthie,' he whispered, 'please, hold on.' He bent his head close to the wall, looked closely at the places where Ruthie's fibrous finger-hold roots were stretching into the loam and mortar. They appeared to be turning brown. He stepped down onto the remnants of the floor, peered over the edge. Far below, in the dim light, the black ash floor had become a sea of pale, slowly writhing roots. 'You need to retreat, Ruthie,' he said, 'once Tom's above your bottom rungs, let them loose. Don't let the Forest get you. Don't let the Forest use you.'

'And . . .Push!' Friz's calls were coming faster as she too saw the churning, seething floor below. Slip climbed down another level as quickly as he dared, hung over the black, charred edge of the floor and held out his hand. 'I can take him,' he said, 'pass the coat up to me.'

Friz tried to do so, instead of climbing a step she pulled the coat up, almost above her head, sweat running in rivers down her coal-black face. Slip managed to find the hem of the coat, grabbed it with both hands and almost toppled down to the floor below. But Tom felt the instability, steadied himself, pushed back hard even though he could feel the step beneath his feet bend. He daren't look down.

'Come on!' Slip yelled, tugging the coat, 'Move!' And Ten did move, slowly, inexorably, as Friz adjusted her grip, as Tom pushed harder, as Slip found a strength he never knew he had. Together they hauled and heaved, managed to manoeuvre Ten over the lip of the broken floor. Friz scuttled after him, Tom was immediately behind.

'We have to keep going,' Slip urged, 'I don't think Ruthie can last much longer.' As he reached the wall, put his hand on Ruthie's ladder, the floor beneath him juddered. He glanced back, the Forest's roots were already appearing, their weight splintering the already weakened joists. 'Now!' he said, 'not far to go!'

Friz was already pulling Ten whose face was pale below the grime and dust. Tom wasn't quick enough. A tendril of root found his foot, curled itself around his ankle. He kicked, but the movement only tightened the root's grip, and it was quickly joined by another, and another. Tom looked up in desperation. 'Just go!' he said.

'Like hell!' Slip yelled, unsheathed his knife and threw himself at Tom. The floor tilted beneath them, Slip slid down the incline and chopped at the roots, cut them clean through. He would have kept sliding if Tom hadn't grabbed his waistband. And the two of them would have fallen if a slender green vine hadn't snaked out from the ladder that was Ruthie and wrapped itself around Tom's wrist.

Friz was already several steps up, hauling Ten after her. 'Some help?' she hissed.

Slip pulled himself up Tom's body, grabbed a rung of Ruthie's ladder, and Tom did the same, used Slip as a means of reaching safety.

'One more floor,' Slip said, looking up to see the guttering flame of the brand he'd left, 'not far.' But the Forest wasn't giving up easily, it tugged and pulled at the remaining timbers, determined to reach its prey or tumble it into the strangling maelstrom of roots below.

Friz was already hunched with her back against the ceiling. Slip was immediately below, he pushed himself beneath Ten. 'You have to reach out with your hands,' he said, 'the wood's solid underneath the scorch marks. Pull yourself up.'

Friz did as she was told, hung in space for a moment, swinging to and fro like a pendulum, then scrabbled for purchase and pulled herself up. Her arms appeared a moment later. 'Ten,' she said, 'can you pass me the edge of the coat?'

Ten was barely conscious, but the words penetrated his pain. His hands waved in midair and the shift in his weight almost caused Slip to fall, but Tom was below, arms raised to support him and his burden. Ten found the coat, held it up, and Friz grabbed it. 'Got him,' she said triumphantly, pulled him up across the jagged, splintering ends of the floorboards and deposited him at the foot of the ladder. Its frame was strong and square, its rungs solid. It was made of cut timber, it had none of the organic roundness of Ruthie.

'Now you,' Friz said.

Slip reached up, felt her strong hand grab his wrists. He twisted and turned as she pulled him up, saw the Forest using Ruthie as a support for its clutching roots. ' Jump!' he yelled to Tom.

As Tom leaped from Ruthie's top rung, so she whipped it away, used it as a catapult, threw him upwards to be eagerly welcomed by four hands who dragged him through the hole in the floor. Slip and Friz dragged him to safety, but only Slip saw the remnants of Ruthie, the slight frame and rungs of her ladder, the frail leftovers of her, tumble and fall into the darkness below.

'She didn't make it,' Slip said. 'After all that, she didn't make it.' He slumped to the ground, head in hands, and began to weep. Friz left Tom leaning beside the ashen-faced Ten, sat down beside Slip and put her arm around him, held him in silence.

It was Ten who spoke first. 'We need to go on,' he said. 'The Forest knows we're here, it'll come after us.' He pushed himself up against the wall. 'I can manage a step at a time, use my arms to pull my good leg up. You're exhausted. We've no food, no water, the light won't last much longer. It's time to go.'

They climbed to their feet. Friz lead the way, up the steps, pushed against the trapdoor which creaked and groaned but opened with a bang. Ten followed, unaided, slow, but determined to do as much as possible. Tom positioned himself to catch Ten if he should fall. And Slip, after one brief look down into the darkness, brought up the rear. He wiped his eyes with his sleeve and picked up the dim torch. He noticed, near to the burnt edge of the floor, something small and green, almost translucent. He bent down, picked it up.

It was a leaf.

It could only have come from Ruthie, blown upwards by the rising warm air. He kissed it softly, remembered the way she'd spoken to him with a touch of her own hand to his lips, and placed it in his pocket.

After three floors Ten had to ask for help.

Two floors later they found, in a corner, some dusty crates containing pewter mugs and plates, stacked against them several bolts of dirty, moth-eaten cloth.

The next two floors were empty. The dust on the wooden boards hadn't been disturbed for a long time. They kept moving up.

'How many floors so far?' Slip asked.

'Don't know,' Friz answered. 'Too many.'

They rested on each floor, and each time it took them longer to recover before starting to the next floor, then the next. Ten spent more time unconscious than awake, that made it easier to carry him but more difficult to judge the damage they might have been doing to his leg. They didn't speak, but each knew what the other was feeling: fatigue, thirst, hunger, an overwhelming desire to lie down and sleep. It was only individual pride that kept them from telling the others of their needs; that, and the knowledge that, if they stopped permanently, they'd never start again.

The flames from the last pitch brand fluttered and died; they climbed by touch, closing each trapdoor behind them; if they fell, they might break a limb but at least the fall wouldn't kill them. They took turns to pull and push Ten; when at the rear Slip considered leaving two doors open, so that when he fell - or jumped, because that would be so easy - the drop *would* kill him. But that would put a greater burden on the others. And that was unthinkable. Except, he told himself, it wasn't unthinkable because he'd just thought it. And if he'd had that thought, then it had probably also crossed Tom's mind, and Friz's, and even Ten's. He gave up thinking, the logic was too difficult to follow, and took up his place pushing Ten to the next floor.

He heaved him through the trapdoor and fell over Friz's legs. 'Wooden boards never felt so comfortable,' he said. 'I could fall asleep standing up.'

'I could fall asleep upside down,' Friz said.

'You're so competitive. I could sleep draped over a barrel.'

Tom was slumped next to him. 'A barrel? Why a barrel?'

"Cos this room is full of them. At least, that's what I'm dreaming. 'Cos I must be asleep.' Slip crawled across the floor. "Cept I can actually feel them.' He pushed against them. 'And there's liquid inside.'

'I can see them too,' Friz said.

'That's because there's light coming down through the gaps in the floorboards above!' Tom joined them. In the dim light they could see more than a dozen barrels of various sizes, all lying on their sides, a wooden bung surrounded by cloth in each. 'It's wine,' Tom said, 'can you smell it?

Friz was already pulling at the bung in the topmost barrel. 'I don't care what it is,' she said, 'as long as it's wet.'

'Careful,' Slip said, 'it'll rush out. You need to tip it back first.'

'A mug? Anyone got a mug?' Tom said.

None of them possessed any container, and the barrel was heavy. Between them, Friz and Tom tipped the barrel backwards and Slip managed to pull out the bung. When the pourers let the barrel down a little, pale, straw-coloured liquid sloshed into Slip's cupped hands. He sipped it, then poured it into his mouth.

'What's it like?' Tom asked.

'Not good. Rough. Feels as if it's burning the inside of my mouth. But it's wet!' He held out his hands. 'More!'

Three more cupped handfuls were enough to take the edge off his thirst and he changed places with Friz. 'The first gulp's the worst,' Slip warned, 'because you're not expecting it to taste so raw, and your hands are covered in ash, so that adds a peculiar flavour, but after that . . .'

'You next, Tom,' Friz said, 'then we need to get Ten to drink.'

Tom grimaced at his first swallow, but the second and third went down more easily.

Friz shook Ten awake. 'We've found something to drink,' she said, 'we need to pull you a little way. Are you alright with that?'

'You could drag me across a bed of nails if there was water at the other side.'

'No, not water. Wine. We must be in a wine cellar, there are barrels of the stuff.' She dragged him across the floor, positioned him below the barrel spout. 'Hold your hands out, we'll pour. Only a little to start with.'

Ten drank eagerly, then they repeated the round. 'Best not drink too much,' Friz said, 'it's definitely alcohol and we don't know how strong it is.'

'I don't care,' Ten said, 'it's stopping the pain in my leg and I don't feel thirsty any more.' He looked around him, lay back on the floor. 'And there's daylight somewhere above, so we'll soon be out of this endless torture, and we might even find something to eat.'

'And a bath,' Tom said, 'it would be so good to feel clean again.'

'A bath? I could drink a whole bath of this wine!' Slip shouted.

'I wonder where we are,' Friz said. 'I mean, it must be a wine cellar. But whose wine cellar?'

I just want some more.' Slip was sitting on the floor beside Ten. 'You want some too?' he asked. When Ten nodded, Slip tilted the barrel forward (it was already more than half empty, some of it drunk, most of it spilled) so that the liquid poured into Ten's open mouth.

'I want to drink it,' Ten protested, 'not wash in it!'

'Sorry!' Slip set the barrel down gently. 'Anyone else want some more? Anyone?'

Not me,' Tom slurred.

'Couldn't drink 'nother drop,' Friz giggled.

'My head's spinning,' Ten added.

Within minutes he joined Tom and Friz in a chorus of gentle snoring. Slip lay for a while, watching the ceiling whirl and turn gracefully. He began to sing in time with its gentle motion, a song with no words and with very little tune. What he lacked in finesse he made up for in volume, and he sang until he too fell into a drunken, dreamless sleep.

He was woken by the sensation of his head being sawn open and someone pulling his stomach inside out. He thought it would be impossible to suffer more, then the trapdoor above was flung open and a spotlight of searing brightness burned his eyes. 'Turn it off,' he begged; his wish was partly granted as a tall figure descended the ladder and stood over him, shielding him from the light. He could see no details of the person's face, only the slim, long-limbed outline.

'Telma! We have visitors!'

'Please, please don't shout,' Slip said.

'Have you been drinking my wine?' The voice was soft and lilting.

'Yes, we were so thirsty. We were in the tunnel and the Forest chased us with its roots, and there was a fire. Ten's got a broken leg and . . .'

'You came from below? Interesting. I think I'll bring my wife. Please don't leave.'

'Don't leave?' Slip said to himself. 'I can hardly walk. Tom, Friz, Ten? Can you hear me?'

There was no response.

Two figures descended the ladder this time. 'Who are you?' a woman's voice asked, singing as pleasantly as her husband's. 'You came from below?' She sniffed. 'You don't smell too good. And your friend is ill. And you're all dirty. *And* you're drunk on wine that's too new.'

'My name is Slip. Ten has a broken leg, Friz's the girl asleep in the corner, and that's Tom. I'm sorry we drank your wine. We were so thirsty.'

The woman made a decision. 'Husband, I think they can tell us their stories later. I'll heat water, see to the injured one. I think they need to bathe and rest first.'

'I agree, wife.'

'Thank you,' Slip said, 'Thank you so much.'

'You're welcome.' The woman turned back to the ladder. 'Kalevi, I'll send Antero and Ilmari to help you,' she said as she climbed, 'I suspect only the talkative one will be able to make his own way up. Venta and I will prepare for our guests.'

The tall man turned to Slip. 'Telma has spoken, so her words become commands. Now then, can you climb the ladder yourself?'

SIXTEEN

The room was small. Billowing curtains at the single window
let in dappled light. Tom blinked. His head was sore, though
not as bad as it had been. He could remember drinking wine,
feeling ill, and being pulled, pushed and carried up a ladder.
He thought he'd been washed, bathed even, because his hair
smelled clean and his skin felt fresh. He was lying in a bed, a
long narrow high bed, close to the white painted ceiling, and
the sheets were slightly rough against his arms and legs.
'That means,' he thought aimlessly, 'that someone undressed
me and washed me, put me to bed. The last person to do
that . . .' He swallowed, closed his eyes, tried to conjure up
an image of his mother. But all he could manage were a few
scattered memories: the warm smell of her, the way she
laughed, the way she teased him and ruffled his hair. The
way she'd wink at him when she passed by, the way she fell
asleep when reading him bedtime stories, the worried look
she wore when trying to do the accounts. And she'd never
let him down, she was always there when he needed her,
but never too close when he had to be independent. And her
voice was always calm and gentle, he could hear it now.

'Tom,' she'd say, 'Tom, it's time to get up.'

'I know,' he mumbled, 'just a few minutes more.'

'Tom! Wake up!'

His eyes shot open. Friz was staring at him, shaking him.
'What's the matter?' he said.

'This is the matter,' Friz said, took a step back. 'Look.'

Tom lifted himself onto one elbow. Friz was wrapped in a
sheet that she'd obviously taken from her bed, and that bed
was the top bunk opposite his. Slip was snoring softly in the
bottom bunk. Tom leaned over, looked down, and found - as

he expected - that Ten was asleep in the bunk below his own.

'We have no clothes,' Friz said. 'And we're clean. That means . . .'

'I already worked that out,' Tom said.

'But I can't remember who did it!' Friz hissed. 'And I'd rather know who took my clothes off and washed me!'

Tom wrapped his own sheet around him and slid down to the floor. There was a woven rug on the bare wood, his toes felt its oily roughness; at the foot of each of the two bunk beds was a plain pine bench; other than that, the room had no furniture. Directly opposite the window was a simple, though very tall, ledged and braced door. 'Have you checked the door?' Tom asked.

Friz shook her head.

Tom lifted the latch and opened the door, stepped through into a room with a stone fireplace in one wall and an assortment of basic chairs and benches crowded round a table. Two of the chairs were occupied.

'Hello, Tom, did you sleep well?' The man who rose to his feet towered over Tom. 'I'm Kalevi Aaltonen, I helped carry you from the outhouse basement. I washed you and put you to bed. Your friend Slip was the only one of you who was capable of speech and independent movement, but neither the speech nor the movement was particularly coherent. I've washed your clothes, they're drying on the line. I hope that answers your immediate questions.'

'Thank you,' Tom replied, unsure of what to do next.

The woman in the other seat also stood up. She was as tall as her companion and she lowered her head in a slight bow. 'In case modesty is uppermost in your mind,' she said to Friz, 'I did the same for you. I'm Telma Aaltonen.'

Both wore their elegance easily. Their hair was long and white (though not with age), it flowed over their shoulders almost to the middle of their backs. Their skin was smooth and pearly, almost translucent, with only a little colour in their lips and cheeks. In the middle of such paleness their eyes were wide and flecked with ocean green and electric blue. Their height and their looks might have combined to make them seem aloof, but both wore smiles that dispelled that possibility.

Kalevi pulled two chairs away from the table, motioned Tom and Friz towards them. 'If you'd care to sit,' he said, 'we'll bring you food and drink, wake your friends and carry Ten through.'

'He needs to rest his leg,' Telma added, 'though it has been well set. I cleaned the wound, treated it with a herbal poultice. He's suffering no pain.'

As their hosts left the room, Tom and Friz shuffled awkwardly to the table and hoisted themselves onto their proffered seats; their feet didn't touch the floor.

'What do you think?' Tom whispered.

'We don't even know who they are,' Friz replied. 'They seem friendly, but so did Zeke and the others at first.'

Telma reappeared carrying a tray laden with food: bread and butter, various jams, fruit and jars of pickles, cheese, nuts, bowls full of unfamiliar cereals. 'Kalevi and I are Walkers.' It was as if she'd been listening to them, though they'd spoken softly. She hurried away, brought back mugs and pitchers of water. 'I'd offer you wine, but . . .' Both Tom and Friz screwed up their faces.

'Morning everyone.' Slip was blinking as he entered the room.

'I think you'll find it's long after midday.' Kalevi followed close behind, Ten looking small in his arms. 'But time is of little importance at the moment.' He placed Ten gently on a chair, hooked another with his foot to place beneath Ten's newly splinted and bandaged leg.

Telma drew the curtains wide to reveal a meadow of long grass, a line hung with all their clothes stretching from a tall pole to the corner of a squat stone building. In front of the building a young man was shelling peas, another was weaving long strands of wood together, and a young woman was chopping wood. 'Our children,' Telma explained. 'Venta's our daughter. Antero and Ilmari our sons.'

'The outhouse over there is where we found you,' Kalevi explained. 'If it hadn't been for your singing we wouldn't have discovered you. We weren't aware the cellar was so deep.'

'It was particularly tuneless singing,' Telma added, smiling at Slip, 'more akin to groaning. I thought it was an animal in pain.'

'And when we found you,' Kalevi continued, 'you were all very drunk, only Slip was capable of speech, and he told us things we thought, at first, was the wine talking.'

'But now we aren't so certain.'

'So refresh yourselves, then we'll listen to you all together.'

The couple bowed gracefully and left the room. Ten raised his eyebrows and smiled at Friz; Tom held out his hands to show he knew only what the rest of them had been told; and Slip protested: 'My singing isn't that bad.'

'I suddenly feel hungry,' Friz said, began loading a plate with food.

'I think we should do as they said,' Tom added, 'eat and drink. We don't know when we'll be able to do that again.'

Slip stretched and yawned as he reached for his plate. 'They seem pleasant enough people. But very tall.'

Ten drew everyone's attention by clearing his throat. 'I'm just happy to be alive,' he said softly, 'so thank you all. It would have been so easy to leave me behind.'

'No it wouldn't,' Tom answered through a mouthful of bread, 'we need someone to insult.'

'And make fun of,' Slip added.

'Face the facts. You're one of us now.' Friz handed him the plate she'd been filling. 'Get stuck in. We need to think about what we tell our hosts. And what we don't tell them as well.'

Slip seemed a little embarrassed. 'I might already have told them a lot,' he said.

'Might?' Friz said.

'I can't actually remember what I told them.'

'About us? About Maia? About the Emperorium?' Tom couldn't hide his annoyance.

'At least I hadn't passed out! And what did they say? If they hadn't heard my singing they wouldn't have found us at all!'

'Children, children,' Ten said, 'didn't someone just say we were a team? I don't think it matters what we tell them. Telma fixed my leg, I can feel no pain at all. They've washed us and fed us, they've let us sleep. They could have done anything they wanted, but here we are, almost fit, rested, unharmed. They feel like good people, and that comes from a person who normally sees the worst in everyone and everything. I think we should trust them.'

'The Vanjelists were kind to us at first,' Friz said, 'and look what they wanted to do to us.'

'That was different. They were after Maia, and she isn't with us. We don't even know where she is, so we're no use to them, we certainly aren't a threat to them, but they've still treated us well.'

'I don't trust anyone now,' Tom said.

Ten spread his hands wide. 'Tell us what to do, then.'

'I don't know. We need to think and talk and discuss, work out a plan.'

'Tom,' Slip said, 'we can't plan anything because we don't even know where we are. We don't have the Map any more. We don't have Shard to guide us or protect us. We need someone to help us. Perhaps, just perhaps, these people will do that.'

Tom sulked. 'We need to find Maia so we can help her. I need to find the Bazhka who killed my mother. And then we need to get back to the real world.'

'So let's ask if Kalevi and Telma will help us in some way towards any of those goals. We have nothing to lose.'

'Except our lives,' Ten added cheerfully, 'but in the grand scheme of things I don't think they're worth that much anyway.' His brow furrowed as he puzzled which unfamiliar fruit he should try next. 'I'm with Slip here.'

'Me too,' Friz joined in, 'I just want someone to tell me where to go and what to do.'

Tom's mood blackened further. 'I can't stop you doing or saying anything, but you can't stop me doing what I want either. Be careful.' With that vague threat hanging in the air he turned his attention to eating and drinking, ignored the awkward silence and anxious glances that filled the room.

When all five Aaltonens reappeared they showed no sign that they'd noticed the unnatural quiet. They asked if their guests had had enough food and, on finding that they'd all eaten their fill, quickly cleared away the plates. The adults brought in two more chairs while the children squatted on the floor, long legs folded neatly beneath them.

Telma began. 'Honoured guests,' she sang, 'Kalevi and I must apologise. When we left you earlier we implied that you might wish to tell us your story. But, having discussed the matter, we realise that you might not wish to say anything at all. And we have no wish to bring any pressure to bear on you.'

'We know a little about you,' Kalevi added, ' through what Slip told us yesterday.'

'But most of that we could have surmised from simply meeting you.' Telma smiled happily. She reached long fingers across the table to hold her husband's hand in hers, though neither of them seemed aware of the contact.

'The ways you speak and dress tell us,' Kalevi went on, 'that you certainly aren't from our Land, and may not even be from our world. You're outsiders. Your journey here has been dangerous. Ten's damaged leg, your cuts and bruises, the condition of your clothes . . .'

'He means,' Telma interrupted, 'the stains and rips . . .'

'And your lack of personal cleanliness. They all suggest a difficult journey.'

'We're aware of dramas and crises in our world. News travels. There have been - how shall I put it - tremors in the fabric of our existence. And we suspect these may be connected in some way to your own misadventures.' Telma motioned to Venta, Antero and Ilmari. 'That is why we've asked our own children to be present. If they must live in dangerous times, we want them to know of the perils they might face.'

'What have you heard?' Tom asked bluntly. 'What are these "tremors"?'

'Nearest to home? Our Bazhka neighbours have disappeared.'

'Bazhka? You have Bazhka for neighbours?' Friz asked uneasily.

'Not "have" but "had". They've left.'

'But Bazhka are murdering savages.' Ten's voice was surprisingly calm. 'That's one of the reasons we're here. Bazhka killed Tom's mother, in our world. They probably killed my father too.'

Kalevi nodded. 'We also know that the Library has been attached by a Bazhka army. Facts are difficult to ascertain, but there is a rumour that they were searching for a girl. An outsider. A human whose name is Maia. That is a name we now associate with you.'

Tom erupted with anger. 'Slip, you idiot! You and your big mouth!' He climbed to his feet, as if he intended leaping across the table to attack Slip. 'Even if we'd wanted to keep certain matters secret we find out that you . . .'

'Tom,' Kalevi said, 'please sit down. We're a peaceful people, we don't countenance the threat of violence. And the name Maia wasn't uttered by Slip. It was you who called out that name as I watched you fall asleep last night.'

Tom did as he was asked, sat silently, his anger forced inwards.

'If you wish to fill in the gaps in our knowledge, please do so. If you'd rather not, or if you prefer to be selective, then that's up to you. None of these pathways will have any effect on the way we treat you: you're our guests; we're Walkers; our home is yours for as long as you wish.'

Telma nodded her agreement. 'But we're also aware that you aren't familiar with us or with our traditions. If you'd rather we explain these to you first, then we'll do so.'

'You might as well tell them,' Tom said to Slip, 'they already seem to know almost everything about us.'

Slip looked at Friz and Ten in turn; each nodded their silent approval; and so Slip began their story. At times Ten added some information, or Friz corrected some small matter. Only Tom said nothing. When Slip had finished, Kalevi and Telma were still holding hands, but their grip seemed to have tightened, to have become more urgent. They looked anxiously at their children.

'Some of your story is beyond our comprehension,' Telma began, 'the world you come from is completely outside our experience. It's something Kalevi and I must discuss together at length. Of course,' she bowed her head to her husband, 'we offer our condolences for your losses.'

'Nor were we aware,' Kalevi added, 'that matters within this world were quite as bad as your story suggests. The

Bazhka have certainly been restless of late. Preoccupied. Uncommunicative.' The heel of Kalevi's free hand was resting on the table, his fingers seemed to be counting and sorting invisible motes of dust, moving in a rhythm that was a counterpoint to his speech.

'We have human neighbours as well,' Telma said. 'None of them seem to have been infected by this epidemic of Vanjelism you speak of.'

'Mama,' Venta said, 'may I speak?'

'Of course, daughter.'

'You don't normally ask,' her father grinned.

'We were at the Byalis' house yesterday, Mrs Byali's just had a baby and you asked me to take her some tonic.'

'The Byalis live in the nearest village,' Kalevi explained, 'a few miles from here.' He nodded to Venta. 'Go on, my dear.'

'Jawa Byali was teasing Antero and Ilmari, calling them names. Making fun of their tallness, their pale skin, their white hair. He said they weren't human.'

'Sometimes people do that,' Telma said. She left her chair and squatted on the floor beside Venta. 'They fear others who are different. We've taught you to ignore such childishness.'

'I know, Mama. But then Mr Byali came out, he'd heard what Jawa said, but he didn't scold him or tell him off. He said he should go inside. Then he asked me and the boys to leave. He said thank you for the tonic, and I went up the steps to say goodbye to Mrs Byali, but he stood in the way. He wouldn't let me in the house. And then he said it would be best for us if we stayed away for a while.'

Telma pulled her daughter into a hug. 'He was probably angry with Jawa. Wanted to speak to him privately.'

'That's what I thought at first. But we had to come back through the village, and no-one said anything to us. Normally there's noise and laughter, someone will shout to us, tell us a joke.'

'Humans think we have no sense of humour,' Telma said.

'But there was nothing. Should I have mentioned it to you earlier?'

'No, love, if you had, we would've said exactly as we have done now. People are strange.'

Kalevi ran his hand through his hair. 'Perhaps I should go out to see Param Byali. See if there's any problem. And I might wander out past the Yuguolos' as well. See if there's any sign of why they left so quickly.'

'I'll come with you, Papa,' Venta said.

'I don't think . . .'

'Let her go along,' Telma said.

'Can I come?' Tom asked.

'I'd hoped to travel quickly,' Kalevi said, 'it's mid-afternoon and, in the circumstances, I'd rather not be out in the dark.'

'I can keep up,' Tom said. 'I'll get my clothes, get dressed. Five minutes.' He hurried out, tripping over the sheet he'd wrapped around him, almost embarrassing himself.

'I can chop some wood,' Friz offered, 'it doesn't feel right to accept your food without offering something in return.'

'I'll wash up,' Slip said, 'unless there's something else to do?'

'I think I'll just lie here and concentrate on healing,' Ten said.

Kalevi's idea of travelling quickly was an understatement; Tom realised within minutes why his host's people were called Walkers. The length of his stride matched his height, and Tom had to run to keep up. Kalevi was almost two feet taller than Tom, something that hadn't been as noticeable when they'd been in the house. But outdoors he seemed uncoiled like a spring, and full of easy-moving energy. Tom

387

had to run to keep up with him, and it was only after a few minutes that he realised the Walker was actually moving at Venta's pace; she was only a foot taller than Tom.

'Do you walk everywhere?' Tom panted. 'Do you ride horses?'

Kalevi shook his head. 'We don't treat animals as beasts of burden, Tom, nor do we use them as food. Our human friends do so. They eat meat, they drink milk, they catch fish. Our lives are much simpler than theirs, we don't strive as they do, we simply exult in being.'

'So you grow crops?'

'No, we aren't farmers. We're healers. We're teachers. We're writers and solvers and storytellers. We're entertainers and law-bringers and judges. We're newsgatherers. We're Walkers. We own no land, we have no property save what we wear and we carry. We strive to cause no hurt, no harm, we bear no creatures any ill will. We answer to no-one but ourselves.'

Tom could only keep up by running, but Kalevi and Venta, striding out on each side of him, didn't seem aware of his discomfort. 'But your house,' Tom gasped, 'and the things . . . in it. Don't you own those?'

'No, they aren't ours. The house isn't ours. We occupy it for a few months then we move on to another, if we can find one. Other Walkers will use the house and its contents if they wish. We are nomads.'

'People give us food,' Venta explained, 'and we help them in return. Mama's a healer, she can care for the people we visit. Papa teaches their children to read and write, and he helps the adults with other things, like how to build better houses, and raise stronger livestock. We perform plays and tell stories. We tell them what's happening far away.'

'When we meet other Walkers,' Kalevi continued, 'we exchange gossip and news, swap information. Few people

388

travel in this Land; Walkers do nothing but travel. And so we know things others don't know, can't know. Like a new way of building a plough, or how to pull out a tooth painlessly.'

Tom digested what Kalevi and Venta had told him: Walkers were the internet of the Emperorium. They brought news, they were a source of information, they taught and healed, they tried to solve people's problems. 'You must be . . . very popular . . . wherever you go.'

'We don't try to be popular. We try to be honest and helpful.'

'Please . . .would you . . . slow down?'

Kalevi came to a halt. 'We've already been moving far more slowly than we normally would.' He reached behind him, grasped a long wooden staff held in place by a loop on a leather shoulder belt. Venta did the same. The staffs were plain with a slight curve at each end, the wood smooth and polished. They bore no decoration, no embellishment. 'Can you manage his weight?' Kalevi asked Venta; her grin was the reply he wanted.

They adjusted the straps around their shoulders so the loops were the same height, low on Kalevi's back, high on Venta's. One of the staffs was hooked through the loops so it was about Tom's head height; the other hung in the bottom curve of the straps. 'You stand on the bottom one, hold onto the top one,' Kalevi said; his words were an instruction, not a request. 'Keep a firm grip; bend your knees. We'll run.'

Tom had run for his school, cross country. He could keep up a steady pace for an hour or so of about eight or nine miles an hour. But the Walkers belied their name, they were running at least twice as fast as he could manage and doing so in step with each other while carrying him over rough ground. That in itself required Kalevi to shorten his stride; without that, without the burden, Tom was sure he would have been able to run at over thirty miles an hour. Yet neither of the Walkers was breathing heavily, they weren't sweating despite the warmth of the day.

After a while Tom found the motion more comfortable, he could focus less on holding on, look around him. They were travelling along a track of some sort, it was rutted in places and well worn. On both sides grass grew tall and lush, and there were several times when Tom saw animals grazing in the distance, though they were too far away to be anything but dark smudges on an uneven horizon. There were stands of trees too, and stumps where some had been cut. He could even hear birdsong. He lost track of time but could feel no slowing in the Walkers' pace until they came to a river, willow trees bending over its banks, reeds clustered in its shallows. Kalevi and Venta waded into the slow waters which didn't even reach to Tom's feet. On the far side he was told to dismount.

Kalevi bent down, cupped his hands and sipped a little water from them. 'Beyond the trees is Birrapur, the village where Param Bilyali and his family live. They're friendly people, I was here four days ago to do some teaching. They gave me some of the food you ate this morning.'

'Do you want me to wait here for you?' Tom asked.

'I see no reason for that. Neither you nor I have anything to hide. Honesty. Transparency. If that's the currency we offer, then we can expect to be paid in the same coin.' This time he walked more slowly, allowing Tom to keep up, three strides to his one.

The village that appeared was made up of single storey houses, mud walls painted in bright primary colours, some roofs of red tiles, others thatched with reeds. The larger buildings had shady verandas supported by stout wooden poles; smaller homes had their overhanging roofs extended a little. Most windows and doors were shuttered, while bright woven curtains hung above them. A maze of paths ran from each building to every other building, but the grass between them was short and well kept. The village seemed welcoming; but there were no people.

'There must be a meeting,' Kalevi said, 'in the Hall.' He led Tom and Venta towards the largest and tallest building, the eaves far higher than the top of Kalevi's head. As they drew closer they saw that the doors making up most of its four walls were flung open to allow those sitting on the ground outside to hear what was being said. The Hall was full. A sea of waving fans and sleeves and hands and pieces of paper tried to keep the air moving.

'Everyone must be here,' Kalevi said, 'from all the smaller villages as well. They must be discussing something important.'

Someone was speaking from the depths of the Hall. Tom could hear a strident female voice, though her words weren't clear; but the audience was quiet, listening attentively, and there was brisk, enthusiastic applause when the speaker paused.

'I think we should move closer,' Kalevi said, marching forward without waiting for Tom or Venta to respond. They found a spot in the shade of a tree where they could sit and listen unnoticed.

'As I said earlier, your kindness to me, a stranger in a strange land, shows how much you care about hospitality. You are a warm and generous people. You have given me food and water, a place to lay my head, and I have been able to offer you nothing in return save my thanks. But there is something else I can give you. I can give you something you've had in the past, but which has been taken from you. I can give you a sense of your own worth, of your individuality as a people, of your ability to succeed without the assistance of those who are not like you, who do not share your culture, who use you for their own means.'

'She speaks well,' Kalevi admitted. 'She holds her listeners. She appeals to their needs.'

'This is the third time I've spoken to you since I arrived here. Already there have been changes. The Bazhka, your oppressors, have gone. Their houses are empty. They will trouble you no more!'

Those words brought a cheer from the audience. 'Until recently,' Kalevi commented, 'the villagers would not have thought the Bazhka to be oppressors. Indeed, in return for small favours, the Bazhka provided great services. I didn't realise there was such deep-seated resentment amongst the villagers.'

'I resent all Bazhka,' Tom said, 'they killed my mother.'

'You are speaking from the heart, not the head. In the first place, your mother was killed by two individual Bazhka; you cannot visit the crimes of individuals on a whole nation. Secondly, you owe your life, according to the tale Slip related to us and which you did not contradict, to Shard, a Bazhka. And thirdly, you do not yet know the circumstances under which the Bazhka and humans coexist here.'

The speaker continued, her voice stronger, more authoritative. 'People of Birrapur, you have been blessed with intelligence, you can see that this beautiful land is your destiny. It is your right to enjoy the fruits of your labours without interference, without owing anything to any outsiders who impose themselves upon you. Do you need Bazhka to protect you from mercenaries and wild animals? I see no wild creatures near your village! I see no armies desperate to attack you, save perhaps the savage Bazhka themselves! Yet you allow them to belittle you, to imply that you cannot care for yourselves!'

This time the audience's cheers were louder.

'And what do you do in return? You give them food that they can't be bothered to grow themselves. You feed them. You care for them. You treat them as your equals.'

Cries of 'No!' and 'Shame!' filled the air.

'But that will happen no more, my people of brave Birrapur. I came to spread the word of your power, of the Maker's power; and now the Bazhka have gone!'

A chorus of 'Praise the Maker!' spread through the crowd.

'My people, my people. There is more!' The Speaker waited for silence.

'She is clever,' Kalevi said.

'She's dangerous,' Tom added. 'Anyone who suggests the Maker is anything good is dangerous. And she's got the crowd worked up, it's her crowd, she can get them to do what she wants.'

'I know these people, Tom. Telma and I have visited them regularly whenever our Walking has allowed. She's helped them into life and eased their passage to death. I've taught them reading and writing and arithmetic. Telma has cured their ills and soothed their pain. I've shown them new and better ways of constructing houses and growing crops.'

'Do you believe in the Maker?' Tom asked.

'I believe in no deity,' Kalevi said quickly. 'Gods are myths.'

'Some people, especially humans, need myths.'

'I will talk to them. They are sensible people. They will listen to me.' Kalevi rose to his feet but was pulled back down again by his daughter. 'Listen, Papa. Listen first. Listen to what she says.'

The woman was speaking again, powerfully, passionately. 'There is so much more, my people. Who do you employ to make your homes and work your land?'

'Giants!' came the swift reply.

'Indeed, Giants. And they take a portion of your harvest in return. You build especially for them as well, is that not true?

393

Isn't this very Hall used by Giants when they force themselves upon you? Isn't this where they sleep? Isn't this where you feed them?'

'Yes!'

'Yes, it is!'

'I thought so. I can . . . I can . . .' The woman breathed in deeply, a stage inhalation, heard by all. 'I can smell them! I can smell their animal stink! And I will ask you, do you need them? Do you not have the ingenuity to do your own building and ploughing, to cut timber, to use beasts to aid you? Because that is why the Maker put animals on this world: to serve humankind!'

'This is not good,' Kalevi said.

He was drowned out by loud cheering, and the stamping of feet, which the speaker quickly hushed. 'And who else enslaves you? Who else are you forced to pay for tasks you can easily carry out yourself? Are you incapable of teaching your own children? Can't you care for your sick, your ill, your tired and needy? Do you need white-faced skeleton ghosts to tell you stories?'

'I think she's talking about us, Papa,' Venta said.

'The Walkers come amongst you, my friends, acting like your lords and masters. They give you a snippet of information here, a drop of medicine there, they tell you to do things in a different way, they take food from your table. And then they're gone! Until the next time, and the next time, and the next time. And look at them, friends, look at them! They make no pretence at being human, with their white hair and their long limbs and their staring eyes, they glorify their strangeness. They refuse your meat, that's not good enough for them. They will not fight for themselves, they're cowards. And yet you treat them as demigods! They are nothing of the sort! They are not of the Maker. And if they are not of the Maker, if they won't even acknowledge

394

and honour his existence . . . then there is no place for them in this Land!'

'This is wrong,' said Kalevi. 'I can't stand by while this woman preaches lies to my friends.' He rose to his feet. 'Wait here,' he ordered.

'Is it wise to interrupt the meeting at this moment?' Venta asked.

'Wise? Probably not. But it would be wrong to leave her unchallenged, and many in the Hall would challenge her if someone spoke up first. So I must speak on their behalf.' It took him no more than a few long-legged seconds to reach the nearest opening and disappear inside.

'I think we should go after him,' Tom said.

'But he told us to wait here.'

'We have done. Now it's time to think for ourselves. We don't go into the Hall, we stay outside, just in case we're needed.' He found a broken branch, shorter than the Walkers' staffs but heavier, swung it once or twice to feel its heft.

'We don't fight,' Venta reminded him. 'If attacked we defend ourselves, but we do no harm to those who assault us.'

Tom was gloriously overconfident. 'That's alright, you defend yourselves, leave the harming to me. I feel as if I need to harm someone.' He led the nervous Venta after her father.

SEVENTEEN

The woman in the Hall was in control. She was younger than Tom had imagined, perhaps in her mid-thirties, smartly dressed in dark grey cotton trousers and tunic, a scarf wrapped around her black hair and shoulders. She was self-assured, conducting her audience, marshalling their thoughts, their responses, making them sing to a tune they'd never heard before; but she knew all the notes; she had written the melody and the words, she knew exactly how to bring this to a climax.

'The Maker cares for you.'

She spoke softly, her words like caresses, making her listeners lean closer to her.

'The Maker knows you for good and honourable people. The Maker welcomes you to his fold, to his love, to his protection.'

She increased her volume, not in a shrill, forceful way, but with a resonating, comforting solemnity.

'And what must you give him in return? What demands does he make on you? What must you pay him?'

She looked at them, smiled at them, and each felt her warm affection as her gaze passed over them and through them.

'He seeks nothing from you, my friends. The Maker does not demand your worship. He doesn't want you to kneel before him, he doesn't want you to sing his praises. All he wants is that you see in yourself the way forward. He wants men and women like you and your families to accept that you need only yourselves to realise your full potential. You don't need Bazhka or Giants or Walkers, you don't need the Tschagen, you don't need Sarens. Now is the time to stand up for yourselves, to shun the non-believers, to remove

396

them from your lives.' She took a deep breath, closed her eyes and held her hands up to the sky so she appeared like a letter Y. 'Now is the time to live for yourselves!'

There was a roar of agreement, of excitement, of appreciation, but it died more quickly than it ought to have done. The woman's lips twitched with aggravation as she opened her eyes to find Kalevi standing in front of her, looking at her, a quizzical expression on his pale face. Although she was standing on a platform (several tables had been pulled together to form a stage) she still had to look upwards to see into his eyes. 'And even now,' she said quickly, 'even as we talk about your future independent of these aliens, one marches into your midst. Unbidden. Uninvited.' She spat out the last word. 'Unwanted!'

'Ah,' Kalevi said, 'I see! You're employing rhetoric. Rule of three. And alliteration too. Very good. But weren't they meant to applaud or cheer after you said "Unwanted"?' He turned his back to her, surveyed the faces staring at him. He recognised most of them, could put names to about half. 'I'm sorry to interrupt this meeting. I had come to find out why the Bazhka had left, and then I saw you all here . . .'

'Go away!' someone shouted, 'you're not welcome!'

'Leave us alone!' another voice called. 'Walk away, Walker!'

Kalevi raised his voice. 'I overheard what this woman was saying . . .'

'This woman has a name! I am Tasma Dainay Wala!'

Kalevi turned to face her again. 'What are you trying to do?'

'He asks me,' she shouted, 'what I'm trying to do! Such arrogance! He knows what I'm doing. I am telling you the truth! I am offering you your freedom!' Her eyes were wide, her skin shone with sweat, and her smile was triumphant. In front of her the crowd began to shout her name, 'Dai-nay! Dai-nay! Dai-nay!' emphasising each syllable.'

'Let me speak to them,' Kalevi insisted.

'They won't listen, Walker,' Dainay said softly. You should leave.'

Kalevi looked around at the baying villagers and nodded reluctantly. 'Very well. I will return when emotions are less fraught.' He managed only two paces when Dainay spoke again. 'See your power, friends! He tries to flee!' Kalevi found his way blocked. Those in his way might have positioned themselves to stop him or they could simply have been trying to see what was happening; the effect was the same.

'He will bring others,' Dainay yelled, 'they will seek to kill your independence, kill your freedom, kill your very existence!'

The intent of the words was clear and they achieved their purpose. A chorus of 'Kill! Kill! Kill!' rose up immediately. Kalevi glanced around. Some of the village elders were silent, still sitting, legs crossed. They were looking at their neighbours, bewildered and confused. Others had risen to their feet and had their arms outstretched, they shook their heads to show their disapproval, patted the air in an attempt to bring calm. But the majority, mostly young men, would not be calmed. They exulted in the righteous anger Dainay had given them.

Kalevi saw the quickest way out. He reached for his staff and used it to vault over Dainay's stage. If he'd succeeded his escape would have been straightforward, but Dainay's surprise at his sudden leap caused her to topple backwards. The table she was standing on fell with her, and Kalevi caught one foot on it, tumbled to the ground beside her. For a moment they lay beside each other, staring at each other. 'Thank you,' Dainay hissed, 'you have won them for me.' As Kalevi struggled to his feet Dainay was already screaming.

'He attacked me! Help, my friends, help, the creature attacks an innocent woman!'

Kalevi wasn't used to irrational behaviour. He'd experienced suspicion, but never hatred. And as he crawled to his knees he realised that the crowd surrounding him wanted only one thing: to kill him with their bare hands. There were screams of victory as he tried to stand but a blow from a chair forced him back to the ground. He was kicked, again and again, he raised his hands to protect his head, pulled his long legs up to his chest, but the blows kept falling.

Then they stopped.

'On your feet!' Tom was standing over him, heaving the weighty branch around his head like a battle-axe. 'Come on!' Tom shouted, 'Move!'

Kalevi ignored his bruises, found his feet. There were far fewer people behind the stage than in front and that was where Venta was, keeping a retreat clear for them, jabbing her staff like a spear. 'Where's mine?' Kalevi asked, searching for his own weapon.

'Leave it,' Tom said, grabbing his sleeve.

'I can't. It's part of me.'

A heavily built man thrust Kalevi's staff into his hands but kept hold of it as well.

'Param?'

The man nodded, frightened, wild-eyed. 'Pretend to fight me! Take the staff from me!'

'I can't fight, Param, you know that. I might hurt you.'

Param pressed forward. 'I tried to warn Venta. I told her not to come back, and I know she told you. But you're so pig-headed.'

Tom moved between them. 'I don't need to pretend,' he said. He raised his club and Param let go of the staff, backed away. 'What do we do now?' Tom growled.

'Escape,' Kalevi said. 'Run!'

The villagers weren't used to fighting. It required only a gesture with the Walkers' long-staffs or a raising of Tom's club to make them fall back, despite Dainay's screaming that they should be captured. Within seconds they were out of the Hall and running back along the path they'd taken only an hour before. But they were being pursued. Thirty or more young men were on their trail, and they'd paused to pick up axes and knives, fishing-spears and cleavers, anything they might use as a weapon. They were moving quickly as well, slowly catching them up.

On their own the Walkers would easily have outdistanced them. But Tom was feeling the aches and pains he'd gathered over the previous days begin to reassert themselves, he was slowing the Walkers down. 'Go on without me,' he managed to gasp.

'We don't leave our own,' Kalevi said. 'Throw away your club.' Tom hurled the wood to the ground and, as he did so, Kalevi picked him up and threw him over his shoulder onto his back. 'Hold on,' he said, and he eased himself into a loping gait. The running was more urgent than before, and from his vantage point Tom could see why. Away to one side and slightly ahead of them were other runners. They weren't dressed in the soft browns and umbers of the villagers, they wore darker shades of grey and black similar to Dainay's clothing. And they would reach the shallow river crossing before Kalevi, Venta and Tom.

'Go ahead,' Kalevi said to his daughter. 'You'll reach the river before them. Escape.'

Venta kept running at the same pace, ignored her father's instructions.

'There are no more than ten of them,' Tom said.

Venta looked over her shoulder. 'But they'll hold us up while those behind us catch up.'

'We will not fight,' Kalevi said, 'we will not cause harm. We will only defend ourselves.'

They were close to the river, but Dainay's men were closer. Tom saw them wade through the water and spread themselves out on the far bank. They were armed with clubs and knives, staves and daggers, not agricultural tools press-ganged into service.

The Walkers didn't pause. As they rushed through the water Kalevi shrugged Tom from his back, saying only 'Stay behind us, be safe!'

Dainay's men were surprised, they'd thought that the Walkers would stop before entering the river, so their response was uncoordinated. Those furthest from the crossing point could only watch as Kalevi reached out with the end of his staff and tripped two of the fighters before whirling and, with his weapon parallel to the ground, pushed two others back into the river. Venta used her staff to vault directly over the heads of two of her opponents; then she swept the stick round in a semi-circle a few inches from the ground, catching both men on their ankles. 'Sorry,' she said as they fell to the ground, then neatly flicked their fallen weapons away from them into the river.

There were four men still standing but they were all armed with blades. One of them, standing behind the others, threw a knife at Kalevi; the Walker knocked it aside with his staff, did the same with a second from the same man, then thrust the end of his pole into the sand immediately in front of the man's legs. It required no more than a twitch of Kalevi's wrist, magnified by the length of the staff, to raise a cloud of sand and dirt into the air and into the man's eyes.

Those fighters already knocked down were rising to their feet. Tom found himself at the centre of a whirling wall of protection, the Walkers' weapons preventing any of their adversaries from getting closer. But the attackers were wary now, they remained more distant, encircled their opponents. One of them, muscular, his hair cropped short, seemed to have taken charge. He urged his men on individually, by name. When one assault was being dealt with, he ordered another into the gap, then another. Venta was hit on the leg by a club, a glancing blow but enough to bring her to her knees. Kalevi blocked other blows as his daughter regained her feet, but they were both slowing, both weakening.

The leader called out several names, at his command they all drove forward together. In fending off their blows Kalevi and Venta left themselves open to the second wave, focusing on Venta. Kalevi tried to help her, but in doing so one of the attackers ducked under his arm, managed to draw a knife across the Walker's chest; a thin line of blood stained Kalevi's tunic.

Another blade cut Venta's forearm. There were cheers from the assailants, a greater yell from across the river where a crowd of villagers had gathered. That caused Kalevi to double his efforts: he disarmed two men in quick succession, but they merely retreated a short distance to find their weapons then rejoined the battle.

'Hit them!' Tom yelled, 'do some damage!'

'No . . .deliberate . . . harm!' Kalevi grimaced as a thrown club hit him, paralysed his shoulder for a few seconds, and his guard dropped. One of the men saw his opportunity and dived into the gap, dagger raised.

Tom saw the club fall to the ground and swooped on it, rolled as he grabbed it and brought it down hard on the attacker's knee. 'Walkers might not want to hurt you,' he growled, 'but I do.'

The fighter crawled away and Tom grabbed his dagger. The short-haired man saw his companion retreat but wasn't sure why, he urged his men onwards, made Venta the object of their attack. Tom crept in front of her. 'Don't let them hit me!' he yelled, and relied on her dexterity, her whirling, fast-moving staff, to protect him. If she was his defender, he was her weapon. Each blocked blow gave him the chance to retaliate with club or knife or both. He broke a fighter's arm, gashed another's side, drove the knife down through a leather-clad foot, knocked one attacker unconscious. And all the time Venta was there, suddenly rejuvenated, exulting in the small victories.

Tom slid in front of Kalevi, waited for his moment, scuffed sand in the eyes of a fighter intent on avoiding Kalevi's staff, then followed through with a kick that winded him and bent him double. He raised his club, then noticed that his victim was no more than a boy, perhaps a year younger than him. 'Enough!' he shouted, and to his surprise the battle stopped. Kalevi and Venta, both bleeding, both breathing heavily, stared at the four men still standing. 'Let us pass now,' Tom said. 'We are three, you are four, but we are Walkers!'

The leader glanced at his men. They all took a step back.

The villagers were still on the other side of the river. Some of them, young men, those who had found weapons, took a step forward. But Param Bilyali, who counted himself as Kalevi's friend, who had tried to give him back his staff, was at their head, his arms outstretched, his hands raised. 'People of Birrapur!' he yelled. 'The Walkers and their Laraku,' he nodded at Tom, 'have crossed the river. They have defeated Dainay's fighters. They have earned the right to go in peace.'

There was a rumbling of discontent, a collective muttering that was silenced by the looks of the elders who stepped from the crowd to stand with Param.

'We are an honourable people, my friends. And we have much to discuss.' He stared at Kalevi. 'Do we have your word of honour that, if we allow you to leave, you will not return?'

Kalevi took a deep breath. Tom could hear the words he intended speaking, that Walkers had the right to wander wherever they wished, that they had been a force of good for the village and its people, that force of arms would not prevail over logic and reasoned argument. And Tom knew that these words, or others like them, would result in the younger villagers attacking them. They would see themselves being insulted, patronised by a condescending alien with a superiority complex. And the elders wouldn't be able to hold them back.

'For once,' he spat at Kalevi, 'shut up!' Before the Walker could object Tom took a step towards the villagers; they retreated, and Tom realised that he and his weapons were spattered with blood. He held up his club and his dagger. 'I am the Walkers' Laraku,' he shouted. He wasn't sure exactly what the word meant, but he guessed that it carried a certain amount of respect. 'I am one of many Laraku who will accompany the Walkers from now on. Not all are as gentle as I am. We will not return to your village, that is my word of honour. But you will not cross the river, you will not lay a hand on any Walker, you will leave us in peace.' He glowered at the crowd. 'Or you will have me and my kind to answer to!'

He turned quickly. 'Come on,' he urged his companions, 'before they decide I'm just a kid with a big mouth.' He led them away. As they passed the injured fighters Kalevi and Venta bowed their heads. 'We feel your pain,' they said, 'we bear only shame at your injuries.' Tom looked up at them, turned his gaze to the men lying on the ground, or sitting with heads in hands, or standing slumped with fatigue. 'I have no shame,' he barked, 'no sorrow, no apologies. Tell that to your leader. Tell Dainay to leave the innocents of this world alone. Or answer to the consequences.'

Kalevi led the way and, despite his fatigue, Tom was happy to jog along at the Walkers' side. Venta kept looking up at her father, as if waiting for him to speak. When he did it was with an air of confusion. 'I've spent my life following my people's beliefs. This isn't a written code, there's no compulsion that certain acts must be carried out. But the underlying principles are these: firstly, treat others the way you wish them to treat you, but don't expect such reciprocation. And secondly, do not harm or hurt or, by inaction, cause harm or hurt to any sentient creature. These are the ethics which have guided my life.

'I have, infrequently, had to defend myself when others have offered me physical violence. My height, my speed, my efficiency with the staff, have all combined to make fighting largely unnecessary. I have made it a rule that I avoid situations where fighting might occur. And being labelled a coward because I ran away from a fight has never been a problem for me; there's no logic in being a dead fighter rather than a live coward.

'But today brought new circumstances. I was faced with people who sought to hurt me and my daughter, to kill us even, simply because we aren't like them. Because we aren't human. And we couldn't run because we were obliged to stay with you, Tom, to protect you. But in protecting you, in defending you, we were in danger of losing our lives with no ultimate benefit to you or to ourselves. To triumph, we needed to hurt our attackers. But that is contrary to our beliefs.' He shook his head. 'There is no logical way out of this argument.'

'Perhaps,' Tom suggested, 'your original premise was wrong.'

Venta smiled. 'Be careful, Tom. My father isn't used to anyone challenging his beliefs.'

'Which premise would that be?'

'Do no harm. There are times when you have no choice.' Tom tried to think of an argument that would impress Kalevi. 'What if one of your family was in danger from someone? If they were threatening to kill them? And if you were the only one who could save your wife or daughter or sons? But to do that, you'd have to hurt the person attacking them? Would you do nothing?'

'That is reasoning I've heard before. My response has always been that I would try logical discourse first, then warnings and threats, and then some defensive action. Only as a last resort would I consider actual harm.'

'And by that time,' Venta said, 'I'd be dead. You spend too much time thinking, father. Too much time considering moral virtue rather than doing what's right.'

'So you're advocating violence, daughter?'

'In the face of a greater wrong, yes.' She linked an arm with that of her father. 'Your teaching did not consider someone like Dainay, preaching hatred. Because hatred of that type is illogical. Perhaps it's time to forget your ideals and your principles when necessary.'

Kalevi sighed. 'I'll think about this.' He waved them to a halt. 'This is the home of the Yuguolos. I did mention them to you, I said that we'd visit them. They're Bazhka.'

Tom had been focusing on the conversation, on making sure he didn't trip on the rough clumps of grass, and hadn't noticed that they were approaching a dwelling. It would have been easy to miss anyway, it was a small building lying low, half-buried in the ground at the top of a small mound fringed with scrubby trees.

'How many Bazhka live there?' Tom asked nervously, his hand creeping to the knife he'd tucked into his belt..

'About thirty,' Kalevi replied.

'In that hut? It's not even big enough for two humans.'

'The hut is merely the top of the dwelling. We are already standing on the roof.'

Tom looked around. There was, as far as he could see, no door or window, no way into the dwelling. But Kalevi motioned him two steps further on and he was standing at the top of a deep cut in the ground, curving away on both sides. Large steps descended to the path at the bottom in which wooden framed doorways and windows were regularly placed. There was no sign of life.

'The place is indeed empty,' Kalevi said, 'had the Bazhka been here they would have already welcomed us.'

'Welcomed? Is that a euphemism for attacked?'

'I don't use euphemisms, Tom. The Bazhka here are hospitable.'

'I can't believe that.'

Venta was leading the way down the steps. 'You mentioned a Bazhka, Shard by name, who was protecting and guiding you and your friends. Wasn't she hospitable?'

Tom reflected on the question. 'In her own bad-tempered way, yes. But she had protection. She wore a necklace which stopped the Maker from forcing her to do things. Like kill people.'

Kalevi followed his daughter. 'To me, Tom, that's fanciful. I know stories of the Maker, of course, but I've always treated them as myths. And many faiths have elements such as magic protective amulets, perhaps your Shard believed that wearing such a trinket granted her free will.'

'Perhaps you're right. The Emperorium isn't my home, I know only what I've seen and what I've heard. That's why I think most Bazhka are murderers.'

The steps were too deep for Tom to manage easily. He had to watch where he placed his feet, so it was only when he stood at the bottom that he realised how impressive the dwelling was. At one side of the walkway water flowed in a stone trough to each of the windows; each room was light and airy, but sheltered from wind and rain. He looked warily through one of the doorways; inside were two large wooden beds with mattresses, sheets lying discarded on a stone floor; a wooden table was cluttered with bowls, plates and goblets; two chairs were tucked under the table, while two others lay upturned on the floor. There was a smell of decay in the air; the plates were full of rotten food, flies hovered over them, maggots moved sluggishly across the surface of putrid meat.

Tom ducked out of the room. 'They left in a hurry. Could they have been attacked?'

'No signs of bloodshed,' Kalevi said, holding his hand over his nose. 'And on the walls, look. They left some weapons.'

Tom peered through the window into the room Kalevi had just vacated. He saw, hanging on wooden hooks in the stone wall, axes and longbows, pikes and spears and swords. 'Clearly not of the non-violent variety,' he said.

Kalevi ignored Tom's sarcasm. 'Bazhka don't leave weapons behind. Something is wrong.'

'And why are you concerned about Bazhka?'

'They're our neighbours. We live together in a balanced society, all of us, Humans, Bazhka, Walkers, Giants.'

'Not "live", father, "lived". First the Humans have changed, now the Bazhka. The balance has disappeared.'

'There must be an explanation.' Kalevi was troubled. He pursed his lips, seemed about to speak but said nothing.

'Father, if the Bazhka aren't here then they must be elsewhere, and if the Humans have suffered some group madness, then the same might have happened to the Bazhka. Many of them need no weapons, they're armed by their own bodies, their claws and teeth; and although some weapons remain, others have been taken. Our family, your family, may be in danger. I think we ought to return.'

'Wise words, daughter.' Kalevi leaped up the stairs, Venta and Tom struggling to keep up. They passed more trenches cut in the earth, invisible until they were almost upon them. There was still no sign of life.

'All gone,' Kalevi called, 'young and old alike. See down there, a sword and a whetstone lying together on the ground. Someone was sharpening a blade and left abruptly. This is *wrong*, Venta was right, your friends and my family may be in danger.'

Tom didn't object when, after negotiating the trenches of the Bazhka dwelling, Kalevi and Venta lowered their staffs for him to clamber aboard. They ran faster than previously, but Kalevi was still able to talk. 'This is not as peaceful a land as it seems. There are wild animals that prey on Humans. Tigrays, Wolves, Gryphons, packs of hunting Kodiaks, Vrines. The Bazhka are fighters. They hunt down these wild creatures. They forage far beyond human settlements and bring delicacies that humans desire. They give humans pelts to keep them warm, skins to fashion shoes, metal ores. They help humans live in the way they wish. And in return humans trade their crops, their fabrics, their expertise. But it would seem that the balance has been overturned. Destroyed.'

'And you, Kalevi, the Walkers, where do you fit into this?'

'I have already said, we are judges and healers, teachers, counsellors.'

'To all?'

'To all who need us, who ask for our help.'

'And the Bazhka don't kill humans?'

'There's no need.'

'So what's happened to them?'

'I don't know. I fear that, if they have succumbed to the same madness that has afflicted the villagers of Birrapur, then all our lives are in danger. We must hurry.'

Kalevi and Venta ran on, Tom balanced between them. The journey was far less comfortable than it had been: the Walkers were moving faster and they were tired, they stumbled, more than once Tom thought he'd be thrown to the ground; his limbs ached and his grip on the upper staff was weak; and he was thirsty, his lips cracked, his mouth dry. But he didn't want them to stop. If angry Bazhka were seeking humans, then the nearest were Tom's friends.

When the Walkers' home appeared on the horizon and came rapidly closer a sense of relief spread between the runners and their burden.

'Everything looks alright,' Tom said through parched lips.

'I can see Antero and Ilmani,' Venta huffed, her breathing laboured for the first time.

Venta's brothers noticed their father and sister, sped towards them yelling.

'Mama say come quickly . . .'

'She needs you to see what's happening . . .'

'There's a Bazhka and he wants to kill the Humans . . .'

'But Mama just wants to fix his legs . . .'

Kalevi and Venta slid to a halt. Despite being as dirty and dusty as Tom, and bearing the scratches and blood stains of a few hours before, they seemed calm and in control.

'Where is this Bazhka?' Kalevi asked.

'In the yard with Mama.'

'Venta, take these two into the house. I think we need some water, they can help. Tom and I will find out what's happening.'

The look on Venta's face told Tom that she'd rather find out herself what was happening by remaining with them, but she did as she was told. Kalevi and Tom walked round the house to find Telma squatting in front of a Bazhka who seemed to be lying unconscious, face down in the dirt.

Telma rose to her feet when she saw them, threw herself at Kalevi. 'Husband,' she said, 'you're injured! Your clothes are torn. What happened?' She looked around for Ventna. 'And my daughter, where is she? Is she . . ?'

'She's with the boys and she's safe, thanks to the interventions of Tom here. I'll tell you all in due course.' Kalevi bent down and touched the back of the Bazhka's neck with his fingertips. 'This one seems to be alive. He seems familiar to me. Why's he here?'

The Bazhka raised his head a little. 'I'm here,' he rasped, 'to kill you and eat your heart and do the same to all those in your care.'

'His name is Gulo,' Telma explained. 'I visited him a few days ago, he was in a fight with a Tigray and it broke both his legs.'

'And it suffered for that,' Gulo said, 'I ate its heart as well!'

Telma ignored the interruption. 'I set and splinted his legs and gave him medicines to speed the cure, as well as poultices to ease the pain. There were no signs of this antagonism. But now? Apparently he crawled from the Yuguolos dwelling, it took him three days. I asked him where he was going and he said, "Where the Maker tells me." But not quite as politely as that.'

'And where are your companions, Gulo?' Kalevi crouched down in front of the Bazhka. 'You can't be comfortable. Would you like us to help you into the shade? Some water, perhaps?'

The Bazhka managed to roll onto its side. Its head was shaped like a dog's, but with the teeth and jaws of a small dinosaur. Its familiar blue skin was dirty, its eyes flecked with pain. 'I want nothing from you!' it managed to growl. It stretched out its muscular arms and dug long claws into the earth, pulled itself forward by a few inches. 'I'm coming, Master,' it grunted.

'If you let us help you,' Kalevi continued, 'give you water, feed you, then you will grow stronger and you will more easily continue your journey.'

'If you help me,' the Bazhka whined, 'then I may reach the Maker, but it will be too late and he will punish me. If I keep going, then each small inch brings me closer to him.' He scrabbled in the earth again. 'The others of my tribe wouldn't wait for me, the Maker's voice is too strong in their minds, in their heads. He calls us and we must go. And when I say "I'm coming, Master", it will be the truth.' Gulo winced and closed his eyes, yowled to the sky. 'Only when I move does the pain cease,' he whispered. He lay down again, almost unconscious, but his clawed fingers continued to twitch and creep, shredding the thin grass beneath him.

Telma had a bowl of water by her side, she dipped a cloth into it and dribbled water onto Gulo's head. She tried to trickle water into the side of his mouth, but it dripped to the ground. Kalevi placed his fingers again on Gulo's neck, and this time the Bazhka didn't respond. The Walker shook his head, stood up. 'I will bury him,' he said to his wife, 'if you and Venta will help me move his body.'

It was almost sunset when Gulo's body was rolled into a shallow grave. Tom, Friz and Slip had all helped, and that gave Tom the opportunity to explain what had happened in the Human village. Later, after they'd all washed and eaten in comparative silence, Tom raised the matter of what they would do next.

'Unless I'm mistaken, Plains was a peaceful place until recently. But everything's changing. The Vanjelists are at work amongst the Humans, the Maker is summoning Bazhka, even those who were previously part of a stable community. Something bad is happening.' He looked at Ten. 'I think we need to move on as soon as you're able. We need a cart of

412

some type to put you in, we can take turns pulling it, perhaps even find a horse or a donkey. I think we should make that our aim, finding some form of transport. Once we've done that, I'm sure Kalevi and Telma will give us enough food and water for a few days.'

The Walkers nodded their consent without needing to consult each other.

'And where might we be going?' Ten asked. 'I'm not concerned for myself. I just want to know what our intention is, our direction.'

'That's the other thing we can do while we're looking for something for you to ride in,' Tom said. 'We need to talk to each other, listen to the advice of Kalevi and Telma. After all, they know this place well. And as long as we're here, I don't know about the rest of you, but I feel safe.'

'Thank you, my friend,' Kalevi said. 'I agree that further discussion is necessary. I feel that I could help you more if I knew more about you and your own world, about your friends Maia and Pencil and Shard. Then we could devise a plan to help you.'

'This land is no longer safe,' Telma added, 'I feel that we too ought to move on, husband. We could travel with these young people, there's safety in each other's company.'

Kalevi looked at his wife and his children. 'I agree. We'll leave in the morning. Together.'

'Tomorrow we find your coach, then,' Slip said to Ten, 'drawn by a team of a dozen white horses. Or possibly dragged by Friz and me.'

'You'll be travelling like a king,' Friz added.

'Can I have a sunshade as well?' Ten asked. 'With frills on the side. And Tom can fan me as we travel, to keep me cool.'

'You'll never, ever, be the slightest bit cool,' Tom said. 'Come on, we need to sleep. There's a long day ahead.'

The moon was a low sliver of pale in a sky littered with stars. The air was cold and still and smelled of fresh linen; dawn was still a long way off. The night was filled with strange noises, of insects and small fearful animals, soft-winged birds and sliding, slithering reptiles, of guttural barks and distant howls. The ground beneath Tom's feet was a little damp and scurrying beetles luxuriated in its moist stickiness. He'd taken the spare clothes laid out for Ten (all he had was what he was wearing), the food left over from the evening meal, and a flagon of water. He still had both the knife and club he'd taken in the fight with Dainay's men, both were tucked in his belt. He tried to remember the way to the Bazhka dwelling, there would be an opportunity there to choose a better weapon and find clothing more suitable for a long trek. And then?

He had a plan, of sorts, but not one he'd been willing to share. It was too dangerous, and he couldn't force even greater danger on his companions. But first he had to get away from the Walkers' house, they'd be sure to look for him when they found the note he'd left. It had been so easy to imagine the track he should follow, but in the dark, with no obvious landmarks on the vastness of the plain, he was soon lost. When a section of shadow detached itself silently from the low bushes directly ahead of him, rose up huge and wide, he realised the folly of his expedition. His hand reached for his knife, he held it, shaking, in front of him.

'Can I guide you on your way?' Venta's playful voice asked.

'You . . ! How long have you been following me?'

'Since you crept noisily out of your bed. I was outside, wrapping myself in the night.' She held her blanket wide again, showing why she'd appeared so broad as well as so tall. 'The Bazhka home is this way.' She pointed at right angles to the direction Tom had been heading.

'How did you know I'd be going there?' Tom asked, stepping long to match her stride.

'Logic. You're an impatient creature, Tom, and when you spoke so eloquently about spending time preparing for your journey, I felt there was something wrong. I thought about your alternatives. You're desperate to find your friend Maia, and you know where she's going.'

'To seek the Maker?'

'Exactly. And who else is beginning that same journey?'

'The Bazhka. Am I that transparent?'

Venta giggled, a sound Tom could never imagine would pass her father's lips. 'It's easy to know someone when you fight alongside them. Laraku. And you haven't yet learned to hide your feelings.'

'I didn't know Walkers recognised feelings. Just logic.'

'Ah, that's because we've learned to *hide* our feelings. Anyway, I suspected you'd want to find and follow a group of Bazhka. Very dangerous, Tom, especially when they're consumed by this madness.'

'That should make it easier,' Tom said, 'thinking logically. All they'll be doing is heading for the Maker. And he wouldn't send for them unless he was telling them where to go. A bit like a beacon?'

'I can see your logic. You might be a Walker yet. If you grow fast.'

'Humour, Venta? You might be a Human yet.'

'If I shrink a little?'

'Shrink a lot.' Something fluttered in the air around Tom's head and he waved his hand to frighten it away.

'Insects that drink blood,' Venta explained, 'travelling at night has its problems. Here, I brought this for you.' She dropped a hat on his head, he could just see long braided hairs hanging from its brim. 'I'm sure my father will make another.'

415

They walked in silence for a while.

'So why am I going to the Bazhka' place?' Tom asked.

'Easy.' Venta counted out the items on her long, thin, elegant fingers. 'Weapons. Extra clothing. A leather shoulder sack to carry everything. And possibly a track to tell you which way to go.'

Tom nodded. 'I think you know my intentions better than I do.'

'I do. That's why, once you find what you need, I'll do the same. I'll find a weapon. I think I might need some type of armour too. I need to prepare myself for the journey ahead of me. I'll come with you, Tom.'

'You won't. I won't let you. It's too dangerous.'

'I will; you can't stop me; and danger doesn't worry me.'

Tom stopped in his tracks. 'You father will come to look for you, take you back.'

'That's an unreasonable argument. I know him, Tom, I know the way he thinks. At some time in their lives, when they're about the same age as I am now, every Walker feels the need to wander. That urge has been with me for a while now., and my father recognises it, understands it. And there's more. His love for me and his wish to have me return will be balanced by my usefulness to you. I think he knows that our world is changing fast, and that you have a special part to play.'

'You can't be certain of that.'

'I can. I didn't take his hat. He gave it to me. For you.' She breathed in deeply. 'Can you feel the warmth approaching, Tom? Daylight will be here soon. And we're almost at the Bazhka village.'

'Did your father say anything else?'

In the dim greying of the morning Tom saw Venta's face break into a smile, but there was sadness hidden in there. 'He said we should take care of each other, learn from each other. We work well together, we must work better together, anticipate each other's thoughts and movements. You must give me some of your braveness; I must share with you my wariness.'

'So we complement each other?'

'His words exactly Tom.'

EIGHTEEN

The Maker wasn't human.

He didn't experience the emotions humans suffered, or perhaps enjoyed; but he did know about them.

He was aware of their existence.

Centuries ago, in a past he often wished to forget, his intellect drove him to seek information about the world surrounding him. He decided that it would be interesting to feel that world through the very limited senses of humankind, and so he built a human body and took up residence.

That was the form in which he appeared to the Truthsingers who sought him out.

They were unlike the other humans he knew.

They were curious and clever, they neither feared nor respected him, and they certainly had no wish to worship him despite him showing them some of the powers he possessed. He remembered wondering what it was made these Truthsingers different to the other humans who grovelled at his feet; he had become curious. And wasn't curiosity a human trait? Perhaps his human body encouraged the growth of human emotions.

When they asked him questions he replied honestly; he hadn't yet learned the art of deception. Yet they were experts in the art of lying. They lured him to the cave where his powers were at their weakest, they tempted him, they exploited him while he was in his human form.

One of them lay with him. She said she wanted him to experience the joy of what she called the 'essence of humanity'. The things she showed him were without doubt joyful. And the pleasure (again, his human body was dictating what his mind was feeling) of lying with the woman, of falling asleep in her arms, the sense of understanding, of happiness and contentment, all combined to make him feel more secure than he was.

Perhaps that was what it was to be human.

He woke with hands and feet in porcelain manacles. He was alone, in bonds he couldn't break, behind doors he couldn't open. Only his mind could wander and wonder.

His first thoughts turned to revenge.

He built the Bazhka and the worlds they inhabited, gave them a lust for destruction and a hatred of humankind. In return the Truthsingers imprisoned his creations in the very world he'd created; they called it the Emperorium, though its Gateways were also known as the Bizarre, the Ferorum, the Beranda, the Kyosker, La Bourselette, Arcadia and others, depending on their location in the Truthsingers' own world.

The Maker came to recognise the Gatekeepers: Klein, the most powerful of them; Pettit and Pequena, Vogel and Mali, Malyenki, Mikro and Beag, Bach, Parvus, Malgranda and Ndogo. Twelve of them, each with their own personality, their own passions, their own vanities and delusions. But he could do nothing to attack them, to persecute them, or to free himself from the prison they'd created.

He tried to fight them with his mind, but he was weak. And so he retreated. He left his worlds to fend for themselves, he left his Bazhka to starve.

He lost interest.

He was aware, on the periphery of his existence, of small changes. He knew that human lifespan was short, he sensed when Ndogo died and his place was taken by another who shared the same blood. Malyenki's successor, however, though powerful, was not related to the original Gatekeeper.

In truth the Maker didn't care.

In truth, the Maker was barely alive.

Centuries later something disturbed him, raised him from his torpor. He was still imprisoned, that was certain. But his mind seemed more able to explore his own domain, the world of the Emperorium. He found that only six of the Gatekeepers – and six of the Gateways – still existed. It was as if he had been liberated, and he began to consider the reasons for this.

The original Gatekeepers had been the humans who had sought him out and who had then imprisoned him. He'd been naïve and understood nothing of the nature of humankind at the time. But now he could see more clearly: the power they'd used to create his prison was his! They might have stolen it; it was possible he'd given it to them (he could remember little of the events); or they could simply have absorbed it from him. Part of that power had given them far longer lives than the usual human lifespan. But they were still dying! Some were dying without passing on their power to their descendants or to their chosen successors. And a part of that power was returning to him!

He experimented.

He couldn't destroy or bend or break his chains; he couldn't bring down the walls of his prison. But he could control his Bazhka, those nearest to him, the old Bazhka, the ones he'd made rather than the ones produced by breeding. He could speak to them, he could influence their movement, he could experience the world through them.

He began to plot. He used his Bazhka to attack the Gateways he sensed were guarded by the weakest Gatekeepers. At first his creations were defeated easily. But the constant attrition began to bear fruit, and first Mali, then Vogel fell.

The Maker had imagined that he would be able to send his forces through the unprotected Gateways and into the world beyond, but he was thwarted by the actions of the other

Gatekeepers who rallied in support and destroyed the unprotected Gateways.

But still the Gateways fell.

Still the Gatekeepers died.

Until only one was left: that cared for by the Klein.

The Maker was stronger than he'd ever been, but Klein was powerful in herself, and old, and experienced. But she was also over-confident, disdainful, proud. If it had occurred to her that, when she died, there would be no other Gatekeeper to destroy her Gateway, then she appeared to be making no plans for that event. When that happened – and it was inevitable, it *would* happen – then the Maker would have access to the outside world.

And so he learned patience.

He turned his attention inwards, towards the myriad Lands he'd created, and was surprised to find them populated by beings other than Bazhka. Humans had crept into them, some deliberately, some left behind when the Gatekeepers had ventured into the Emperorium. Others seemed to come from elsewhere, and the Maker began to suspect that there were means of access to the Emperorium that were beyond his perception, beyond his control. How else could he explain the presence of Giants, of Walkers, of all the other creatures who co-existed (sometimes peacefully sometimes not) with his Bazhka. It would have been possible for him to organise a pogrom, to have the Bazhka destroy them completely; but that would have involved using his strength, his resources and his Bazhka for something that probably wouldn't have brought him any immediate advantage. So he watched and listened, he tolerated these parasitical newcomers, he occasionally toyed with them; but most of the time he ignored them.

Still the Klein wouldn't die.

The Maker searched his memories to see if there was a reason why she should be so long-lived, why she should remain so powerful. She could, he knew, create her own new worlds; he'd seen them blossom and grow, then suddenly wither as if she'd lost interest in them. They were, for a brief moment, inhabited by phantasms. He suspected that, if she was inclined, she could make new worlds as he could. The human part of her didn't realise the power she possessed.

And still she wouldn't die.

The Maker became aware of a new type of human.

He'd been happy to let the Bazhka cultivate the hatred of humans he'd sown in their fertile minds. But humans fought back. They organised themselves into militia and armies. They claimed Lands as their own. And they sought explanations for the world they lived in. It required little effort to tell them of his existence. They made him in their own image. They made him into a God. Once again he was worshipped. And it was GOOD!

The Maker realised that Klein might live as long as him, and he could see no end to his own life. So he began to search for a different way to free himself.

His worshippers called themselves Vanjelists and detested Bazhka because they fed on humans and had shapes and forms abhorrent to humans.

The Bazhka hated humans because they had been created by the Maker to detest those who had imprisoned him. This antipathy was wasteful. So the Maker exerted pressure on those he controlled.

His direct control over the Bazhka meant he could summon them at any time.

His indirect control over the Vanjelists meant that he could expect them to do as he wished.

His plan was that both Vanjelists and Bazhka should combine their forces in Arx to physically destroy his prison.

There would be no need to wait for Klein to die, no tiresome drip drip of assaults on her Gateway. He would wait. He would wait to be freed by Bazhka and Vanjelist together, and then he would allow them to turn on each other, to destroy each other. It didn't matter if only one survived. The most important thing was that he would be free to use all his strength and power to vanquish Klein and turn his wrath on the world of the humans.

Revenge would be sweet and delicious.

But then Klein made a mistake.

She spent too long inside the Emperorium and something happened in her own world that disabled her Gateway.

It was the moment the Maker had longed for, and he was unprepared for it.

His attention was elsewhere.

And in that moment a new variable arose.

The Maker could sense the female human he later found was called Maia.

It was the first time he'd ever sensed a human directly, other than the original Truthsingers, the Gatekeepers. His conclusion? That she was a Gatekeeper. And yet she wasn't familiar. Where had she come from? Why did her existence flare into his perception and disappear almost as quickly? She was inside the Emperorium, but where?

Her presence was a distraction, but a captivating one. Those she was with were of no importance, but she piqued his curiosity in a way that he recalled from that long distant night when he'd taken human form and lay with a human.

He decided to push ahead with his plan and summoned those of his Bazhka in the wider Emperorium to return to Home, to Arx. If the Bazhka themselves could destroy his prison he would have ordered them to do so; but the doorways were framed with porcelain, and Bazhka couldn't even approach them without becoming vacant, uncontrollable. His Vanjelists could tear down the doors of his jail, but they lacked the numbers and the physical strength to do more.

So they would work together, because it was his will that they do so.

It would be their crusade.

And the girl Maia? What could one young girl do that might hurt his aspirations? But she interested him, so he would watch, he would send out word that others should watch, and he would listen.

As for the Klein? She was still able to prevent his Bazhka from passing through her Gateway into the human world beyond. It wasn't necessary for her to die; indeed, his instructions had always been that she should not be harmed.

He wanted the last Gateway to be opened, not destroyed.

He wanted the Klein to be delivered to him alive. There were so many ways he wanted to torture her.

About the Author

My name is Alan Dunn. I was born in Newcastle-on-Tyne, spent a large part of my adult life in Cumbria, and now live in Somerset. I've been a professional writer for over thirty years and have had novels published in the UK and the USA. I've had short stories anthologised since I began writing.

Few novelists can make a living solely from writing. My other jobs, the ones I've done to allow me to write, have seen me work as a hospital administrator, insurance salesman, director of a double-glazing company, GP surgery manager, and teacher of Creative Writing, English Language and English Literature at secondary and adult levels. Although my reading (and writing) tastes are wide-ranging, I've been devoted to SF and Fantasy since I was a teenager.

'The Porcelain Necklace' is the first of three novels (the others are 'The Search for Home' and 'The Battle for Darkness') making up the 'Madame Klein's Emperorium' series. These last two will be published as e-books and paperbacks.

My time is also spent playing folk music and painting. If you want to see my art you can find me at:

www.pinkpenguinart.co.uk

Printed in Great Britain
by Amazon